mCath

THE
CARDINAL'S
SIN

Also by Robert Lane

The Second Letter

Cooler Than Blood

THE
CARDINAL'S
SIN

ROBERT LANE

© 2015 Robert Lane

All rights reserved.

ISBN: 0692356517
ISBN 13: 9780692356517
Library of Congress Control Number: 2014960162
Mason Alley Publishing, St. Pete Beach, FL

Sticks and stones will break my bones,

But words will never harm me.

Children's rhyme

THE CARDINAL'S SIN

CHAPTER 1

I killed a man in London who did not die.

"Forgive me my sin," he said as I towered over him with my gun. It was an odd request from a cardinal.

"Your *sins*, you pompous ass," I corrected him.

We were in Kensington Gardens by the Peter Pan statue. It was thirty-five minutes before sunrise, and I was eager to finish my assignment before the light gave birth to more joggers. It wasn't a location I would have chosen, but I carried no vote. Nor was it how I envisioned spending the final morning of my European vacation with Kathleen.

The cardinal wasn't really a man of the cloth. He was an international assassin with numerous disguises, including this ridiculous cardinal caricature. He'd recently been tied to several deaths in the United States. Instead of targeting his victims, who were current and former members of special ops—the latter a card that I carry—he assassinated members of their families: the elderly parents of one, the girlfriend of another, and a sister of a third. Action was required. He had to go. It was my assignment to make the world a better place. Vacation or not.

I had stalked him for ten minutes and then, from the shadows, called his name. He hesitated and turned. I shot him.

"Please," he said. The strength of his voice surprised me. The first bullet had to be within inches of his heart. It was hard to believe he was still functioning. "Forgive...forgive me my sin."

His last-ditch effort for clemency—from me, of all people—didn't particularly strike me as unusual. Death, when it arrives with no escape clause, brings out strange spirits in people, but I expected something harder in his soul. His eyes were seeing the last of the world. Such eyes do not take in but allow everything out. Even in the waning dark, I didn't like the desperate pleading of his eyes, as if instead of fearing or challenging me, he was trying to communicate something with childlike innocence. It didn't seem right. Screw it. I was on a tight schedule and dismissed my intuition. I was paid to kill, not to hear deathbed confessions or spout my opinions on the metaphysical.

He lay on the ground, wrapped in his vestments of a black cassock and scarlet fascia. His right hand clasped a piece of paper. He muttered some final words, some mumbo jumbo about the pope and his guardian. Staying in his role until the end. What was the point? He brought up his right arm, his outstretched, closed hand yearning for me. I reciprocated by leveling my gun.

"Forgive me my—"

"Save it for never-never land."

I squeezed the trigger.

CHAPTER 2

I jogged at a leisurely pace toward my rented flat on Green Street and ducked into a parking spot just past Dunraven Street, where the designated Dumpster was. I stripped off my outer T-shirt, snatched off my baseball cap with the fake ponytail, and stuffed them—along with my latex gloves—into a plastic bag half-full of garbage and teeming with maggots. The gun and clear glasses were next. I knotted the drawstring on the bag and, reaching into my pocket, took out the scrap of paper that had been in the cardinal's outstretched hand. Did he want me to have it? I hadn't been able to resist prying his fingers open and now was unsure what to make of it: a faded graduation photo of a young woman, brunette, the colors barely hanging in. Creased and worn by years. Who was she? A daughter? Lost lover? It went back in my pocket.

At the Starbucks on the corner of Green and Park Streets, I purchased a French Roast Grande. A tipsy, round table by the window served as a perfect place to read the *Times.* A few minutes later, a lorry with wood sides and an exposed bed rumbled down Green and swung right onto Park. A hodgepodge of old tires, discarded lumber, and garbage bags was in the back. My bag was there. It would be incinerated within the hour. When it was light enough outside to read, I relocated to a table squeezed between the building and the curb. The table was level, solid like a rock.

Kathleen was upstairs in the flat and had another hour to go before she entered the new day. We were flying back to Tampa and had a comfortable schedule except for one issue: the time Kathleen requires to pack is directly correlated with the time allotted to accomplish the task. She's in a rush whether we leave at 6:00 a.m. or p.m.

I got my phone out of my shorts pocket and sent a text to the colonel:

the bird is dead

Sirens screamed from Oxford Street, two blocks away. They kept going. I went inside and purchased a banana and a lemon pastry that negated all the calories I'd burned during the last half mile of my run. When I returned outside, a man was three feet from my table and closing. We made eye contact. I shook my head. He moved on.

More sirens, now on Bond. Like everyone else, I kept my head down when they passed. They did pass. I didn't like what I had just done. The deed didn't bother me, but it had been hastily arranged, and Kensington Gardens was far too public a place. More important, it had been the intention of Kathleen and mine four-week European vacation to spend time together without the vagaries of my lifestyle interrupting us. So much for that. Wherever I go, I follow.

The target, tentative time, and location had been communicated to me in Paris. It came while we shared a raspberry parfait over glasses of Chablis at Les Deux Magots. We watched a man with a cane—the Caned Man, Kathleen dubbed him—navigate the scurry of shoppers, tourists, and workers that swamped Boulevard Saint-Germain. We clanked our glasses to his success, and Kathleen wondered if he lived alone. I thought it an idle question; she seemed to truly care. The waiter palmed me a note.

The next day we picnicked by the tower with a baguette, Mimolette Cheddar, and a bottle of Château du Terte. Our lunch lasted for three hours, and the longer we stayed, the smaller the world became, as all I saw was her smile. When I think of the City of Light, I think of that smile.

In Rome she insisted on dragging me to a nightclub across from the Hotel Cosmopolita, where we were staying. There was no sign over the single metal door on the side of the nondescript, faded-yellow brick building. At midnight the door opened. She filled the room and the night with her laugh. It was nearly dawn before we left. The next day I missed my early-morning run through the narrow streets.

That afternoon, on the left side of the Spanish Steps between the wall and the concrete divider, a woman wearing a white dress and holding a green parasol brushed past me. She handed me a folded piece of stationery. Her fingers felt chafed, and I didn't expect that. The stationery held the name I would use when I registered for my flat on Green Street. I was assured that my previous registration had been erased. The people I work for like that word. *Erase*. It's simple. Effective. On a good day, they can spell it. I sat on the steps and burned the piece of paper.

When I think of Rome, I hear her laugh. I also recall the day I didn't run. It wasn't worth giving up for the nightclub, but I'll never tell her that.

When we arrived in London, I wanted to shield her from knowing that I was using an alias. Before our contact arrived to open our flat, I dispatched her to the store for grapefruit juice and beer, insisting she go immediately.

Small things mask great deceits.

Kathleen knew that my partner, Garrett Demarcus, and I did contract work for our former army colonel, but this was different. This was our vacation. I wasn't searching for a kidnapped young woman or shutting down a sex-slave import business while retrieving a stolen Cold War letter—a pair of previous undertakings. I wasn't sure how she would react, so I opted to not give her a choice. It wasn't a well-thought-out decision, but it was an easy one—a classic example of how I seek the path of least resistance. Harp on me all you want, but we all do it.

From London we took a train north to York to escape the mass of civilized international humanity. The northern England weather was waiting for us, and she bought a gold scarf. She circled it around her neck so her head sprouted out like a spring flower pushing through winter ground. She was the sexiest damn thing in Yorkshire County. Ever. And it's an old county. She was cold and wrapped in the scarf when we stumbled into an eighteenth-century tavern with a seven-foot ceiling and fortress walls. It was small and warm. We were looking for a quick dinner before we caught the train back to Paddington. We took a room upstairs. Dinner was quick; everything else slow. I insisted she keep the scarf wrapped around her neck. We missed our train.

My final confirmation of place and location came the next day along with the dinner check at La Genova. I was glad I didn't have to extend my stay and make up some bullshit excuse for Kathleen. Why would that bother me? I'd been deceiving her since Paris.

I checked my watch. Time to scoot. I took my coffee up to the second-floor flat. Kathleen was in the living room, shoving clothes into a stubborn and argumentative suitcase.

"Ready to fly?" I said.

"Next time we travel, I'm bringing a steamer trunk."

"You could buy less."

"No." She gave a huff and looked up from her task. Her hair was somewhere between tied back and unbridled freedom, like a country in the midst of a revolution. She wore tight jeans and a white, untucked shirt buttoned halfway up. No shoes. The black, wood dining table behind her was strewn with newspapers, souvenirs, euros, and maps of colored tube routes that looked like an ant farm someone had poured dye into.

"That has nothing to do with it. How was your run?"

"Uneventful." I gave her a good-morning peck. That wouldn't do. No way.

"Car comes at eight thirty, right?"

I went to the eight-foot patio doors and swung them open. The bustle of a summer morning in London filled the flat. I turned around and pulled off my shirt.

"What are you—"

I was on her and kissed her savagely. My adrenaline had gotten no release, no satisfaction, from killing the cardinal. My instincts and body had been prepping for battle for over two weeks, but an assassination is a passive act—like hitting the mute button on a person's life. I crumbled us onto the floor and tore into her clothes, both acts absent of any delicate consideration.

She pulled away. "Slow down, stranger. Do you even need me?"

"One's a lonely act."

"OK. Well, gee, this is one of those times when a little lie comes in handy."

"I don't lie," I lied.

"The curtains are open. The buildings are so close they—"

"Let's give them something to remember." I arched her body off the floor.

"Jake?"

"Yeah?"

"I don't think you ran fast enough this morning."

I like making love to Kathleen on a hard surface, but I'm not sure that's what I did.

We were putting on the last of our clothes when the cleaning crew, a woman and a man using their own key, came in without knocking. Kathleen, as if someone had smacked the red button, went into travel-mode panic. She dashed to the bedroom and out of earshot.

The woman was missing her front tooth and had steve-dore fingernails. She looked as if she'd spent the last forty years cooking in the galley of a freighter. The young man had a buzz cut. His baggy clothes couldn't disguise his impressive physique.

"You're early," I said to the man.

"I'm in charge here," the sea hag said.

I turned to her. "*You're* early. You know what you're doing here?"

"No, honey. I've been with the agency since Khrushchev, but I got no bloody idea what I'm doing here." Her teeth were a testament to nicotine. Her skin was drawn and tight, but her eyes were sharp, as if she'd never known doubt or indecision. She struck me as a remnant from an early le Carré novel.

"Why the time change?" I demanded.

"You dump your gear around the corner?"

"I did. Answer me."

"New plans. Your car's fifteen minutes out. What does she know?"

"'New plans' doesn't cut it."

"All I know. *You* answer *me*; what does—"

"Nothing."

"OK." She turned to the man. "Until she leaves, strictly normal. Start with the kitchen. After they're gone, wipe it all down. Take all the bedding, bath towels, kitchen towels—even the unused ones—with us. Get to the van the second they're out of my life, and bring up the new linens, all in that box. Don't stand there, move." She pivoted and looked up at me. "You."

"Yes?"

"Shoes?"

"By the door." I was glad they were taking my running shoes. The last thing I needed was some zealous Scotland Yard detective inspector tracking me down through my shoes.

"Don't make the mistake of putting them—"

"I won't. I—"

"Don't interrupt me. Anything unusual I should know?"

My eyes wandered over to the spot on the floor where Kathleen and I had just made love, or whatever that had been. Her eyes followed mine. I asked, "You wipe the floors, right?"

"When?"

"Five minutes ago."

Her gaze shifted back to me. "A real Don Juan. Any other place?"

"Just there."

"I'll take care of it. Keep to the bed next time. Women don't like doing it on the floor, only men. Why are you standing here?"

She went to the patio doors, closed them, and drew the draperies. The man had already drifted to the kitchen and was loading the dishwasher. I hustled to the bedroom and closed my suitcase. I had been packed since four thirty that morning. I wondered if her comment about the floor was accurate—and how the hell would she know?

"Aren't they early?" Kathleen complained as she rolled an article of clothing into a cavity she'd found in her second suitcase. "I thought you said that—"

"I forgot I moved our ride up. I did it through the rental agency, so they must have notified the cleaners. Besides," I wanted to move on and not get into too much detail about the arrangements for the flat, "it's rush hour. I'd rather be at Gatwick an hour early than sitting in the car, staring at the Tower, and wondering if—"

"I'm ready." She popped up triumphantly from her suitcase. "I'm sending the whole pile to the cleaners. No matter how you fold them, they always come out ruined at the other end." She draped her scarf over her shoulders. Her unbuttoned shirt was tucked in, although I'd seen better jobs.

"Buttons."

"What?"

I ran my fingers over my chest. She looked down, and her nimble fingers worked her buttons with zipper speed. I picked up her suitcase. "How'd I do?" she asked.

"We'll call this one Little Ben."

She blew out a puff with a nod indicating that that was my problem. She trudged past me with her carry-on.

I lugged Little Ben around the corner to the front hall and nearly plowed her over.

"We didn't even use those," she said to the man in the kitchen. He had emptied all the drawers and placed the clean, unused towels in a box. He froze and looked up from his work. Kathleen gripped the handle of her smaller suitcase in the living room as well as her carry-on. "There's no need to clean them. We never touched them. And why put them in a box? The unit has a washer."

I cut the lady a look. She gave a glance toward the man and then returned my hard look. She turned her attention back to the man. "She's right. They didn't use them. You can put those back in." She pivoted to me. "Have a nice trip, Mr.—"

"I'm sure we will." I let go of Little Ben, gently placed my hand on Kathleen's lower back, and guided her out the door. I retrieved Little Ben and my own suitcase and slung my travel bag over my shoulder. I wanted to get out before the sea hag inadvertently called me by the alias I had checked in with. Little old twit knew better, but I didn't trust her.

We settled into the backseat of the car, and the tension evaporated from my body. I wondered why my departure had been moved up. The commercial flight certainly had nothing to do with it. Maybe the cleaning crew had another trail to erase. As we headed toward the airport, Kathleen finished dabbing on her makeup while I checked my phone. Nothing. I leaned my head back against the headrest and stared out the window. As frantic commuters scurried about on bike and foot, backpacks weighing them down, the cardinal's last words played in my mind. I couldn't decipher exactly what he'd said.

Not that it mattered.

CHAPTER 3

I stretched out in my first-class seat and, before the plane backed away from the gate, reviewed my deed.

The faux cardinal's name was Alexander Paretsky, although there was little trace of any such man. He was a paid assassin (as, evidently, am I, although we're going to let that slide) whose modus operandi was that he rarely appeared as the same person. He even varied his height with an extended heel in his shoes. He could enter a scene at one height and leave it three inches shorter or taller.

Birth parents unknown, he was adopted in France and raised by his adopted sister after their parents abandoned them. They hopscotched to various parts of Eastern Europe and then disappeared from public records. He purportedly killed for any cause that was proficient at wiring money to various bank accounts throughout the world. The only picture I'd been shown of him was taken in the Caymans, time unknown, as he walked out of a bank in George Town. He hadn't looked much like that picture this morning, except for something about his eyes, but it had been dark.

According to the colonel, Paretsky had previously never operated against US interests. However, after a security breach had leaked the identity of numerous US personnel, he started a new game. Paretsky, and whoever funded him, nurtured greater diabolical desires than merely hitting hit men.

My brethren's parents were executed as they left a Publix grocery store in Venice, Florida. That alarm sent US intelligence agencies to parade attention. Hope that it was a one-time event was decimated when, three weeks later, a young woman was cut down in Conifer, Colorado. On her finger was her new engagement ring from her special ops fiancé. Next was a sister in San Antonio. Taught third grade. Teacher of the year. Mother of three. She was a recipient of a head shot from two hundred yards.

The message was clear. Our enemies had taken a page from the Mexican-drug-lord playbook. There *is* something worse than dying: causing the death of those you love. The witnesses, few that there were, gave varied and often diametrically opposed descriptions.

Even different heights.

Paretsky was put on the short list. Whether he was acting alone or abetted by an accomplice, we didn't know. A tip came in. Paretsky, for unknown reasons, would often dress in full cardinal wardrobe and stroll through Kensington Gardens an hour before sunrise. London had long been suspected as one of his homes. Whether his holy stroll was a new ritual or not didn't matter. The source, who purportedly knew things that proved his intimacy with Paretsky's history, was positive. The current location of all cardinals was tabulated, and the ones on British soil were trailed for two weeks. None had the early Kensington habit. Our information was deemed to be accurate. My number came up.

Vacation or not.

The plane started its backward motion; there is no power on heaven or earth that can keep me awake when that occurs. My eyes closed. I was back at Kensington Gardens. The cardinal—Paretsky—faced me. He had thin eyebrows, like a woman's. He mumbled again about the pope and his guardian.

Forgive me my sin.

I bolted up as my head tumbled forward like a loose rock.

"Would help if you slept at night," Kathleen said. I looked past her out the window and saw England leaving us. I'd slept through the thrust of jet engines defying gravity. "You bounced around like a busted bag of popcorn in a microwave. Bad dreams?"

Her hair was tight behind her head; not a free strand had survived the revolution. The scarf was wrapped around her neck, and she wore a pale-blue blazer. Regardless of the temperature, Kathleen was always cold in airplanes. I caught a faint whiff of perfume, just enough to make me want more.

"No," I lied again. "Looking forward to being home?"

Instead of answering, she glanced out the window. She knew I often threw a question back in response to one I didn't want to address. I doubted I had fooled her now. I doubted I had ever fooled her. "How does it go?" She turned back to me. "Forever lies a corner of England?"

"'That there's some corner of a foreign field. That is forever England.'"

"I like that. And I always thought you could substitute whatever you felt like for 'England.'"

"I think that Brooke would approve."

She smiled, and my eyes, as always, were drawn to the edge of her smile, where a thin line of age was just starting. It was not an indication of what was leaving her as much as a promise of what was to come.

"I am," she addressed my question, "looking forward to being home. Fall in Florida is my favorite time."

"The fields of yellow mustard, the sunset maples, the—"

She swatted my shoulder. "You know what I mean. The humidity's gone, and the winter crowds haven't arrived. I do wish, though, that I'd bought that dress at Harrods. The black-and-white one? I just couldn't decide."

"You want it more because you didn't get it." I crossed my ankles. She had looked stunning in it. I was surprised when she passed, but she claimed to have enough black-and-white dresses. "What's the book?"

She lifted the book off her lap and showed it to me. It was *How Green Was My Valley* by Richard Llewellyn. "So far," she said, "it's good. I think you might like it."

"I believe I read it. My rare first edition contains pictures of nude Welsh maidens frolicking in the country—"

"What can I get you two?"

I turned as the stewardess was upon us. "Bloody Mary." I impolitely jumped in front of Kathleen. "The sooner, the better." Kathleen requested coffee.

The stewardess moved back a row and repeated her question in the same chirpy yet indifferent tone. She could have changed her pitch a bit, made us feel a little special.

"And you?" Kathleen said.

"And me what?"

"Reading."

"Later," I told her as I rummaged through my carry-on bag and extracted a pair of earphones. I wasn't going to attempt reading. I was beat. I selected a playlist from my phone. "When I fly, I like to fly."

"I was going to tell you something."

"What?"

"I forget. It'll come to me."

When the drink landed in front of me—under a minute, not bad—I gave the stewardess a five without leaving my world where music was making me comfortably numb.

We landed at TPA and found a young man waiting for us with my name on his tablet. He was dressed in black and looked as if he were going to a junior high prom.

"You old enough to drive?" I said.

He nodded and smiled. "*Si*."

"Wonderful."

We collected our overweight luggage and followed Junior to his black Suburban. I asked him if he needed a stool to get in with. He nodded and smiled. It would have been the same reaction if I'd told him I got his sister pregnant. An iPad mounted to the dash gave him directions to Kathleen's condo in Spanish. She lived in downtown St. Pete, nine floors above Tampa Bay. My block bungalow was on an island less than half a mile from the Gulf of Mexico. We opted to decide later if we were getting together that evening. "Let's decide later" was our code for each of us staying in our own homes. We never broached discussing our secret message; it worked, and we were either content with that or too afraid to bring it up. Probably both. We pulled up under the building's portico. I instructed Junior to wait. Nod and smile.

"I got your sister pregnant," I said in a cheery voice.

Nod and smile.

"Jake, that's mean," Kathleen said. "What if he understands some?"

"I wasn't talking to him."

She punched me—hard. We got out of the SUV.

Her private elevator was undergoing repairs, so we took the general elevator to the ninth floor. It opened into a small library.

"Not a bad little reading room," I said. "You ever run into any of your cellmates out here?" The condo association, Kathleen had explained a week ago, had converted each floor to a themed library while we were gone. Looking for a means, I assumed, to justify the $1,200 monthly HOA fee.

"I'm the only one here right now. Other two units are empty."

I recognized some of the titles and then picked up on the theme. "War books?"

"*That's* what I was going to tell you on the plane." She fished for a key in her purse. "I received an e-mail last week. Each floor houses a collection, and I got Genghis Khan. Just below me? The poets. Above? O'Connor, Austen, Brontë. But nooo...I get the testosterone room."

"Not a bad draw," I said. "After all, war makes rattling good reading. Peace, not so much."

"That's not you, is it?" She unlocked her door.

"Hardy, and not the boys." I couldn't remember the exact line of the quote. That bugged me. I must be slipping. Too much booze?

I placed her two suitcases on stands in her walk-in closet. Her carry-on went on her bed. My phone buzzed an incoming text. I ignored it.

"Sandwich?" she asked from the kitchen.

"I'm fine."

I went to her window and gazed out over the waters of Tampa Bay. I like extended travel—relocating myself for several weeks at a time. Hemingway said homes were good for coming and leaving. His point was well made, but I need a base. We all do. Mine is the salty, sandy strip of the west coast of Florida.

"You sure?" Her voice came again from the kitchen. She'd make a good mother; she never took no for an answer when trying to feed someone. It had been a waste explaining to her that I was a highly functioning human being, fully aware of the consequences and meaning of my answers. Her voice again from the kitchen: "I can whip something up real fast."

What do you do with that?

"I'm gone," I said, as I entered the kitchen. I bundled her in my arms and gave her a kiss. Our trip, so eagerly planned, was over. I placed a finger over the line at the corner of her mouth. "Paris is dim," I said, "and crying without you. Rome's senators are back in chambers collecting a tax to pave in gold the streets that your feet graced. English poets are rising from the dead to pen words they sought for eternity to describe you. Your—"

"No."

"No?"

"Us, Jake. The poets have never seen anyone like us, not even in their itty-bitty-witty poet brains. Besides." She gave me a return peck. "When did you get so Victorian? Paris cries, Roman senators bow, and English poets burn their pens."

"OK." I stifled a yawn. It was all catching up with me. "Works for me."

I told her I'd give her a call tomorrow, a totally useless comment, and hit the elevator. I gave my address to Junior, a totally useless exercise, then grabbed the iPad and punched it in. Fifteen minutes and two bridges later—my pad's on an island off another island—I entered my base. Hadley III, my cat, greeted me by promptly yowling and darting out of sight. Cats. Missed you too. Don't think I paid money for the furball or rescued her from some shelter; I'm temporarily watching Hadley III for a friend who permanently moved away. Usually while I'm gone my neighbor Morgan looks after her, but Morgan was sailing, so my other neighbor, Barbara, had graciously accepted the honor.

While unpacking, I came across the wallet-sized picture that had been in Paretsky's hand. I didn't recall him reaching into his pocket to retrieve it. Did he routinely clutch the photograph while taking his predawn stroll? That didn't seem right. I stuck it in a drawer.

I poured a few ounces of Graham's 20 Year Old Tawny Port and headed down the dock. I'd started drinking port in Europe and learned to differentiate between the ten-, twenty-, and thirty-year vintages. It was a challenge picking up the nuances, but I was dedicated to the task. I think that's what they mean when they say you should continually grow as a person and embrace being a Triple L: Lifelong Learner. I might tackle opium next.

It felt strange not being with Kathleen after spending the last month together. Did she feel the same way? It felt like a question a fourteen-year-old would have. I thought of jumping back in my truck and going to her. Instead I took a seat at the step-down at the end of the dock, my toes a few feet off the water's surface.

The red channel marker came on for the night. A dolphin blew; I hadn't heard that sound for twenty-seven days. Hadley III arrived beside me. I took a sip of the port. Life was good. Maybe I'd do some fishing tomorrow. The only thing going on was that I was expecting a call any day to schedule delivery, within a two-hour window, of my new guest-bedroom furniture. I'd already donated the old bed and dresser to the local thrift shop. Better not inconvenience me too much; I detest being beholden to someone else's schedule.

My phone rang. It was Garrett.

"Want to come down, do a little kitesurfing?" I asked.

"You read the text?"

My phone had buzzed at Kathleen's, and I'd forgotten about it. Something in Garrett's voice urged me to get to the point of his call. "Tell me."

"From the colonel, he copied me—"

"And?"

"Your job in London?"

"What about it?"

"You clipped the wrong bird."

CHAPTER 4

"You there?" Garrett said.

"Playing with me, right?"

"Sorry, Jake."

His use of my name eliminated any doubt about a sick joke. Besides, Garrett was humorless. "You—they sure? Positive ID? It wasn't Paretsky?"

"Got the same message you did. I checked the British papers. Take a look yourself. You plugged Cardinal Giovanni Antinori. Thirty-two years with the church. The—"

"No way." I stood and faced my house. "No fucking way." He could have used a more sympathetic word than *plug*. Why care about nomenclature at such a time? "You're telling me some real cardinal just happened to be at the exact spot at the wrong time. I don't buy—"

"Get online. They—"

"I was set up."

I punched out my breath. A fish jumped to my left. Was it leaping to get food or to keep from becoming food? It goes both ways. My own mind was leaping around at a frenzied speed. There were so many questions jostling for attention I didn't even attempt to prioritize them. I threw it back to Garrett. "What now?" As I asked the question I knew that in all likelihood he had exhausted his knowledge of the situation.

21

"Not sure. Just wanted to make sure you saw the text. Knew you were traveling today."

"What do you make of it?"

"Rule out a coincidence. That—"

"What a shit show. No way was this Antinori bird not complicit in some manner."

"No one's saying he wasn't complicit. He just wasn't the mark. That leaves us with a couple of choices. Someone who knew we wanted Paretsky dead also wanted Antinori dead. That's a stretch. What's not implausible is that Paretsky got wind of it and sent out a decoy. Somehow he convinced Cardinal Antinori to take an early-morning stroll. Paretsky, assuming it's him behind this, wants us to know that—"

"If we go after him," I said, picking up the thread, "the most innocent and undeserving will die." While I spoke I thought, *I murdered a cardinal.*

"That is the new war. He used the cardinal to deliver a message that he'll do what he wants, and our interference will only cause harm. And in an ugly twist..."

He had pulled up short of hanging me, so I did the honors. "We're the ones who plug the innocent."

"Looks like it." He didn't need to agree that fast, either.

"He wasn't surprised."

"Who?"

"Ani...Is it Anitori or Antinori?"

"Antinori."

"He was calm, like a man who knew his time had come. How do you explain that?"

"I bear no explanations. He—"

"They checked, right? For two weeks they trailed the cardinals, and never once did one of them do the Peter Pan route."

"That's correct. Did—"

"Fucking shit show."

"—he question the gun?"

"Unbelievable. I assumed that Paretsky recognized when his time was up." I was trying to convince myself, but I knew it was a losing effort. *His eyes…he was trying to communicate something with childlike innocence.* I slapped away my second-guessing, but I knew that sucker would circle around with a Louisville Slugger. "What do you have on Antinori?"

"Mary Evelyn is rounding up everything there is on the man; you can look him up."

Garrett was a corporate lawyer in Cleveland—that was his bottle. Mary Evelyn was his assistant.

"Keep me posted," I said and disconnected. I was too disgusted to talk any further.

I stood at the seawall and gazed out toward the end of the dock where I had sat just minutes before, sipping my port, counting my lucky stars, and wondering during what two-hour window of a totally unencumbered day some smiling shitbag was going to ring my doorbell, whistle in with a bed, and then urge me, as he waltzed back out, to go online and take a customer satisfaction survey. That life was gone.

I'd killed a cardinal.

What do you do with *that*?

I looked at my house. My grass. My boat, *Impulse.* The familiar objects soothed me, provided me with a sense of calm that I desperately needed. I thought of contacting the colonel. He distrusted satellite phones, which are not positively secure. I could be at MacDill within forty-five minutes and use one of the SCIF phones. The air force base was headquarters for SOCom; Special Operations Command. Garrett and I believed that was where the colonel's funding came from, but he never confirmed or denied our allegation. On more than one occasion, we had flown in and out of the base and also utilized its communication equipment.

Forget it. I did my job. Someone else screwed up and owed me an explanation. Make them reach out. I wasn't wasting my time. I went into my sanctuary, took a seat in the screened porch, and pulled up Cardinal Giovanni Antinori on my iPad. He had a fountain of hair, a Madison Avenue smile, and that permanent tan that God bestowed upon the Italians as compensation for their lack of self-governing acumen. If the church shtick hadn't worked out, Hollywood would have welcomed him.

He was also a goner. And in the corner of England that I had just come from, his demise was big news. I perused the headlines.

Cardinal Gunned Down While Taking Morning Meditation Walk

Execution-Style Murder Reminiscent of Mob Hit

Eyewitness Points to Mystery Ponytail Man

That last one was of particular interest to me. A woman jogger who had passed me from the opposite direction while I was trailing Paretsky—really, Antinori—claimed that she saw a runner with a ponytail and glasses. She remembered him because "you don't see many guys running with eyeglasses on."

I remembered her. I'd kept my eyes down as we passed each other. Tube socks. Who the hell wears tube socks? And she was on me for wearing glasses? If that was all they had, I wasn't worried. But the investigation was ongoing, and the police only release what they want the public, or the perpetrator, to know.

What was Cardinal Giovanni Antinori doing taking such an early-morning stroll? It wasn't his habit. No one was aware of him doing it in the past, and his reason for being there remained shrouded. Yet I'd been told that Paretsky did take a customary morning stroll. Someone dressed like him had obviously duped us—put a lot of thought and effort into the deception. How did Paretsky lure him out there? Blackmail? A benign request for a clandestine meeting? Would I ever know?

Antinori was instrumental in championing food for infants and farming skills in Africa. He'd settled past sexual impositions of Catholic priests and was credited with moving the stoic institution into the new millennium. "Religion," he was quoted as saying, "is not an institution administered by man for the benefit of the administrators, but, rather, religion *is* the common man. It must address the questions and temptations of the modern world and cannot cling to outdated and unsubstantiated beliefs." That last comment had landed him in hot water. After all, what was religion if not "unsubstantiated beliefs"? Antinori was adamant that the church must face its own past transgressions. That brought more cries for censure from Rome and applauds and accolades from the crowd. His popularity seemed to have exploded over the past couple of years.

He was labeled 'The People's Cardinal.' His official residence was Granville Estates, north of London, where he held an annual fund-raiser for children of low-income families. It was an old-fashioned church bazaar held the third weekend in June. He'd been a young priest at a nearby parish early in his career and had started the carnival during that tenure. He personally manned an ancient high-striker attraction where contestants swung a sledgehammer in an attempt to ring a bell at the top of the tower. Several pictures on one site showed a smiling Antinori through the years, surrounded by children in front of the high striker. One picture, taken a little over twenty years back, before he became a cardinal, caught my attention. Everyone smiled at the camera except for an attractive young woman in a white sweater, who stood off to his side and smiled at him. Something about her...I plowed ahead.

He'd spent six months trekking across the globe, including a three-week sojourn in the Swiss Alps, before the age of thirty.

He still heard confessions.

Celebrated Mass at his childhood church.

Dropped unannounced into a kitchen for the homeless and toiled for hours.

A seven handicap—oh, come on, now.

I flipped the lid shut before the man fed Africa with a loaf of bread and clocked a four-minute mile.

I couldn't sit. I jumped in my truck. Half a mile later, I parked and hiked over the arched boardwalk that connected the parking lot and the beach, keeping foot traffic off the dunes and sea oats. I took a seat on a concrete bench. It had a plaque with the name of a dead person on it. That would be me someday. On the gulf, a light above the surface slid south—the top of a sailboat's mast. If a boat serves to facilitate coming and going—like Hemingway's house— but someone lives on it, what direction is he headed? I'd leave those issues to Morgan. He grew up on a sailboat and claimed movement was his natural state. I kept my thoughts at bay.

Farther out on the gulf, lightning streaked the sky. It was distant and small. Yet, if you were caught in the isolated storm, the tempest would be anything but inconsequential. A woman giggled off to my left. To my right the pink hotel stood against the dark black, its Moorish towers giving nothing away.

Somebody used me.

That person would pay.

Alexander Paretsky was still alive.

That wasn't my problem. Unless Paretsky had been the one to set me up. The Garrett theory.

I rearranged the questions, hypothesized on what might be, and accomplished nothing. After a while I stood and defiantly faced a stiff breeze that had swept in off the gulf. I bid the plaque a good night's sleep and went home.

He came to me that night, like he had on the plane when I'd dozed off as it pulled back from the gate. His back was to me, and his cardinal vestments fluttered in a breeze, but there had been no breeze the morning we had met, and I knew that wasn't right. I told myself—in the dream—that I was dreaming, but that admission in no way empowered me to break free. He reluctantly turned. He did not speak. His eyes pleaded for resolution.

I tried to wake myself up, but I was a prisoner in a different sphere and powerless to leave.

"Why are you here?" I demanded.

He did not answer. Instead, Cardinal Giovanni Antinori said, *"Forgive me my sin."*

I bolted up. My room was dark except for the light from the moon's reflection on the bay filtering through the slats of the venetian blinds. My window was cracked open so I could hear the sound of the water, but all was still, and I heard nothing. Hadley III appeared at my door. She hesitated, her green eyes catching a streak of light. She backed away. I was sweating as if I'd broken a fever.

It was wrong. All wrong.

If Garrett's theory—that Antinori was somehow coerced by Paretsky to take the walk—was correct, wouldn't it be the other way around? Wouldn't he be forgiving me? After all, my gun was drawn when Antinori turned. Even in the dim light, he certainly saw it. And who the hell only has one sin or a sin that outweighs all the others?

I do.

For I have killed a cardinal of the church.

CHAPTER 5

It was the second time I'd found him nesting at the end of my dock.

A year after Garrett Demarcus and I left the army, Colonel Janssen parked himself on the bench that ran across the back of the twelve-by-twelve deck at the end of the dock. The December sun had broken the horizon directly across the bay. His arms were spread out on the bench like a bird drying its wings. He asked me if I had enjoyed my yearlong drinking binge. I told him to hit the road. He recruited me for clandestine work. Now he was back at the same spot, but today the late-summer sun broke the horizon far to his left.

I finished my run and rinsed under my outdoor showerhead at the side of the house. I put on a pair of shorts and a V-neck T-shirt, brewed a pot of coffee, and poured a cup. I strolled down the hundred feet of my dock. I took a seat at the opposite end of the bench. He was long, gangly, and pale—like a great white egret with clothes. Beltway born and bred, he wore khaki pants, loafers, and a white, long-sleeved shirt with the sleeves rolled up. Two pens stood at attention in his shirt pocket. To his right was a rust-colored attaché case with a leather handle. It looked as though it had been thrown under the bus a few times, dragged behind a stagecoach, put through an industrial washer, and finally donated to the zoo's gorilla exhibit.

29

"Under Florida's 'stand-your-ground' law," I took a sip of coffee; I had not brought him any, "I could have put a couple of rounds in you from my rear porch and walked a free man." There was a small patch of white, baked-on bird shit between us.

He didn't bother to look at me but kept his eyes on a blue cruiser churning the waters toward the bridge across the bay. Its loose aft curtain flapped violently in the wind, as if trying to tear away from the boat.

"We catch more heat killing a civilian in Iraq," he said, "than someone does for wasting his neighbor in Florida. God's waiting room has some real cowboys up in Tallahassee."

"That's a considerable insult to the cowboys."

"What do you know?"

"You sent me on a mission in which I killed an innocent man."

He turned to me. Drops of perspiration dotted his forehead. "Yes, you did." He looked older than the last time I'd seen him; I wondered if he thought the same of me and why I cared. It didn't escape me that he was fine with my statement implicating myself, but he wasn't about to share the guilt. *Yes, you did.*

"When we got word, we hustled you out of the flat in order to get you through airport security as fast as possible," he continued. "The collateral damage is unfortunate. That's not what concerns me."

"Concerns me."

"You'll get over it. If not, there are plenty of stolen boats to recover."

He was referring to a side business I have of recovering missing boats. "If all you do is issue orders based on compromised or incomplete information, then I'd rather be chasing boats."

"We were a hundred percent positive and—"

"You were a hundred percent wrong."

His jaw tightened, and his face scrunched. He gazed over the water. I kept my eyes on him; I wanted to be waiting when he came back to me.

"You got a leak, Colonel," I continued. "That's why Paretsky knows the location of his targets. Why he knew I was coming. Your ship's taking on water, and you don't know where. Or do you?"

A sailboat with a dog sticking its nose over the bow glided by us. His eyes followed the boat. "We don't know how he gets his information. Your assignment was known to only a very few. No one in that group talked. We—"

"Someone sure as hell did."

He turned to me. "I will remind you that when conducting business with me, you are still—"

"Someone spilled. That needs to be your primary focus, your obsessive focus—not my lack of protocol."

"We're working on that. That's not your problem."

"Like hell it—"

"*This* is your problem."

He pulled an envelope from his attaché case. He tossed it in my lap, and it nearly slid off and onto the composite decking. I opened it and extracted a picture. It was dark. Grainy. Nonetheless, I could make out my back as I stood over the fallen cardinal. I turned it over. Nothing. I brought it back around so the picture was facing up. I returned it to the envelope and tossed it back onto his lap.

"They'll never make me for it," I said. He had not bothered to pick the envelope off his lap. "I was layered so thick with disguise that I wouldn't even recognize myself."

"It confirms Paretsky as our man and that he knew you were coming and set us up. We received similar pictures through the same channel when the couple south of you was hit, as well as the Colorado girl and the teacher. It's his way—"

"And you're positive those were him?" It didn't escape me that he didn't offer a supportive remark after my statement that I couldn't be identified in the picture.

"No ques…as positive as we can be."

"Recent events indicate that's not saying much. Maybe someone knows Paretsky's habit and is trying to pin it on him."

"That's overanalyzing. We—"

"Your lack of analysis is why we're sitting here."

"You want off this?"

"I want to kill Paretsky and, if it wasn't him, whoever set me up to kill the cardinal."

"Then listen, soldier. Paretsky knew we were coming after him. He wants us to know; otherwise, why send the picture? He's telling us that any attempt on his life will be met with the death of another, and that—"

"You're avoiding the issue." I interrupted him despite his instruction. "Your leak is closer than you thought. You knew there was a leak that led to the previous deaths, but this tells you the leak is in your inner—"

"His source of information that led him to his other targets is not necessarily the same source that gave him knowledge of your presence."

"And that is why the army keeps recruiting. You need fresh bait to spin your bullshit on. Explain how this went down without it being the same leak."

"We can't."

I started to resume my attack, but his reasoning was correct. The cardinal job likely was from the same leak, but not necessarily so. Assuming it was the same leak could lead us down false paths. He'd reached that deduction before I had. That would put me in a foul mood all day.

He picked up the envelope with the picture in it and placed it back into his attaché case, which was packed with red, white, and blue folders.

I asked, "What color am I?"

Janssen kept his case open. "We fear that Paretsky may be recruiting a team to do hits on US soil. Not on agents but rather, as we have begun to witness, the immediate families of agents. We suspect that money remains his primary motivation and that he is likely financed by the world's latest religious nuthouse, PTO.

"Our primary goal, which you failed at and as of now are still engaged in, is to erase him. You are red. I don't plant my ass on a dock in this suffocating freak show of a state for whites and blues." He bent his head down, brought up his right shoulder, and wiped his forehead with his shirt.

I decided not to contest his assertion that I had failed or defend against his slanderous assault on my home state. "Your source," I said. "Who tipped you off that Paretsky would be in Kensington Gardens?"

"Don't know."

"Don't know what?"

"Who he is."

"What type of operation do you run, Colonel? You sent me on a job, and you didn't verify your source. That is what you indicated, correct?"

He took a breath and seemed to settle down, as if the worst was behind him. A pelican dive-bombed the water. Janssen ignored it. "He gave intimate details." I sensed the first hint of an apologetic and conciliatory tone, as if he too had been duped. "The source knew things about Paretsky's past that only we knew. That only someone who knew him could possibly know. We didn't have time to verify. That he knew Paretsky was never in doubt. We traced the movement of other cardinals that were in the known area. It made sense; he'd disguised himself as clergy in the past. We did our background work to ensure that—"

"Paretsky," I cut in. "He led you to himself so he could sacrifice someone and teach us not to mess with him. Played you like a dime-store harmonica, didn't he?"

"He'd have nothing to gain by doing so. He kills for money, not kicks and giggles."

He withdrew another envelope from his still-open attaché case and handed it to me. I opened it and took out a picture of a young woman. She had thick, dark, shoulder-length hair. Her bangs hung over her eyebrows to her lashes. Pale-green eyes and plump, red lips. Not a ruby red, but soft, like a rosé summer wine. She looked like the girl next door who'd grown up into a runway model. She was with a man whose back was turned and head was down.

"We believe," Janssen started in, "that's Paretsky in the photo and he's been spending time with that woman. Therefore, she might have been our anonymous tip. And even if not, she could lead us to him."

"Who is she?"

"Renée Lambert. American. Sometime model. Used to favor the islands, casinos in Macau, and nightlife in Dubai. Last couple of years, she shed that skin and has taken up social issues. A do-gooder. We've been able to produce two more sightings of Paretsky: one with Ms. Lambert and the third," he pulled out a color eight-by-ten, "with this lady."

He held up a picture of a blonde with sunglasses half the size of her head. She stood on the deck of a yacht. Paretsky was behind her and slightly off to her left. He wore tan slacks and a black, short-sleeved shirt. That told me he spent his boat time in the air-conditioned stateroom. His frame was small, almost delicate, but his eyes, under pencil-thin brows, were dark, and his face was tight.

"We think that when he's away from London, he spends considerable months on the water; boats of different registries and names make it even harder to pin him down. One more thing." He paused, obliging me to go in.

"Yes."

"Renée Lambert's father, Donald, is living the American dream. Shuffleboard. Florida sunshine. Two-for-one every day. Moved to Treasure Island four years ago."

"You withheld this from me?" Treasure Island was the spit of sand north of me.

"We didn't know if it meant diddly-squat, and we still don't know."

"You led me to believe that you only had one picture of Paretsky."

"This is recent, and—"

"Not that recent."

He extracted another picture from his attaché case. "Last night we came across this picture of Ms. Lambert with this unidentified man. He's not her father, and he appears too large to be Paretsky, but as you can see, his turned head makes identification difficult. Paretsky, as I'm sure you've noted, is of a smaller stature. This man," he handed me the picture, "is quite large."

The background looked familiar: boats to the left and a park of some sort directly behind them and lower. It registered. "The mezzanine of the Valencia," I said. The Valencia is a grande-dame hotel built in the roaring twenties in downtown St. Pete.

"Correct. We—"

"When was it taken?"

"About two weeks ago." He handed me another folder. Thicker. Who knew, maybe the whole bloody briefcase was for me. He stood. I did likewise. "Find Paretsky, Erase him."

I'm telling you, they have a limited vocabulary.

"The cardinal," I said.

"What about him?"

"Why was he there?"

"Not an exigency for us."

"Is for me."

"That's on your dime."

"What aren't you telling me? What are the answers to the questions I'm not asking?" His face remained rigid. "Forget it. Who else is working this? I can't be tripping over other—"

"It belongs to you and Demarcus. Multiple teams create too much disturbance, too much wake. We obviously underestimated Paretsky's intelligence capabilities." He paused a second and then said, "He has connections to your little corner of this swamp. Find him. Finish your job."

"I was paid to—"

He stepped into me. He smelled of fresh mint. Beads of sweat dotted his forehead like water on the outside of a glass. "I pay you to think, and I suggest you start doing that."

"I did—"

He stuck his nose within an inch of mine. "You knew. You *knew* when you pulled the trigger that morning that something wasn't right. You might not admit it to yourself, and you sure as hell won't admit it to me, but you knew." He leaned in even closer. Next stop was Eskimo kissing. "There is no goddamned way that a cardinal went down like a world-class assassin. You want to tell me otherwise, son, make a go of it. Right here. Right now. I'm listening. I don't hear you. *I don't hear you.*"

Prick.

He nodded his head a few beats, backed off a couple inches, and then shut it down. "Don't screw up this time." He pivoted and strolled confidently down my dock.

A little over a year ago, the colonel had acted off the grid, pulled a mother lode of favors, and arranged a new identity for Kathleen. The Chicago Outfit, her deceased husband's business partners, was pursuing her. We staged her death and gave her a new identity: Lauren Cunningham became Kathleen Rowe. At the time I'd thought it a great act of charity. A real pal. I know now that he was acting in his best interest. He owned me for life.

Good thing for him that my love for Kathleen astounded my senses. Otherwise, I'd hide behind 'stand–your-ground' and drop him into the salty water that lapped up against my seawall. I had murdered a cardinal. I sure as hell wasn't going to blame myself.

Good luck with that stiff breeze.

CHAPTER 6

Donald Lambert lived in a single-story ranch house less than a half mile from a public beach access. The house had a fresh coat of yellow and white paint. His lawn and landscaping appeared to have just come from the barber. I rang the doorbell. The Westminster Quarters chimed inside. I couldn't imagine listening to that every time I wanted a pepperoni and green olives.

I rapped my knuckles on the door. I hiked around the house. It backed up to a canal where a gray dock, put in around the time *Thriller* was released, hugged the property parallel to the water. No boat or lift, but a half-submerged bait bucket with a yellow line tied to it bobbled in the wind-scrubbed water. A great white egret staked out its claim by the bait bucket. Across the canal, a man worked on his twin-engine Wellcraft, *Knotty Girl* in script on her side. The sticky, humid air clung to my skin like a wet suit.

I continued following the circumference of the property until I returned to the front porch. The door was open, and a man stood, arms folded, leaning against the doorframe.

"Nice tour?"

"What's in your bait bucket?"

"Bait," he said. His hair was buzzed on the sides, nothing on top.

"That would be a fine place to keep it." I thrust out my hand. "Jake Travis."

"Lambert, Donald Lambert." He shook my hand purely out of obligation. "What can I do for you, Travers?"

"Tra*vis*. Travers wrote *Mary Poppins*." I flashed him my Florida PI license. "I'm looking for your daughter, Renée. Harvey Boswell Chevrolet has retained me. They're a mega-dealer over on the East Coast—must have a thousand cars on that lot. Nothing your daughter did, Mr. Lambert, but they had some purchases using fake IDs. All cash. Your daughter's ID was used. I'm guessing her dream's not a dual-exhaust, cherry-red Silverado 3500. If so, thank you for your time." I opted for the cover and soft opening, instead of proclaiming that his daughter might be in grave danger, as I didn't want to alarm him. Nonetheless, I sounded like an actor who knew he was blowing the audition.

"Wouldn't the police be involved?" He wore a washed-out blue T-shirt with a pocket. I like T-shirts with a pocket, but they're hard to find.

"I assume they are." I put my license away. "But Boswell hired me to expedite the process, you know, kick it into high gear. With the Patriot Act crawling up everybody's ass, they're eager to get this behind them. You don't have something to drink, do you?" If he checked with Boswell, I was cooked. But I'd have my information by then.

Lambert took a second with that and then surprised me. "Sure, Poppins, come on in."

We went through a living room of uncluttered furniture. Lambert didn't strike me as a man who spent a lot of time in a living room, although, as traditional homes go, that room got naming honors. A large picture window occupied the front wall. The blinds were raised tight against the ceiling, and a prominent, trimmed hedge blocked the lower half of the view. I doubted the blinds had been touched in years. We entered the kitchen, where a bucket rested on the tile floor next to the oven. The bucket was filled with water, and a mop leaned out of it like a crooked palm with no fronds.

"Didn't answer when you knocked; I was in the shower. Up early and done fishing by nine. Water OK?"

"Appreciate it."

He opened his refrigerator and handed me a bottle. "Just getting ready to do the kitchen. I put that bucket in the shower and use the water it catches to do the floor."

I unscrewed the lid and took a swig. "That's certainly an energy ef—"

"Nothing newfangled green about it, either. My wife, she was British, grew up using the bathwater. You always walk around people's property who you don't know?"

"No, and I apologize if I offended you. I live on the water, about two miles south of here. I wanted to see your setup."

Lambert seemed to consider that as he poured himself a mug of coffee. The chipped, stained cup had *Dad* on it in large letters.

"Pinfish," he said and took a sip. "In the bait bucket. Couple of blues as well. Nothing this morning, though. Good-size gag grouper yesterday, enough for two dinners. What do you pull out?"

"Little of everything. Flounder, lately. I got sea grass, and they like the edge just where the water turns deep beyond the end of my dock."

"We don't get them back here."

"I'll bring you some next time I hook one." I took another drink from the bottle. "Hate to press and all," I said, "but do you have a number for your daughter? Like I said, whoever is using her identity is using this address, and we'd like to get in contact with her."

"Follow me." He strolled out the back door to a covered, concrete patio, where he claimed a metal chair. I settled into a chair next to him and leaned back. It nearly flipped over, but the back of the chair hit the wall of the house.

"You ever go out on *Knotty Girl* across the canal?" I said.

He stared across the narrow water. "Old Linwood," he said. "You can't tell that fat boy nothing." He looked back at me. "Yeah, we used to go out friends and come back enemies, but that ain't what fishing's about. We have a good time now 'cause we recognize that in each other. Nothing more important in a relationship than knowing your counterpart and accepting him for what he is."

I wasn't sure what to say, so I went with, "Do you know how I can reach your daughter?"

"You say you catch flounder."

"I do."

"On the edge of the sea grass where it gets shallow."

"Deeper. They like the deeper edge."

He nodded. "And this Boswell has thousands of cars on his lot?"

"He's got a few."

A man and a woman on separate Jet Skis motored down the canal toward the open end. The woman kept revving her engine and spurting forward. Lambert took another sip and put his *Dad* mug on a wrought-iron side table. He leaned forward with his elbows on his knees, steepled his fingers, and said, "Here's the deal; I believe what you said about the fish, but nothing else. Only reason I invited you in was to find out who the hell you really are."

Time to jettison my cover. "She might be in danger."
I leaned in and mimicked his position, elbows on knees.
"We—and I cannot discuss who *we* are, but we fly the red,
white, and blue—believe that she is associated with a very
nasty person. I need—"

"You don't give a rat's ass about Renée. You want her
because of that fellow she was seeing."

"That's correct." I wanted to respond quickly to his accusation so as not to alienate myself any further.

Lambert leaned back. The great white egret on his dock
took a slow-motion bird step in our direction. Lambert paid
it no attention. "You working with that other guy?"

"No clue who you're referring to."

"Came round yesterday?"

"Tell me about him." I couldn't imagine that the colonel would send me in twenty-four hours after someone
else.

Lambert got out of his chair and lumbered out to his
dock. I followed. The great white egret, not intimidated
by him, took a single step back as he passed. My bet was
that they were fishing buddies, and he fed the bird. Lambert
turned his back to me, raised his bait bucket, poked around,
hesitated, and lowered it back into the water. He gazed out
toward the open water where the Jet Skis had just taken a
corner. Their engines shattered the morning. He spoke with
his back to me.

"How do I know," he said, "which one of you to trust?"

"You go to Sea Breeze for breakfast?" He faced me and
nodded. "Ask Peggy. She'll tell you everything about me,
and when she's done, you'll no doubt have higher aspirations
for your daughter than me, but you'll trust me."

Peggy, who works the counter at the breakfast joint, doesn't know that much about me. Few people do. But that wasn't what he was really fishing for.

"I might just do that," he said. "This other guy, he was like you, all muscles, but not as tall, and a shaved head. No twinkle in his eye, either. Said he was a friend of her boyfriend, and her boyfriend hadn't seen her for a few days. Said they were both concerned."

"He here?" I ignored his twinkle remark.

"Who?"

"Her boyfriend."

He snorted. "Never met him."

He tossed a pinfish to the egret. The bird took a step forward and caught it in its mouth. "I keep hoping that she's just waiting for the right one to bring home. You got kids?"

"No."

"Married?"

"No."

"Then you don't know. All you ever really want for them is to be happy and maybe bring someone good back to the nest. Just someone who cares the world for them."

"She's in with the wrong people," I said, returning to the reason of my visit and sounding rude in the process.

Lambert kept his eyes on the bird and then glanced up at me. "I believe you're right. Let's go back in the shade. I need a refill." He motioned with his empty cup.

Lambert disappeared into his house while I reclaimed my seat. The egret tracked his movement. I picked my water up off a fish magazine on the wicker side table where I'd left it. It was the same sportfishing rag I get, three issues back.

He stepped out from the kitchen and settled back into his chair. He kept his mug in his hand. "Renée, she doesn't come around much. Last couple years she calmed down a bit, took life more seriously. She was close to her mom—my wife committed suicide six months back—and settled in London. Elizabeth, my wife, was originally from around there, little place called Harlow. Visited the place couple years back. Me? I like this part just fine. But Renée, she's young and good-looking. Got a personality that can light up a room."

"My condolences regarding your wife." I recalled reading that Giovanni Antinori was also from around Harlow. As a young priest in that area, he had started an annual carnival. I dropped it in a mental file. Problem is, that file has a hole in the bottom.

"She's finally at peace. Her mind was a rough place to live. Anyways, one day Renée calls me and says she's been spending time with some fella in Europe. Told her to bring him by next time she was home."

"And did she?"

"Said she would, but no, never got around to it."

"Talk much about her new friend—what he did?"

"No, sir."

"Name?"

"No."

I brought up the picture on my phone—I'd taken a picture of all the pictures the colonel had given me—of Renée Lambert at the Valencia with the indistinguishable mystery man. I handed it to Lambert.

He asked, "When was this taken?"

"We believe around two weeks ago. The Valencia." The colonel hadn't told me how he came into possession of the photo. I wouldn't be surprised if NSA had tapped into Facebook and done a portrait search. I scrolled to a picture of Renée with Paretsky. "This man your visitor?"

He took my phone and studied it. "No. He was bigger, more like that first one you showed me, but no way of telling from that shot." He handed my phone back. "She was to come by, but she called that night—late—and said she couldn't make it. I haven't heard from her since."

"Since when?"

"Pardon?"

"When was the last time you talked to her?"

"That night. Little less than two weeks back."

"And the last time you saw her?"

He shrugged and gazed out toward the water. "Half a year, maybe? When her mother—"

"Is that unusual?"

"What?"

"Being in town and then begging off and not dropping by."

"Why do you think I'm yakking to you? You think I normally let lying strangers walk around my property and then invite them in?"

"How did she sound on the phone—when she called you at the last minute and begged off?"

He brought his left hand up and rubbed his cheek as if conducting a shaving test. "Like she didn't want me to worry." He switched hands. His left went down by his side, and his right hand came up to his right temple. "I almost asked her if everything was all right. I should have. It was late, I was tired, but I should have."

"You had no way—"

He waved his hand at me. "Save it."

I shifted my weight and stuffed my phone back into the front pocket of my cargo shorts. Music played in the house; it was soft, and I couldn't make out the tune. I hadn't heard anything when I walked through. He must have flipped it on when he got a refill.

"Have you called her?" I said.

"Her phone's off. Or she doesn't answer it. I don't know one from the other." He leaned in again, elbows on his knees. He had a pen in his T-shirt pocket that hadn't been there when he answered the door. Above his right shoulder hung a slightly crooked picture of a beaming Donald Lambert with his arm draped around a woman I assumed was his late wife. I wondered why he kept it outside, but then I knew. This was where he lived. His living room.

"Nice picture." I nodded toward the wall and momentarily thought I'd seen the picture before.

"That was us a couple years back," Lambert said. "I tracked down a few of Renée's old friends, but they haven't heard from her. Told them to call me if they did."

Although I enjoyed Lambert's company, I hadn't learned much. I was eager to see if Mary Evelyn had found anything more on Cardinal Antinori. "Tell me about your other visitor."

Lambert leaned back into his seat and took a sip of coffee. He considered my request like we were in a play, and he had momentarily forgotten his lines. "He walked into my house..." He paused and gazed out toward his dock. "Didn't give two shits 'bout me." He gazed back at me. "Never looked me in the eye like you do. Jake, you're one of the worst liars I've ever met."

I'd been told that before and never took it as a compliment.

"Said she was in danger. Kept moving. Touching things. Opened my cupboards, took my phone, and ran through it. Threatened—"

"Why didn't you call the police?"

"You ever watch old Western movies?"

"*The Searchers.*"

"Those big long pistols? He drew one from under his coat the second he stepped through my door. Kept it on me the whole time. Said if I went to the police, he'd find out, and I'd never see her again."

"Yet you let me in."

"Bad guys don't wear shorts."

I didn't know what to do with that other than that I needed to start wearing black jeans in order to be taken more seriously in this world. And practice lying. About the only person I do that well with is Kathleen.

"Tell me everything," I said. "Every detail."

He didn't have much. Cropped hair, solid build. Dark clothes. Lambert stated that his visitor claimed that he and Renée's boyfriend were concerned that she had dropped off the grid. That their concern manifested itself with a six-shooter didn't escape Lambert. If Lambert knew where his daughter was, he wouldn't tell them, nor, I decided, would he indulge me, shorts or no shorts. No way. Two guys, back to back, looking for his daughter, and Lambert did what any dad would do: battened down the hatches.

I'd be walking out with not much more information than I'd walked in with. We both stood, shook hands, and I gave him my card. I told him to call if he remembered anything or heard from his daughter. I reminded him to have breakfast at the Sea Breeze. At the door I turned and faced him. Behind him, outside the sliding glass doors that led to his patio, the great white egret stood, no more than three feet from the glass. He might have lost his wife and was missing a daughter, but he had a bird for a friend. Whatever that was worth.

"Trust me," I said, and it sounded so lame I hurried up my speech so those two words wouldn't pollute the air. "Give me something about your visitor with a gun. His entrance into your life is not good for you or your daughter."

He brought his right hand up as if to touch his face but then brought it back down to his side. "I'd l-like you to leave now."

I knew I'd be back.

CHAPTER 7

Peggy dropped my breakfast in front of me on the lacquered counter in Sea Breeze. I crop-dusted the plate with pepper. The windows were open, and bushy red geraniums in the window boxes spilled into the booths like frozen fire. The syrupy air hung heavy with the smell of grilled bacon, onions, and potatoes. I picked up a paper someone had left and flipped to the weather page. I noted the tides, gulf temperature, moon phase, sunrise, and sunset. I thought about tackling sports, but I just didn't care.

I'd decided the best way to earn Lambert's trust was to respect his wish that I leave. I planned to give him some time and circle back. I already doubted that blueprint and wished I'd insisted that he join me for breakfast. He was hedging, maybe flat-out lying, and a little one-on-one might help dissolve him. My phone rang.

"What do you got?" I asked Mary Evelyn. Garrett had told me she was compiling information on Cardinal Antinori.

Mary Evelyn was third-generation, East Side Cleveland, Ohio, Irish Catholic. Garrett, against my judgment, shared everything with her. She had validated his decision numerous times. I had no clue how she would take the fact that I had accidently on purpose wasted a cardinal.

"I'm sending you a doc on the cardinal," she said. "I assume at this point that you know most of it, but there might be some details about his early life and career that you haven't come across. Whether that helps you or not, we'll see."

"You know what occurred, right?" I thought I should say more but held back. The ball was in her court.

"I do. Don't worry, Jake."

Her use of my name startled me. Mary Evelyn and I had a running game in which I tried, always unsuccessfully, to get her to call me by my first name. This was only the second time she had ever done so, and like the first occasion, it was unsolicited and at a time when I was vulnerable. "Garrett gave me the details," she continued. "Accidents happen."

"Accidents?"

"You deal with it in your way, and I'll deal with it in mine. And Mr. Travis?"

"Yes?"

"Don't screw up this time." The line went dead.

Seems to be a universal instruction for me.

I started to take a forkful of eggs, but her last comment spurred me forward. I placed the fork down, but not before the saliva started running in my mouth. I called FBI Special Agent Natalie Binelli. I had worked a case with Binelli, and we'd developed an informal arrangement whereby she would assist Garrett and me. I left a message. I did the same with Brian Applegate, a security analyst at MacDill.

"When's the big day?" Peggy demanded as she refilled my coffee.

"You'll be the first to know," I said, picking up my fork for another pass at the eggs. "You got a good summer crowd today."

She plopped the coffeepot on the counter. "Don't change subjects with me. You better grab that woman while you can, or else."

"What?" My mouth was nearly drooling with anticipation. I shoved the eggs in.

"What?"

"Or else what?" It came out a little garbled.

"Don't be smart with me, either."

"Listen, you don't think I have a twinkle in my eyes, do you?"

"I've seen no proof of a light inside your head."

She picked up the coffeepot and did a refill on the guy next to me. He hadn't bothered to pepper anything on his plate; that severely limited my interest in him as well as his contribution to society. Peggy wasn't done with me. She planted her left hand on her hip and squared off. "Not a woman out there—you listening to me?—not a single one out there, no matter what they tell their man, that don't wanna walk that aisle."

I thought of the sea hag in London lecturing me that women don't like making love on the floor. And now Peggy chiming in on marriage. I realized that I knew precious little about Peggy other than that she served me breakfast and urged me to marry Kathleen. I took a bite of crispy bacon, and my world became a better place.

"Tell me what your—" My phone rang and jiggled next to my coffee, cutting me off...Binelli. I looked up, but Peggy was off barking at someone in the kitchen.

Binelli volunteered to send me what she had on Paretsky, but I doubted it was anything more than what the colonel had already provided. She was between meetings and briefly questioned the source of my curiosity. I deflected her questions, and she hung up on me. That woman *never* said good-bye.

Applegate called back as I was finishing the hash browns and sports; I'd gotten bored, so I memorized the winning percentages of all the Major League Baseball teams. He was aware of the hunt for Paretsky. He regurgitated what he knew, but it was identical to the colonel's spiel. They were reading from the same dossier. We disconnected. My plate was empty, although I didn't remember taking the last bite. Where's the enjoyment in that? I left an extra five on my seven-dollar breakfast and instinctively lowered my head on my way out the door.

It was disappointing that neither Binelli nor Applegate had anything, but not disheartening. The chances of Applegate having a thicker folder on Paretsky than the colonel did were slim. Binelli would take some time, ask some questions, and scout around. She'd be back. She was a player.

I passed under the filtered shade of a pine stand, where a pair of fat-tire beach bikes leaned against the trunks, and headed down Eighth Avenue toward the beach.

Renée Lambert was AWOL. That didn't surprise me. I'd perused the packet the colonel had left me before I dropped in on Lambert. Her London flat had been searched as soon as they realized that I shot the wrong man. Maybe sea hag got that call as well. Nothing of consequence was found. It was under surveillance now in the event that she returned. I thought of catching a flight and taking a peek myself but didn't consider it a wise use of time. Whoever searched it was likely far better at those things than I was.

Hard to imagine—anyone better at anything than me.

That left me with Lambert. Someone had paid him a visit. Might do so again.

I called PC. He and his sidekick, Boyd, did grunt surveillance work for me. They were high school dropouts, and PC packed a kick-ass IQ. It had gotten him thrown in the slammer twice before age sixteen. He and Boyd had proved to be valuable assets, more than capable of improvising and looking out for themselves. PC had also become a worthy chess adversary. I wanted to keep them on the right side of the law and knew that idle time was the devil's time. The path he was heading down when I'd met him was a hard one to back out of.

"Jake-o-man. Still hunting rogue cops?" PC and Boyd had recently been instrumental in helping me locate a missing girl who had been kidnapped by a sheriff's detective.

"He's doing twenty. Got a job for you."

"Shoot."

"Need you to watch a house. Treasure Island. I'll text you the address." I slowed my pace so as to stay under the overhang of the stores.

Two women passed me on the bikes that had been outside of Sea Breeze. One of them wore a hat so wide it cast a shadow over her entire body. The other had thin arms and long, slender legs that pumped up and down in a mesmerizing motion, her ponytail swinging in rhythm like a metronome. I fell deeper in love the farther she got from me. Glamour and lust, after all, both feed on distance.

"Twenty-four-seven?" PC terminated my affair.

I hesitated. Wouldn't hurt, but it would be hard to remain undetected—not that Lambert would ever report anything. "Maybe twelve, eighteen hours a day. Next few days." It seemed a little wishy-washy for me, but I justified it to myself by thinking my actions were strictly precautionary in the first place. "Start immediately. I'll—"

"No can do. We're—"

"Don't tell me that. You—"

"Breathe deep, Jake-o."

"When?"

"Tomorrow. Noonish. We're at Disney with a couple of babes, real Space Mountain junkies. And cotton candy. No idea that chicks were that passionate about pink whipped sugar." He paused. "That OK?"

There wasn't any sense in disrupting their trip. I hadn't planned on keeping tabs on Lambert, but once I'd learned that a man with a gun had imposed himself and that initial inquiries to Binelli and Applegate were air balls, I wanted an eye on him.

"Tomorrow's fine," I said. "Say hi to Goofy."

"You mean Boyd?"

I hung up.

I gazed down the street, but the legs, and my lust, were gone.

At home I fixed a cup of coffee and took my laptop to the screened porch. The double, sliding doors were open, and there was little discernable difference between the outside and interior air. The legal profession calls it 'difference without distinction.' I occasionally turn the AC on at night, but otherwise I like living with a roof over my head and open walls. This arrangement, enhanced by a nonlatching, screened-porch door, creates a vibrant gecko population within the house, but Hadley III is a formidable huntress. A dead one was on my seat. The seat faces southwest toward the open waters of the gulf. I avoid seats that face north; I like the sun in front of me. When I dip beneath the equator, I adjust my habit appropriately.

I picked it up—the gecko, not the seat—kicked open the screen door that didn't latch, and tossed it out under the wild red hibiscus bush. I'd just finished putting a new pneumatic closer on my neighbor Barbara's door; it would have been nice if my latch had gone before I made the hardware run, but it doesn't work that way. Next big blow that came along, the door would bang all night. I perused the doc that Mary Evelyn had sent to see if it meshed with what the colonel had provided. There might be slight differences—albeit without distinction—but sometimes those slight differences are misleading.

Cardinal Giovanni Antinori was born in Castelfiorentino, Italy, about an hour out of Florence. His family moved to Manchester, England, when Giovanni was three. His father worked at an engineering firm while his mother stayed home to raise their son and his older sister. Raised by devout, old-country Catholics, young Giovanni charged into the priesthood. My interest waned. After all, I knew the end of the story.

I tried to grind on, but it was like trudging uphill carrying two pairs of snow skis. After surveying the salient facts, I capitulated. His career was an Oscar-highlight film. I forwarded it to Morgan with a note to analyze. He was due back any day aboard *Moon Child*, his forty-two-foot Beneteau. He'd taken off for St. Kitts a month ago, while I was in Europe. Whether or not he could access the doc before he returned was another matter. He was unaware, naturally, of my association with the deceased cardinal. I merely inquired in my note if he could find anything unusual in the recent past. I'd have to reveal the root of my curiosity, but I didn't want to think about that. Not yet. Perhaps unbiased eyes could find a clue as to why Antinori was in Kensington Gardens that morning. Something in his past linked him to Paretsky.

The perversity of the thought struck me. *If something in your past is that influential, then it's obviously not in the past.*

Hadley III pounced on top of the grill, cautiously wiggled her back end down, and stared at the water. I reviewed the photographs the colonel had left with me. There were several pictures of Donald Lambert. One picture of Paretsky and Renée was marked Covent Gardens, London. Time unknown. The shot of Paretsky with the unidentified blonde on a boat was labeled Key West, with a question mark. In neither picture were Renée or Paretsky the focus of the photographer. I pushed them away. I had a far more serious issue.

An issue that, every minute of every hour of the day, had caused my mind to short out like a faulty circuit board.

I gave *Impulse* a double layer of wax. That was easy to do on the port side as it faced the dock. The starboard side was a real workout as I hung over the gunwale until I nearly joined the fish. She didn't need it, but I needed to do it. Needed to avoid thinking about that evening, about what I truly cared about. About the only damn issue I'd really thought about all day.

Kathleen and I were to have dinner that night; I'd told her I'd pick her up at half past six. The hours of the day had carried a mindless emptiness, as if they were cognizant that they served no purpose other than to advance the clock. No matter what I did or where my thoughts wandered, the sole intent and momentum of that day had always been the evening. I would have to tell her. My deed. My deceit. My everything.

Before I left, I remembered to text PC Lambert's address.

CHAPTER 8

"Where would you like to go?" Kathleen called out from her bedroom.

She was in the final stages of prepping herself, as was I. I was into my second straight Irish whiskey—Jameson Black Barrel. We'd adopted the drink in London. Even took a bottle in a cab and had a jolly good time.

She must have hustled out and bought some. Peggy was right; I'd better grab this woman. Whether she'd want me after tonight was a question that two layers of boat wax couldn't address.

"That's the right stuff, isn't it?" She asked a second question before I answered the first.

"It is. Shall we grab a cab tonight?"

She poked a smile around the doorframe. "*That* was fun. What's on the agenda?"

I thought, *Have I got a surprise for you*, but said, "How about the Valencia? Steak house on the lower level." In the event that things turned out poorly, I didn't want to go to Mangroves, our default restaurant.

She slipped back into her bedroom. I helped myself to a tin of cashews and tossed down a handful. Lightly salted, my ass. A few moments later, she swirled out of her room and circled me in a cream, sleeveless dress. A small scar was visible on her upper left shoulder where the bullet had passed clean through. Whether I ever tell that story, I can't say. A circle of pearls dropped low on her chest, and a red sash wrapped her waist. I was glad I'd exchanged my shorts for beige linen pants and a navy silk shirt. I never know when she's going to dress to the nines.

"Perfect," she said as she lifted a glass of chardonnay off the granite countertop. I wondered why she hadn't taken it in the bedroom with her. "It's cozy and dark. Just like that place in York." She clanked her wineglass to my nearly empty tumbler. "To cabs in London and nights in York." She leaned in and gave me a quick kiss. "Hopefully it will be less stress than the last time we were there."

Oh…shit.

I'd forgotten. Kathleen, under false pretenses (not that I harbor any resentment), had hired me two years ago to locate her missing friend. He was really a hit man from the Outfit, sent to—well, erase her. I confronted her and her pack of lies while we had dinner at the bar in the steakhouse. We survived a disastrous first act to our relationship. What a dickhead decision to go back there. For a smart guy, I make my share. Furthermore, I've begun to suspect that my stupid decision-making ability is like the universe—ever expanding.

She said, "You remember, don't you?"

"I recall that you lied about everything since we met at the D—"

"You couldn't keep your eyes off me," she teased. She was riding high tonight. Maybe I should table my confession that I committed murder on our vacation—killed old what's-his-face. Why waste an eight-ounce center cut over such trivial affairs?

I downed my drink. "I can't keep my eyes off any good-looking woman."

"Your eyes are totally free. It's your heart that I want. Besides," she took another taste of wine, "love looks not with the eyes but with the mind."

I put my arms around her and gathered her in, her soft body melting with mine. She smelled fresh. A hint of perfume that wasn't there from six feet out, but up close—you'd be a damn fool to let her go. I hovered my mouth over hers and tripped on the edge of passion. I searched my brain, but it wasn't there.

"Keats, Byron, Muhammad Ali?" I said.

"I *got* you." She pulled back. "You don't know, do you?"

"I know Twain implied what could be construed as an opposing opinion. Tell me."

"No."

"No?"

"I'll make it ea—"

I kissed her as if it were my last act on earth before being led to the chair. I had held back long enough and wasn't at all confident about what the end of the night would bring. I released her.

"OK. Sometimes…" She paused and let her breath out. "Sometimes I think that just does it for me."

I put her arm through mine. "Shall we?"

"Wherever you go."

We'll see about that.

We rode the elevator down and then strolled out of her condo and onto the hustle and heat of Beach Drive.

We headed, without discussion, straight to the bar. Kathleen and I like eating high, and the steakhouse has massive, high-backed, cushioned stools. The amber, whiskey-wood walls did remind me of our special place in York, except—

thank God—the New World didn't tolerate seven-foot ceilings.

I ordered a bottle of 2005 Château Haut-Bages-Libéral, a Bordeaux that was a nice compromise between the heavy reds that I prefer and the lighter ones that Kathleen gravitates to. I normally stick to American reds. After all, the French refused to allow us to use their airspace when we did the world a favor and bombed Gadhafi in 1986. American crosses—count 'em—forever gazing over the frigid waters of the English Channel. I'm not implying that grants us carte blanche, but when those—

"I said," Kathleen said, interrupting my binge in which I was thinking of anything other than what I needed to focus on, "are we reprising our signature night here? I believe you got the eight-ounce, and I opted for lobster tail, and then we split."

"Perfect."

"You seem distracted."

The bartender, in a black jacket and bow tie, arrived with the prize, and I sampled the Bordeaux. I gave him a nod, and he filled Kathleen's glass and then mine to the appropriate level. We ordered, and he expertly spread black napkins like placemats in front of us. Silverware and water with lemon followed. All set up. Nice and neat. I made a strategic decision. Tell her after dinner. No way was I going to step in front of surf and turf.

Dinner was a waste.

While Kathleen babbled about God knows what, all I could think about was my entry point. We were into the second bottle, and that was stupid as hell. Sinatra's "Hello Young Lovers" sneaked out of the speakers. I bet the Big Boy in the sky got a snicker out of that. I know what he thinks of me.

"What I like about lobster," she said, as Bow Tie cleared our dinner plates, "is that it necessitates eating butter."

I tabled my wineglass and faced her. How should I tell her? Five years in the army had left me with this: be brief, be bold, be gone.

She said, "Let's take a walk. I—"

"I need to tell you something."

"What?" Normal voice. No idea what was coming. The bombers are overhead, and in Dresden the little children sleep.

"While on our trip," my voice sounded distant to me, "I received a message, an assignment." Her eyes were focused now. I felt bad for her. What a pretty picture we had, and look what I was about to do. I hoped it wouldn't go down that way, but I knew I'd been kidding myself. I do that some-times—live within my delusions. The problem with that is you have no say in when reality kicks down the door, blows the roof, flattens the walls, and nukes the illusions you've built to keep it away.

I went in fast. "I was assigned to kill an assassin, an evil man who has killed many."

"You didn't tell me?"

Be brief.

"I didn't want it to spoil or interfere with our plans."

"OK." She moved her head back. Just a bit. The first step. "That's wrong on so many fronts I don't even know where to start. When was this?"

Bow Tie asked if we wanted dessert, and I waved him off. He sauntered down to the end of the bar where a blue sports coat sat with a toothpick in his mouth and a drink in his hand.

Be bold.

"London. Kensington Gardens. While you slept."

"Jake, you're serious?"

"I am."

She leaned back into me. "Why didn't you—"

"That's not the story."

"Not the story?" she ricocheted back at me. "How can that *not* be the story?"

"The man I was supposed to kill was disguised as a cardinal. I was given his precise location. After we returned, I was informed that the man I killed, who was *exactly* where the assassin was supposed to be, was in fact a real cardinal. We have no idea why he was there or what he—"

"You killed a cardinal, a Catholic cardinal?"

I nodded.

Her hand flew to her mouth. She froze for a few brief seconds before she unleashed. "Oh my God. I read about him. You? It was *you?*" She recoiled away from me as if I carried the next plague that would wipe out a third of humanity.

I didn't know what to say; in the event she'd missed the pertinent point, I added, "I had no idea. Someone set me, set us up. I'm engaged now in finding what went wrong and completing the assignment."

"It was *you?*"

"Keep your voice down. I was set up. Some—"

"Oh God, Jake."

She brought her arms tight across her body and slumped in her chair as if her power cord had been yanked out. Kathleen was always a lady at a table, erect with a straight back. It seemed odd, her mentioning my name while self-hugging.

As if the very connotation of me had metamorphosed into something ugly and foreign. I had decimated her evening, and the look on her face and what it did to me were things I was unprepared for. I didn't recall seeing such pain or disappointment in the cardinal's eyes as he lay dying, and that man had taken a bullet.

Words cast from lips cause more damage than bullets fired from guns. Take it from me. I'm proficient in both. We discover, at the strangest and most unpredictable times, the atomic particles of truth that implode and rearrange our world.

"Complete the assignment?" she said. "Do you believe what you just said? Do you even hear your words?"

"It's what I—"

"While I slept?" She shook her head.

"It's what I do."

"During your run?"

"I had no say in the time."

"No say in the time? What about the deed?"

"It was an accident." I was tossing shit at the wall.

"*Accident?* What kind of comment is—"

"Listen, kid. I'm in the real world. I don't live in books."

Her eyes narrowed as if I were out of focus and she was straining to see me. "Oh, great. We're back to that?" She straightened up and unwrapped her arms. "I've got to move. I need a moment." She stood, shoved her stool back, and pounded off to the ladies' room.

What the hell was I doing? My last comment was a dagger. Kathleen held a PhD and taught literature at a local college. I had advised her once, when she rightly questioned my profession, to go back to her books if she couldn't stand the heat. It had been a crude and crass remark, and now I'd laid it down again. But I was ticked. Didn't she know I felt remorse for my act? It was on me. A smidgen of sympathy would have been nice, and I hadn't gotten a crumb from anyone. Words. They will fuck you six ways from Sunday. They should give you a certificate when you complete an English class. *You are now licensed to kill.*

I took the opportunity to hit the head myself. When I washed my hands, I didn't look up—I wasn't a virgin.

I was waiting for her when she returned. I could tell by her gait that everything had changed. She didn't sit. She placed her hands on the back of her stool. She'd been crying, although she tried not to show it. I know that look. It's not something you forget, especially when you're the source.

"The cleaning crew," she said, and then I really knew my boat was going down. "They were part of it, right? I mean, they were taking everything out of our flat and—"

"I wanted—"

"Don't." She shook her head like a schoolmarm addressing a child who knew better. "I need some time."

"I know—"

"No. Listen." She placed her hand on my left shoulder. "We've come so far, so fast. But I need to slow it down, Jake. Your world...we're alike in some ways, yet so hopelessly...so frighteningly different in others."

"You know I didn't—"

"Oh, babe. I know." She brought her hand up over the left side of my face. "But you did. Your job..." She withdrew her hand and shook her head. "That is so stupid. It's not a job. It's your life. It's who you are."

I wanted to plead my case, but what if I didn't have one? What if the best thing for Kathleen Rowe was that she never saw me again? I stared into her hazel-green eyes and con-gratulated myself on allowing a lobster to die in vain.

"Kathleen."

"No. Do—"

"The book remark. You know—"

"That hurt, Jake. I don't know why you do that when you know it hurts. It's as if, down deep, you think your life is superior to mine—but look what you do. My books are looking pretty nice compared to your story. I like my books. I like them just fine. I—I've got to go."

She turned and started to walk.

I said, "Shakespeare, isn't it? Love with the mind?"

She stepped back toward me. She raked her hand through my hair like it was a distant object, her eyes following her hand. "Such a beautiful mind." She brought her other hand up against my cheek and nailed her eyes to mine. She pivoted and strode out the door, nearly breaking into a run, but not before I caught a shudder in her slender shoulders.

All those years I spent in the army, and it was Kathleen who was brief, bold—and gone.

CHAPTER 9

Nothing, with the exception of partying until four in the morning in Rome, interferes with my morning exercise. That includes a hangover, hurting the one out of seven billion people I care for more than the rest of the asylum combined, and enough booze in one evening to meet my weekly quota.

I ditched the pool at the pink hotel and swam in the gulf for thirty minutes. That was followed by a three-mile, barefoot run on the beach in record-slow time. My body felt like a busted-up coconut, and I was fortunate that my insides stayed there. I washed off under the outdoor shower at the hotel and let the semicool water carry the heat from my skin. The lounge chairs on the front row of the boardwalk were covered with towels and magazines that staked territorial claims for the day. A man sat in one with a coffee to his side and a newspaper spread before him. He battled the gulf breeze for control of the paper.

"Trade places with you," I said as I twisted the shower handle. His reading glasses were halfway down his nose.

"Come again?" His eyes shot up to mine.

"Nothing."

I dried off with a towel, pulled on a T-shirt, and tried to justify my existence. Like a song stuck in my head, all I could think of was last night's closing scene. I didn't like the way

Kathleen had sprinted out the door. Confident. Purposeful. Marching out of one life and into a new one. No, sir. I did not like that at all.

Kathleen's scar came into my mind. You can see a scar. I prefer that; you know where you stand. Words leave ghost scars—unseen and omnipresent. Bound to reappear down the road at the most unpredictable moments.

I threw my towel in the dirty hamper and thought it would be nice if I could do the same with my troubles. My phone rang. Binelli.

"What do you got?"

"You just don't learn, do you?"

"What do you got, please?"

"Why are you interested in Paretsky?"

"You're not in my cir—"

"Retained to erase him, aren't you?"

"Apparently me and half the armed forces." I recalled the colonel's testament that it was Garrett's and my job, no one else's. Total fabrication. "I need to know whatever you can find. My agency gave me a set of docs. I know it's not one big, happy party with everyone bobbing for apples, cheering at the kids' soccer game, and doing their neighbor's wife."

"Might be your lucky day."

"How so?"

"Paretsky was our responsibility until we turned him over."

"Why's that my lucky day?"

"'Might,' I said, and, like you, I don't think the competing agencies get stars by their names. I wouldn't be surprised if we retained some pieces of information. Something that might give us a leg up in our effort to locate him. Make us the heroes. Increase our funding."

"So young. So cynical."

"The way of the world."

"He's killing innocent people and—"

"Gear it down. Why do you think I cooperate with you?"

"What do you got?" I sat down on an unclaimed blue lounger. Behind me a deliveryman unloaded cases of beer cans at the beach bar. Its steel curtains wouldn't rise for another two hours.

"Nothing, now. But I'm having lunch with a woman today who may know more than what we put in the file. I'll give you a ring later. Here—"

"You called just to say—"

"Do you have any friends?"

I stood up and walked past the hot tub, where a rotund man reclined in a frothy sea of bubbles. "I'm listening."

"We believe there are two men. Paretsky and another. Is this news to you?"

"Tell me."

"That's what my lunch date is for. Some branches think Paretsky's a lone wolf. We don't concur. It's information that even if we *did* pass along—and we really do cooperate more than you think—whoever received it might disregard it if it didn't parallel their own intelligence. We share intelligence, but the next guy might toss bits and pieces into the recycle bin. There's no shortage of arrogance on the Beltway. Are you chasing just Paretsky?"

"As far as I know."

"I'll be back." She disconnected.

The hotel has facilities that allow me to use it like a country club. I changed in the locker room and fixed a cup of Colombian. They hadn't gotten any bananas in for the day, and that knocked my mood down a few notches. I jumped in my truck and headed back to my house.

The aroma of coffee and bacon greeted me when I entered through the garage door. Morgan sat in a cushioned chair, reading a stack of stapled papers.

"When did you dock?" I said.

"Two a.m. Calm seas the whole way. Angelo gives his best."

"You tell him he can have Hadley back?" I plopped down beside him.

"Hadley Three. He didn't ask. I told him she was good for you."

A coffee mug and beer can sat on the wood side table to his left. Morgan drank half a beer every morning and threw the other half away. He claimed the distaste for it kept him from drinking until later in the afternoon. He'd seen too many lives ruined by alcohol, including that of his father, who never said no to a bottle. Morgan called alcoholism the Caribbean flu. Like a flu shot, he was convinced, a little live virus every morning kept it away.

"What are you reading?" I said. A twin-engine dual console went by with three men in it. A battalion of fishing rods sprang victoriously out of the rocket launchers attached to the back of the hardtop.

"The file you sent me on Cardinal Giovanni Antinori." He took a sip of his beer and pushed the can away. "Want breakfast? I made extra." He got up.

"Refill, too." I handed him my Styrofoam cup. "And a bottle of water."

He returned with a bottled water in his cargo shorts pocket, my coffee in one hand, and a plate of peppered eggs and still-warm bacon in the other. He handed me the goods and then took his seat. He'd dropped a record in the Magnavox, and Bobby Darin's voice competed with the screech of the osprey that likes to defecate on my boat. I'd just completed my collection of Darin albums and had been contemplating whom to conquer next. Didn't matter now.

"Speaker's still out," he said.

"I know."

"It's going to be hard to find anyone who knows vacuum tubes. Want to try and tackle it ourselves?"

I took a long drag from the bottle. The Magnavox was a 1961 floor-model record player and radio with twelve-inch side woofers. It was stuffed with vacuum tubes and weighed in at around three-hundred pounds. I put the water down and picked up my coffee. "I've got other issues."

"So I heard."

Did he know? "Kathleen?" I said. It came out harsh, even bitter. I had never spoken her name in that manner. "I thought you didn't get in till two?"

"She left a voice mail. I called her after my meditation."

"She up this early?"

"Never went down."

That's what she gets for walking out on me. "Tell you everything?"

He placed his coffee on the dusty glass table and turned to me. His hair was in a ponytail, a moon talisman hung around his neck, and he wore a sun-bleached, crew-neck T-shirt. No pocket.

"One never knows, but in the spirit of your question, yes." Morgan held my eyes in a steady gaze. Although I was used to him now, when we had first met—he walked in the door without knocking, confiscated a beer from the fridge, stuck out his hand, and introduced himself—his intensity took me by surprise. He is fully engaged with a person when listening. A quote from David Augsburger hung in his boat's cabin: "Being listened to is so close to being loved that most people can't tell the difference." I thought that was about as thick as it flowed, but I'd been beginning to reevaluate a few things in my life. No rush. Don't want to bite off more than I can chew. Maybe a new thought every year or so.

"The cardinal?"

"Everything."

The bad speaker kicked in, and Darin went up a dozen decibels. "Look over those pages and photographs," I said. "See if you can find anything that might give me a clue as to why Antinori was in Kensington Gardens that morning. He must have come across Paretsky—that's the assassin who was supposed to be there. But how and when, I don't know. If I did, it could help lead me to Paretsky and—"

"As well as explain why, assuming he had a choice, the cardinal wanted to die. That's the real mystery, isn't it?"

Morgan rarely interrupts people. The speaker went out. Darin went down, and I stood up. "Let me know what you think."

"I think you should apologize to her."

"Really? In case something got lost in translation, I had no idea the man was not who he was supposed to be."

"About what you said about going back to her books."

"What's that got to do with anything?" But I knew. Knew that it was everything.

"When we lived on a sailboat," he picked up his coffee and glanced at me, "on more than one occasion we cruised into uncharted waters, battled unpredictable weather, and brandished firearms to keep pirates off the deck." He took a sip. I almost interrupted but hit the brakes. "A lot of inherent danger living on the seas, but my father never warned against it. He never even told me to be careful at the helm;

to the contrary, he urges curiosity and risk taking." It wasn't unusual for Morgan to refer to his deceased father in present tense or to mix the tenses when referring to him.

"But my father treats words as delicate creatures, pieces of fine crystal to be passed between people. The only thing he tells me to be careful of is words. Imagine that. All that uncertainty, danger, unknown ports, thieves, not to mention the often angry and unpredictable Poseidon, but words are the only things that he advises I exercise caution with."

His dad was a drunk, too, but I didn't say that. Instead I added, "I liked you better when you were a thousand miles away."

He countered in a lively tone, as if another speaker had kicked in. "What time's dinner?"

"Seven?"

"Works for me."

He stood and slipped out through the screen door that refused to latch, gently shutting it behind him, and headed around the fence to his house. I hustled out of the house; I had a full agenda for the day. Twenty minutes later I parked my truck in Donald Lambert's driveway. I started to get out but involuntarily collapsed back into my seat.

Brief, bold, and she was gone.

I forced myself out of the truck, but it was hard.

CHAPTER 10

"What's the deal, Poppins—different day, same story?" Lambert threw out when I came up behind him on his dock.

The great white egret moved a few paces to accommodate me. Considering my weight advantage, it did an admirable job of holding its ground. Lambert had two poles stuck into PVC pipes drilled into his pilings. Lines from the poles floated in the breeze and eventually threaded into the water. As I approached, he quickly dropped his bait bucket back into the water and took a seat in a cloth tailgate chair. It had a cup holder on the right arm that held a plastic travel mug. Coffee, I assumed.

"No." I sat down on his dock, arms on propped knees, and angled myself so that I partially faced *Knotty Girl* and Lambert. "Just trying to sell myself today."

He let out a huff. "I don't give you much chance of that, although I admire your directness. She said you're a bona fide hero around here. Dropped a pair of drug runners a couple years back." While recovering a stolen boat for an insurance company, I had killed two men who tried to outrun me in a Donzi. The affair got unpleasant when they hit a sandbar, and it had brought unwanted notoriety. "Said you were straight up, but to stick to your good side."

"Who said?"

He cut me a look. "Your girl, Peggy. Down at Sea Breeze."

"You checked me out."

"I did." He took a sip from his mug, but the lid must have been closed. He pulled it away from his lips, slid open the flap, and made another pass. "Used to have a second chair out here, but I don't need it much anymore."

"I'm good. Your daughter might be in trouble."

"There's a hell of a s-statement. You just wake up?"

He had stuttered on his closing comment to me yesterday. I wondered if it was always there or brought upon by stress. Or me. Or if they were one and the same.

I got up, took a step toward him, and lowered myself into a knee bend so my face was level with his. My left knee emitted a ripple of cracks. He hadn't shaved. The great white egret took a step back. It was about four feet behind Lambert and, despite the two lines in the water and the bait bucket off to the side, the bird kept its eyes on the man.

"The six-shooter. Try to recall his every word."

"Said that he'd be back."

"Why? What does he gain?"

"That's what I told him." His voice was strong. "I told him he could stick his gun up my ass, but I wouldn't tell him nothing about Renée and didn't know anything about…"

"About what?"

He hesitated. "Nothing. That's just it. I don't know anything about where she is."

I let it go. "What did he say to that?"

"Said—said I'd be lucky. That's what he said. Said I'd be lucky if all he did was s-stick a gun up…" Lambert spit on his dock. I didn't take him to be someone who spit on his or anybody else's dock. "Said he'd give me some time to think about it, and when he came back I'd better have…information for him. Said she was in danger, and the sooner I cooperated the better off she would be. I didn't believe him, and he knew I didn't believe him. Said he was her guardian. He laughed at that like it was some kind of joke. Said his job was to protect Renée."

"Guardian?" Hadn't Antinori muttered that word?

"Something like that. Trying to get me to buy in that he was protecting her."

"And what did you say?"

"Well, Jake, I told him..."

His body shuddered, and he looked away from me. I reached out and touched his arm. It was awkward. It's not a move that comes naturally to me, and I can't help but think that when I do it the recipients realize that. The great white egret took a bird step toward us. "She'll be OK," I said. "I'll—"

"She's a good woman," he asserted, as if someone had challenged his daughter. He brought his eyes back to me. "She told me when she was jus—said she was thinking of going back to school, wanted to do counseling for kids. She was real adamant about helping children who are bullied, especially young girls. That's a great thing for a person to be involved in. I suppose she gets her interest on account of her mother never being right. Always saying it went back to her childhood. Verbal abuse when she was young." He gave a shake of his head, as if trying to rid himself for the thousandth time of something that he could never comprehend and he'd grown weary of the effort.

"Help me, Donald," I urged him. "He have a way of speech? A tattoo? Give me something."

"Cleared his throat. You know, like a smoker, but he didn't smell."

"Cleared his throat?"

"Yeah. Habitual…no, more than that. Like a reflex, and he couldn't help it. And he smelled—"

"I thought you said he didn't s—"

"Like Hall's. You know, a throat lozenge."

"Maybe he had a cold."

"I don't think so."

"That's it?"

"Yeah." He gave a dismissive shrug and shifted his gaze out to the water. He changed tack. "Just got that bait bucket about a year ago." He glanced back at me. "Got some good blues in it, some other gems as well. It'll hold about anything you want."

I stood and thanked him for his time. "Call me," I said. "Anytime. You understand that?"

He remained silent.

"You under—"

"I got it."

I turned to leave and remembered a comment he had made. "You said he wanted information from you. What information?"

"You know…where Renée was."

That didn't seem to fit with how he had said it, but I couldn't—

"Don't worry, Poppins. I'll let you know if I hear anything."

I left Lambert on the dock and climbed into my truck. I hit PC's number and confirmed that he and Boyd were to start surveillance on Lambert that afternoon—told him to make it twenty-four seven.

"No sleep?" PC asked as I navigated the new bridge that was still being constructed.

"It's overrated. One off, one on. Get a rental so you're not in the same wheels. Play chess. Don't get spotted." I didn't want to put PC and Boyd in harm's way, and being scruffy teenagers helped their cause. It was difficult, at face value, to take them seriously. "Anyone approaches the house, give me a call. Do *not* get caught. Do *not* take—"

"I'm not old enough to rent a car. I can use my fake—"

"Don't. Use a friend's."

"Sure. Or we can—"

"Don't wire one, either."

"We're good. Any new books?"

He meant chess books. "Try Terekhin's new book."

"Any relation to Tartakower, or do you just like the Ts?"

"Coincidental. But you can read Savielly repeatedly. He goes beyond chess."

"'No game was ever won by resigning.'" PC quoted Savielly Tartakower, my favorite chess master. God as my witness, I swelled with pride.

"Keep me posted." I disconnected.

No game is ever won by resigning. If Kathleen thought she could walk out of my life, that lady was in for a surprise.

From 275 North, I took 375 to Beach Drive and swung into a parking spot facing Straub Park. I lifted the center armrest and pilfered through dry cleaning and ATM receipts for quarters. My efforts yielded five. I fed the meter and headed across the street to the Valencia. In my leather shoulder bag, I had the folder the colonel had left me. It contained the pictures of Renée Lambert with Paretsky and with the mystery man taken at the Valencia. I also had the picture

77

of Paretsky on the boat with the unidentified blonde. They were much easier to view than the copies in my phone.

A cavalry of bicyclists, intent on taking the corner as a solitary mass, swooshed by me. They all leaned to their port side at the exact same degree. I strode across the street, skipped past the valet stand, and hopped up the stairs to the front porch. I was glad the steakhouse was in the dungeon. That was where it belonged. I'd been there twice with Kathleen, and she'd cried both times. No one wins when a woman cries.

I took the wide stairs, two at a time, from the end of the grand hall up to the mezzanine level. The outdoor mezzanine was deserted. It was used primarily for large functions in the evening and an occasional lunch. It ran the length of the hotel and had an expansive view of the park and Beach Drive. I went to the space where the background matched the one in the picture. Renée Lambert had stood…here. Her companion stood…like this, head down, shoulders turned. He was certainly aware of the picture being taken and wanted no part of it.

I returned through the double French doors and took a seat at the bar in the upstairs lobby. I took the photograph from the Valencia out of my bag and laid it flat on the counter. I pulled out another sheet from the colonel's packet. It was a list of all corporate functions the hotel had held on the mezzanine level over the last ninety days. Forty-one events. I focused on the last twenty-one days, during which, Lambert told me, Renée was in town but neglected to drop by. Even odds that he was lying, but not much I could do about it.

"Are you sailing?"

A brunette with her hair imprisoned tightly behind her complemented the other side of the bar. She wore a bartender's black vest and a white shirt buttoned one button short of the hotel's employee manual requirements. Her eyes were Spanish black. Her body poised and relaxed. Orange nails. No ring. No pale skin or indentation where a ring might have been.

"I am," I replied.

"What pleasure's your port of call?"

"A Bloody Mary would fluff my sails."

"Got your mast up this early?"

"I do. Never know when a blow comes."

"Suppose not. Want to feel her?"

"I want to eat her."

She smiled in approval. "I like mine with a steak knife."

She started constructing my drink. If she had been a he, I would have stuck with an iced tea, as last evening wasn't yet flushed out of my body. But it seemed a wimpy drink, and who knew, maybe I was single again. I sank my head back into the list.

The colonel, with the cooperation of the hotel, had done admirable legwork. The events were subdivided into corporate functions, weddings, and "other." It was difficult to imagine that she'd be in town for a wedding and not mention that to her father. Maybe she had, and Lambert had lied to me. I skimmed over the weddings and concentrated on the past month. The National Association of the Self-Storage Association of America. That's NASSAA to the members. Southeast Trial Lawyers. Award trips for insurance brokers, all with impressive names: Chairman's Group, Director's Circle, Owner's Club.

"Give that a try for me."

My Bloody Mary appeared off to the side, placed squarely on a hotel napkin. A celery branch poked high out of its side.

A skewer with a cherry tomato squeezed between two alpha green olives—all the same size—leaned against the other side of the glass. A thick cut of summer sausage rested on the edge of the glass, supported by a toothpick that vanished into the murky red. I stuck the sausage in my mouth and placed the toothpick on the bar.

The nametag said Vicki, but, with those eyes, I'd go with Spanish. As attractive as she was, I was suddenly overcome with distaste for her entire line of the species, but I needed her. I took a sip of the red sludge. Horseradish, Tabasco, Worcestershire, salt, pepper, tomato juice, and lemon jock-eyed for position on my overstimulated and outmatched taste buds. The vodka was like a liquid conductor keeping everything in line. It was a kick-ass Bloody Mary. Classical guitar came through the speakers. I caught a whiff of sweet perfume.

It's not easy being depressed in paradise.

"She your girlfriend?" Spanish said with a nod toward the picture.

"No." I got out my PI license and laid it on the table. "I'm being retained by her father. She's missing. We know this picture was taken here."

She picked up my license, gave it a studious look, and placed it back exactly where I had put it. "A real private dick," she said, and I couldn't tell whether she was toying with me or not. "Shouldn't you be nursing an iced tea instead of drinking on the job?"

"I wanted to see what you were capable of, and an iced tea hardly seemed a challenging measure of your talents."

"I see." She picked up the photograph as if she were con-sidering buying it. "Stunning," she said to the photograph.

"Love those eyes." She lifted her eyes over the picture to me. "Who is she?"

"Name is Renée Lambert. Mean anything to you?"

"No." She put it down.

"You work functions?"

"I do."

"If I found out what function this picture was taken at, could you point me in the direction of who worked that evening?"

"I really don't do that many." I'd come on too fast. Too late now to change gears.

"I don't care about many. I need to talk to someone who worked the one that Renée attended. Two weeks back, give or take." I hoped that by dropping Renée's name, I made myself less threatening.

"We get a lot." She instinctively lowered her head and started washing glasses. I couldn't imagine any being dirty this time of the day. I decided to give her time. I scanned the list again.

What did Lambert say Renée's interest had migrated to? Working with bullied kids? Children's psychology? I didn't think much of it, but the incongruity hit me now. Jet-setting around Europe, a sometime model, and suddenly her interest turned to child psychology? But what did I know? Recent events would indicate precious little. I scanned the list again. Florida Teachers Association. Twelve days ago.

Spanish said, "She in trouble?"

"No. Her father's worried. She's not answering her cell." I was going to pad that but decided to let it go. Less was best. "She's interested in kids. Maybe she attended the teachers' conference."

81

"That's a biggie, all right. But I didn't work it."

"Who did?"

"I don't know—"

"They can decide themselves what to tell me."

She stepped back, tilted her head, and placed her hands on her hips. "You didn't tie up here looking for a drink, did you?"

"Does anybody?"

"Go see Adam. Front porch bar."

"He work that evening?" I had no evidence that Renée Lambert had attended the teachers' conference, but it beat starting with the Mortgage Association of Florida's Annual Symposium on Underwriting and Liability Practices. Hard to believe that as children we all had dreams.

"If not, he would know who did. Adam—how shall I say this? Not much escapes him." She gave a crooked smile, the right side of her face scrunching up. "That's tired," she came back in, "and doesn't do his passion justice. It's genetic with him. He *has* to know everything that happens and, naturally, offer his opinion on it. Anyways," she gave a shrug, "I'd be surprised if he didn't work it. He lobbies for every event. Needs it to pay for his wardrobe."

I pushed away from the counter.

"You sailing solo?" she said.

"Right now...I don't know."

"Too bad. That's the only answer I stay away from."

I left a twenty on the bar. I grabbed the hurricane glass and went searching for Adam.

CHAPTER 11

The bar was in the Atlantic Time Zone of the front porch. A couple that had walked out of a Fitzgerald novel occupied the side that looked back over the porch.

I claimed a stool on the opposite end and parked my Bloody Mary in front of me. My phone buzzed an incoming text. I retrieved it from my pocket. Binelli said her lunch date was shoved back a day. I texted back *OK*, even though that in no way conveyed my frustration. I tried to squash my irritation over the delay. Waiting and I don't get along.

Lady Fitzgerald laughed and placed her hand on the man's shoulder. She was ten to twenty years older than her male companion. Her wispy black hair was shoulder length, and she sported a pair of pronounced Germanic cheekbones. A narrow, braided orange headband circled her head. I liked it. She looked good. Vicki's nails were orange. Must be the new color, although I bet it was called something different. Her companion couldn't keep his hand off his drink.

The bartender approached me. "I see you've met Vicki."

I fast-forwarded from the 1920s to the man in front of me. "What gave me away?"

"A lone cherry tomato with two olives. That's her signature. We all put a different twist on our Bloody Marys that identify us. Management's clueless. It's just a little fun we have."

"She also gave me a chunk of sausage."

"You can thank me for that. I initiated that carnivorous addition."

"Thank you."

"You're welcome, my friend."

"Are you Adam?"

"Adam, I am."

Adam sported the identical uniform that Spanish wore, but he was buttoned all the way up. A light-blue bow tie balanced perfectly between the collar points. His buzzed hair served to accentuate his angled face. He was as gay as the tie was blue.

"Spanish," I told him.

"Pardon me?"

"Vicki. I call her Spanish. Eyes that dark don't come around that often."

He bobbed his head in approval. "She does have a set. No doubt about that."

He slid off to my left to attend to a lady who had just sat down. She ordered a mimosa. She crossed her legs, brought up her phone, and disappeared into her 4.7-inch world. At the other end, the Fitzgeralds laughed in harmony. I extracted the picture taken at the Valencia from my bag and placed it on the counter.

Adam rotated back to me. I gave him the same pitch I'd given Spanish. I handed him the picture and inquired if he'd worked the teachers' conference or remembered seeing the woman in the photograph.

"I did and I do," he answered, without taking his eyes off the picture in his hand.

"Come again?"

"I worked the teachers' shindig, and I remember her." He shifted his focus to me. "Her night was the opposite of yours."

"What do you mean?"

"Not much gets past me, you know?" He cocked his head as if to will me to understand. "I like pouring drinks because of the people and the stories they bring."

"Tell me."

"Her night was different from yours; that's what I'm saying." He lowered the picture onto the bar.

"You're going to have to bring it home, Adam." I reached over the bar, snatched a cardboard coaster, and placed my drink on it. I didn't want the condensation leaking onto the picture. "I wasn't there that night. Never met her."

"No, my friend," he said in a voice that made you believe that he had reserved all his sincerity just for you. "You were not there that night. I'd remember you. And I do remember you. You came in last night with a lady and left alone. Your brown-haired beauty there," he tilted his head towards the picture, "she came in alone and left with that man. See what I mean? Opposite of you."

There was no need to dwell on his observation of my solo exit, as I had no interest in rehashing last night. I was taking denial pills. Four every two hours.

I slid my glass away from the picture. "Tell me about that night."

Before Adam could launch, another woman joined Mimosa, and Adam snapped to attention in front of her. She ordered what her friend had, and the friend ordered a second. I took a few ounces from my drink, congratulated myself on the quick recovery from last night, and leaned back into the chair. Across the street in the marina, a seventy-foot cruiser was stern in. A woman with blond hair and wearing a white robe came out of the stateroom. She was a good-looking woman on a good-looking boat. My eyes are drawn to boats. And women. In the smorgasbord of walkers, joggers, condos, trees, cars, and the constant bustle at the valet stand, my gaze naturally migrated to the classic lines of the *Southern Breeze* and the lady on the back deck. She flipped her hair, brushing off the night, shed the robe, and took a seat on a chaise lounge in the full sun. The black script letters *SB* were embossed on the head of each chaise lounge. She was nude and rubbed oil on her skin. I wanted to rub oil on her skin.

"She's a lonely girl." Adam had rotated back to me.

"Who?"

"Please—the woman you're gawking at. She and her man keep to themselves; she whines that he never leaves the boat. She came up here once with a posse of girlfriends, and after a few drinks, you know, when others got high? She got low, know what I mean?" He gave a slight shrug. "Don't really blame her. Her man, from here at least, looks like a real dweeb."

"I was actually admiring the boat, *Southern Breeze*." The lady did look a tad familiar, but I like to believe that I can say that about any nude on any boat. I gave her a parting glance as she rolled over on the recliner, her buttery breasts gleaming in the sun. Booze, boobs, bacon, and boats—all before noon; I'm telling you, it's hard being depressed in paradise.

Adam said, "Uh-uh."

"Tell me, Carnac the Magnificent," I said, placing my elbows on the table, "about the night Renée Lambert walked in alone and walked out with a man."

"Wasn't her choice."

"Explain."

"The man she walked out with? He was a party buster. No way did he belong at a teachers' convention, unless he taught gym. He had bolt-on muscles and a face that never knew a smile.

"I spotted him when he appeared. He scanned the room." Adam tilted his head and raised his eyebrows. "Sadly, he passed right over me. But your beauty buddy—Renée, right? He went straight to her."

"You're a pretty observant guy, Adam-I-am."

"That I am. Unfortunately, it gets a little fuzzy after that. We were swamped. I lost track of them."

"Do you know who took the picture?"

"No, but all these functions have photographers wandering around."

"What can you tell me about the man?"

"I thought you were interested in the girl."

"She's missing."

He shrugged and placed a dry glass down. "Not much. Short hair. Buzzed. Black T-shirt. Nice, like silk, not cheap. Once he saw his mark, his eyes darted around the room—not like he was searching for anyone else, but more like a nervous habit."

"That's not much?"

He arched his eyebrows. "Not in my book."

I took a green olive and stuck it in my mouth. "And their exit?"

Adam pulled away as a man settled on the far side of the mimosa twins. He ordered a beer. I gave Adam credit—no one at his watering hole needed to vie for his attention. He checked on the Fitzgeralds. Zelda said something to him and reached across the bar, touching his hand as she spoke. Adam circled back to me, checking in on the mimosa twins along the way.

"I saw them leave." He fingered his bow tie. "He held her elbow, like in the old movies. Guided her out the door. I can't say she went willingly, but he didn't drag her, either."

"Did her demeanor change after he entered the room?"

"Don't know, boss. Didn't really pick up on her before then."

"Anything else? Pierced ear? Someone else he talked to? Hear his voice? Anything that—"

"He coughed."

I leaned in on the bar. "Tell me."

"Nothing, really. I heard him clear his throat when I was passing by with a dessert tray. I'm like, I hope this guy doesn't sneeze on this tray, you know?"

"He smell?"

Adam crinkled up his nose. "Like...BO?"

"No," I said, remembering what Lambert had said about his visitor coughing and smelling like cough drops. "Like he was sucking a throat lozenge."

"Naw, I mean, who goes around sniffing people? You're scaring me, man. I was worried about my raspberry-swirl minicheesecakes. That's about it." He picked up the picture of Renée. "Just look at those windows. I can't imagine the pain behind them."

He put the picture down and wandered off. I glanced at her eyes. Looked like eyes to me. I pulled a ten from my wallet and placed it on the counter. I'd taken the man's time, and he'd been cooperative. He caught me doing so out of the corner of his eye and broke off from a conversation he was having with the twins.

"Keep it." He scooped up the ten and handed it back to me. "Happy to help, if that's what I did."

I stuffed the bill back in my billfold and said, "I do appreciate your time." I gave him my card. "If you recall anything else, or see either person, call me."

He took my card. "I'll do that."

I was a few steps away from the bar when he said, "She cried, you know."

His words spun me around. "Who?"

"Your woman..." He glanced at my business card. "Jake. When she walked out by herself last night? She tried to keep it together, but she was crying. Crying a river. I don't know what you said, man, but you hurt her. Hurt her bad."

CHAPTER 12

A lime with wheels and a windshield—whatever became of the nation that put a man on the moon?—momentarily blocked my path before I scampered across the street. I took an outdoor seat under an umbrella at Mangroves, ordered an iced tea and a grouper Reuben sandwich, took out my iPad, and tried to forget Adam's parting salvo.

I spoke with two women at the Teachers Association. The first handed me off to Samantha, who gushed without solicitation that she had just adopted a cocker spaniel from a rescue shelter. "Named her Mary Jane. I'm hooked on Tom Petty like the day I first heard him in Tallahassee."

She divulged that Renée was attending the conference as a member of a group called Words Against People and that she sat on a panel. Samantha also volunteered that she'd been divorced twice, had a mastectomy, and had seen Petty thirty-seven times. She lamented that there was precious little new talent in the world, a dire situation that she blamed for her rocketing blood pressure. Some people carry their life in a glass of water and splash it on everyone they meet.

"Try Bugg," I said. "Two Gs."

"Excuse me?"

"To lower your blood pressure." I swiped a napkin across my mouth after a particularly disastrous attempt at a bite. "Tell me about WAP."

"Who?"

"Words Against People."

"Oh, yes. I get it. Here's the description they provided us. You ready?"

"Breathless."

"What?"

"Go on."

"Words Ag—WAP is an international organization that supports individuals who have been verbally abused and who claim that such abuse has led to mental and social stress. Such stress often results in emotional difficulties that are as real as physical ailments and hinder those individuals in performing normal functions within the society in which they live."

Samantha went on to explain that the teachers' organization formed an alliance with WAP because verbal abuse fell under bullying. Bullying, it appeared, was the hottest new topic in public education since the Scopes Monkey Trial. Bullying had also leaked beyond the schoolyard boundaries and into the workplace. WAP and the teachers' group were striving to raise the visibility of verbal abuse and to create an acceptable method for victims to come forward without shame or hesitation. They were constructing a formal list of words and phrases that would not be tolerated.

Sounded a little wishy-washy to me. In my old hood, you bullied people with land mines, bullets, knives, drones, and anything you could lay your hands on in order to inflict physical pain and death before they returned the favor. We called it "protecting freedom." They cheered and waved flags when we returned home. Gave us discounts on car insurance. Wrote country songs about us.

We disconnected. I tracked down WAP and placed a call. As the phone rang, I gave an affirmative nod to my waitress regarding a refill on my iced tea. A young man walking an immense, panting dog passed on the sidewalk. I felt bad for the dog. It shouldn't be south of Canada.

"Words Against People, where every word counts, this is Bretta. May I help you?"

"Bretta, Frank Bernard here. I'm a principal who attended the recent conference you had in Saint Petersburg. I had a discussion with Renée Lambert of your organization and was impressed with her. I would like to have her speak at a local meeting. How may I contact her?"

Bretta informed me that the only information she could parcel out was what was in the program guide or on the website. She did mention that Renée had joined around two years ago and was not that active in the organization. She inquired if I'd like to leave a comment that Renée might view. I sat up straight, unaware that I'd been slouching.

"How does that work?"

"You can post comments on our members' board. You know, success stories, things like that. You can address your comment to anyone who is listed or post a general comment. Is there something you'd like to add?"

"Is Renée active on that forum?"

"I don't know and couldn't say even if I did."

I gave that a second and then said, "Tell her—"

"You can log on yourself with your password and do your own post. We pre—"

"Machine's in the garage. Dumped a Diet Coke on the keyboard."

"Ouch."

"Second time in a month."

"Might want to be more careful."

"Copy that. Do you mind?"

"Go ahead. I can post without your password. If she does reply, it will be as a general comment."

"Just say that, as an attendee, I was moved by her talk as well as the story she shared about the young man who joined her for the evening. The one she departed with. If she'd like to continue the story and discuss her association with the man, I'd love to hear from her."

I gave her my number and repeated it. I told her that I'd lost my program guide, and she reminded me that I could bring the itinerary up on the website when my computer was fixed. I thanked her and disconnected.

It was a shot in the dark. I was betting that the man Renée left with wasn't there for the event. Might have even been the visitor at her father's place, although Adam's observation that Renée's escort cleared his throat wasn't enough to hang a hat on. If she needed help, maybe she'd give me a call. You don't catch any fish until you cast a line in the water.

A chunk of ice slid into my mouth with the final swallow of iced tea. My teeth gave it an audible crack as I considered my next move. I sprang up and hiked down Beach Drive. Kathleen's condo was two blocks south. I took the general elevator to her unit on the ninth floor—the private one was still inoperable. I marched through the war room and knocked on her door. I had no idea what I would say. She wasn't in. Didn't expect her to be. I perused the titles and borrowed the untranslated *Last Letters from Stalingrad*. It was a 1962 first edition. How'd it end up there?

I swung by Donald Lambert's home to make sure PC and Boyd were maintaining their vigilance. They had parked a block away and were skateboarding the neighborhood. They couldn't do that for hours. Despite my desire to have his house under constant surveillance, it wasn't practical. The street was too packed with seventy-five-foot lots. After I roped them in, we settled on drive-bys every fifteen minutes in alternate vehicles, coupled with walks and skateboard trips. Anything more would invite unnecessary scrutiny on them. I showed PC the pictures of Renée with Paretsky, Paretsky on the boat, and the single picture of Renée with the mystery man. I instructed him to be on the lookout for either man.

"She come around often?" PC said and stepped to within a foot of me. His social radar didn't know north from south, and he habitually invaded other people's space. He viewed the picture of Renée that was taken at the Valencia.

"No. Her father said she was supposed to drop by a couple weeks ago, but she was a no-show." I had little choice but to accept what Donald Lambert told me, despite my growing skepticism.

"Shame," he said, studying the photograph. He wore a T-shirt that had a black-and-white silhouette of Bill Murray's face on it. Boyd, who now sported a beard that looked like an S.O.S pad glued to his chin and a moustache, was off to the side tossing SweeTarts in the air and catching them in his mouth.

"Be careful," I urged them. "Be on the watch for anything unusual."

"You're a broken record, Jake-o," PC said.

"Both men are dangerous. Don't go poking around. Call me if you—"

"Want us to do the other," an airborne SweeTart landed in Boyd's mouth, "street, too?"

"What other street?"

"One behind this house." He tossed another Tart in the air. "We already", he paused as it found its mark, "scouted it. We can see between the homes and actually get a pretty decent view of the backyard."

"Do that."

PC studied the picture of Renée Lambert. "Those eyes. What is she? Sad? Afraid?" He glanced away from the picture and back at me. I recalled Adam making a similar comment. He took his phone out of his cargo shorts pocket and snapped a picture of the picture. He put his phone back in his pocket and handed the photo back to me. "In her life, Jake-o, it's not Christmas morning."

I glanced at the picture. Just a good-looking woman to me. Between Adam's and PC's observations, I wondered if part of my radar wasn't operational. Bet Kathleen would cast a strong vote on that.

Morgan was late for dinner. I fixed a small pitcher of margaritas. I dropped Etta James on the turntable and took a seat on the screened porch. I drained the drink, poured a refill, sliced off some chunks of Welsh cheddar, and snatched some cashews, crackers, and a cigar. Dinner. I returned to the porch. I slid the cigar out of its cellophane wrapper and sniffed the open end. I gave it a slight squeeze to gauge how moist it still was—it wasn't—clipped the end, and torched it.

The red channel marker blinked on, signaling the night's arrival. The charter sunset boat, *Fantasea*, flying the flags of a half-dozen nations, cruised in from the gulf. Hands pointed as several dolphins, on cue, fluidly broke the surface off the end of my dock.

Morgan came through the side door, latched the handle, went into the kitchen, and came back with a glass of wine.

Neither of us spoke for several minutes. We rarely invent conversation. He helped himself to a chunk of cheese.

"Did you see the margaritas in there?" I said.

"I did. Did you talk to her?"

"No."

"Why not?"

"Didn't get around to it." I didn't feel like telling him I'd dropped by her condo. Hadley III leapt on top of the grill. Her wide eyes surveyed her domain.

I exhaled smoke out of my mouth. It went a few feet and then wafted into the air like a fog bank. "You read that file I gave you?"

"Cardinal Giovanni Antinori." He took a cracker and popped it in his mouth. "Quite a career." He took a few chews. "But you know all that." He propped his bare feet on top of the glass table. It needed cleaning. It always needed cleaning.

"I do. What do you see that I don't?" He wouldn't question my tenet that he and I experienced and saw things differently.

"Antinori changed. Transformed. About two years ago."

"How so?"

"You know of his progressive views?"

"I do. The critics in Rome censored him. He was like a Broadway hit; everybody hated him except the audience."

Morgan nodded. Hadley III jumped onto his lap from the top of the grill. Damn cat walks all over him and Kathleen but glares at me like she's waiting for me to drop dead.

"Precisely." He took a slow sip from his glass. Morgan was never in a hurry with food or people. "And that love stemmed not only from his gregarious personality but also his liberal views on religion. Those views and opinions, and hence his immense popularity, started around two years ago."

"What are you telling me?"

"You won't understand what I'm telling you unless you understand Giovanni." He took another bite of cheese. "Dinner, right?"

"You're looking at it."

"You know the law of preceding generations?"

"You just made it up."

"No, what—"

"Enlighten me."

"We receive our initial set of values and beliefs from our parents. Language, religion—both indoctrinated into us. Passed down, often unquestioned, from one generation to another. No one passes along science theory over the dinner table, nor do we engage in traditional science holiday gatherings. Therefore, science, unburdened with yesterday's dogma, is free to explode ahead. Indeed, it's expected to change."

"Can we skip?"

He stroked Hadley III's back, and the furball fired up her diesel. "Understand, Antinori's parents were Old Catholic. They embraced beliefs that for the most part had gone unchallenged not for mere generations but centuries."

"And about to change."

"Radically. Not many priests these days peddle indulgences. Yet at one time they were blatantly abused to help finance Saint Peter's Basilica. A sham that, in part, led to Martin Luther and John Calvin initiating the Protestant Reformation."

"Was this part of the hundred?" Morgan had been required by his parents to read one hundred books of their choosing before he left the sailboat and traveled on his own. I hit the bottom of my glass and remembered that my liquor cabinet was running on fumes. Might have to take a run tomorrow and restock. My mood lightened. Buying alcohol always cheers me up; the mere thought of it puts me in Happyville.

"Religion was a fascinating segment, although, admittedly, not up with the war books." He claimed the last chunk of cheese. "'War makes rattling good history, but peace is poor reading.'"

"That's it." I shot him a glance. "You get that from Kathleen?" I hadn't been able to recall Hardy's exact quotation when I'd stood in the war room of her condo.

"No. Why?"

"I had to paraphrase—never mind. Two years ago, Antinori, the man, not the wine."

"It all changed for him. His comments—did you read the one, 'If there is only one god, there can be no gods'?"

"I missed that."

"My father says that. If one religion is right, then all the others must be wrong. Therefore, no one can believe in their god if there is just one god."

"Unless you picked the winner."

"You're missing the—"

"I got it."

He gazed out to the water, where there was nothing except the lights across the bay. Twenty-eight streetlights span the bridge. I count them every night.

He turned back to me. "Something happened in your cardinal's life two years ago to force him to make such an abrupt turnaround on his beliefs. Something that—"

"Perhaps he'd been having doubts for years."

"We all do. But there was a triggering event in Giovanni's life that caused him to become outspoken. He is—was—a bright guy. He was aware of the consequences of his words, the reverberation of his speech, the impact of his dissension. Something tipped the man, and he was never the same again."

"And this has what to do with why he was at Kensington Gardens?"

"Haven't a clue." He put his wineglass down. "You still got red filets?"

"I do." He had hooked them as he brought *Moon Child* in the other night. They went in my refrigerator, as my screened porch—my *living room*—also served as the ad hoc dining room.

He stood, and Hadley III darted into the house as if a Florida panther was hot on her trail. "All I'm saying," he said, "is the man you killed was two years old. He held very different beliefs than he had ever known. Look at me."

I'd been mesmerized by a center console idling past the end of my dock. I turned my head and met his eyes.

"This man's beliefs," he continued, "were all he had, everything he was. Like you and I harbor the sun, the moon, the water. How these define our world? His world was his beliefs. His job, his standing in the community—everything centered on his beliefs. You can*not* imagine how traumatic it must have been for him to renounce what he was born into, to renounce the faith of his father—to blaze a radical new path. Do not make light of that. Fire up the grill."

I started to protest—not his comment about the grill—but couldn't muster the effort. He vanished into the kitchen. I was glad he was gone. There are times in our relationship when, quite unintentionally, I'm sure, Morgan makes me feel inferior—as if everyone's laughing except me. I drained my glass and opened the Weber's heavy lid.

Richard Harris's voice came from the Magnavox. It was one of Morgan's father's favorite albums. As I snuffed out my half-smoked cigar, Morgan came back with two empty plates, forks, and a plate of red filets bathed in olive oil and lightly seasoned. He also carried a bottle of red and the margarita pitcher. I took the filets before he dumped it all and placed them on the fish tray. A few minutes later we sat eating as the drawbridge across the bay opened and closed like a heart valve in slow motion. Barbara's side door quietly latched. She'd let her dog, Happy, out for the last time.

After the fish and the wine were gone, the Magnavox was silent, and the rustle of palm fronds filled the night, Morgan stood and said, "You got it?"

"Two years, right?"

"Two years. The cardinal buried one life and started another."

"Got it," I replied more to please him than as an affirmation of my belief. "Port?"

"I'm good."

"Do it again tomorrow?"

"I'll pass. Tomorrow," he drained his glass, put it down, and gave me a nod, "is another good night."

He vanished through the door and across my dark lawn. Hadley III snuck out with him. Morgan's comment affirmed our joint belief that the sweet spot of the day lay toward the end. I wondered if he, Kathleen, and I would ever see those days again, get that rhythm back.

I took my twenty-year-old port to the end of the dock.

Two years ago, Antinori decided that his beliefs were a house of cards. Renée joined WAP. It was if I had a file folder labeled 'Two Years,' but it held more questions than answers, more mystery than substance.

None of it getting me closer to Paretsky.

I'd forgotten to bring up the program itinerary on the website that Bretta had mentioned to me. I wanted to talk to people who had served on the same panel that Renée had. Tomorrow. I was finished for the day; when the day is done, I'm done with the day. I corked the bottle before I went in too deep.

He came again that night, but this time Cardinal Antinori didn't speak. He looked upon me with merciful pity, as if my stupidity summoned his empathy. I tried to talk, but my jaw was frozen and sluggish, and no words came out. His face was kind and sad, and he kept peering at me like we were brothers. I got tired of the mind game, brought up my gun, and shot him in the face. It had no effect. I shot again and again and again as if I were at a carnival shooting booth, and if I hit the clown's head in an exact spot I'd win a stuffed animal for the girl who was no longer mine.

CHAPTER 13

B inelli said, "My source expects a two-way street."
"No promises." I traded my phone and banana peel,
shifting the phone to my right hand and the peel to the left.
I was sitting on the balcony of the hotel after another brutal
workout in which I tried to kill myself and failed. Keep the
faith; there's always tomorrow.

"I'm not playing games with her," Binelli said. "I'll tell
her what I can deliver and not one iota more. Understand?
If you expect to use these people in the future, you need to
establish and practice fair reciprocity."

"I was never good at reciprocity."

"Time you learned."

I rubbed my head. I wasn't in the mood for reciprocity;
I didn't even like the sound of the word. "I don't know if I
have that much to offer, but tell her I'll play."

"Already did. Ball's in your court."

"I thought you weren't meeting until lunch?" A
woman at the table two down from me lit up a cigarette,
crossed her cigarette legs, tilted her face toward the sky,
and exhaled.

"She called and moved it up. I didn't think you—"

"What do you got?"

"Two."

"Two?"

"More like twins. We—"

"Two what?"

I stood, tossed my banana peel at the seashell waste can, and moved away from the smoker. I rounded a corner to the front of the balcony that faced the resort's two pools and bar. The smell of breakfast emanated from the restaurant off to my right. On the flat waters of the gulf, a paddleboarder made her way south.

"You listening?" Binelli prodded me.

"All ears." I sat on the concrete love seat.

"The FBI thinks that Paretsky works with a partner—serves as a sort of bodyguard for Paretsky, or at the very least a decoy. We further believe that his partner may even carry out some of the kills himself. That's why it's been so hard to track or identify him. It's not one man—it's two."

"Why would my organization only feed me information on one, and what do you have on the second man?"

"I can't speak for whatever branch of the bloated uncle you work for. I can say this: we—and by that I mean the people on our end who are hunting Paretsky—believe there are two men. Others do not. Perhaps they feel that pursuing two will only hinder their cause. Sometimes madness has a method, usually not. It's a big world, buster, room for lots of opinions, and you need to consider then all. That *is* why you befriended me in the first place."

Considering Lambert's visitor and the man who corralled Renée Lambert at the Valencia—possibly the same person—I was warming to the two-man theory.

"OK," I said. "My agency decided to send me after one man because they may not swallow the two-man theory, or maybe they just think I can run faster after one. Maybe they sent another team after two. Doesn't really matter. Tell me what you know about Paretsky's supposed partner."

"Nearly zilch."

"Come again?"

"You heard me."

"How can you build a theory on zilch?"

"*Nearly* zilch."

The concrete bench was hard and I traversed back around the corner. Cigarette Legs was still there. Her right leg was crossed over her left, and her right foot bounced in the air like a nervous habit. I said, "What constitutes *nearly*?"

"We caught a break eight months ago. Busted a guy for drug trafficking. Turns out he was close to doing a deal with Paretsky. He was eager to trade us information for a lighter sentence. He didn't have much, but he said Paretsky indicated another man he worked with might be the one to actually pull the job. We didn't think much of it until the Venice hit, south of you. Know about it?"

"I do. Couple walks out of a grocery store and smack into two head shots. Their son was in covert."

"Exactly. My source has reason to believe that Paretsky was 2,500 miles away that day and—"

"Doing what and where?"

"Not sure on the first, and Europe on the second. But if he works with another, it explains a few holes we've needed patched for some time."

"Name? Description? Anything?"

"Not much. They had handles for each other. Paretsky supposedly called his colleague the Guardian."

"Say that again." Both the cardinal and Lambert had used the word. I had dismissed it. A common word, not meant to connote a single person. Was the Guardian an actual man? If so, who was the Pope? Paretsky?

Binelli cut through my thoughts. "Called him the—"

"Who called who what?" I walked over to the garbage can, picked my banana peel off the side, and dropped it into the container. For the life of me, I cannot make that shot.

"I said, Paretsky referred to his partner as the Guardian, and that guy referred to Paretsky as—"

"The Pope," I blurted out as I remembered Cardinal Giovanni Antinori's last words to me. Words I hadn't paid attention to at the time, and now I wished to hell I had.

"How'd you know?" Binelli came back in, but I wasn't listening. It was my turn to hang up on Natalie Binelli. I sprinted down the steps and across the street toward my truck. I gunned it down Gulf Boulevard to Donald Lambert's house. When I was five minutes out, PC called. I didn't answer. I knew I was too late.

CHAPTER 14

PC's Camaro with the Endless Summer plate and flame-painted sides was tight against the curb. He and Boyd got out of the car. I quietly closed the truck's door.

PC said, "I tried to call you jus—"

"I know. What do you got?"

Nothing appeared unusual at Lambert's house. Perhaps my paranoia had gotten the better of me. It's often like a fire alarm blaring in the middle of the night. It has also saved my life on more than one occasion, which is a decent trade-off for a few false alarms.

"A boat," Boyd said. He usually let PC take the lead. They both wore the same clothes they had on yesterday. "I saw it come down the canal, from the open end, you know?" He arched his back, reached under his T-shirt with his left hand, and scratched his chest. "Didn't think much of it. Twenty—thirty minutes tops—it saunters out real slow like."

"Idles," PC said. "Boats idle, man. Not saunter."

Boyd considered the point. "I thought that was when Caesar was killed."

My eyes drilled Boyd. "Why do we care about the sauntering boat?"

Boyd stared at me with a brew of guilt and fear in his eyes. "It never went past the house, Jake. You know? We didn't think anything of it until after it left, and then we realized—"

"Maybe the guy anchored and dropped a line," PC said in his clipped speech. "Maybe he had engine trouble. Who knows? Here's the thing, Jake-o." He glanced at the house and kept his gaze there as he spoke. "Those blinds in the front? Never down. Even at night. But we noticed after the boat left that they were down."

The living room blinds were down. The same blinds that I'd noted earlier looked permanently open because the trimmed hedge neatly blocked the lower half of the window.

"We checked," PC continued. "The view of the back of the house from the other street? The rear blinds are drawn as well. Maybe he's going someplace, and he closes up shop before he leaves. We can't say for certain when those blinds were drawn. Follow me?"

I went to my truck and got my Belly Band holster out of the backseat. I strapped it around my waist under my T-shirt and put my Smith & Wesson into one of its two sleeves. My five-inch, folding Boker knife went in my shorts pocket. *Bad guys don't wear shorts.* I got a pair of latex gloves from a box and reached over the seat and grabbed a pair of old boat shoes. I had just bought a new pair and didn't want to wear them into the house. A habit of sprinting out of the house in bare feet and had taught me to keep the last few pairs in the truck.

"I'm going in," I said, but the hopes of a false alarm were crashing. I smelled smoke. "PC." He looked up at me. "Leave. Go now. If there's any problem, I don't want you two around. Leave and—"

"Jake-o, if I listened to people, I'd still be wasting away in chemistry cl—"

"If the heat comes, you want to introduce yourself?" PC and Boyd had a couple of juvie arrests on their records. "We'll draw too much attention out here. I'm sure everything's fine. I'll go in and talk to Lambert and call you later. Vamoose."

Boyd turned around and headed back to their car. PC did likewise but not before he shot a glance at the latex gloves in my right hand. He knew. And he knew that I knew that he knew.

My gloved finger rang the bell. The Westminster Quarters chimed. I pounded the door before the second quarter. A white van crawled down the street. Plumbing. Most likely scouting for an address. It slowed and pulled to a stop five houses down on the opposite side of the street. I tucked around the corner of Lambert's house. The great white egret was standing at attention at the sliding door. The blinds were drawn. The bird didn't give any ground when I approached. I could have reached out and patted it on what little head it had. I drew my gun and slid open the door just enough to allow myself in. I closed it behind me.

Lambert lay on his kitchen floor in a pool of blood. His open eyes stared up, as if in death he was fascinated with the popcorn ceiling. I stepped around him and cleared the house. Every drawer was empty, every closet trashed.

Lambert had been shot in the right knee, the chest, and the head. Despite the condition of the interior, the mop and water bucket stood upright against the oven. Lambert's left hand stopped just short of the bucket, as if in his last act he'd tried to touch that simple and unassuming thing that, different for us all, is what we want to be left alone to do and seems so little to ask of the world.

My guess was that his assailant knew torture would be a waste of time—what man gives up his daughter? But why kill Lambert if you gained no information? Was there some reason he needed to be dead, or was whoever committed the deed merely not taking any chances?

"I'm sorry," I said, gazing down at the body. "I should have—" My shoulders drooped, and my breath blew out. I took in a slow, deep breath. I smelled cough drops.

The scent of a man who was no longer there.

Combing the place for clues while not overstaying my welcome was a delicate task. Who knew what some neighbor had seen and whether he had already dialed the police? I hurriedly searched the mess that used to be the man's home but came up empty. No computer. I scrounged through his pockets. No cell phone. The Guardian had taken Lambert's electronics.

It was a crime scene, and I needed to exit. I opened the rear sliding door, and the great white egret stood waiting for me. It bent its neck in, took a step toward the body, but then stopped, one long stick-leg frozen in midair. It snapped its head toward me and lowered its leg like a low-geared motor. "Sorry, buddy." I grabbed the picture of Lambert and his wife that hung on the outside wall. They were grinning, like we all do when we face the camera, clueless as to what the future will bring. *Smile, we're toast in two years.* I'm not sure why I did that—swipe the picture—other than an impending sense of failure to protect Donald Lambert was already gathering within. Perhaps the picture would sharpen my focus.

When I left, the bird was peering into the house.

CHAPTER 15

Remember this: *Beware the following sea.*
When on the water, always check your rear so a wave doesn't swamp the stern and send you to Davey Jones's locker. I had bundles of things to do, but first I needed to protect myself.

At home, I started a small brush fire and burned the gloves and shoes I'd worn in Lambert's house. I doused the fire with water and shoveled the ashes into the bay.

I retrieved a burner phone from the safe and called the police. I didn't want Lambert's body waiting for the cleaning lady. The phone went into the bay—after a thorough wipe down.

PC was next, and I told him to meet me at Riptide. We needed to scout out boat rentals and work the neighborhood to see if anyone saw anything that would help me find the Guardian. It was a safe assumption at this point that Paretsky did have a partner referred to as the Guardian, and that man was looking for Renée Lambert. He had killed her father, likely after Donald Lambert refused to give him any useful information, or maybe after he sang—there was no way of knowing. Furthermore, Cardinal Antinori somehow knew and was connected to both men. I didn't even waste a wild guess on that one.

What had Antinori said? *Beware the Pope; he has the Guardian?* The Cardinal's death would have to take a backseat. If Paretsky or his partner was near, I needed to double my efforts.

On the way to Riptide, I hit Garrett's number.

"What?"

"Next flight."

He hung up.

PC and Boyd were on high, wood stools that faced the gulf. The black man with dreadlocks who sold paintings was setting up for the day under his bright-blue canvas. We exchanged nods. A girl in a bikini and a pierced belly button, Riptide's signature outfit, danced over to the table.

"SweeTarts?" she said, staring at Boyd, who had just taken a sleeve from his pocket.

"Want one?"

"*Do* I?" She placed her order pad on the table and held out her hand. Boyd dropped a few sugar tablets in it. "So," she said, popping one in her mouth and cracking it. "What can I get you gentlemen?"

My appetite, which had taken a serious blow at the sight of Lambert, roared back. I ordered a grilled fish sandwich, fries, water, and a beer. PC and Boyd followed. Belly Button Ring didn't bother to write anything down.

"He's gone, isn't he?" said PC.

I kicked off my new shoes—they were still stiff—and freed my toes. It was already steaming out. "Don't blame yourselves. There's nothing you could have—"

Boyd said, "We were paid to be his guarding angel and—"

"*Guardian*," PC sliced in with a tone that conveyed his disgust with their efforts, not with Boyd. "And—"

"What the hell, man?" Boyd cut PC a look. "You always gotta—"

"—we failed."

"—get on my case just because—"

"Enough," I interjected. "*If* you failed it's a damn good thing, otherwise..." Belly Ring came by and dropped three waters and three beers on the table. The water glasses were sweating like sieves. I took half of mine in one gulp. A chunk of ice went in my mouth, and I rolled it around with my tongue.

"Otherwise," I bit down on the ice, "you'd be dead as well. Listen, boys." I leaned in across the table. They were kids—the heck was I doing putting them in harm's way? But, on their own, all they had managed to find the time for were prank tricks that had gotten them room and board in the slammer. That's not where you want to be making friends. I wanted them off the street. Unfortunately, my line of business wasn't stocking chips on shelves. "I told you up front. I decide what you do, and I'm the only judge of your conduct. You did fine." I cracked the remnant of ice in my mouth. "Just fine."

Belly Ring dropped off our lunches, and no one spoke as we consumed our food while our thoughts consumed us. A song came over the speaker stating that one was a lonely number. *One's a lonely act*, I heard myself telling Kathleen on the floor of our London flat. Was there no element in the constellations that in some manner didn't connect back to her?

"Who does that?" Boyd asked, and I was relieved for a conversational bridge to get the two of them back together and get my mind off the floor.

"Three Dog Night," PC answered.

Boyd wiped a napkin across his mouth. "Never," he said, and balled his hand, still clasping the napkin, into a fist and poked it into his stomach. He emitted a mild belch not worthy of the prelude and continued, "Heard of them. They new?"

PC shook his head. "Sixties, early seventies. They——"

"What's their name again, Three..."

"Dog Night. A night so cold you need to sleep with three dogs to stay warm." He pushed his plate away and looked at me. "What can we do?"

I finished an appreciative draw on my beer. "Whoever killed Lambert left a trace, a crumb. We need to find it. Check out the boat rental places within a mile of here. Tell them your buddy went out...hell, you figure it out."

"You think he rented a boat, gave a card number, and then wasted a guy?" PC said. "Maybe provided a home address?"

"Do *not* blame yourself." I picked up my empty plate and placed it on the table next to us. "He likely stole one, and with luck you might get a description. But luck isn't free; you've got to sweat for it."

"We'll canvass door to door," PC replied. "Boyd-o," he turned to Boyd, who was nodding his head to the beat of the song and keeping his eye on the waitress's belly button, "remember when we did our Bible thing to get into that house a year ago?"

"Mormons, man. Once," he spread his hands out, "we were young and Mormons." His head kept a steady beat. A solitary gull approached us by foot and blasted its plaintive cry. It was odd; they are usually tentative and quiet when working solo.

"We'll conjure something new." PC turned to me. "We hit the boat rentals and both streets, the one he lived on and the one on the other side of the canal. Anything else?"

"Want the standard lecture on being safe and not doing anything stupid?"

"Naw, in fact," he rose and pushed the stool back toward the table, "safe begats boredom."

Boyd got up and nodded at me. "Thanks for lunch." He took two steps and turned back to me. "Sorry, Jake. PC was sleeping. It was my watch. I saw the boat and knew right away that it didn't creep out on the other side of the house. I just figured that—"

I stood up, went to him, and put my hand on his shoulder. It felt more natural than when I had touched Donald Lambert's arm. Maybe I just needed a little practice. "Forget it, hear me? There was nothing you could have done or foretold."

He held my eyes for a second, turned, and trailed PC. I settled the tab and climbed into my truck just as a late-morning cloudburst dumped on it like it was in the middle of a car wash. I sat but didn't twist the key. The water cascaded down the windshield.

It was possible that the death of Donald Lambert would bring his daughter out of hiding, assuming she was still alive and not afraid to show her face. I doubted it, but that didn't keep me from fantasizing about an easy break. I turned the key, and the wipers came on. I wondered if Lambert mopped his floor before he was killed.

CHAPTER 16

Remember this, too: *Don't be afraid to see what you see.* Credit goes to Ronald Reagan's farewell address. Or maybe it was Daffy Duck arguing with Bugs about whether it was rabbit season or duck season. Does it really matter?

This does: I saw nothing.

Nothing that connected Cardinal Antinori to Paretsky. Nothing that connected Renée Lambert to Paretsky other than that she, at one time, had been his girlfriend. Why did Paretsky and the Guardian want to find Renée? Did they routinely erase all former girlfriends?

"What do we have?" Garrett demanded as he came in the side door. Monk parakeets, as if they sensed his presence, screamed from a palm tree. He carried no suitcase, having, I presumed, dropped it off at Morgan's. He stayed there to allow Kathleen and me our privacy, not that it mattered anymore. Just as well—I was short a bed as my guest-bedroom suite hadn't yet arrived.

I took my eyes off the diagram I'd been doodling and gazed up at Garrett. He wore jeans and a black T-shirt. About the only time he wore something different was when he and Morgan went kitesurfing. The whistling sea breeze swung my door open.

I said, "Donald Lambert took three bullets this morning."

"I thought you had someone on him." He walked around the perimeter of the screened porch. A wood sailboat came in from the gulf with only its main up and cleared my dock by about a hundred feet. Two couples sat in the cockpit.

There was no way of knowing if they were couples. Two men and two women; after that, my mind jumped to the convenient and logical conclusion, which was not necessarily the truth.

"I can't find any connections," I said, ignoring Garrett's accusation. I reviewed with him the scene that morning and mentioned that PC and Boyd were working the neighborhood.

"You need to find Renée Lambert," he said. "She's—"

"I know that."

"—our best lead. If she's gone, or they beat us to her, we've got nothing. So far, we got zilch."

"*Nearly* zilch." I plagiarized Binelli's words as I stood up.

I'd forgotten to look at Words Against People's website to see who else was on the dais with Renée Lambert. Should have been on that sooner. I opened my laptop and in a few minutes had the itinerary for the conference. Renée shared the platform with two women and a man. By cross-referencing the three names, I found the two women lived within a couple hours, in opposite directions, of the greater Tampa area. The man, Joseph Vizcarrondo, was in Pompano Beach, north of Ft. Lauderdale. He was also the moderator of the panel. I printed out two sheets and handed one to Garrett. Within ten minutes, we secured addresses and phone numbers.

Morgan cut across my lawn and firmly closed the screen door behind him. He collapsed in a chair with his bare feet propped up on the glass table. I filled him in. I didn't tell him about the great white egret peering down at the body of Donald Lambert. He would have insisted that the bird in some manner comprehended the situation, and I just wasn't up for that.

"We should each visit one," he instructed as I handed him my sheet with the three names on it. "Far more likely to get information in person than with a phone call. See what they know about Renée Lambert, what she might have said, where she might be staying."

"We can do a face-to-face," I said, "with all three and be back here by tomorrow evening. Find out everything they know about Renée. With a little luck, between PC and Boyd scouting for leads on the boat, and these three—who at least had some contact with Renée at the WAP conference—we should get a solid bite."

"Call them first," Garrett said. "Make sure they're available."

"I'll take it. What's my story?" Morgan asked me.

"Say we've been retained by the teachers' organization to do a follow-up interview. Some spin about making next year's conference even better, and can we have thirty minutes of your time. If we go in saying we're assisting someone investigating a murder, they'll clam up and have more questions than answers."

"They'll wonder why in person."

"Tell them we're in the neighborhood. Buy 'em lunch. Whatever. I'll take the moderator, Vizcarrondo. There's half a dozen flights a day from Tampa to Lauderdale."

"I'll take April Woltmann, in Rotunda West," Garrett said. "That leaves you," he nodded at Morgan, "with Tracy Leary in Winter Park."

Morgan took the sheet into the living room. Fifteen minutes later, he emerged with the details. Joseph Vizcarrondo would meet me the next day at Brazenhead's Pub on East Atlantic in Pompano Beach at half past noon.

"Upstairs," Morgan instructed me. "Said you'd find him camping by a window."

I booked a round trip. My return flight was the last in the day, and I hoped to make it back before then but wanted to give myself ample time with Vizcarrondo.

CHAPTER 17

If bad guys don't wear shorts, then a representative of a firm retained by the teachers' organization to elicit feedback from its conferences wouldn't either. I wore summer khakis, a white shirt, and a blue blazer. I was six deep in the queue at the taxi stand at Lauderdale when I shed the coat and rolled up my sleeves. The stiff in front of me had on a dark suit and cuff links. He glanced over his shoulder. His suit was buttoned, and his knot was tight under a gold collar bar. A real corporate storm trooper. I thought they were extinct.

Pompano Beach was a short drive up I-95. The cabbie, a young, bearded man from Turkey, was glad that LeBron James had gone home to Cleveland, even though the cabbie himself had no intention of returning home. He took the East Atlantic exit and dropped me off in front of Brazenhead's. Wherever you go on the surface of the globe, there is a piece of Ireland. Never have so few people spread so much joy to so many as the Irish. Brazenhead's had Guinness on draft and a toboggan run of a bar that, according to the laminated sign, was from a shuttered hotel in Dublin.

Vizcarrondo was upstairs at a two-top that fronted a double-hung, open window at the far end of the room. I strode over to him. A framed picture of girls in psychedelic dresses and ringleted wigs, some in midair in a step dance, hung above his head next to the dark-stained window trim. He wore shorts and a green polo shirt. Lucky guy.

I shed my jacket and draped it over the back of my chair, which inconveniently faced north. Vizcarrondo was halfway through a beer so dark it would block the sun on a clear, bitterly cold January day. We exchanged pleasantries.

"Please, just Rondo," he insisted. "That's been my handle since my first group of junior high buds." Rondo had an osprey nose and slivers of uncut hair that begged for scissors. The right hinge of his glasses was held together by tape.

The humidity climaxed in a downpour. I reached for the window. "We'll be fine," he said. "There's a big overhang. Unless it goes horizontal on us, we'll stay dry."

How many times had he sat there in order to confidently make such an observation? The waiter dropped by. Rondo caught me checking out his beer.

"Think less of you if you don't," he said.

"I'll have what he's having."

He flicked his eyes up at the waiter. "Don't let me see the bottom."

As the rain formed a liquid curtain a few feet to my right, I apologized to Rondo for realizing that I was out of business cards. I kept it short; I'd been told that I didn't lie well. I explained that the Florida Teachers Association was soliciting suggestions on how to make the conference even better next year.

"You do that face-to-face? I already got an e-mail. Five pages of questions."

"And what did you do with that?" The beers arrived, each with a one-inch head.

"Deleted it."

I spread my hands. "As does nearly everyone. You, being the moderator—"

"But you're sending someone to interview April as well."

"April?" I feigned ignorance.

"Woltmann."

"Guess I didn't draw that name."

News travels fast. I glanced at his hand. No ring. Were he and April Woltmann an item?

"We're just an outsource firm hired by the FTA," I said, forging ahead. "I won't argue with you; that's some budget they have. If you don't mind." I opened my notebook. On the jump across the interior scrubland, I'd jotted down some questions. I didn't want to spend any more time than necessary on my fictitious assignment but wanted to ease into my questions regarding Renée Lambert.

I took Rondo through a litany of questions and had him rate a few items on a one-to-five scale. Standard trash about the accommodations, communications, what we could do better, and feedback he'd received from others. The rain stopped, and the noise with it. The sun illuminated our cozy upstairs alcove. I glanced at my pad and up at Rondo. His glasses were slightly crooked, as if the tape wasn't quite up to the task. Time to dive in.

"We were unable to locate one of the individuals with whom you shared the table, a Renée..." I glanced down at my pad. "...Lambert."

"Don't know much about her."

I felt my posture weaken. He finished his first beer and, in a continuous movement, picked up the second and took a sip.

"Do you know how we can contact her?"

"No. I've been with WAP for five years. She's fairly new. You see her? I'm telling you," he shook his head "she's a beautiful woman. Smart, too. That's the thing, you know. For some reason she kept to herself. Not married. No kids. Not that any of that's a prerequisite for WAP; it's just that the most common type we draw is someone whose kid's been bullied and verbally abused."

"What's your story?" I wanted to return to Renée but knew I couldn't afford an unhealthy obsession with her if I was to gain his confidence.

"My son," he said, and took another quick drink. "Lost him about seven years ago this coming May third."

"I'm sorry." *About* seven years ago this coming May third. Bet he knew the hour.

He waved his hand. "I'm fine with it. That's what we're told to say when we realize that we'll never be fine with it. That things will never be the same, and we have accepted that and can move on. What do you think of that?"

"I'll defer to your judgment."

"Then you think that's total bullshit. Thick and deep, and once it's in the tread of your shoes, it never comes off." He reached for his mug but drew his hand back, although he kept his eyes on it. I had to say something, so I threw out, "Traffic accident?" even though I couldn't imagine how it would lead him to join WAP.

"What?" He glanced up at me.

"What hap—"

"No." He waved his hand. "Benny, name was Benjamin, had…some troubles. Good kid, bad crowd. Shitty timing." He didn't deny himself this time and picked up his mug. "That is a wicked combination. Yes, sir. A *wicked* combination."

"I didn't mean to pry. You don't—"

"Oh, hell." He looked up at me. I wondered if I would be out in time to catch standby on the earlier flight. "I don't mind. He peddled child porno. Lot of money in that. He got caught, did time. Embarrassed himself to hell. Couldn't hardly look at his sister, let alone his mother." Rondo stole a glance out the window. "He gets out," he came back to me, his eyes tired behind the crooked glasses, "doing fine, you know. Got a job. One day he's busing tables, and some big birthday party walks in. One of the moms, she stops cold in her tracks and demands to see the manager. Pulls him over and pounds holy hell into the man, right there in the middle of the restaurant, yelling at him that he had a pedophile working there.

"Turns out one of the pictures Benny had was of her daughter. Someone had set up a camera inside a girls' locker room at a gymnastics studio. This lady recognized Benny from his trial. She goes balls-out ballistic on the manager. Acts like she's King Fuckin' Tut. Creates a scene. Patrons start to peel out. He fires him. Believe that? Fired him on the spot. On the way out the door, the lady, she's screaming at him—this is just what people tell me, I wasn't there—calls him a threat to society."

"I'm—"

"Hung himself a week later. My wife found him in the coat closet when she went to get the vacuum because I spilled potting dirt. Before she opened that door, she was pretty ticked about the mess. Not so much afterward. No, sir, not much at all."

I looked out the window and wondered what I was doing with my life and couldn't understand why that thought hit me at that time.

"Anyways." He brightened up. "Didn't mean to pee on your snow cone, but it happens. My wife and I joined WAP. Good group—not good enough to save the marriage, though—but I suppose the whole sorry-ass thing just revealed problems that were already there. They told us a tragedy like we went through could bury us, that we needed to find and remember who we really were. Problem was, who we really were wasn't much in the first place.

"Those words," he stole a glance out the window and quickly came back at me, like he didn't like what was out there, "stripped me of everything except my mortgage. They killed my son and torpedoed my marriage. Did more harm than anything he ever had on his hard drive. Think those pictures ever killed anyone? Think they put *that* lady in jail? Brought her up on charges? Think that bitch even feels regret? And I'm told to remember who I am. Fuck that, man. Yes, sir. You can fuck that."

I didn't think there was a question in there that expected an answer. I let Joseph Vizcarrondo come out of his thoughts on his own. I'd lost control of the conversation. I wondered again what my odds were for standby on an earlier flight.

"That," he said, as he picked up his mug and tilted it toward me, "is my story. Some people have constipation of the mind and diarrhea of the mouth. And they're killers, my friend, just like the kind we put in jail. Sorry you asked?"

"No. I—"

"Sure you are. Renée? Her story was her mom. Said her mom was verbally abused as a young girl, ten, twelve, whatever. Not cuss words, she said. Not loud words. But soft and gentle words, that's what she said, 'soft, gentle words.' Those words eventually took her down. Her mother committed suicide as well. We talked about it, but not much. No sense having a cry fest every time you meet someone in the organization."

"How did you select her for your panel?"

"She called me, lobbied to be on it. Said it was her hometown. Chance to see her dad."

Donald Lambert had lied to me. No way did his daughter lobby for a gig in her hometown and not drop in on Dad. I should have challenged him on that.

"Do you have any means of contacting her other than her cell and e-mail?" I fondled my beer. "She's not responding to either."

"Nothing." He farted. "Excuse me."

"Never married, right?"

"Not that I know of." He gave me an appraising look. The waiter dropped by. I glanced at Rondo, but he waved the man off.

"Boyfriends? You said she was a head turner."

"Don't think so."

"Was she with a man that night? Muscular, short hair?"

"I wouldn't...there *was* this guy. Where's your shed?"

"Pardon?"

"Where do you live?"

"West coast. Saint Pete Be—"

"And you came here to talk to me?"

"Yes, sir. We—"

"Bullshit."

Busted.

"She's missing." I shifted my weight. "I've been retained by the family to locate her." No need to tell him that Renée's father bled out that morning on his kitchen floor, reaching for his mop bucket while a great white egret mourned the loss of its food source.

Rondo leaned back in his chair and smiled. It was the first time I'd seen him do that. "I thought," he said, and bobbed his head up and down like an oil pump, "when I saw you strutting toward me, tall and fast, like you owned the world? No way, I thought, someone like him is working for some outsource poll-taking firm. You play ball?"

"No."

"Really? Whatja do?"

"Army."

"How was that?"

"Three meals a day."

"I hear you."

"Tell me about the man."

"Yes, sir. I knew." He bobbed his head some more. Guess he wasn't done with his self-congratulatory accolades. "The second you made those top two steps in one stride and took the corner, I knew."

He tented his hands in front of him and leaned in. "Came in late." He picked up his pace. "Hustled her out. Not friendly, but not unfriendly. Like they knew each other, you know?"

I did. It was the same record that Adam, the bartender at the Valencia, had played for me. Benny Mardones's hit single, also his single hit, came over the speakers, and I hoped Rondo didn't catch it. I pushed my beer aside and waved away a gnat that displayed curiosity in my barley and hops. Rondo and I locked eyes.

"Did you overhear anything, see him before, catch a name?"

He sucked in his lower lip and shook his head. "He said he wanted to explain. I was heading to the bar, and I overheard as I brushed past them. He said something about some other guy not wanting to hurt her...no, that wasn't it, more like he would *never* hurt her. He had her by the elbow and was saying this other guy just wanted a chance to talk to her. Said to give him a chance, that after all they'd been through, he deserved at least that."

"Must have been a slow brush," I said.

He nodded his head in approval of my observation. "I hung around the bar and eavesdropped. What else you gonna do?" He shrugged. "Go back to the room, turn on the tube, and watch a bunch of tattooed cooks get cardiac arrest in a kitchen? You gotta see this lady. It wasn't just that she was a stunner. She had a normalcy that belied her appearance. Just a real nice girl, you know? Usually it's the ugly ones that got the great personality, God's little joke on men—you know, my man, exactly what I'm talking about—but from the little I hung with her, she'd make any father proud. Speaking of," he tilted up the sagging side of his glasses with his right hand, "is he worried?"

"Who?" But I knew.

"Her father."

"Doing OK."

It appeared the only thing I was going to get out of Rondo was a sad story. I stole a glance at my watch. Should be able to make standby for the earlier flight. I was anxious to hear what Garrett and Morgan had unearthed, as well as PC and Boyd. Certainly someone had something.

I shifted my weight and closed my notebook. "Anything else?"

"About it." He gave a light shrug of his shoulders. "He did mention something about a disc. She said she didn't know what he was talking about. He got a little peeved at that. Said the sun disc was missing. We had an afternoon free, and they bused us to the beach. I didn't know whether he was referring to a paddleboard, WaveRunner, or—"

"What about the disc?"

He nudged up his glasses. "I think she said she didn't know what he was talking about, said she didn't take it, but really? It was loud, you know? That's really it."

"Did he accuse her of having the disc?"

"I'm not—"

"What exactly did he say?"

He leaned back. "I don't know. Hey." He shrugged his shoulders. "Wish I did. It was like he was accusing her of something."

I stood, thanked him for his time, and gave him my card. He made me promise to keep him informed. I turned to leave when his voice came from behind me.

"You never touched it." He nodded to my beer.

I shrugged. "Guess I didn't." It's a game I play sometimes. Put the devil in front of me and walk away. *You owned me once, but not now.*

"Mind?"

"All yours."

"That bitch?"

"Pardon me?"

"The bitch. Squealed on my—"

"Right."

Joseph Vizcarrondo picked up my mug of beer and tossed the golden liquid out the second-floor window and onto the sidewalk below. He placed the mug back on the table with a thud.

"She can rot in hell. That's how I deal with it," he said. "That's who I am."

I strutted out the door.

CHAPTER 18

"I think Renée Lambert stole a SanDisk USB flash drive from Paretsky," I announced to Garrett over the phone.

I'd made the earlier flight and was into my second beer at an airport bar, squeezed between a woman in a navy pinstripe business suit who buried her head in a laptop and the Marlboro Man: long coat, boots, sequined shirt, handlebar moustache, Stetson on the counter, and a face that was a living testament to Wyoming winters and the long-term hazards of ignoring skin moisturizers. If my bar mates copulated, their offspring would ride horses and use Google maps.

Garrett said, "Vizcarrondo tell you that?"

"Not in so many words, nor can I be positive. He overheard talk about a disk and the sun. Lambert's place was trashed this morning. Most—"

"Easy thing to hide. Tough to find unless you squeeze a guy for hours, even days."

"The Guardian didn't have the time to torture *and* search the house. I would have done what he did: shot the guy in the knee, let him get a taste of real pain, and spend as much time as possible searching for what I came for. Head shot on the way out the door."

Business lady gave me a cursory glance and then sank back into a pie chart. "We can look," Garrett said, "but there's no way of knowing whether the Guardian already located it."

"I'll go with this: Lambert told me that he hadn't seen his daughter in close to six months. I think he lied. His daughter was in town more recently than that. If Renée stole the disc, it had to be during the last two, three weeks, tops. Paretsky wouldn't be pulling off those previous hits if he thought his information was compromised. I think she was in contact with her father and went underground after he was murdered."

Lights out for business lady. She packed up her toys and bolted. She landed about eight stools down, around the ninety-degree angle of the bar. Her perfume stayed behind, as if she now occupied two seats.

"If she has a disc," Garrett said, "and if that disc contains information on Paretsky's group, bank accounts, and clients, then she's more valuable than Paretsky."

"No wonder Paretsky and his buddy are on her trail. What did you find?"

"Zilch."

"Prefaced with a 'nearly'?"

"No."

We disconnected. I hit Morgan's number. It went to voice mail, and I left a message. If he was on I-4 on his Harley racing back from Winter Park, I wouldn't get to him before I got home.

PC was next. No boat rental business reported renting to a single man or having a boat stolen. No one in the neighborhood had reported a stolen boat. I hung up and picked over a salty mix of bar snacks, selecting sesame-seed sticks and peanuts. I tossed them in my mouth and followed them with a swig of beer.

"What's your story?" Cowboy asked.

I gave him a glance. You could take a Weedwacker to his eyebrows, but his eyes were as blue and clear as any I'd ever seen.

"Domestic dispute."

"Didn't sound like that to me." He leaned over and peeled back his coat with his left hand. He had a holster that bulged with a cannon-sized revolver that Lee would have forked over his family farm for at Gettysburg. And a badge. A big, brassy, badass badge.

"Federal marshal," he said. He removed his hand, and his coat closed like a stage curtain. If he blinked while looking at me, I missed it.

"No kidding."

"No, sir."

I reached back into my wallet, extracted my card, and handed it to him.

"Beach bum," I said.

"No kidding."

"No, sir."

I introduced myself, told him I'd served five years in special ops, and was a Florida PI. You never know when you're going to need a federal marshal on your side. He handed me his card, but I didn't read it.

"Wayne." He stuck out his hand. "John Wayne."

I tried not to smile but couldn't help myself. "John Wayne?"

"Yes, sir." He tilted his head and curled up the left side of his lip. "Dad wanted John, and my mom wanted anything *other* than John."

"How'd he take that hill?"

"Bought her a pink AMC Pacer. Made her heart spin."

"That's painful, John. It was an ugly car the day it was born and a better world the second the production line was shut down."

"I know," he replied, without a hint of a smile.

"Listen, I have no idea when I might need a federal marshal from Wyoming, but if I do I'll give you a call, and if I can ever be of assistance, don't hesitate to dial me."

"Wyoming?"

"Just a guess. What brings you here?"

"My mother's not well. Flew in to see her."

"Pretty long trip."

"Yes, sir." He took a sip of water. "Pretty long trip from Wyoming."

I got up, took a few steps, and then spun around. "Your mother." He raised his eyes to mine. "She going to be all right?" He certainly realized that although my question was directed at him, my body was already leaning away, but after Rondo's beer toss, I felt—hell, I don't know what I felt.

He didn't answer right away but seemed to be appraising me for the first time. "I believe she's going to be. I thank you for asking."

I hustled to my gate and promptly saw that the plane was delayed by fifteen minutes. Morgan hadn't gotten back to me. PC, Boyd, and Garrett all whiffed. And I? Maybe Renée Lambert took a USB flash drive from Paretsky. Other than that, the day was a bust. I glanced at John Wayne's card before I stuck it in my wallet.

Edward Jonathan Wayne

United States Marshal, Northern District of Florida

A Tallahassee prefix. *Pretty long trip from Wyoming.* John Wayne had had a little fun with me. I thought of the words the colonel had spoken at the end of my dock. *God's waiting room has some real cowboys up in Tallahassee.*

If only he knew.

CHAPTER 19

There was no sign of Garrett or Morgan when I entered my house. They had cleared out, and I saw why. Kathleen sat on the end of the dock. Leave it to a woman to scatter your buddies like a gas blower on dry fall leaves.

I didn't want to face her, mainly because I held delusions that everything was fine. Delusions and hopes are often my best friends. When they disappoint me, they're easy to rekindle. I grabbed a bottle of red, two glasses and headed down the dock.

Good thing I brought supplies, as she had nothing to drink. As our bare feet dangled over the edge, I poured two glasses. I didn't know whether to be glib, serve up a humorous comment, or gush a sincere apology.

I said, "I don't know whether to be glib, serve up a humorous comment, or gush a sincere apology."

Her hair was pulled back so tight it looked as if it were threatening to secede from her forehead. She wore beige shorts and a red, sleeveless top that I didn't remember seeing before. I ran my hand down the side of her neck. She turned, and the slightest of smiles formed.

"I'm a major screw-up," I jumped in. "My mistakes, I'm sure there'll be more. You know I hold no malice or intention of hurt. To the contrary, my actions—perhaps driven by irrational thoughts—nonetheless, were construed to protect you—"

"The man you were supposed to kill?" Thank heaven she interrupted me. My bumbling and rambling speech was nothing more than incoherent parts, like notes that didn't make a melody.

"Paretsky?" I took a sip of my wine. No idea where she was coming from. I lowered the glass halfway and brought it back up for a second offering.

"He's still alive, right? How bad is he?" Her words came out in a rehearsed tone, as if the questions were neatly lined up and would be delivered in order. I went with the program.

"The worst. The longer he lives, the more innocent people die. Not just frontline intelligence operatives, but their parents and loved ones."

"OK. And you didn't tell me." She gave a minuscule shrug of her shoulders and glanced at me. "Why? Why not tell me the truth? Is it that hard?"

I couldn't do it, play the rapid-fire Q-and-A game with her. "Do you have *any* idea," I said, starting in on a speech for the ages, intent to stir a poet's grave, "what your voice, your smile—"

She placed her hand lightly on my mouth. "Answer the question."

"I thought it would have spoiled a time that was never in my dreams, for I knew of no such things to even dream about."

A little thick—I'll give you that. But desperate times, right? Let's see what she—

"Can the crap." She gave a slight shake of her head and gazed out toward the blinking red channel marker, then at me. "You getting an assignment while we're on vacation?"

"No choice."

"Not to receive it, but you did in accepting it."

"True."

"Could have come to me, told me about it."

"Could have."

"But you didn't."

"And say what? 'By the way, I gotta knock this guy off before toast and tea, hope you don't mind'?"

She pinned my eyes with hers. "Listen, dingleberry, that is exactly what you should have done. If that is who you are and who *we* are, then don't sugarcoat it."

Dingleberry? Things were looking up for the world's second-most-important person. Might even get a sleepover out of the evening.

"From now on I'll—"

"None of that is the issue, Jake." She spit my name out. "It's what you said, not what you didn't say. It's your words, not your omission of words."

"The books?" I threw it out, because I always knew.

"Do you know how that makes me feel?"

There's not a guy on the planet who can field that question from a girl. Twice, when we'd hit rough patches in our relationship, I'd told her she could withdraw back into her books. Once was bad enough. But twice?

A dolphin blew behind me. Probably Nevis casting a vote for Kathleen. A waxing moon, two days from full, had broken the horizon, and its light whitened and sparkled the dark waters of the bay.

I waited for her to rescue me, but it wasn't going to happen. "No, obviously, I don't know," I said in a voice I didn't recognize. "If I did, I never would have said it."

"That's nice, but it doesn't cut it."

"You're really steamed, aren't you?"

She jerked her head back. "Steamed? No, Jake, I'm not *steamed*."

I wished she'd stop using my name. I took the opportunity to pour more wine into my glass and sneak in a gulp. I was tempted to skip the glass and take the bottle straight to my mouth. The sunset sailboat *Magic* came in from the gulf. A couple took a selfie off the stern: a white flash, and then laughter. Assholes.

"When you say that," she said, staring ahead at the wide swath of illuminated water, "that I can always go back to my books, it makes me feel...small. Like your life is larger than mine."

Eleanor Roosevelt's comment that no one can make you feel inferior without your consent flirted in my head. "You know—"

She raised her hand like the lead rider of the cavalry. "As if," she turned and looked squarely at me, "I'm an object, and when things get a little dicey, it's beyond my head. My intellect. My ability to cope. My image in your head of who I am."

"Kath—"

"Don't. You killed a cardinal. You show no remorse, but I know it's there. There had to be a reason he was there. You were set up. I don't hold you. You want to shield me. I don't agree, but I get it.

"But underneath, I'm a minor character to you who can't handle the big issues. That is your image of me that surfaces at the most unguarded moments. That I am a person better off reading about moral ambiguities, because I sure can't handle them. A condescending attitude, buried so deep you don't know it's there, and you have no control when it flares."

"That's horseshit."

"No." She shook her head. "I don't think so."

"I make some regrettable, off-the-cuff remarks, and you extrapolate those into—"

"You repeated the regrettable, off-the-cuff remark. I'm not extrapolating anything. I'm struggling to see things as they are." She stood up. "I suggest you do the same."

Don't be afraid to see what you see.

I rose and put my hands on her shoulders. I wanted to shake her until everything was right; I don't like it when my world doesn't work that way. "Tell me what I need to do." The left side of her face was in full moonlight, and the right was dark. I leaned over and hovered my mouth over the corner of her lips. "Tell me."

I pulled back, and we locked eyes. "I need some time." She turned and started walking. My hand slid down her arm and found her left hand. I didn't let go. She swung her head back to me.

"I won't let go."

"I know."

I let go.

She strolled down the dock. Brief, bold, and gone. That girl owned it.

A sailboat came in from the gulf. It passed under the moon, and for a brief time, I could make out the two people in the cockpit as if they were under a spotlight in a play. The boat slipped back into the dark, and they were gone.

I tried to get her out of my mind and focus. I was chasing two men, not one. I wasn't gaining ground on either. I had misjudged my adversary, and Donald Lambert had paid the price. Tomorrow I'd check in with Bretta at Words Against People on the chance that Renée Lambert had taken the bait on the message board. I'd push PC and Boyd until something came up. I still hadn't heard back from Morgan. I wanted to go back to Lambert's and—

I'm struggling to see things as they are, and I suggest you do the same.

Was my distraction with Kathleen leading to a half-assed effort? Was Donald Lambert's last act on earth reaching for his bucket of dirty shower water because of my prancing? Either I was in the game or I wasn't. I picked up Kathleen's wineglass. She had not touched it. I took a page out of Rondo's playbook and threw the glass into the bay.

CHAPTER 20

The cardinal didn't visit me that night. That was no great surprise, as neither did sleep, which was a prerequisite for his nocturnal visits.

I was in the hotel pool at half past five, did my swim and run, and was back at the house by seven. I sat down in the screened porch, picked up a notepad, and collapsed into a deep sleep.

Morgan startled me as he came through the side door, holding his morning can of beer. Except for the morning throwaway, he never drank out of aluminum.

"Wake you?"

"No."

His bare feet slapped against the floor, and he claimed the chair next to me. I picked up the notepad I'd been studying before I did my version of Wynken, Blynken, and Nod. A breeze off the water made the palm fronds rattle like unbalanced, warring ceiling fans.

Morgan said, "Coffee?"

"Didn't get around to it."

He hopped up and disappeared into the kitchen. I viewed my pad. April Woltmann. Tracy Leary. Bretta. PC/Boyd. Lambert's house. Cardinal Antinori. I scribbled notes by each entry. Morgan returned and placed two cups on the table between us. He lowered the blind a few feet to block the sun's rays from searing our faces. The day had started at muggy and promised to never look back. I put my pad on the side table.

"Where's Garrett?" I said.

He took a sip of his beer. "Kitesurfing. Out before dawn." He put the beer down and gave it a definitive shove. "Was Kathleen waiting for you last night?"

"She was."

"You tell her your life is a meaningless pit without her?"

"I wouldn't go that far."

"Do you know your life's a meaningless pit without her?"

"Tracy Leary. What did she give us?"

Morgan glanced up as a fifty-foot boat with a yellow hull and a soaring tuna tower created swells just off the end of the dock. Dolphins jumped its wake as if it was burning gas just for them. *Impulse* rested in her lift a good ten feet off the water. She looked small. Neglected.

He shook his head. "Tracy, Tracy," he said. "Such a sweet thing. We're getting together in a few days—"

"Wonderful—I sent you to a redhead?"

"You did."

When in the vicinity of redheads, Morgan was like a Geiger counter at Chernobyl. His excuse, he had once enlightened me, was that on the bow of his parent's sailboat (a Morgan, hence his name) was a figurehead of a woman, nude from the waist up, with flaming red hair. Her eyes, ancient mariners believed, scanned the horizon for enemies and angry weather. As his parents sailed into Caribbean sunsets, young Morgan, tethered so as not to tumble off, would straddle the lady while his hands, for stability, cupped her smooth, wooden breasts as the bow rose and fell with the gentle swells. Without realizing what was happening to him, Morgan's first sexual climax, at a very young age, came from riding the back of a redhead. "Freud," Morgan had said, "would get no arguments from me."

"That, however," he cut me a look, "did not in the least impede my mission. To the contrary." He took a sip of coffee just as the yellow boat's rolling wake crashed into the seawall and sent a great white egret aloft. "We had a meaningful discussion."

"I'm sure you did. Didn't bother with a cover, did you?"

"Never really planned to."

"She have anything?"

"Her story was—"

"She know anything about Renée Lambert?"

Morgan eyed me and took another leisurely sip of his coffee. I jotted another note to look into the funeral arrangements of Donald Lambert, although I'd decided no way would Renée show herself after the murder of her father. I'd tossed the picture I took from Lambert's house into my truck and hadn't looked at it. I made another note on the pad. I drew a stick figure with a gun in its hand, but the gun looked like a banana.

"Renée," he started in, and my phone rang. PC. I hit the button, said, "Call you right back," and disconnected before he had a chance to reply. "You were saying?"

"She knows Renée. Said Renée joined the group after the suicide of her mother. Her mother got verbal abuse from the most unexpected source and in the most unexpected manner. She didn't spend a lot of time with WAP but wanted to be on the panel at the Valencia so she could drop in on her dad."

"Did she?"

"What?"

"Drop in on her dad."

"Didn't say one way or the other."

"What was the unexpected source and manner?"

"I questioned her on that. She said Renée didn't elaborate, nor did she press."

"Anything about the man she was with that evening?"

Hadley III landed on his lap. "Tracy and Renée met in the ladies' room toward the evening's conclusion. A chance encounter. Tracy said Renée was upset and had been crying."

I leaned forward with my elbows on my knees, as if the intensity of my body language coupled with the sincerity of the request would in some manner contribute to a satisfactory response. "Tell me she got *some*thing out of her."

"Tracy asked if she was having boy problems. She—that is, Renée—blurted out, 'He's not my boyfriend.' Tracy had seen Renée with the man somewhere around the bar area."

I thought of Rondo's statement that he had seen them both at the bar. Same with Adam. Morgan hadn't given me anything new.

He mimicked my position, which sent Hadley III sprawling to the floor and darting out of the room. "Renée told Tracy that she'd made a terrible mistake, a 'judgment' she called it, and that both her boyfriend and his friend were professional killers, and that if—"

"She told this to some woman she barely knew while they powdered noses?"

"Washing hands."

"Pardon?"

"Side-by-side sinks, and I never said they barely knew each other. I said they met that evening by a chance encounter."

"Correct."

"They knew each other from a previous meeting and had shared several dinners together. In the ladies' room, Renée just spilled. Tracy said she talked faster than the water came out of the spigot, like she broke and just couldn't keep it in anymore."

I stood up. "What else?"

"This." He arched his back, reached into his pocket, and handed me a bar napkin. "Renée took a pen out of her purse, jotted this, and handed it to Tracy. When she gave it to her, she said, 'He knew.'"

"Who—"

"Flip it over."

Antinori's name was written on top of Paretsky's. The napkin was partially torn at the letter *A*.

"What else did she say?" I asked, without lifting my eyes from the napkin.

"According to Tracy, two other ladies came in, and Renée went mum. On the way out the door, Renée said, 'If anything ever happens to me, these men are connected. Paretsky is doing Antinori a favor, and Antinori knows what's coming.' Something like that. She couldn't recall the precise words. Tracy lost track of her after that."

"Tracy up to speed? She realize that Antinori's dead and in the news?"

"Tracy," Morgan leaned back, "never heard of Antinori, nor did I tell her of his recent demise. She assumed that Renée's note referred to boyfriend issues. She took it totally out of context."

I glanced again at the napkin. "The hell I'm supposed to do with this?" I tried to hand it back to Morgan, who waved it off. I placed it on the table between us. "She question her? Talk to her later?"

"Not that evening—lost track of her. In the following days, Tracy tried to call Renée but said she couldn't get hold of her."

Although it was news, it wasn't. I'd known since that morning in London that the cardinal wanted me to kill him. Assisted suicide. I'd been in denial, telling myself that I didn't have the luxury of questioning the man. And now a napkin on which Renée had scribbled his name. I couldn't understand the ménage à trois of Giovanni Antinori, Alexander Paretsky, and Renée Lambert.

What if I never could?

Morgan took *Impulse* to the marina around the corner for a pair of new batteries. He asked before he left if I needed him for anything. I wished I could have given him an affirmative answer, but I was piling up questions faster than I was closing ground on Paretsky.

I worked my list. Garrett said Woltmann was a bust. Tracy Leary gave me a napkin bearing the name of the cardinal I had killed. Rondo spun a sad tale and raised the distinct possibility that Renée had a flash drive that belonged to Paretsky. That got a couple of stars next to it on my pad. I called Bretta at WAP and left a voice mail. I wanted to know if Renée, like a spy coming in from the cold, had responded to my message.

I'd already dismissed funeral arrangements for Donald Lambert as a dead end. If Renée was on the lam and in danger, assuming she was still alive, no way would she pop up for her father's funeral. A few phone calls confirmed my theory. No one had claimed the body of Donald Lambert, nor were they able to contact his daughter.

PC called again.

"I forgot," I answered. "What do you have?"

ROBERT LANE

"We're at Riptides."

I thought of just drilling him on the phone but decided to meet them and then hit Sea Breeze for breakfast. "Be there in five." I climbed in my truck and thought of Lambert's picture of himself and his wife that I'd tossed in the backseat. I'd give it a look after I talked with PC.

PC and Boyd were at the same high table as last time. Their shoes were on the sand-dusted plank floor beneath them. The playlist was country, but as I joined them, it changed, midsong, from Willie to classic rock.

A waitress—they were starting to look annoying—inquired, while smacking gum, if I wanted anything. I told her I was fine. She pressed her belly on the table. "You sure?"

"Positive."

She popped her gum and spun around.

PC, munching on a cheese bagel he had brought with him, explained that several people mentioned noticing a boat, but seeing a fishing boat on the canal was as common as seeing a bird in the air. No one reported a stolen boat.

"The guy across the canal who owns *Knotty Girl*, he see anything?"

"No. He was out of town for a few days. Just got back." He picked up his bagel but didn't bring it to his mouth. "But all's not lost. We ran smack into Slammin' Tammy."

"Slammin' Tammy?"

"Slammin' Tammy Callahan. Longest drive on the WPGA tour in 1981. Know how we know that?" He took a bite.

I waited, but either he wasn't going to let me off the hook or the information wasn't worth delaying a bagel bite for. "Tell me."

146

Boyd put down his beer and broke in. "She unloaded on us two seconds after we rang the doorbell, showed us the plaque, the picture of her—"

"Two doors down," PC said, cutting him off. "Broadcast her fifteen minutes of fame before you could catch your breath, but after that not a bad lady. Knows all, hears all, even fed us. Told Boyd he needed a haircut."

"It *is* about time." I checked my watch. Garrett had texted me and was due back any moment, and I wanted to meet with him. I leaned on the table, and it rocked away from me. "You didn't bring me down here to tell me about the longest women's drive of 1981."

"You said that she, Renée, hadn't been around for two months, right?"

"Six months. Lambert heard from her around two weeks ago, but he insisted that he hadn't seen his daughter for close to half a year. I think he lied. Tell me I'm right." Not only had recent events led me to that conclusion, but, as I recalled from my initial conversation with Lambert, he had broken eye contact and looked down.

"Roger that," PC said. "Slammin' Tammy said Renée was there 'bout two weeks ago."

"She positive?"

"No doubt, claims she knows her. Came in a cab, ten, ten thirty. We're talking ante meridiem. Slammin' Tammy says the cab waited twenty minutes tops. Saw Renée walk out, get in the cab, and exit stage left."

I heard Lambert's voice the second time I'd met him: *She told me when she was jus*—Had he been on the cusp of admitting that Renée had just visited him? Instead of feeling vindicated for my theory, I felt like an idiot. I should have seen it earlier.

I abandoned the boys and headed to Sea Breeze. I wedged my truck between a '57 Chevy and a Fiat that could fit into a wheelbarrow. I took a seat on a backless stool at the counter facing the 1930s pine siding. An obnoxious car ad filled the air.

"Usual?" Peggy asked as she blurred past, neither waiting for nor expecting a reply. I grabbed a disheveled paper someone had left, tore through it, and placed it back on the counter in better shape than I'd found it. I got off my stool, retrieved my writing pad from the truck, and ducked back inside. Breakfast was waiting. I dumped the red bowl of grilled onions over the eggs and hash browns and then let loose with the pepper shaker.

A few bites into it, I called Binelli and left a voice mail. Bretta, at Words Against People, was next. She answered just as I was about to stick my last slice of crispy bacon in my mouth. What was I thinking, using the phone while eating bacon? I reacquainted myself with her and inquired if Renée had left any comment on the members' message board.

Bretta explained that she couldn't tell me what Renée posted on the board but that I was free to log in and view it myself. Unlike our previous conversation, she wasn't going to perform the task for me.

I punched Rondo's number, and he picked up on the third ring. I explained what I'd done and asked if he would check in on the message board and get back to me as soon as possible. He said he was out running errands and would log in when he returned home. Binelli returned my call before I'd put the phone down.

"What do you got?" I answered.

"You called me."

"I think Renée Lambert has a disc drive that belongs to Alexander Paretsky."

"You *think?*"

"Conversations were overheard. You know her father's dead." I realized I should have informed her of that earlier but then decided she had her sources and already knew.

"No thanks to you. I heard from—"

"You need to search his house. I can't do it. I have no authority, and even if I broke in, a flash drive might be impossible to find. You need to get a team there and scrub every—"

"Pretty sure that's on the agenda, but I'll tell them about the disc. Tiny little sucker. Who did him?"

"The second man. The man who goes by the moniker of the Guardian."

She didn't say anything, so I prompted her. "Still there?"

"Sorry." She smacked her lips. "Some idiot brought in sausage burritos for breakfast. Some sins are totally worth it. The two-man theory."

"Looks like it."

"What are the chances that Lambert's daughter is still breathing?"

Peggy swooped up my plate without breaking stride. "I can't find any funeral home that is taking care of Lambert. My guess is that Renée is too smart and too scared to bury her own father. If someone comes forth and claims that body, that person may lead to Renée. You need to keep an eye on that."

"Hot dog! Am I ever glad you're on our side."

"Just tell me."

"We thought of staging a funeral, the old mob trick, you know? Hang around with a camera and see who shows up.

We decided it would be a waste of time and resources, but we're keeping tabs on the body."

"The flash drive," I said, returning to the pertinent issue. "You know how small those flash drives are? Tell them they have *got* to—"

"I know." She hung up.

I wiped my mouth with a napkin. Lambert had lied to protect his daughter, but why not tell me she'd dropped by? I thought I had won his confidence on my second trip there. I'd thought wrong.

Something else, though, was bothering me. Swelling and building like an offshore tidal wave.

If Paretsky's modus operandi was to target the loved ones of intelligence personnel, and he got wind of me closing in on him, would he go after Kathleen? I'd gotten up last night, when sleep avoided me like a winning lottery ticket, and finished the final book in Churchill's six-volume opus on World War II. Kathleen had bought me a first edition, and although it wasn't necessarily good history, it was worth the read. *Triumph and Tragedy.* Good news—the Germans are conquered. Bad news—the Russians are in the house.

Good news—we found the flash drive. Bad news—it contains a flattering picture of Kathleen, along with her address.

I called Morgan on the way out the door and told him to be prepared at a moment's notice.

"What if she objects?" he said.

"She'll have no choice."

CHAPTER 21

I slammed my truck door and started for my house. The picture.

I spun around and got the picture of Donald and Elizabeth Lambert that I had taken from Lambert's rear patio. When I entered my screened porch, I tossed it on the chair next to the one Garrett sat on. Morgan was hosing down *Impulse*. I hadn't expected him back so soon, or I would have told him in person instead of the phone call.

"Morgan told me your plan," Garrett said, without lifting his eyes from a newspaper.

"I have a plan?"

"Kathleen."

"Right. And?"

He put the paper down. "You think he's got the drop on us? We're not close enough to sniff him downwind in a hurricane."

"If that's the case, then he's looking smarter every day, and that only reinforces my decision."

Morgan slid through the door, pulling it tight behind him. He picked up the picture. "Renée's parents?"

"Elizabeth and Donald Lambert," I said.

"So much like her mother."

He showed me the picture, and I noted a faint resemblance, but only because of his leading assertion.

"Lambert," I said, "told me it was taken about two years ago."

"They're at the carnival," Morgan said and glanced over at me. "Don't you think so?"

"Antinori's?" Garrett said and shifted forward in his seat.

Morgan placed the framed picture on the glass table in front of us. Donald and Elizabeth Lambert stood on a trimmed lawn. Behind them was a brick estate camouflaged with centuries of vines. A dozen or so people milled around in the background. "See, right there?" He pointed to the back right corner of the picture, over Elizabeth Lambert's left shoulder. "Isn't that—"

"The high striker."

That was us a couple years back.

I seized the picture and brought it closer to my face. "The building must be Antinori's residence. This picture was taken two years ago at the annual fund-raiser that he held on his estate. Lambert told me his wife was British. Some town...Harlow. Think she knew Antinori?" I passed the picture to Garrett, stood, and started pacing. "Two years. The Lamberts attend Antinori's fund-raiser, his beliefs take a radical turn, and Renée Lambert drops the club life in favor of helping verbally abused children. Besides," I slapped my hand on the top of my grill, "you always go back to the scene of the crime." I shot Garrett a glance. "Keep an eye on her for two days."

"Our job is to finish Paretsky, not discover why Antinori was at Kensington that morning."

"There's a connection between Antinori, the Lamberts, and Paretsky, and I'm not going to find it lounging around here. Whole damn group knew one another. I can be there and back in forty-eight, and right now we're tanks in mud."

"Our world's getting smaller," Morgan added. "Harlow's a stone's throw from the late cardinal's residence, Granville Estate. You read what Mary Evelyn sent you?"

"More or less. Heavy on the less."

"Antinori was a young priest there." He had my iPad on his lap, and he hammered at it. "They might have known each other from decades past. You can still make it."

"Tell me."

"British Airways direct to Gatwick. Leaves at eighteen fifteen."

"Right. I've taken it. Return the next day at eleven fifty-five British summer time."

"You got it. GMT plus one. Premium economy still available, but it will set you back a pretty tuppence."

I didn't bother to answer but went into my bedroom and packed.

A few hours later, I sat at the gate and prepped myself for what I was about to do: return to the scene of my crime in a foreign country.

CHAPTER 22

It wasn't until my first few steps past the customs booth at Gatwick that I realized how tense I'd been.

I rented a car and took off on M23 to M25 and M11. Ninety minutes later, I gave my name at the Granville Estate gatehouse and proceeded to motor up a blacktop drive that, like a meandering river, couldn't decide which direction to swerve next. Sculptured boxwoods framed in dark mulch lined both sides. The drive and the landscape curved in unison, as if they both had been squirted out of a giant caulking tube. The estate was the official residence of the late cardinal and, I presumed, his replacement, although I hadn't researched that. The aged, brick mansion was wrapped in insulating summer vines and bedded in thick shrubs. The vines were snipped around the windows, creating dark, reflective eyes.

I'd called ahead and requested a meeting with a representative of the house. I stated that I was investigating the death of Donald Lambert, whose wife was originally from the area. It took some cajoling on my part to convince the lady on the phone that I had no reason to believe the death of a man in Florida was in any way related to the cardinal's residence, but, you see, I just happened to be in town, and I would appreciate the opportunity to possibly tie up some loose ends.

"I won't waste anyone's time," I'd pleaded. "I know his wife was British, and they spent time in the area and on the property."

"How do you expect us to be of assistance?" the lady replied.

"I'm not sure. It's just that I don't expect you to *not* be of assistance."

It was a weak ticket, but I got it stamped.

The blacktop gave way to a circular cobblestone drive. I pulled under a portico and into one of the numerous visitors' parking spots off to the side of the carriage house. Two of the five massive garage doors were raised, and I caught a glimpse of a fleet of automobiles. I retrieved my leather shoulder bag and blue blazer out of the backseat, put the blazer on, and walked—I tried not to strut—to a side door as the man in the gatehouse had instructed me. Security cameras caught every move. The air was crisp and thin—like someone had sucked all the water molecules out of it—compared to my corner of the world. I went through a double entry, took a left, and found myself in a sitting room with worn carpet, buckling lead-glass windows, and the musty smell of wood that was around when Charles Edward Stuart and the Duke of Cumberland engaged in the last battle to be fought on British home soil. That battle, in 1746, effectively put the lid on the Jacobites.

"May I be of assistance?" A primly dressed, middle-aged woman sat erect behind an English ladies' writing desk. *Had I met her?* The desk held a laptop, pad, pen, and phone. No nametag. Her hands framed each side of the computer. No wedding ring.

"You may." I presented my card. "Jake Travis. I called yesterday expressing my desire to speak with someone concerning the death of Donald Lambert." She wore an unalluring, lightweight, white sweater over her dress and a single layer of beads around her neck. Her maple-blond hair was pulled behind her head, and the ends of a white bow stuck out on each side. I'm a sucker for a single bow in a woman's hair. A solo strand graced the soft nape of her neck. "Are you the lady I had the pleasure of speaking with?"

She examined my card with genuine curiosity. "Yes, I believe I am." She placed the card squarely on the corner of her desk. Her finger flipped off the corner of the card, and it made a light smacking sound as if to accentuate the precise movement. "Will you have a seat, please, Mr. Travis?"

"Thank you."

I turned, ignited a squeaky floorboard, and settled in a spindle-back chair with a useless, worn, red pad on the seat. She raised her phone, announced, "Your appointment is here," and returned to her computer. I crossed my legs, picked up a magazine, and put it back without opening it.

She looked up. "May I inquire as to your interest in Mr. Lambert?"

"Routine questions. Did you by chance know the Lamberts?"

"Excuse me?"

"Elizabeth Lambert." I popped up, flipped open my shoulder bag, and extracted the photograph of Elizabeth and Donald Lambert. I held it up for her to see. "She grew up around here. About your age, although I admit I struggle with ages. You know her?"

She looked startled, as if I had breached her sense of propriety. "I...I really—"

"Mr. Travis?" I turned to my right, but not before I registered curiosity, perhaps even a tinge of sadness, in her eyes.

The man who had enunciated my name with flamboyant annoyance complemented the bottom side of a crescent wood frame of an inner doorway. He was in the vestments of his trade: black robe, high, starched collar, and long sleeves. If there was a wrinkle in his garments, it was not detectable. If there was sunshine in his personality, likewise. He looked like a prize-winning gourd.

"Yes?"

"*I* will be assisting you."

"I appreciate your time." I stuck out my hand. "Jake Travis."

"I am—was—Cardinal Antinori's personal secretary, Father Thomas McKenzie." He clenched his teeth and curled up his lip in a failed attempt to smile. He was a man not accustomed to introducing himself. In his backyard, people knew him. We shook hands. I had to let up on the pressure. His hand was soft, an appendage not to be utilized for anything other than self-service. "You may call me Thomas."

You may call me Thomas. As if he had bestowed a great honor upon me—although it pained him to say his own name.

"Thank you for seeing me, Thomas, and my condolences on the cardinal's death. A tragic affair. Do they have any suspects?"

"Sadly, no." He folded his hands in front of him. "There are mad little men whose cowardly deeds destroy greatness. It has always been thus. Please." He extended his right arm toward a side door. "Let's take some fresh air."

I glanced back at the lady behind the desk, but she was feverishly typing away, her head down. I put the picture of the Lamberts, which I had held at my side and slightly behind me, back in my shoulder bag and snapped it shut.

Thomas stood like a statue, his right arm, in the event that I'd forgotten where the door was, extended like that of a traffic bobby.

We strolled outside, and he took the lead once we cleared the door. A winding, speckled, gravel path bent around the carriage house where a vast lawn opened before us. The cardinal's annual carnival. I envisioned the high striker. Donald and Elizabeth Lambert stood—

"What may I assist you with, Mr. Travis?" His hands were clasped behind his back. He walked as if a flagpole served as his spinal column.

"Please, just Jake."

"It is Jacob, is it not?" Our path had only graced the edge of the expansive lawn, and we now turned right into an English garden. It was at the height of its glory, a tangled, orchestrated bedlam of green, disrespectful of territory, every plant battling for the sun's light.

"It is."

"What can I do for you, Mr. Travis?"

"I've been retained by the family of Donald Lambert to investigate his recent death. He and his wife, we believe, frequented these grounds. She grew up not far from here in Harlow. I was hoping you could shed some light on any associates or friends they might have. I realize it's not much, but we're at wit's end trying to solve his murder."

What little information I had on Elizabeth Lambert came from Mary Evelyn. She'd politely pointed out that she had previously sent me information on the Lambert family. It was after the section on Antinori.

"I'm afraid I can't help you," he said in a challenging tone. "And you're not the police."

"I'm a private investigator hired by the family."

"Yes." He stopped and, with his foot, flicked a piece of mulch off the path and back under the foliage. "I'm not sure how I can be of assistance." He resumed his pace.

"We know they attended the carnival two years ago."

"Mr. Travis, a great many people attend the cardinal's carnival. I'm afraid that I am not familiar with the Lamberts."

"Would Cardinal Antinori have known them?"

He halted again and turned to me. "I was the cardinal's personal secretary," he said, in case I hadn't caught it the first time around. "If he knew them, then so would have I." He blinked hard, as if each blink was a conscious act.

"I believe she, that is Mrs. Lambert, was in Cardinal Antinori's parish while he was a young man." I was throwing stuff on the wall. I had one more person to talk to, and if that person and Tommy were dead ends, I might well be wasting two days.

"Again, Mr. Travis, a great many people were blessed to have crossed paths over the course of their lifetime with the late cardinal. I do not know why you think any of this has anything to do with your murder investigation, but I can assure you," double-hard blinks, "that the Lamberts were not in his social or business circle."

"Was Alexander Paretsky?" I reached into my bag.

"I don't know that name."

"Know this face?" I brought out a picture of Paretsky.

Father Thomas McKenzie froze. His lips parted, but nothing came out. He blinked and said, "That is...no, I don't recognize him."

"I think you do."

"No." He shifted his weight. I was surprised his uniform didn't crack from the movement. "For a brief moment I thought I did, but I've never seen that—"

"You're lying."

"I *beg* your par—"

"Look again." I jiggled the picture.

"I have no..." He glanced at the picture and back at me. "The name and the picture are unfamiliar to me." He straightened his back even more—an incredible feat. "Is there anything else I can help you with? I have a meeting that starts shortly."

"Didn't mean to ruffle your feathers, Tommy."

"It's...never mind. You didn't—"

"How come you didn't ask me?"

"Ask you what?"

"Who Alexander Paretsky is?"

"Because I never heard of—"

"Or the identity of the man in the picture?"

"I assume that is a picture of your Mr. Parrot—whatever his name is."

"Did I say that?"

"Well, no. But one would expect—listen here, Mr.—"

"One would expect curiosity as to why I showed you the picture and threw out the name. Don't you agree, Father McKenzie?"

He hesitated, as if expecting me to say more, but I remained silent. I placed my left hand in my jacket pocket. I felt a ticket stub. A show at the Mahaffey?

"Mr. Travis, what does this have to do with Elizabeth Lambert?"

"I was hoping you would tell me."

"I am afraid I must disappoint you. Please," he said, and he extended his arm as he'd done earlier. "I do need to be getting back."

I remained motionless. "Do people always move in the direction of your arm?"

"Are you always so impudent?"

"I thought we were getting along just swell."

"Good day, Mr. Travis. I do hope that you find whoever killed Mr. Lambert. I am afraid there is nothing here to help you, and I can be of no further assistance." He lowered his arm and started back on the path toward the great house. I came up beside him.

"How did you know her first name?"

"Whose?"

"Elizabeth Lambert's. I never mentioned her first name, and you said you weren't familiar with her."

"My secretary provided me with their names." He didn't skip a beat; I'd give him that.

"She that pleasant lady sitting behind the desk who greeted me? The one with the white bow in her hair?"

"No, that is not her. Cynthia is our receptionist and nothing else." I wondered how Cynthia felt about being "nothing else."

"I'll pass along your condolences to Mrs. Lambert."

"But she's d—" He trailed off, and his eyes narrowed.

"She's dead, of course." I stopped walking, which forced him to do the same. "But you're not supposed to know that, seeing as how you're not familiar with the Lamberts—your words, Father—and I only said I was here to investigate the death of Mr. Lambert. What are you afraid of? Why are you lying to me?"

He shook his head as if he had no patience for any of this. "What I am afraid of is that I am out of time. My secretary did provide some background for...your visit. I see a great many people every day, and I try to be as accommodating and informed as I can be. Nothing else should be implied. Pity my efforts are met with such rude cynicism. I apologize, Mr. Travis, if I misled you in any way. Do have a safe trip back across the pond." He strolled away before I had a chance to counterpunch.

"Thomas." I raised my voice after him and walked briskly up to his side. I don't like others having the last word. "You said you were Cardinal Antinori's secretary."

"What of it?" Guarded now, knowing that he had stumbled badly on the battlefield.

"Why was he in Kensington Gardens the morning the madman found him?"

He abruptly stopped. "Jacob?" He pronounced my name as if introducing me to a royal court.

"Yes?"

"I thought you were investigating the murder of a Mr. Lambert."

McKenzie strikes back.

I had to be careful. Standing in front of this man, I was not without sin. I certainly didn't want to raise his suspicion of me and suffer the consequences of his influence and power. I handed him my card. "If you ever feel the urge to confess, Father, give me a ring." He held my eyes with his while his hand found the card and took it from me. He stared at it for a long moment, but he couldn't have been spending all that time reading. It contained only my name and phone number.

He brought his eyes up to mine. He said in a different tone, as if he was sitting around the dinner table with his family and friends, the bottles empty, and the yawning begun, "Jake, if you ever find what Giovanni was doing by Peter Pan's statue, please give *me* a ring."

He held my gaze long enough to let me know that he trusted me about as much as I trusted him and that he knew we were playing the lying game.

He turned, and this time I let him go. I felt as if I'd won the battle and lost the war.

He knew Paretsky. Bet my last pair of sneakers on that. He covered well when I mentioned the name, but he couldn't mask his recognition of the photo. He knew the Lamberts. There goes my record collection if I'm wrong. He did not know why the cardinal had been there that morning. That hurt Father McKenzie. He knew everything about the man—it was his job—and yet the cardinal had secrets, and dark ones at that.

Under normal conditions I would extend Father McKenzie's and my special time together, inflict the necessary pain, and find out what he was hiding. A nasty piece of business that I'm not fond of but is often required. But not here. Not in this country, where my previous deed was still headline news. Not with a well-connected man whose vestments put him beyond reproach.

I wandered back out to the lawn and took a seat on a concrete bench by a sculpture of Aphrodite. A reproduction, of course. Kathleen and I had viewed the original in the Louvre. I wondered what she was doing right now. Kathleen, not Aphrodite. Garrett planned to shadow her for protection. There was no reason to believe that Paretsky knew I was on his trail—that would be a real compliment considering my snail-paced progress—yet if he did know, I had to circle the wagons around her. Did she still love me? A juvenile and silly thought. I glanced up at Aphrodite for guidance, but she had her own issues, namely that she was missing both arms.

I was contemplating how to approach the other person
I wanted to see when she rounded the corner, clutching her
handbag and scurrying down the path as if she were late for
the Mad Hatter's tea party. She halted in front of me.

"Mr. Travis?"

"Yes, Cynthia?" If my use of her name startled her, it
didn't show.

"Follow me. Be quick."

CHAPTER 23

Her version of quick did not exactly sync with mine. I trailed her to the far end of the gardens by a curved, wooden gate with a single tarnished, brass lamppost on the right side. Brick columns supported the gate, and the hinges looked as if they could be melted down into bridge trusses. She popped off her high heels, took out a pair of flat shoes from her handbag, slipped them on her feet, and stuffed the heels into the bag, acting at once bored and put off with the whole process.

"Do you have a car?" she said.

"One might call it that, but I have serious reservations." She gave me a puzzled look. "I've got wheels."

"Wheels. Yes, well, very good, then. You'll need to use them. Meet me at Red Lion, London, Audley and—"

"N Row?"

"You know?" Another puzzled twist of her face, but this one was accompanied by a nervous glance around me, over me, and just about everywhere but above me.

"I do. Why there?"

A young girl pedaling a bike with a white bunny in the basket strung between the handlebars came from the opposite direction. The girl half sang and half hummed a song, like you do when you don't know all the words. As she approached, she rang the bell on her handlebars. Cynthia seemed mesmerized by the girl and then broke away from her trance and faced me. "One hour," she said and bustled away.

I cautiously entered the Red Lion. I was familiar with it; it was just around the corner from the flat where Kathleen and I had stayed. I was sure this was coincidental, but I wouldn't be the first or the last person to make a false assumption and walk into a trap.

The bar, roughly the size of the top deck of an aircraft carrier, ran along the left side of the pub. I strolled to a back room that was elevated a few steps and took a seat overlooking the lower room. A side door was on my port side in the event I needed to make a mad dash. A pair of afternoon drinkers anchored the stern of the bar. An electric guitar riff from the speakers competed with the constant, tuneless hum of gasoline engines coming in from the side and front doors, both propped open.

I got up and checked out both the men's and the ladies' rooms. The stalls were empty. No windows. I returned to my seat.

A girl with blue hair, red lips, double-pierced ears, and a tattoo across her chest planted herself in front of me, popped out her right hip, and said, "What's it gonna be?" I told her a water and a pint. She turned and got a few paces away from me.

"Wait," I called after Blue. She pivoted her head, opened her mouth, and sprung her eyes wide as if she were breathless with anticipation. A real clown. "Fish and chips," I said. She poked out her other hip, gave a thumbs-up, and flipped her blue hair over her left shoulder.

Cynthia came in ten minutes later, just after I had doused my fish with vinegar and taken a bite. Her eyes wandered around the pub, found me, and kept wandering. I put my fork down. Shoved away my chair. One of the drunks at the bar glanced over his shoulder. Two young men came through the front door. One of them caught my eye and looked away. I stood. Cynthia's eyes scanned the pub, clearly expecting someone else.

I stepped toward the side door. A flying leap and I could be out of the place. I mapped out my—

"Mum!"

Blue bounded out of the kitchen and embraced Cynthia, who wrapped her arms around her, and they stood like that, suffocating each other as if the whole world had melted away. The drunk's head returned to home position. The two young men, laughing, took stools at the bar. I reclaimed my chair.

Cynthia and her daughter raced through some foreign dialect of English, and then Cynthia broke off and joined me. I rose as she approached.

"Mr. Travis," she said as she took a seat.

"It's Jake." I nodded to where Blue stood talking to a couple who had entered while she was jabbering with her mother. "Your daughter?" I sat down. I'd noticed at Granville Estate that she didn't wear a wedding ring. I wondered if she was divorced or widowed. I decided to slip in the question if the opportunity presented itself—if I cared.

Cynthia glanced at her and shook her head. "My only child. I'm *so* proud of her." She turned back to me. "I do hope you didn't mind driving in. You seemed a little, well, shocked, when I mentioned the pub."

"No problem at all. I'm actually staying in town." Why did she look so familiar?

"I haven't seen her in a week. We're very close, you know, and a week is such a long time. I just had to see her."

"I call her Blue," I said.

"Don't you just love it?" Cynthia gushed. "She was red a year ago. I never had that nerve when I was her age," she let out a humph, "let alone the residual of it now. All I managed to do was go from a brunette to a blonde, and that took me thirty years."

Cynthia was dressed in the same white sweater over a knee-length skirt. I placed her in the neighborhood of forty-five to fifty-five, but as I've admitted, I don't do age well—don't see the point. She was borderline matronly, which is enigmatic ground to occupy. She could swing either way, and I fought the urge to lean across the table and untie her hair, see who was really there. "Lizzy," she said with a shake of her head. "I'm so lucky to have her."

"Here, Mum." Lizzy positioned a pint in front of Cynthia. "Still shopping this Saturday?"

"If you have the time."

"Always. My flat at noon? We can do an early dinner, too. I'm not going out till later." She glanced over at me. "Those chips OK, Yank? Not too soggy?"

"Perfect," I replied. "They serve as a vessel so that I may dine on vinegar."

"A vessel for vinegar." It came out well paced as she nodded her head. "There's a *man* for you." She leaned in a bit and lowered her voice. "Betcha these kids," she gave a nod to her left where the couple sat, "will dip them in ketchup—just watch." She straightened back up. "Usual, Ms. Cynthia?"

"The usual will be fine."

Lizzy spun and waltzed into the kitchen like she was dancing on air. I took a swig from my mug. "You have a wonderful relationship with your daughter."

"No. I have a *jubilant* relationship with my daughter." She took a draw from her glass, and a good fifth of it disappeared. Must have been a hard day at the factory. "She's my best friend, I can tell you that."

"You and your husband must be proud."

"I'm divorced." *Where had I seen her before?*

"Sorry to hear that."

"No need to be. Not everything's made for distance; we barely made a lap but, voilà, a daughter forever."

She smiled, and that brought it home. She was in the picture of a young Antinori at the high striker with everyone grinning at the camera lens, except for one young woman off to his side, who kept her eyes on Antinori. She had worn a white sweater then, too.

She was that woman. Was she?

Whether or not that meant beans, I hadn't a clue. I blurted out, "Why did you want to meet me?"

"It's Mr. Travis, correct?"

"Please, just Jake."

"I suppose. You Americans always pick brevity over form."

"We're a nation in a hurry. It's in our DNA. It is Cynthia." I spread my hands out. "Is it not?"

"Yes, my goodness, I failed to introduce myself. But how did you know my name?"

"Thomas. We bonded. Instant karma."

She squinted her left eye, waited a beat for it to sink in, and then let out a staccato laugh. "Oh, that is so good, Mr.— Jake. Yes, Father McKenzie. A real charmer, isn't he? He can freeze butter on a hot day."

ROBERT LANE

"I didn't get your last name."

"What an example of manners I turned out to be. Richardson." She extended her hand across the table, and I met her halfway. Her handshake was firm and confident. She'd take Father McKenzie down any day. "Cynthia Richardson, but please, just Cynthia."

"Pleasure to meet you." She held my hand a beat too long, and I thought of her flipping down the corner of my business card.

I sat back and took a drink of the stout. Lizzy served her mother a fish sandwich with a side salad sans dressing. She inquired if I wanted another, and I gave her a thumbs-up. She cocked her head, raised her eyebrows, shot one back at me, and frolicked away.

After a few moments of partaking, Cynthia pampered her lips with her napkin and said, "It was me you were supposed to see today. We get so many requests for, oh—visitors, donations, tours, jobs—they routinely go to me. And I," she sat up straight with mock authority, "am the 'no' person. They enter the door, I smile, sympathize with their cause, and, with professional politeness, usher them back out." Her body relaxed, as if she'd been acting the part. "But Father McKenzie, as he occasionally does, perused the list and saw that next to your name I had written 'Elizabeth Lambert.' He inquired as to why you called, and I told him that you were investigating the death of her husband, Donald Lambert."

"But you wrote Elizabeth's name?"

"Yes. Well, we'll get to that."

No reason why we couldn't get to it now, but it wasn't like I had anyplace to go. "He recognized the name," I pointed out. "Otherwise, he wouldn't have questioned you

170

any further." McKenzie had denied knowing the Lamberts, insisting that his secretary provided the background material. I knew that shiny, little gourd was lying.

She took a second with that. "Yes, but I wasn't surprised. I assumed he recalled her from an incident a couple years back. He asked if you were coming for any business other than the death of Mr. Lambert. I said not that I was aware of. He asked why I thought that you thought that we would have any information on Mr. Lambert's death. Did I say that right? What I—"

"You did. And what did you say?"

"I told him I hadn't the faintest idea of why you were coming beyond what I had stated—that you were investigating the death of Donald Lambert."

"Does he normally intercede with random visitors, even if he knows them?" I gave her a little latitude on her comment about a past incident two years ago to see if she fit it naturally into her story.

"No, that struck me as odd. It *was* odd. Father McKenzie—how shall I say this—is not a man of the people. He likes being the silent power, the lever of authority. Long before he took the stage, I was Cardinal Antinori's secretary. That, mind you, was centuries before he became a cardinal, and I..." Her eyes briefly left mine but returned just as quickly. "I was a young woman. Father McKenzie always maintained a streak of jealousy because Cardinal Antinori and I shared a history that superseded his own involvement with the cardinal by over two decades."

Something in her last statement urged me to slow down, but I rushed ahead, a flag bearer if there ever was one. "And yet he wanted to see me. Why? What was the incident you referred to?"

Lizzy brought my second and picked up my first. She addressed her mother. "Suzette just texted me and wanted to know if I had plans this weekend. Mind if she joins us for shopping on Saturday?"

"Oh, that would be wonderful. I haven't seen her since she came by the house at Christmas."

Lizzy smiled, bent over, and landed a kiss on Cynthia's head. "Thanks. Already gave her the green light." She hustled off back to the bar, and Cynthia's eye followed her. She rotated back to me.

"Suzette is her close friend from school. The three of us have a marvelous time together. Where were we?"

"McKenzie wanted to—"

"That's right," she exclaimed. "He commandeered your appointment. Why would he do that, Mr. Travis?"

I took a long draw from the cold stout. I wasn't sure how any of this information was going to get me closer to Paretsky. "I don't know." I threw it out there just to stay in the game. I recalled Cynthia's eyes when I had mentioned Elizabeth Lambert earlier that day.

"You knew them," I said in an accusatory tone. "The Lamberts. Or at least Elizabeth. You knew I was coming to inquire about them, and you were looking forward to talking with me. That's why you put her name down in the appointment book."

"Yes." She said it with a tinge of regret, as if entering a sad chapter of a book she'd previously read. "Yes, I knew her. This is the part where we get to it."

She placed her fork down, slowly and with purpose, as if the act of placing a utensil upon a table was not to be taken lightly. "You know," she said, raising her eyes to mine, "she's from Harlow, and we spent some time together before her family moved away. We were childhood friends."

"Do you know Alexander Paretsky?" Before I rehashed her childhood, I might as well discover if she knew anything about what I cared about.

"Who?" She looked startled.

"You know who." I shot it out in a confident tone, hoping to gain a confession from her. "Paretsky. Friend of the late cardinal."

She blinked and held my eyes, although it seemed an effort. "I...I'm afraid I don't know who you're referring to."

She looked confused, wounded. I backed down. "Never mind. You were saying you knew Elizabeth Lambert?"

I glanced at my watch. My interest didn't reside with Elizabeth Lambert, but it occurred to me that for an inexplicable reason her name kept popping up. I thought of Stalin's comment, "You may not have an interest in war, but war has an interest in you." Maybe I didn't have an interest in Elizabeth Lambert, but, dead as she was, Elizabeth Lambert had an interest in me.

"Yes," she said, still recovering from my abrupt charge.

"Tell me about her," I said with as much enthusiasm as I could summon. "Tell me about Elizabeth."

"I don't know if it means anything. After all, you're looking into her husband's death. Such a shame to think that both of them are gone."

"Did you know their daughter, Renée?" I asked, swinging for the fence.

Her once-vibrant eyes were now shadowed and withdrawn.

"I do. She and—"

"Is she friends with Lizzy?"

"No, I'm afraid not. Elizabeth moved to the states years ago when she was a teenager."

"Do you have a means for contacting her?"

"No, I don't."

So close. It was like feeling a solid tug on a line, and for the briefest moment it's fish on—then it's fish off.

"So…" I shifted my weight, started to check my watch, but caught myself. "You've never heard of Alexander Paretsky. You were secretary to Antinori before he became a rock star. You spent some childhood years with Elizabeth prior to her family being transferred stateside. You're afraid you have no idea where Renée Lambert hangs her hat. And an incident a couple years back brought Elizabeth Lambert to the attention of Father McKenzie. Is that correct?"

Cynthia Richardson considered me for moment, looked as if she was going to say something, but remained silent. I reached for my wallet to settle the chit.

She pushed her plate off to the side and placed her hands neatly in front of her, mimicking her position at her desk earlier that day. "If you don't mind me saying, Mr. Travis, you're asking all the wrong questions, and your penchant for speed—well, sometimes, as they say, you get there fast by taking it slow."

I tilted my head. "OK. Why don't you ask some questions of me?"

"No need to be snotty."

"My apologies."

"You are interested in Elizabeth Lambert."

"And Renée."

"Why Renée?"

"I'm not positive she knows of her father's death."

That paused her. She glanced out the side window, where a motorcycle swerved between two cars. "You should be asking," she said, "why a powerful man like Thomas McKenzie wanted to handle you today."

"I thought I did. The answer?"

"About two years ago—as I was trying to say—the Lamberts returned, came over for a holiday."

"How did you reconnect with her?"

"Facebook," she exclaimed, as if she had just discovered the key to the universe. "I had not seen her since we were little girls—or young women—somewhere in that time slot. We all went to the cardinal's carnival together. Every year he—"

"I'm familiar with it." I also recalled Lambert telling me that he and Elizabeth had been back. *Visited the place a couple years back.*

She gave me a quiet stare. "Very well." She folded her hands in front of her. "There was an altercation between Elizabeth and the cardinal. Words, loud words, were exchanged." She shook her head. "No, that's not right. Elizabeth screamed in his face. It was...it was just a terrible thing. Elizabeth snapped and started yelling about Renée, shouting, 'You killed Renée.'"

"I don't get it. Did Antinori know Renée, and why would Elizabeth think her own daughter was dead?"

"No," Cynthia said and shook her head. "Not that Renée. Not the one you seek."

"There's another?"

"The one she's *named* after, Mr. Travis. The one who died."

CHAPTER 24

It was as if every effort I expended, every calorie I burned to get closer to Paretsky only served to push me further away. I wasn't sure where the Lambert/Richardson chronicle led, but my curiosity was piqued, and with luck the more I learned about the family trees, the greater the likelihood that one of their branches would enter my world. I made a note to not bid her good night until I inquired if she had any clue as to why Cardinal Antinori had been in Kensington Gardens that morning.

Lizzy came around and cleared the table. She and Cynthia laid out a preliminary schedule for their girls' day. A light rain sprinkled the sidewalk, and the air turned summer damp. I realized that I'd never heard from Rondo regarding a posting Renée—the living one—left on the WAP message board. Maybe he forgot. I checked my phone to make certain that I had not received any calls or texts.

"Do you wish to go on?" Cynthia said.

"My apologies. Business. By all means." I pocketed my phone. "Two Renées—please, continue."

"We were a tight little group."

"Who are you referring to?"

She placed her elbows on the table and linked her hands. She gazed at me, but for the first time that evening she seemed to drift away.

"Elizabeth, Renée Sutherland, and myself. We grew up not far from Granville Estate. All on the same street. We were very close, although we went to separate schools. Elizabeth and I were Catholic, and Renée's family was Protestant. This was nearly forty years ago, Mr. Travis, a different world, a transitional world. Great progress on the surface, but underneath, people's beliefs—*some* people's beliefs—remained relatively unchanged from centuries ago."

"Such people exist today," I reminded her.

"They do." She placed her hands down. Although her pint was still half full, she shoved it away. "And, I'll remind you, in religion there is a fine line between honoring one's heritage and traditions and—well, the more oppressive and even aggressive nature that often accompanies unquestioned beliefs. Do you follow me?"

"Seems to be a major issue in the world."

"I'll give you the short version. I think," she gave me a coy smile that confirmed my enigmatic but borderline-matronly I-want-to-let-my-hair-down diagnosis, "that you are a man who would appreciate that."

"Take as much time as you'd like."

"Hmm...yes. Well, we, the three of us, played nearly every day. Girls with dolls and not a care in the world." She waved her hand at me. "You wouldn't know." The rain had stopped, and the smell of the Old World hung in the air. "We promised that when we had children of our own, we would name our daughters after one another. Little girls making big promises.

"Renée's body had other plans. Life and death, Mr. Travis, I've come to believe are the same. They are identical twins separated at birth and destined to reunite. Death kick-starts the heart in the womb and vanishes, leaving you with the beating illusion of life, and only later does it dawn on you that it's a ticking clock that's been left in your chest, charged with holding your memories, your loves, your lust—all the while counting down the seconds. Renée's clock didn't tick very long. She got cancer and died at age twelve. Renée and Elizabeth were very close; I was two years older and always felt like the third person. Although I was close to Elizabeth, she and Renée were inseparable. God forgive me, but when Renée died I was thankful that I was the third. It hit Elizabeth so very hard…that age, you just can't imagine."

"I'm sorry. That must have been—"

"Long time past." She straightened up. "Little over a year later, the Mastersons—that's Elizabeth's maiden name—moved to the States. I wrote to Elizabeth, and we visited them once, but the magic of youth was gone. For Elizabeth, it died with Renée."

"Lizzy," I said, as it hit me.

She smiled. "Yes. Her name is Elizabeth, and Elizabeth Lambert named her daughter after Renée Sutherland."

"It seems that little girls can keep big promises."

"On our own, we honor every word."

I leaned in. I needed to see if this story was a dead end or not. "Tell me about the cardinal and Elizabeth's shouting match. Did they previously know each other?" I recalled reading that Antinori's first parish was close to Granville Estate.

"You see it now, don't you? He was in charge of our parish. He counseled young Elizabeth in her attempt to cope with Renée's death, although I can't say it ever did any good or she ever got over it. He…"

"He what?"

"So sorry. Lost track of where I was."

"Did you go to counseling?" I wondered what had distracted her.

"No."

I waited for more, but nothing came. "Just no?"

"My father was what you would call a progressive thinker. He didn't want the church counseling me. Elizabeth's parents were devout, and they insisted that she attend. My mother wanted me to see our pastor, but my father was an Easter and Christmas man. He was a young boy on the East Side of London in 1940 when the Huns in their flying machines tried to burn the city. They drove his family, like rats, to the tunnels. You know your history, Mr. Travis?"

"My share."

"Yes. Well, my father didn't discuss it much, but he wasn't one to ever conjure up an image of a supreme being watching over us. He wasn't the only one. Do you know that Churchill, when addressing Parliament at the end of the war—that exalted and glorious moment of victory—never mentioned or evoked God? Not once? The church, at that time, was still infected with residual thinking, like a medieval virus, from centuries back. My mother wanted me to get counseling, but my father said I'd be better off drinking poison."

"What exactly did Elizabeth, two years ago, shout to the cardinal?"

She hesitated and then came in with a defiant tone. "As I said, that he ruined her life and killed Renée, forever. An ugly pall over the day for anyone unfortunate enough to witness it."

"I don't get it. Killed Renée forever?"

"Her words."

"But she had cancer."

"Nothing to do with the physical death, I'm quite sure."
What other death is there? "How did he ruin her, Elizabeth's, life?"

"The words he said when she sought him out for counseling. I'm not sure exactly what those words were. Perhaps her daughter knows. I wasn't privy to that." It tumbled out fast. She moved on. "Her husband, Donald, at the carnival that day, had to restrain her. It got quite ugly, I must tell you. Quite ugly, indeed. Father McKenzie summoned security, but the cardinal waved them off. Mr. Lambert finally led her away, but not before she turned, just as they were leaving the entrance, and her screaming—oh, one should never have to hear such things." She let her breath out and reached over for her mug. She took a gulp. She brought her eyes up to mine and lowered her voice. "On the way out, Elizabeth screamed, 'My mind's on fire. You burned it. You burned my mind.'" She held my eyes as if I was expected to understand that she had just answered the central question of the universe. Problem was, I didn't know the question.

Morgan's voice in my head. *Something happened in your cardinal's life two years ago to force him to make such an abrupt turnaround on his beliefs.* Now Donald Lambert describing his wife: *her mind was a rough place to live.* Did the cardinal's encounter with Elizabeth Lambert alter his beliefs? Did his first encounter with her as a twelve-year-old girl lead to her madness and eventual suicide? Did his altered beliefs have anything to do with him using me to kill him? The whole mess sounded like a cheap tabloid story.

I skipped ahead to the salient point. "Why was Cardinal Antinori in Kensington Gardens?"

Lizzy cut into my question as she placed a hot tea in front of her mother. I thought it an odd follow-up to the beer.

Cynthia glanced up and said thank you, but Lizzy was gone. The joint was filling up. My afternoon drinkers had abandoned ship, and the after-work crowd circled the barstools with an energy and enthusiasm that the day drinkers had long since lost or never possessed, which led them to being afternoon drinkers in the first place.

"I have no idea," she replied to my question.

"You were his secretary for years."

"Nearly a decade. But during that time I took a sabbatical to France. I was gone for over a year. When I returned, I worked for him for less than a year. He was short-listed for greater things and placed on the fast track. When he returned years later as a cardinal to reside at Granville Estate, he arrived with his entourage. He inquired if I wanted to resume some sort of secretarial position with him, but we—I requested the receptionist post. It's a plum job. No pressure, great pay."

"The 'no' lady."

"A polite 'no' lady."

"And you never heard of Alexander Paretsky?"

"That name you ambushed me with earlier? No."

"I didn't mean to be so harsh," I said.

"Of course you did."

"You haven't heard from Renée Lambert?"

"I have not, but if you do find her, please tell her my thoughts are with her."

"Why did her mother commit suicide?"

"You do jump around, don't you?" She leaned back and crossed her legs. "I don't know why. I never saw her again. It was nice seeing her at the carnival—they actually stayed two nights with us—but we weren't close. Too many years. Although my husband and Mr. Lambert certainly hit it off, but you men can do that, can't you? Smack that little white ball, hit a pub, and find common ground so effortlessly. You seem like a resourceful man, Mr. Travis. Do me a favor?"

"Gladly." I reached for my shoulder bag.

"Keep me apprised. I would love to meet Renée someday. I'm not sure why. Perhaps to close the circle."

"I'll do what I can."

"Thank you for meeting me. You were, I believe, familiar with this place?"

"Here about a week ago."

Her eyes narrowed as I pulled out a picture of Renée and the Guardian at the Valencia. I placed it on the table, thinking I should have told her I was last here a month ago.

"I know his back is turned," I said, "but does anything look familiar about the man she's with?"

When I glanced up at her, she was staring at me. She quickly focused her attention to the picture. "No. She's beautiful, isn't she? Elizabeth shared photos with me and posted on Facebook, but it's been a while. You said you were in London a week ago?"

"Closer to two." I modified my statement, sensing dangerous ground. I took out the picture of Renée and Alexander Paretsky that the colonel had given me. "And you never saw this guy, right? Alexander Paretsky?" I checked my watch again. I might give Rondo a call. Try PC and Morgan as well. I wanted to believe that while I sacrificed two days some progress was being made in my absence. "We believe that he poses a grave danger to Renée. Perhaps fatal."

"Oh, my—" Her hand flew to her mouth. It struck me as a staged move—my single-bow friend wasn't a theatrical person. "Why, that's—that's Mr. Hoover."

"Who?"

"Mr. Hoover." She pointed to Alexander Paretsky. "He's...
an old friend of, or was, I should say, of Gio—the cardinal. I
never knew that he..."

"What? That he what?"

"Went by a different name."

I leaned back, grabbed my mug, and treated myself to a
hearty drink. The first break in any investigation is the hard-
est. This one was a long time coming, but it was a doozy. A
real zinger. Cynthia's words echoed in my head: *Get there fast
by taking it slow.*

"Tell me," I said, as Cynthia Richardson leapfrogged to
the second-most-important person in the world spot, "all
about Mr. Hoover."

CHAPTER 25

"He's a sweet man, really."

"This guy, right?" I pointed at Paretsky. "You're sure? He's the candy man? Sammy Davis Junior?"

She gave the picture a cursory glance. "Oh, yes, quite. So soft-spoken. You think he'd hurt Renée?" She drummed her fingers, a new act for her.

"They have, or had, a relationship. How they met, I don't know. Does Father McKenzie know of Mr. Hoover?" McKenzie had done a fair job of hiding his recognition of Paretsky's name and picture.

"I can't imagine how he would *not* know of him. He's a major financial supporter."

"Paretsky?"

"Who—you mean Mr. Hoover?"

"They are the same."

"Yes. Well, Father McKenzie is well acquainted with him."

"Yet he, like Peter, denied knowing the man three times."

"I'm afraid you'll need to take that up with Father McKenzie. Did you show him the picture?"

"Yes."

"Yet he denied?"

"Thrice."

"I don't know why."

"From the top, Cynthia. *Every*thing you remember."

"I don't understand what this—he, has to do with Mr. Lambert's death."

"That is precisely what we are trying to find out."

She explained that there was no day one, or if there was she certainly didn't remember it. I thought of interrupting her over the nonsense of that statement and pushing her to recall the first time she saw Hoover/Paretsky, but refrained.

Mr. Hoover, according to Cynthia, strayed into the cardinal's life when he returned to Granville Estate. "He would come by to celebrate Mass," she concluded, "but mostly he attended dinners and events that were reserved for our big donors. He was well-heeled and gave generously to the cardinal's causes. His gifts were—"

"Did they have a personal relationship outside the church?"

"Your question," she tilted her head, "if you don't mind me saying, exposes your ignorance. For people like Giovanni Antinori, there was nothing outside the church. The church, you see, is not a location, it is their life."

"What did Cardinal Antinori say about Mr. Hoover?"

She hesitated. "Very little, only that Mr. Hoover was generous with his money." She shifted her weight and placed her arms on her lap. "His gifts, as I was trying to say, were always unrestricted. Believe me, those are the most desirable kind. Everyone wants to give food to the poor, but precious few wish to donate funds to buy the gas and insurance that the van needs to deliver the meals, let alone a token of appreciation for the driver. His gifts carried no strings. He became increasingly prominent at the dinners. Furthermore, Mr. Hoover came to confession, although only when Gio— the cardinal—was hearing."

ROBERT LANE

"How did he know that the cardinal was hearing confessions that day?" I recalled reading that Antinori still heard confessions.

"That's a very good question. They must have shared private words."

"Did Mr. Hoover confess to anyone else?"

She hesitated. "No...well, it's not something I would know."

"Mrs. Richardson?"

She tilted her head in a playful manner. "Mr. Travis?"

"Did Mr. Hoover confess to anyone else?"

I was eager to place Antinori and Paretsky in a private setting where Paretsky might spill the beans: confess that he was a paid assassin, plead for forgiveness, and then for some God-unforeseen reason hatch the plan where I snuff out the cardinal. That scenario didn't provide a reason for Antinori wanting to die, but at least it gave structure to the events.

Cynthia glanced down at the table. She wasn't one to break eye contact, and I gave her time. She didn't need much. Her eyes found mine.

"No."

I felt like I'd scored a meaningless goal. "What else did the cardinal divulge about Mr. Hoover?"

"There was one time—you have to understand that Giovanni was an especially closed man—nonetheless, we found ourselves in the garden, and he mentioned that he was...troubled by Mr. Hoover and things that he, that is Mr. Hoover, said to him. Giovanni thought Mr. Hoover had a dark soul but seemed..." She gazed down at the table. "I often wonder," Cynthia said to the table, "if Giovanni and..." She rubbed her hand over her right temple.

"What?"

"Pardon?" Her eyes flicked up to mine.

"What do you often wonder?"

"Terribly sorry. I was drifting there."

"More like blowing out to sea. Most candy men don't possess a 'dark soul.'"

"He displayed nothing other than exemplary manners and courtesies when around Giovanni and me."

As the night progressed, she had dropped the titled name and become more comfortable with Giovanni the man versus Antinori the cardinal. Did she push away her drink out of habit, or was her abstinence limited to this conversation, fearful of what she might spill under the influence?

"Is there any way of contacting Mr. Hoover?" I asked.

"Not that I know of. His contact information was a box number, his money wired from an offshore bank. Unrestricted gifts, Mr. Travis, unrestricted. You just can't imagine the good that does."

"The carnival," I said gently, having previously been accused of ambushing her, "in which Elizabeth Lambert and Cardinal Antinori had words?"

She seemed to consider whether to proceed. I didn't know what had happened to her, but she was like a windup doll that was down to the last few clicks. "Yes."

"Was that about the time that his beliefs took a seismic shift?"

"Pardon me?" She considered me as if I was a new and potentially dangerous acquaintance.

"Around that time," I said, as I recalled Morgan's insistence on how difficult it would have been for Antinori to change beliefs midcareer, "approximately two years ago, Giovanni Antinori renounced—"

"I think that's a little har—"

"Don't quibble. We both know it's correct. He renounced much of the dogma he was raised under and charted new waters. Do you think, Cynthia," I leaned in, "that Mr. Hoover's reappearance in his life or the cardinal's encounter with Elizabeth Lambert had any bearing on the cardinal's compass suddenly losing true north and spinning wildly as the man struggled, perhaps for the first time in his life, to understand his religion and, therefore, his life?" The words didn't sound like me, but I thought Morgan would be proud.

I sat back. Cynthia's jaw dropped, but nothing came out. She closed it. She straightened her back and sat erect.

"Are you with the church?" she demanded.

"No. I told you—"

"Yes." Her voice was curt. "I know what you *told* me. But your knowledge of the cardinal's progressive theological awakening is hardly congruous with a private investigation of Donald Lambert's death."

I gave a slight shrug. Progressive theological awakening. I had no idea that I was even capable of discussing such a thing.

"I will only ask once, Mr. Travis," Cynthia said with an air of authority that was ill-fitted for her, "and, I remind you, I have been extremely forthright and cooperative with you." She paused as if to preface her final act. "Why are you here?"

Crunch time. She had been cooperative; the jury was out on the forthright verdict.

"As I indicated, I'm trying to prevent Mr. Hoover from killing Renée Lambert. That is why I came. There's a good chance that I have already failed."

"I see." She took a sip of tea as if I'd just proclaimed a slight chance of evening thunderstorm. British to the bone.

She said to her cup, "Would Mr. Hoover do that type of thing? Kill another person, one he knows?"

"Yes. Does that surprise you?"

"I...oh, my, I don't know. Tell me what you think."

"In a heartbeat."

Cynthia nodded deliberately, as if I'd confirmed what she previously suspected. She lobbed a few questions about my quest, focusing more on Antinori than the Lamberts, but I fended them with deniability and lies. She professed no other knowledge of Mr. Hoover or his entanglement with the cardinal. "He was," she said, referring to the cardinal, "at the core, as I said, a very private, introverted man. Especially so in the last two years." She inquired if McKenzie knew of my true motive. I said that, although I felt he harbored suspicions, I never confirmed anything other than that I was there to track down Donald Lambert's killer.

"You didn't answer my question," I said.

"Beg your pardon?"

"Was his progressive theological awakening related, in your opinion, to the reappearance of Elizabeth Lambert in his life?"

She buttoned two buttons on her sweater as the cooler night air permeated the pub. "Yes."

"Yes?"

"There's no need to make things harder than they are. I do believe that his seismic ideological shift, I'm paraphrasing your words, was related in some manner to Elizabeth Lambert's reappearance in his life. Elizabeth, in my mind, was the catalyst. I know it's all conjecture, but conjectures aren't necessarily false."

"You seem certain."

"Giovanni Antinori was a man without ripples, Mr. Travis. Elizabeth Lambert was a storm on the sea of his life. I believe that, for Giovanni, the waters never settled again."

"Do you know why he was killed?"

"Certainly not. Why would I know such a thing?"

"But you have a theory?"

"I assure you, I haven't a clue, let alone a theory."

"You're holding back."

"Certainly not."

"I think you are."

"I think you're impertinent."

I thought of Donald Lambert lying to me. I hadn't pressed hard enough. I leaned in across the table. "Talk to me, Cynthia Richardson. Tell me what you're afraid to say about Mr. Hoover and Giovanni Antinori."

She squirmed in her seat. "Now you're just being rude. I assure you, I am done. I am finished here." She shook her head, and her lips quivered as she fought her emotions.

"You know. Tell—"

"Don't be ridiculous." It came out vehemently and as a single word. She cast me an angry look. She summoned her composure, but it took a great effort. "I have told you everything."

I reached for my wallet, tired of the whole damn day.

"Why could it possibly matter?" She shrugged her shoulders as if trying to regain her composure or, more important, questioning her decision to terminate the conversation. "Like Peter's denial. It all just happened, and then," she flicked her right hand, "it is finished."

Her eyes pleaded with mine. There had to be some words that I could spin out that would open her up, but that part of me never was worth shit.

"He was so sullen," she continued, "the last six months or so, like a cloud had settled on his spirit and suffocated all his joy. He was always a man of extreme highs punctuated with unpredictable lows—he fought that battle his whole life—and toward the end his low moments took the field and never yielded. Why could it possibly matter now?"

How about because he used me to end his sorry-ass existence?

We stood and said our good nights. She was holding back, but I didn't see how further questioning would land me closer to Paretsky or Renée. I'd taken her to near tears, and she'd slammed the door.

"The cardinal," she added as an afterthought as her eyes scanned the pub, no doubt searching for Lizzy, "was planning a visit to the States. Your neck of the woods. Florida, I believe. He was so looking forward to it."

"Why was he going to Florida?" I had another question queued up, but it escaped me.

"I don't know."

I extended my hand. We shook. "Yes, you do."

She smiled weakly. "Thank you for dinner."

I strolled out the front door, leaving her chatting with Lizzy. I was about to merge with the sidewalk traffic when she called from behind.

"Mr. Travis."

Cynthia stood under the doorframe, no more than an arm's length away from me.

"Yes?"

"Let me know if you find out who murdered Giovanni. I'm not much for heaven and hell, but there must be a hell for such a man. A conscious inferno."

"I'll do that."

I turned, as did she. Then I spun back to her as I remembered what I'd wanted to ask earlier. "Cynthia?"

"Yes." She halted and looked at me. A man with a red attaché case brushed between us without muttering an apology. I took a step toward her to close the gap.

"What caused the cardinal to be 'sullen' about six months ago?"

"I don't know."

"That was when Elizabeth Lambert committed suicide."

She looked at me blankly, her eyes as guarded as they'd been all evening. "Good night, Mr. Travis. I wish you a safe trip, wherever you're headed."

She blended into the crowd. I allowed myself to be swallowed up by a mass of people on Bond Street who didn't know me and didn't care. It was the perfect place for me.

I slogged through the dark London streets. I couldn't do the hotel room. Not yet. The relationship that Cynthia enjoyed with her daughter struck me as the stuff of dreams, but what do I know about mother-daughter relationships? About anything? Cynthia was holding back, but whether her unplayed cards would help me, I couldn't be certain. If I thought my pensive demeanor would bring forth answers and unveil hidden truths, I was grossly mistaken.

I kept their comments at bay as long as I could, but the game was over. Like a doctor waiting to deliver bad news, after the chitchat you just want to get it over with. Father Tommy McKenzie: *Mad little men whose cowardly deeds destroy greatness.* Now Cynthia. White-sweater Cynthia with a bow in her hair and a solo strand on her neck: *There must be a hell for such a man. A conscious inferno.*

A conscious inferno. Not bad—I liked the ring of that.

I tired of my thoughts, and I was damn certain my thoughts were tired of me. I stumbled back to the hotel bar, where a jazz combo occupied a corner. The bartender set me up with Black Barrel straight. I assured him after the third—or maybe the fifth—that I was staying on the premises. The piano player mesmerized me as his hands electrified the keys. At one point he played only with his right hand, and I would swear that in no way could five fingers do what his five fingers did. I wondered why, amid the smorgasbord of life, he had felt possessed to master that skill and marveled at what a finer thing he did than I. I hoped his future didn't include arthritis.

I should have called PC, Morgan, and Garrett—see if I'd missed anything. I knew that if I had, they would have called. Piss on it. Piss on it all. When that cloud comes over me, it rents me. I went up to my room. It had a *mini*bar. What a mad world.

He came that night. We were at the statue of Peter Pan, and the world was black and white, and I knew that wasn't right. I told him I'd discovered that his sugar daddy was a ruthless killer. "Mr. Hoover?" he said. "We do go back a bit." He spoke with an Irish brogue. I wondered if his accent had anything to do with the black-and-white world and thought I might be dreaming. *Of course you are, you idiot. Now milk this guy for everything he's got.*

"I apologize if my death has caused difficulties between Kathleen and you."

Difficulties. I thought it a strange word to drop into a dream. Proper. Formal. Not dreamlike at all.

"It *is* a strange word for a dream," he replied.

"You knew I was coming for you," I insisted. "You weren't surprised. I did what you wanted me to do. I was your Judas. I have no guilt."

"Did I say you should?"

"Why were you there?"

"I need to ask you something, Jake." How did he know my name? How'd he know Kathleen's?

He got into the paddleboat with the giant swan head that was beached by the pond behind the statue. The other side of the pond was bathed in color, as if Renoir's palette had been splattered across the far shore in preparation for the boating party's lunch. He was younger than he'd been the night I'd killed him. I wondered if I too was younger. I thought of looking for a mirror—have you ever seen a mirror in a dream? I walked over to the boat. He smoothed his robe with his hands.

"What?" I demanded in response to his statement.

"Have you forgiven me my sin?" As he spoke, he gazed across the flat water toward the vivid colors of the promised shore.

"If your sin is that you used me to kill you—forget it. I couldn't care less." It came out like a bad line in a bad movie, the kind they used to only show after midnight. I knew that I was trying to convince myself, but if we can't do that in a dream, then why dream?

Giovanni Antinori glanced up from his boat. "Forgive me my sin." He started pumping his legs, his robe rising and falling with the motion, his vestments dragging in the water beside him. Like the hairs of a paintbrush, they left streams of brilliant color in their wake.

Peter Pan said, "She's here."

I turned. The lady jogger with the tube socks and nice legs stood staring at me.

"I saw you looking at my legs." Her voice was a monotone, as if she too were dead. "I know you. I know you. I kno—"

I bolted up in my bed, my breathing labored. A siren wailed on the street below. I picked up the bottle of water on my nightstand and went to the window. I pulled back the draperies. I searched for a latch, but the window didn't open. I peered down upon the dark streets. The drone of traffic was barely diminished from hours ago. Great cities are the engine room of humanity. I drank the bottle. I took a seat on the cloth chair. I must have fallen asleep, for I was startled awake by the tinkling of a bell from the street below. The sun, for some unfathomable reason, had come back around, if not for me, to at least shine on little girls with white bunnies.

CHAPTER 26

Running is my salvation.
For forty-five minutes, as the ball of fire climbed upward in the clear, summer sky, I atoned for last night's morose. I consumed an English farm for breakfast and stopped by Harrods on the way to Gatwick.

I settled in an empty corner by my gate and worked the phone. Rondo said the message board was down yesterday, and he would check it again. He was on a tee box. Good for him. Beats dumping beer out a second-floor window.

Nothing new from PC. Garrett and I discussed Paretsky's alias. We concluded that he likely had a dozen names. Nonetheless, he would contact the colonel and see if "Mr. Hoover" carried any significance. We assumed the colonel would ask the church for financial records of Mr. Hoover's gifts, and that road would be a dead end. Paretsky was certainly capable of hiding a money trail. I called Binelli and left her a voice message regarding the Hoover alias and recapped the pertinent points of my conversation with Cynthia. She rang back within ten minutes.

"Anything new?" I answered.

"Do you never learn?"

I eased out my breath. "How are you, darling?"

"Sparkling. And you?"

"Splendid. Say, did you find anything on Paretsky's alias?"

"Mr. Hoover," she said, as if opening a book on a grave subject. "We—"

"What do you got?"

"Things get a little interesting in that direction."

"Tell me."

"Not on this line."

"Find anything at Lambert's house? I assume by now that you completed the search."

"Not on—"

"Save it." I blew my breath out. My phone wasn't secure. "What can you tell me?"

"When do you get in?"

"Sixteen hundred." My phone signaled an incoming call.

"Call me when you can. It's nothing urgent, certainly not going to hang the case on it, so don't worry."

I switched to the other call, but it had already gone to voice mail. It was the deliveryman for my new guest-bedroom suite. Please call back to schedule a convenient time. And to think that just a few days ago that was the biggest thing going on in my life.

On the jet, I placed my gift-wrapped box in the compartment above my seat, along with my carry-on. I doubted the colonel would pick up the difference between coach and premium economy, but it didn't matter. Money is not the headache of my life. I wondered if that would always be the case, or if I too might develop some form of arthritis that would threaten my livelihood.

The Bloody Mary was no good. I put on music, never got more than thirty seconds into a dozen songs, and yanked out my earphones. The window seat next to me was empty. Once upon a time a lady with a golden scarf wrapped around her neck had sat there. Enough of that. I got out a blank notepad, selected a blue pen from my laptop bag, and set out to jot down what I knew. I put the pen down. The absence of Kathleen, where she'd sat just a few days earlier, was stronger than her presence on that day.

That was new to me—her absence taking up more space than her presence.

I'm that guy who, when the tram from the gate to the terminal comes to a stop, leads the brigade. Fools block my path. I double marched toward the walkway by the currency exchange that led to the parking garage. He stood midway between the escalators that led down to baggage claim. Jonathan Wayne was dressed exactly how I'd seen him the day before in Ft. Lauderdale's airport. I halted in front of him.

"Mr. Wayne."

"Mr. Travis."

"Not looking for me, by chance, are you?"

"No, sir. You're right in front of me."

I expected a smile, but it didn't materialize.

"It was rhetorical, John."

He squinted and replied, "Let's have a talk."

"You're not here to fly Cayman Airways to George Town? You know they give free rum drinks to everyone."

"No, sir. I'm here—"

"Last time I was on it, a girl waltzed down the aisle, hiked up her shirt, and charged a dollar for guys to 'rum' her tummy."

"I've never—"

"Follow me."

I took off without him and headed toward a restaurant. Only Binelli and Garrett knew my schedule, and I ruled Garrett out. Therefore, Binelli was guilty of siccing

Wayne on me. I took a seat at the bar, and Wayne pulled up beside me. Behind us, at a four-top, a German family babbled away. They had flown in from Frankfurt and were deciding which fantasylands to visit before returning to the beaches.

"Binelli, right?"

"Excuse me?" He took off his Stetson and placed it on the counter on the other side of him. I didn't know much about the man, but I could tell you this: he hadn't bought a new hat since Y2K destroyed civilization. He folded his long coat over the chair next to him.

"Binelli," I said. "She coughed up my schedule."

He gave me that single nod of his. "I can't discuss that."

I stood up and took a step.

"Agent Binelli," he said.

"Our meeting in Lauderdale?"

"Coincidental."

"I don't do coincidences."

"Suit yourself."

I reclaimed my seat, and a heavyset woman with a streak of purple in her black hair planted her body in front of me. I ordered a beer. After last night I'd sworn off drinking for eternity—that's about eighteen hours. I'm always amazed how methodically I recover, but what if that gift goes away one day as well?

"Water, ma'am," Wayne replied to Streak's question as to what cowboys drink.

"Why are you here?" I asked.

Wayne still wore that shining badge the size of Viking breast armor. Still packed Robert E. Lee's cannon. Federal marshals, the oldest federal law group, are used, among other things, to find and transport fugitives. Their duties, however, vary greatly, and I hadn't a clue why Binelli had arranged for our tête-à-tête.

"I understand," he started in, "that you just returned from London." Streak placed my beer in front of me and poured the bottle into a frosted mug. She put a tall glass of water in front of Wayne.

"I did."

"And that you were looking into the death of Giovanni Antinori."

My back stiffened. I took a mouthful from the mug. "Actually," I said, "I did a little shopping." I nodded to the gift-wrapped box that I had placed on the oak floor next to me. His eyes didn't follow. Neither of us spoke for a few seconds. I was considering standing up and announcing my departure when Wayne broke the impasse. "He contacted us."

"Antinori?"

"Not us directly, but a branch. He wanted to come in, said he had a few things to say. It was our job to move him. But—"

"Ease up, slim. He was British. How could you possibly have jurisdiction over any of his movements?"

He hesitated. "I see your point." It was a strange comeback, as if he'd never considered the question of jurisdiction. Perhaps US marshals are granted a longer leash than I know. He addressed my puzzlement. "We're used for a myriad of jobs. In this case, it was deemed that Mr.—"

"He was a cardinal."

"Excuse me?"

"He was a cardinal in the Catholic church."

His tongue pushed out his right cheek; he gave his lonely nod and continued. "Mr. Antinori, we believe, was in possession of information desired by our government. My understanding is that we were more than willing to depose him in the United Kingdom, but that he preferred to travel incognito to the United States, as he had other business to attend to here as well. My job was to escort him. He was killed prior to arrangements being finalized."

"What made you think he had 'desired' information, and why would a man in his position have such information?"

"There's the crux of it. He gave detailed information of a man, a 'tragic and evil' man, he said, that he referred to as Mr. Hoover. We'd never heard of the man. Indeed, there is no trace of any such man, but his deeds were known to us. We concluded that Mr. Antinori's Mr. Hoover must also be—"

"Alexander Paretsky."

"I understand that you also made that connection."

"I did. Second part. How would Antinori come across such information?"

"We do not know. Do you?"

"Paretsky fenced himself off as Mr. Hoover and was a major financial supporter of Cardinal Antinori."

A single nod. "That fits. Was actually one of our theories. How did you arrive at the information?"

"I exercised patience in a London pub."

He landed a quiet gaze and then reached for his water. "You're looking into the death of Donald Lambert?"

I shifted forward and put my elbows on the bar as it dawned on me. "Cardinal Antinori was planning on paying Donald Lambert a visit."

"That's correct. That's why the call came to the Florida office."

That was the moment for a spark to ignite and pull the pieces together. Antinori, Lambert, Paretsky, Elizabeth Lambert, Renée I, Renée II. Two years.

Nothing.

Maybe if I added minor ingredients: McKenzie, Cynthia, J. M. Barrie, Spanish Eyes, Aphrodite, Sammy Davis Jr.

Zippo.

The words swirled in my head like a busted sentence that I couldn't piece together. I felt like a math savant stuck in a literature class.

"Do you know why he was coming to Florida?" I asked.

"You mean, do we know why he wanted to meet with Mr. Lambert? We do not."

"Isn't there a federal marshal district closer than Tallahassee?" I recalled that Florida had three districts.

"There is." He took a sip of water and gently placed the glass back onto the exact center of the bar napkin. "But they wanted me."

Streak dropped by and inquired if I wanted another. I waved her off. The Germans were discussing dessert options. Cheesecake hugged the rail.

"You were assigned to pick up Antinori in street clothes and bring him here to rendezvous with Lambert." I straightened my bar napkin under the mug. "He catches a bullet. Case closed. You move on. But you're not. Why are you meeting me?"

"We want to see what you found out about Mr. Hoover."

Everything was *we* with Wayne. My bet, though, was deep inside he was genetically coded to ride by himself. That was what would come out in a fight. I'd have no problem picking him to be on my side. How much should I tell him? Enough to keep him close if I needed him, but not enough to turn him against me if Uncle Sam got fingered for the Antinori hit and threw me under the bus like the colonel's briefcase.

I summarized my meeting with McKenzie but fudged the facts, telling him that McKenzie confirmed the relationship between Antinori and Hoover/Paretsky. No need to include Cynthia Richardson. If someone ended up with fractured bones over this, I wanted McKenzie, not Cynthia, up for consideration. Unless he talked to the parties involved, Wayne would have no reason to question my version.

He considered my comments while the Germans considered whether to spend an extra day in Disney's grasp or tack on an additional beach day. The daughter lobbied hard for the beach. She carried the moment. The mother commented that the cheesecake was too sweet.

I needed to ascertain that Wayne and I were on the same page. "What do you make of it?" I started in. "Antinori discovers that the man he knows as Hoover is villainous, and he decides to spill the beans. But not in his own country, and not under his title. Furthermore, he decides to drop in on Donald Lambert. Both Lambert and Antinori die within a few days of each other."

"That's correct."

I pivoted and faced Wayne. He rotated his head and stared at me. "It gets a little cloudy at this point," I added. "Why would Antinori want to visit a retired bachelor in Treasure Island, Florida?"

"You tell me."

"I don't know," I lied. I think I lied. Pieces were starting to fall into place, but they were floating down slowly, like snowflakes on a windless day. "Do you have any clue as to how or why Antinori came into his knowledge of Alexander Paretsky?"

"We do not. You?"

"No." Again, I think I lied.

"Mr. Lambert was not on our radar until Mr. Antinori made his request." He turned his body to fully face me. "When the man we are supposed to escort turns up dead and the man we were instructed to escort him to goes through the pearly gates a few days later, our curiosity is piqued."

"Imagine so."

"I understand you discovered Mr. Lambert's body."

"I did."

"Did you search the premises?"

"Not a whole lot of time for that."

"Did you?"

"Only time to pick the low fruit, but nothing there. No phone or computer. You?"

Wayne arched his eyebrows. "Excuse me?"

"Did you search the premises? I told Agent Binelli that a flash drive belonging to Paretsky might be in that house."

It was one of the items that Binelli wasn't going to discuss on my unsecure phone. I wasn't sure of the exact role the Marlboro Man played in all this, but I was willing to bet that, like me, he wasn't showing all his cards. I pushed myself up on the stool. I hadn't been aware of my poor posture. The flight and sleepless nights were starting to make their presence known.

"I did," Wayne answered. "We were alerted to the possibility of a flash drive, but we didn't find one. However," he reached into his shirt pocket and handed me a letter, "we found this."

It was a letter from Cardinal Antinori to Donald Lambert, on plain stationery. It started with a brief paragraph asking permission for his upcoming visit. Antinori got to the point.

Your daughter is dating a man I know as Mr. Hoover. That is not who he is. I believe that you and your daughter might be in grave danger. I cannot undo the past, but you must trust me now.

I turned to Wayne. "Where did you find this?" But I thought, *Why, Donald, didn't you tell me? What should I have done to earn your confidence?*

"The house, as I believe you know, had already been searched. But, judging by the appearance, it was a hastily done job. We found this in the New Testament. Book of Corinthians."

"The greatest gift."

"Pardon?"

"Apostle Paul's timeless treatise on love. Any particular page?"

"Don't know. How do you think Antinori found out that Renée Lambert was dating Paretsky?"

"Don't know. Maybe he showed up at a donor's dinner with her draped on his arm."

Wayne said, "Do you know what he means about undoing the past?"

"Haven't a clue."

"How about a clue on how the Lamberts, Antinori, and Paretsky are related?"

"Drawing a blank there, John."

"Do you know how to contact Renée Lambert?"

"No."

Another nod. "Why do I think that, except for your last answer, you're not being an honest man?"

"Maybe you need a badge to be an honest man."

He took off his badge and tossed it to me. It slid and stopped when it nicked my mug. "Go ahead. I got more.

You tell me if the badge makes the man or the man makes the badge."

"Don't get preachy on me. What were you doing in the Lauderdale airport?"

He hesitated. "My mother is not well."

OK. So the guy was being straight with me. Paranoids don't always get it right, but as a species we've been around a long time, and that's nothing to apologize about.

I said, "There's a man who works with Paretsky—goes by 'the Guardian'—know anything there?"

"The two-man theory."

I leaned in toward him. "Renée visited her father within the past few weeks. He lied to me. Said he hadn't seen her in close to six months. I think she might have left the disc with him or at least told him about its existence. I think the Guardian killed Lambert and searched the house. No way of knowing if he found what he was looking for."

"Why do you believe that Renée left the disc with her father?"

"Because he denied her being there. It was a natural reaction—when people are afraid, they deny. You searched the drains, attic, pillows—you know how small a flash drive is."

He brought his right hand up and rubbed his chin. "I imagine if someone wanted to hide something that small in his house so that no one would ever find it, it wouldn't be a difficult task."

"Imagine so."

"May not even be in his house."

Wayne stood and picked up his coat and hat. We pledged to keep each other informed, but if he treated me with the same distant trust that I afforded him, I wasn't sure how productive our alliance would be.

I strapped my case over my shoulder and extended the handle of my carry-on. Ten paces from the restaurant, I spun around and returned to the bar. I picked up his badge and stuck it in my pocket. He was coming out of the restroom.

"The greatest gift," he said. "Apostle Paul's—what is it?"

"You never read it?"

"I did not."

"Love, John. It endures all."

A single nod, and he was gone.

CHAPTER 27

I needed to call Binelli and review my meeting with John Wayne as well as give Rondo a ring. I decided to wait until I got home. Sometimes when I drive, I just drive.

The cardinal had known that Renée Lambert was dating a dangerous man. Did Antinori threaten to expose Paretsky, and therefore Paretsky set him up to catch my bullet at the Peter Pan statue? Why would Antinori go through with that? Did Paretsky hold something over him to force his hand? It was like trying to stuff ten pounds of flour into a five-pound bag. If he was about to take life's last ride, he might as well take the devil with him. Instead I got *Forgive me my sin* and some mumbo jumbo about the Pope and the Guardian.

I took the small second bridge to my island. My phone had buzzed a couple of times while I talked with Wayne, but I'd resisted looking at it. I pulled into my drive and headed straight to the kitchen. I snatched a beer, snipped a cigar, pulled out my phone, and headed for the end of the dock. Hadley III was crouched like a jungle cat under the wild hibiscus bush. She pounced at my ankles as I strode past. Damn thing nipped me.

Binelli was first. I recapped my meeting with Wayne. She assured me that Wayne was astute enough not to ask me too many questions regarding my involvement with Paretsky.

No one had claimed Lambert's body, but I'd already reeled that line in. I reviewed with her what Cynthia Richardson told me. I gave it to her straight and then told her that I'd spun a slightly different version to Wayne. She didn't question my decision to do so.

"Can I trust him?" I asked her.

"You met him, what do you—"

"I'm asking you."

"With your life."

We disconnected.

I took a long draw on the cigar and blew out the smoke. It stalled in the air and then, like a balloon with too little helium in it, sank under the weight of the humidity.

A dolphin blew off to my right, followed by another. Hadley III jerked her head toward the sound. I didn't even know she had followed me. Probably hanging around to see if I was mortally wounded.

I called Rondo. We traded apologies for not returning calls in a timely manner.

"Did you hear from her?" I asked.

"I did. You posted that you were interested in her story and the story of the man she was with that evening. Is that the right song?"

"That's the gist of it." I couldn't imagine that Paretsky would infiltrate WAP and post a reply just to create the appearance that Renée Lambert was still alive. If she replied, she was alive. I waited, but Rondo needed coaxing. "What did she say?" I took another drag from the cigar and flicked the ashes into the water, where they met their fate with a subdued hiss.

"Hold on, I wrote it down." The canvas that covers the twelve-by-twelve deck at the end of the dock rustled in the sea breeze. "Here we go. She said, 'I don't know what man you are referring to.'"

"That's it?"

"Pretty much."

"Either there's more or there isn't. What—"

"There's one more line. She wrote, 'Who are you?'"

Renée wasn't going to reveal herself. After all, I might be the Guardian or Paretsky trying to flush her out. I needed to drop her a serious clue.

"Tell her," I started in. "You ready?"

"Locked and loaded."

"Tell her that I'm Renée Sutherland." My hope was that by mentioning the deceased friend from her mother's childhood, her namesake, I could convince Renée Lambert that I was close to her family. There was always the risk that she would think Paretsky or the Guardian would have come across that information, or that she had previously told either of them herself, but it was a long stretch.

"I don't get it," Rondo replied.

"I'm trying to gain her confidence," I told him. "Can you enter it now, tonight?" My phone indicated an incoming call.

"Sutherland, right?"

"Right. Give her my number again, and tell her it's secure."

We disconnected. Renée knew her life was in danger. She didn't come forth to claim her father's body, yet she cautiously replied to my posting. The Guardian was likely seeking her. Meanwhile, Alexander Paretsky was as far away from me as he'd ever been.

I went back to the screened porch. Garrett sat next to Morgan. I hadn't heard them arrive. Dusty Springfield came from the Magnavox. I took a seat next to Morgan, who hummed along with the song. I checked my phone for the missed call and saw I had a voice mail. It was the number for the furniture delivery. I deleted the message without retrieving it. Like a new bed would make a difference in my life. I took Wayne's badge out of my pocket and tossed it on the table.

"You've been deputized?" Garrett said.

"Souvenir from a cowboy. Where'd you boys ride in from?" The table lamp was on low and cast a soft light on his dark face. He held a bottle of water, and Morgan cradled a glass of port with both hands.

"We were at Mangroves," Morgan replied, "having dinner with Kathleen."

"She ready to apologize?"

Garrett snorted, and Morgan said, "You didn't even come up."

I couldn't imagine a world where I didn't even come up. What a sad, desolate, ice-capped place. I reviewed my message to Rondo and my conversation with Wayne. Then I reversed and gave a synopsis of my encounters in England.

"Two Renées," Morgan said, after I'd exhausted my interest in rehashing my trip.

"McKenzie," Garrett cut in. "He knows more than he shared."

"I agree. Cynthia confirmed his lie, but there wasn't much I could do. I'd already given him my name and, considering what I committed in that country, I'd—"

"You'd have been a fool to press him. But we need to make him come clean."

Morgan shifted his weight. "Is that necessary?"

"We'll be polite." Garrett stood, pulled out his phone, and walked out the door toward the dock.

Dusty sang that life is like a wheel within a wheel. I'd recently purchased *Dusty in Memphis*. I'd gotten interested in her work after hearing her at Raydel Escobar's house before I helped put him behind bars. He was a sixties aficionado, and his wife, Sophia, quickly became a friend of Kathleen's. They were probably talking about me right now. Laughing, joking, sipping cocktails, and—

"Did you know she was instrumental in signing Led Zeppelin?" Morgan interrupted my thoughts.

"Who?"

"Dusty. During the recording session for this album, she told Atlantic Records to sign them. They did so without seeing the group."

"And you know this why?"

"My father told me a few nights ago."

Morgan's father died of alcoholism—the previously mentioned Caribbean flu—over ten years ago. Morgan was a major fan of dreams and had on more than one occasion, when parting for bed, said he was going to visit his father.

"It's knowledge you already knew," I countered. "Your brain put it in your father's words while you slept."

"Probably right." He glanced at me and brushed his hair behind his head. He took a sip of port. He and Kathleen— Garrett didn't partake—had likely conquered two bottles. And now tawny port.

"But that doesn't make the conversation any less real," he continued. "No more than you or me repeating something to each other that we previously had stated. It was just a conversation we had the other night."

"You'd think he'd impart more knowledge from the great beyond other than Atlantic Records signed Led Zeppelin without seeing them."

"Might be all there is. Besides," Morgan said as he gazed out to the water, "no one dies until the last memory of that person has been swept away. As long as I live, my father lives. We talk and walk, as real as we ever did."

"A real tent revival. You and my ex found the truth at the bottom of the second bottle, didn't you?"

The hell is my problem? Morgan was—is—close to his father, and me taking that away from him, in whatever form he still held the man, was a senseless thing to do.

The bad speaker went out, and Dusty went down a notch at the song's climactic moment.

"Just a conversation with my father." He plunked down his glass of port and stood up. "Catch you in the morning." He strode out the side door, and it bounced open behind him.

Garrett returned and stood on the other side of the screen. "We'll know tomorrow what Father McKenzie really knows. Why'd Morgan leave?"

"Got me."

We reviewed our lack of progress, and he headed over to Morgan's.

My legs ached from lack of sleep. I wasn't sure I'd gotten more than three hours the previous night. Maybe eight in the last forty-eight. I often feel at the end of a day as if that day was a whole life.

That night it was Kathleen and not the cardinal. She was a small, black-and-white head shot, like a sixth-grade picture from the sixties, and it floated under the bottom of a dirigible tethered by a purple string. I tried to catch the photograph, but my legs were heavy, like I was running in waist-deep water. As slow as the dirigible was, I was even slower. There was another small photograph I wanted to see, but I couldn't remember it.

— — —

It was light when I awoke, and that nearly put me in cardiac arrest.

Morgan sat at the end of his dock, doing his meditation thing. I'd learned to never interrupt him during his ritual. Nonetheless, I jumped around the fence and marched out to him. He did not turn. I stood behind him and delivered a few sentences that are nobody's damn business except his and mine.

I tailgated an electric utility truck to the hotel. I swam fast. Ran faster. Afterward, Eddie, the pool man, interrupted my buzzing mind with a tale of a man who'd jumped his fence and sat on his patio furniture. After the third time, the neighbors called the police. I listened patiently, a far more difficult thing to do than either the swim or the run, but I liked Eddie; he'd been spreading towels and raising umbrellas for guests for over two decades, and I still felt bad for being a jerk to Morgan the night before. As if listening to the pool man would absolve me of last night's thoughtless remarks, but that's how we operate, isn't it? I finally broke away, thinking what a tadpole brain I had for considering a moment of genuine concern to be an admirable achievement and personal sacrifice.

I drove to Lambert's house. Breakfast could wait. Wayne's parting comment to me yesterday had been gaining steam. His words had been with me every stroke of my swim, every step of my run. *May not even be in his house.* I had a good idea of where the flash drive might be, or at least where I would have hidden it. Assuming the Guardian hadn't found it. I walked around to the dock. The great white egret stood by the bait bucket.

"Listen, fellow, you need to move on. Your time here is done." It moved a step closer.

Lambert's voice in my head. *Got some good blues in it, some other gems as well. It'll hold about anything you want.* The comment was during my second visit. During my first visit he had turned his back to me when he leaned over the side of the dock and checked the bucket.

I squatted down on my knees and pulled the bucket out of the canal. Water poured out through the holes. I placed it on the dock, opened the lid, and took out a Ziploc bag. Inside the bag was a watertight plastic capsule with a marina's name on it and a small chain. I have a similar one; they're used for boat keys. Mine also holds my boat registration.

I opened it and took out a USB flash drive.

I tossed a pinfish to the bird. He caught it in his mouth.

CHAPTER 28

Garrett ran it over to SOCom at MacDill. I doubted I would ever know the full contents of that flash drive. I was curious to know if it held the names of special ops personnel scattered throughout the world and if we had effectively shut Paretsky down. Not that I would rest on that—I had my own score, like a wheel within a wheel, to settle with Paretsky.

I was also anxious as to whether Garrett's and my name were on the flash drive. If my name was on the list, was Kathleen's as well? The only way anyone would know of her was if there was a leak in the colonel's department. The colonel, when he'd sat on my dock, had evaded that question. With luck, the flash drive would not only reveal information about Paretsky, but also provide a clue as to his source of information.

I was riding high and channeled my momentum into calling Kathleen.

"Hello, stranger," she answered, and my heart flipped like a dolphin coming out of the water.

"Lunch?" I said.

"Can't. Sophia's got that slot."

"Dinner? Whatever you say, do not say no. No is not an—"

"I—"

"I'll sit up straight. Won't pinch the hostess. Refrain from polio jokes."

"I—"

"Just say yes, Kathleen."

"I was trying to say I'll be ready at seven."

"Really?"

"Against my better judgment."

"You know, don't you?"

"What?"

"I'm spec*tac*ularly in love with you."

I hung up before she had a chance to reply. *Hello, stranger*—that was a zinger from the old days. The days before I killed a cardinal, lied to her, and told her (for the second time, as she reminded me) to go dwell in her books.

Morgan dropped in with his can of beer and took a seat. "Eat yet?"

"No."

He sprang out of the chair he had just landed in and bolted to the kitchen. I went to the Magnavox, opened the lid, flipped the two albums that were on it, and joined him. Within a minute Bryan Lee timidly entered the sound waves of the house. His blues exploded when the tubes warmed up. Morgan and I threw together the usual combo of eggs, bell peppers, and onions. I rubbed a bulging potato with olive oil and punctured it repeatedly with the tines of a fork. After microwaving it, I sliced it lengthwise and placed the slices into a hot pan of oil. I sprinkled the pan liberally with ground pepper and salt. Morgan opened a plastic container of mole sauce left over from a week ago and heated it in a saucepan. We didn't have any fish to add, so I panfried thick strips of applewood bacon. We took our usual seats. We dosed the eggs and potatoes with the spicy sauce. We ate like dogs.

I tried to ignore Kathleen's empty chair, but, like on the plane, I felt her absence more than I'd ever felt her presence. I wondered if that was something that wore off or if some people lived their lives like that, sitting in a familiar chair with the empty universe next to them.

Garrett called and said they hoped to break the encryption today. He planned to camp out at the base. The bacon was good, but it's too hard to make the thick stuff crispy. As I chewed, I wondered what Kathleen was doing.

"Seeing her today?" Morgan said. I swear the man owned my mind.

"Dinner. That your Lee album?" He'd been starting to bring his vinyl over to play on the Magnavox.

"My father always played blues on Sunday mornings."

"Honoring the tradition."

"I am."

"Does he still listen to it on Sundays?"

He turned to me and smiled. "He does."

I fetched a bottle of Taittinger and two crystal champagne flutes. On Sundays Morgan broke his ritual, and he, Kathleen, and I split a bottle—sometimes two. Maybe what I missed was the booze and not the woman. There's a thought.

"To your father."

We clinked glasses as an osprey flew over with a large sheepshead clamped in its talons. The fish, as if swimming at fifty feet above sea level, waved its tail, frantically trying to free itself. I put my flute down and called Rondo.

He picked up on the third ring. "Send another message," I commanded.

"Travis?"

"Tell her I found the SunDisk that her father hid and to call me ASAP."

"I don't—"

"Just do it." I ended the call.

"Think that's wise?" Morgan said, after I explained the recent developments. "What if Paretsky or the Guardian is on those pages? You just let them—"

"They don't know whether I'm bluffing, and no way are they on Words Against People's message board. I don't even know what I'm doing on it. Besides," I said, as I turned to him, "I've got to flush him out, or the next sister, mom, or girlfriend to take a bullet's going to be on me."

After breakfast Morgan grabbed some rods and took off on *Impulse*. I would have loved to join him but didn't dare be on the water in the event we got a break. I pestered Rondo, and he confirmed that Renée had not responded to the message board. I staked out Lambert's house to see if Wayne or anyone else came by. I called Adam, the bartender at the Valencia. I reacquainted myself with him, although he cut me off halfway through, aghast at the mere thought that he might not remember me. He had not seen the man I referred to as the Guardian who had been with Renée Lambert that night.

I texted Garrett, but still no break on the encryption. I organized notes that didn't need organizing. I checked my watch every hour. Every half hour. I shaved. I changed shirts three times. Midway through taking the second one off, impatient with my girlish behavior, I ripped off the last four buttons. I avoided alcohol.

I was at her building at half past six.

CHAPTER 29

Her private elevator was still roped off, so I headed for the public one. As I waited, an athletic man in a cream, silk sport coat, a blossoming head of hair, and George Burns glasses came up beside me. He looked sharp. A real dandy. Ready for a night on Beach Drive.

"Be happy when they fix our private elevators." He cleared his throat. "It's been a while."

"You'd think it would be a simple job."

"That's what they told us. Can't imagine what the issue is." His neck was the width of a piling, and his shoulders threatened the seams of his jacket. The door opened, and a lady in black spandex shorts and a dog on a leash exited, the mutt forging ahead. I stepped into the elevator and punched the number nine. Paul McCartney's voice dropped from the ceiling speakers. "All My Loving." A great jingle that was never released as a single. My phone rang in my pocket. The elevator door closed.

"What floor?" I asked as I fronted the only bank of buttons in the elevator.

"Nine."

I hit the button again. I recalled Morgan's comment that when he and Garrett had had dinner with Kathleen, I hadn't even come up.

I'm coming up now, baby.

I took my phone out. Garrett. The phone had died in the elevator. I'd call him at Kathleen's. I stared down at my feet. I nodded my head to the gentle beat of the song. It was the first song that Paul wrote the lyrics to, but that wasn't what struck me; it was the opening song they played on their first appearance on the Ed Sullivan show in 1964, and it floated over the hospital speakers sixteen years later when Lennon's body was rolled in on a gurney after Chapman shot him. Heavy satanic symmetry.

I'm coming up now, baby.

I wouldn't blow it tonight.

Bringing all my loving.

I stared at the digital readout of the number nine. It had seven separate lines that—

Kathleen's words flooded my head, drowning out my Beatles trivia and penchant for counting. *I'm the only one here right now. Other two units are empty.*

I wore glasses and a ponytail when—

Cough drops.

I collapsed to the floor as his fist exploded into the panel where my head had been. My face planted hard on the phone box handle, and it cut into my skin. *PHONE* was spelled out vertically, and the *E,* no more than an inch from my right eye, had nearly worn away.

Grabbing his leg, I burst up from my crouched position. We crashed into the back wall. His right hand held a knife. I reached out with my left hand and clamped his wrist. He brought his knee up into my groin, but I pivoted in time so my left thigh took the blow. I stuck my right hand into his throat. Like the osprey with the giant sheepshead in its talons, I squeezed.

The knife inched closer. His right arm was stronger than my left arm. His left hand locked on my right wrist around his neck. My fingers dug into his throat. My right arm was stronger than his left arm. The knife came closer to my face. He would win by virtue of possessing a weapon.

McCartney entered the middle eight.

I released his right wrist and ducked. The knife swished wildly above my head. He was not expecting me to let go, and his weight followed his hand into the wall. I put him in a rear naked choke hold, wrapped my right leg around his legs, and tripped us both forward so that I fell on him. Now it was his face scrunched up against the phone box. His wig slid down over his left ear, and the glasses fell off. The back of his buzzed head looked identical to that of the man in the picture with Renée at the Valencia.

He was nearly asphyxiated before I was able to wrestle the knife away. I pressed it tightly against his throat.

"How did you know she was here?" I demanded. Blood dripped onto him from my face. I must have cut it on the phone box.

He didn't answer.

"Where's Paretsky?"

Nothing.

The knife drew blood. I needed him alive but wanted him dead. I'd fought that battle before. I put my mouth to his ear.

"You will talk. The only difference will be the amount of pain you receive. Do you understand?"

Nothing.

He stared straight ahead at the carpet, which had a crown pattern, like a remnant from Windsor Castle. He started to roll, but I applied more pressure. I pressed the knife as hard as I dared. An ounce more and it would slice his throat. "Talk to me and save yourself. It's Paretsky we—"

He reversed his resistance and jerked his head forward—he had been holding it back and away from the knife. The sudden release, similar to how I had just freed my grip on his arm holding the knife, caught me by surprise.

I wasn't fast enough. The knife cut deep into his throat, and the blood surged out of his neck, running over the royal carpet like a river that had breached a levee.

"No, no, no!" I shouted as I dropped the knife. I turned him over and applied pressure to his neck. I ripped off my silk shirt—the third one I'd put on and the second one I'd ripped that day—and tried to stem the bleeding. His legs danced as if he was being electrocuted. He smiled. Sir Paul sang. I was losing him. I didn't want to give him the final satisfaction of imposing his will on me. I relinquished my effort. I picked up the knife.

"This is for Donald Lambert." I sliced the Guardian's throat to the bone. "Beware, my ass."

The elevator bell gave a soft, cosmopolitan ring to signal that we had reached the ninth floor, or perhaps that the round was over. The door opened. My phone rang. I dragged the body into the war room.

"What?" I said to Garrett as I hit the button.

"They know. They broke the code, but that's not it. They found the leak. Have reason to believe that our names—"

"I just killed the Guardian on his way up to see Kathleen. Who else is on the list?"

"She was it."

"Morgan?"

"No. Word's gone out. No doubt he has copies, but at least they can protect themselves and relocate. You OK?"

"Fine. The leak?"

"Didn't get it from the drive, but they cuffed him today."

"Tell Morgan he sails in thirty. Understand that?"

"Got it."

"And we need a cleanup in aisle nine."

I disconnected and dropped the body under a collection of Great War titles. Two monstrous olive-branch bookends squeezed a couple of dozen tomes. On the left was Tuchman's *The Guns of August*. On the right, Toland's *The Last 100 Days*. Remarque's *All Quiet on the Western Front* stood alone, propped up in the corner. It was the translated edition, but *Last Letters from Stalingrad* wasn't. Were they from the same source? Why would I think of that now? A heightened state of alert is an inexplicable level of consciousness. Kathleen's door opened.

She wore tight jeans, a sleeveless white blouse, and a sweater. The sweater had no buttons in the front and was trimmed with lace. It nearly hung to her knees, and the sleeves were neatly rolled up to just past her elbows. It was a light, see-through, linen material. A gold-embroidered pattern of leaves and flowers. The back of the sweater came up high where a choker of aqua and brown—Sedona colors— clung to her neck. A matching bracelet was on her right wrist. Her hair was tied back, although some of it was free, I think by design.

She had on high heels and was a good four inches taller than usual. We were nearly eye to eye.

She glanced over at the Guardian's body. It twitched. Her mouth dropped open.

I said, "Bit of a skirmish in the war room."

She glanced back up at me. "Jake?"

"We've got to go."

The color started to leave her face. Shock. I realized I didn't have a shirt on and was smeared in blood.

"I'm fine," I blurted out. "It's his blood, not mine."

"Jake?"

"I'm fine."

"Jake—"

I didn't want to touch her for fear of ruining her sweater. I moved into her foyer and shut the door behind me. "You're not safe here. We leave in five. I'm rinsing under the shower and changing clothes." I kept a few items in her closet. I started into her bedroom.

"Where's your shirt?" she asked.

I pivoted back around. "Elevator."

"Which one?"

"Eleva—"

"No. Shirt."

"Blue one you bought me last spring."

"When I bought you two?"

"Yeah. Ripped the buttons off the other one earlier this— this is nonsense. Go pack. You're leaving."

"Leaving?"

"Five minutes. You need to sit down?"

"What?"

"Sit down. You—"

"I'm fine," she snapped and abruptly collapsed on her leather recliner.

"You need to pack."

"I thought you said to sit down."

"Do both." I left her and bolted into her bathroom.

I rinsed under her shower and changed into jeans and a T-shirt. As far as I knew, Kathleen's elevator was the only one not operating, and everyone used the bank of elevators that opened into their respective units. Nonetheless, I needed the place cleaned. MacDill was less than thirty minutes away, and they had a team there. Garrett, as I'd instructed, would make the call.

I finished dressing. Kathleen crammed semifolded clothing into a suitcase, much like I'd seen her do in London.

"Who was he?" she demanded.

"Man we call the Guardian."

Why not tell me the truth? she had implored me at the end of my dock. Think she can handle it? Fine, let her hear this cannon roar. "He was dispatched to kill you solely based on your association with me."

"I see." She stood a few feet from me and blew her breath out. "I would expect you to perform such a task without creating such a mess."

Damn.

OK, let's see how she handles Fat Man. "It was only by luck that I was in the elevator with him. I didn't know he was coming."

She nodded her head. "An honest and lucky man."

Double D.

"For the record." She turned and slammed shut her suitcase. She pivoted, took a step toward me, and stuck her face in mine. "What I *don't* like is being kept in the dark by someone who thinks I'm a bibliophile incapable of reality."

"Let's go." I took a step forward and grasped her arm. "You're not safe here."

"I said, you un—"

"Yeah, yeah, yeah. We need to hustle."

"Where to?"

"Morgan's waiting."

"I'm sailing?"

"Pronto." For all I knew, Paretsky was waiting for us. Her faux cavalier acceptance of my luck didn't disguise her apparent shock and lack of comprehension of her immediate situation.

"Wait a sec." She dashed off to a dresser and bounded back into the room with two bathing suits, a wide-brimmed, floppy hat, and three paperback books. She unzipped the outer compartment of her suitcase and crammed them in.

OK, so maybe I underestimated this woman.

We hustled through the war room and into the bloody elevator. Kathleen sequestered herself in the far corner, away from the blood.

"Bet this doesn't happen," she said, a corner of her thin lip curling up, "to Emily Brontë and friends."

CHAPTER 30

Garrett confirmed a cleanup for 27B.
Florida was the twenty-seventh state to enter the union. And B? That was Garrett and me. Must be a Group A out there. I often wondered if they were still operational. Still vertical.

Kathleen peppered me with questions on the first few minutes of the fifteen-minute drive from her condo. She gave up after she realized that she wasn't going to scale my wall of silence.

I wanted to tell her everything would be fine. Hadn't she heard what I had said? *It was only by luck that I was in the elevator with him.* She might react with a calm demeanor, but it was unacceptable. I was unacceptable. I should not be in her life.

Moon Child, at forty-two feet, extended well beyond the decking at the end of my dock. I assisted Kathleen onto the boat, and Garrett untied the bowline. I started to turn, but then reversed and hopped on the boat. I grabbed her and kissed her. At first it was a solitary act, but then she kicked in with everything she had. I pulled back. Our eyes locked. I stepped off the boat.

Morgan said, "Anyplace in particular?"

"Get her the hell out of my life."

The screened porch was quiet. No music. No cigars. No Morgan. No Kathleen. My life was more hole than substance.

More of what I'd lost than what I'd accumulated. It felt good to feel sorry for myself. Cheered me up. All I needed was some whiskey, and I could crawl right into funky town. The bullshit thoughts are a dead-end street, but you need to visit that cul-de-sac sometimes to remind yourself that the only way out is to retrace your steps past everything that drove you there in the first place.

No bullshit here—what good was finding the one of seven billion for me if all I brought her was danger?

When I first met Lauren Cunningham, I overreacted, nearly got her killed, and brought about her new identity as Kathleen Rowe. Less than a year ago, while searching for a missing young woman, I again endangered Kathleen when the man who held the woman recognized Kathleen as the previous Lauren Cunningham. Now this.

Screw it. I was lying to myself. She hadn't flinched at any of that. That girl was solid oak. What she did blink at, what irked her, were my crass remarks that she should go back to her books. My insinuation was that she was better at observing life than living it. Not only was I astonishingly wrong— dead bodies, new name, no sweat—but what did she zero in on, what really got under her skin? Words.

Incredible.

No.

Indelible.

I went to the kitchen and built a drink. I plopped three cubes into a glass and drowned them with whiskey—a simple job, no blueprint needed. I dropped an LP on the Magnavox, returned to the porch, and tossed down two shots faster than you can take baby aspirin. Maybe Kathleen wasn't rattled by what just happened, but I was. It was too close. I let one of the ice cubes slide into my mouth and gave it a crack. Garrett came in and sat beside me. Tony Bennett came over the Magnavox. "If I Ruled the World." It was all props, but we need that sometimes. Sometimes it's all we're left with.

"The flash drive?" I said.

"Dozen or so names. More like a loose network. He might be one of many. By shutting down the leak, we eliminate any further damage. The exposed parties just need to cover themselves. Paretsky got lucky a few times, and that turned the battleship in his direction, but even if we sink him there are others."

"Kathleen?"

"Address. Nothing else."

"How many people have that information?"

"Not sure."

"The leak?"

"Low-level, midcareer geek looking for money to pay off an underage girl who threatened to put him behind bars."

"A stiff dick has no conscience."

"Nor legal rights. Somehow Paretsky made contact with the source and traded money for names."

"Antinori," I asked. "He on the flash drive?"

Garrett's eyes cut into me. "No. Whatever reason he was there that morning had nothing to do with compromised information."

It would be nice if, just once, things came easy.

I thought of the colonel's remark on my dock, that the leak or source that led to the demise of agents and their loved ones wasn't necessarily related to Antinori's early morning stroll. I had started to argue with him but pulled back, admitting that events that appeared related should not be assumed to be so. I was becoming convinced that the death of Cardinal Antinori wasn't related to Paretsky's official line of business.

The picture he sent of me? My bet was that Paretsky took advantage of the situation—and why not? It made him look better than he was. Crafty little turd.

I cracked another piece of ice. "Father McKenzie?"

Garrett stood and walked to the screen, facing the dark. "We picked him up, took him for a ride. Questioned him hard on the cardinal's schedule; you knew the man, kept his calendar, the usual muscle bluffing." He turned to me. "Direct questions about Hoover and Paretsky."

"And?"

"Nothing beyond that he knew the man as Mr. Hoover and that he was a generous donor. Said Antinori insisted on handling Hoover, kept him close, and that he, McKenzie, didn't interact that much with him."

"They scare him?"

"Pissed in his robe."

"Holy water."

Garrett snorted a laugh, which is as close as he ever got to the real thing. "The cleanup team should be at Kathleen's place by now. Within a few hours, after they lift the Guardian's prints, we'll likely know his identity, and a whole new line of investigation should open up. Unless the fingerprints and dental records aren't in any database."

"I'm going to forget you said that."

I called Binelli and told her that the man referred to as the Guardian was dead. She said she'd pass the information to Wayne.

Garrett's phone rang as I reached for my drink.

"No," he said. He listened some more. "No way."

His tone alarmed me. I stood. He disconnected.

"Identifying parts of the body are gone," he said. "Someone beat us to it."

"Gone, as in—"

"Hacked off."

"That might be the best news all day."

"How so?"

I drained the last drop of whiskey that wasn't there. "Means Paretsky's in town. Let's find him."

CHAPTER 31

Sometimes a cowboy can come in pretty handy. You'll see what I mean—twice.

Garrett and I discussed how we would dispose of body parts and unanimously agreed taking a boat into Tampa Bay with a few cinder blocks was a no-brainer.

I took out my phone and hit Adam's number. The harbor was directly across from his end of the front porch.

"Any boats go out in the last fifteen minutes or going out now?" I asked him.

"We're hoppin'."

"Look now. Over your shoulder. Tell me what's going on at the marina."

"OK. The babe you saw, you know, the one who digs nude sunbathing?"

"The *Southern Breeze*."

"Roger dodger. She's having a boat party. Smallish crowd. I don't know what to tell you, man. Lots of people strolling in the park and—"

"Forget the park. Focus on the marina. Any boat leaving? Just don't look at the shore."

His voice faded, and he said, "Be right with you." He came back to me. "What was that?"

"The water, man. The mouth of the marina."

"That's it, Jake. The boat party, nothing…the dweeb banker?"

"Who?"

"You know, the girl's man who owns the *S*—"

"What about him?"

"He's motoring out in his tender. Must not like his girl touching other—"

"Say that again?"

"The little intense dude, you know, her man. He's heading out in the *Southern Breeze*'s tender."

My body shuddered.

I saw it. I saw it like one of those pictures that's an illusion because it's two pictures, and try as you might to see the second image, you just can't see it, and then when it pops into view you wonder how you could have not seen it.

An indelible image.

Alexander Paretsky had been under my nose from the beginning. Resided on boats. Rarely came ashore. The lady on *Southern Breeze*. I had thought she looked familiar when I spotted her from the front porch bar of the Valencia but dismissed her as just another blonde on a good-looking boat whose skin I wanted to massage.

I instructed Adam, "Keep him in your sights as long as you can." I disconnected, raced into my study, and retrieved my shoulder bag. I rummaged through the bag and extracted the picture. It was of Paretsky and the blonde on the boat that the colonel had shown me as we sat on my dock. I flashed it to Garrett on the porch.

"I think she's the same woman."

"Who?" He planted himself beside me, studying the picture.

234

"I saw this woman on a boat downtown. Been there for days. Captain is described as a slight, intense man. I bet—"

"Is it her or not?"

Was it? I tried to recall what she had looked like that day, when I nursed Spanish's Bloody Mary, the Fitzgeralds laughed, and the mimosa girl ordered another drink when her friend arrived. The blonde oiled her skin and turned on the chaise lounge. The letters *SB* embossed—

Behind the girl and the man, I could clearly see an *S* in the same font as the one in my mind. "*Southern Breeze*," I said. "He kept one boat too long."

"Same boat?"

"Positive. I saw her a few days ago. Paretsky's there now, taking his dinghy out to the bay. He's been there all along."

"We go by car or boat?"

"Boat." I started for the side door. "If we find him, his dinghy will be no match for *Impulse*. Grab the bag."

I sprinted out to the end of my dock and hit the switch to lower *Impulse* into the water. The lift had one speed: slow. At full throttle, it would take *Impulse* close to twenty minutes to make the downtown marina. I could drive in fifteen—tops— but then I wouldn't have a boat. If Paretsky was on the water, I wanted to hunt him. My twin 250s would scorch him unless he had an insurmountable head start, which was a real possibility. If he pulled up anchor on *Southern Breeze,* I'd board him like a pirate. But what if I wanted to be on land and sea?

This is where a cowboy comes in handy.

I called Edward Jonathan Wayne. I told him about the *Southern Breeze*. He said he'd be at the boat within fifteen minutes. Must be staying in town. Was he dispatched to babysit me?

Two Super Bowl halftimes later, *Impulse* finally floated. I jumped in, flicked the battery switch, and uncovered the helm and seat. The Garmin's ten-inch screen flashed to life, as did an abusively loud Bob Marley. I killed the music. Garrett leapt in with his SASS and Morgan's old red spinnaker bag. It contained a hodgepodge of guns, knives, a first-aid kit, sat phones, passports, and currencies. We never leave home without it. I told him what I'd discussed with Wayne.

"Trust him?" He echoed my question to Binelli.

I held the remote lift control in my left hand and pressed the down button. "Do now."

I threw the twin Yamahas in reverse, and *Impulse* lurched backward, dragging the cradle into the bay, as she still wasn't buoyant on her own. I spun the wheel, headed for the starboard side of the channel marker, and thrust down the twin throttles. She reared up like a racehorse and settled down on an even plane. The bay was smooth, and she sliced the water like a surgeon's scalpel. I didn't slow down under either bridge.

When I approached the entrance to the harbor, my Boker knife was in my cargo shorts pocket, and my Smith & Wesson was in the holster under my shirt. I cut the speed, and Garrett searched the water with the Steiner marine binoculars for signs of Paretsky.

"Two o'clock," he said. I spun to starboard and picked up the anchor light of a boat around two miles offshore.

"Looks like he's drifting. Probably fishing."

"We'll need to chase down every light we see." My phone rang as I was doubting the validity of my plan.

"Tell me," I blurted out to Wayne.

"I pulled up a minute too late," Wayne replied. "She cast off. Leaving the harbor now."

"I'm picking you up." I told him where and disconnected. I turned to Garrett. "We're collecting Wayne first." I wasn't worried about losing track of *Southern Breeze*. Hard to hide seventy feet of fiberglass, even on night water.

A few minutes later, I pulled alongside the public pier, and Wayne stepped on board. I'd never had a cowboy on my boat. I'd never *seen* a cowboy on a boat. Garrett and Wayne exchanged names.

"We'll check out this one boat," I said to whoever cared as I swung the bow back out toward Tampa Bay. "Make sure it's not him. Maybe he told the captain of *Southern Breeze* to take off on his own and create a red herring. We'll see what they know and then chase her." I shoved the throttles down, and the roar of the outboards silenced my rambling.

We came at them fast. Garrett, six foot three and black as night, stood on the forward deck with the SASS over his shoulder and the binoculars around his neck. Wayne planted himself in the stern, his long coat blowing out behind him, slapping the starboard engine's cowling. He held his revolver in his right hand, and his left hand was tightly wrapped around the hardtop's white-powder aluminum railing for support. We came upon the boat. It held three men. The men held fishing poles.

"Gentlemen," I said as I threw the engines in reverse to keep from ramming their port side. One of the men rushed to keep the boats from colliding. The other two remained stiff. I kept my eyes on the man wearing a baseball cap—at night—who kept the boats from hitting. The fishing boat was likely his. "Did you see a man, by himself, in a dinghy?"

"You law?" Baseball Cap said.

"That's right," Garrett replied. "We're law."

"Not game wardens," I said, cutting in. I didn't want them to think we were going to haul them in for lack of a fishing license. "You just need to tell us—"

"Nothin'," a man in the aft deck blurted out. "We ain't seen a thing."

I kept my eyes on the captain. "I'm asking you."

The boats rubbed together, but Baseball Cap kept an eye on Garrett as he pushed away with his left foot.

"Ten minutes ago," he said, looking up at me. "No lights. Maybe two hundred yards off our bow, but hard to say without them running lights."

"Headed where?" I said.

"New Orleans. How the hell I know?"

"You really want to talk to me like that?"

"Hey, I didn't mean any—"

"You know these waters?"

"Born and raised here. We're just out here doing some night fishing, you know? Don't want any—"

"Tell me where he was headed."

He stuck his foot out again to keep the boats from hitting. "Lot of water, man." He glanced back up to me. "But my guess? Those channels by Westshore. Let's put it like this: if he kept a straight course, that's where he would dock. But you're too far behind, even with all that juice on your ass. If that was where he was headed, he's docked and halfway to Mickeytown by now." He nodded at Wayne. "What's with the cowboy?"

"His horse drowned."

I spun *Impulse* around and punched the throttles down when she was still coming out of her turn, throwing my wake into the port side of the fishing boat. I wasn't going to give chase to an unknown boat, in an unknown direction, that I couldn't catch.

In the distance the lights of downtown St. Pete glowed against the Florida night. I switched off my running lights. On the flat surface of the bay, the lights of *Southern Breeze* moved along the shore toward the channel of Tampa Bay and the open waters of the Gulf of Mexico.

She was mine.

CHAPTER 32

S he was also faster than I thought.

She must have had a pair of hell-injected diesels deep in her hull, firing with everything they had. We didn't catch up with her until the Sunshine Skyway Bridge.

I doubted Paretsky was on board *Southern Breeze*, but maybe the dinghy leaving the harbor was a red herring. Even if he had abandoned ship, those individuals still on board should hold information about his operation and possibly even his whereabouts.

I shouted to Wayne, "You pilot a boat before?"

"Bass fishing. Lake Talquin." His left hand, knuckles white, was welded around the aluminum rail.

"Good enough." The three of us reviewed our options, picked the one least likely to get us killed, and unanimously agreed that we would find out if lady luck was on deck or not. I wished Morgan was with us but was thankful that Kathleen was safe. *Unless someone's gunning for them with the same speed I'm closing in on* Southern Breeze. I didn't need that in my head and shut it down.

Southern Breeze went wide open under the bridge, north of thirty knots by my gauges. Someone had a brass pair. The concrete embankments are wide enough for freighters, but to run them full speed at night in a seventy-foot cruiser? Not to mention the concrete bumpers placed on either side of the entrance to protect the supporting structure.

Her name was written in neon blue across her stern in the same font as the initials I'd recognized on the chaise lounges. She sported a rear deck the size of my screened porch that cleared the water by only a few feet. Two Jet Skis were clamped to the transom. The hoist that lowered the dinghy to the water was flopping over the side. I came in fast and dark.

"You're humming in pretty quick here," Wayne shouted.

"Just to get us close," I shouted back. I surrendered the wheel to Wayne and maneuvered to the bow alongside Garrett. The churning wake and convulsing waters caused by *Southern Breeze*'s props supplanted the shrill noise of my twin Yamahas.

"What if she pulls up?" Wayne shouted.

"She's not a mustang. Just keep off to the side," I shouted back at him. "Get us close. Starboard side."

"Now," Garrett shouted, and he leapt onto the swim platform. I started to follow, but *Impulse* bounced away. It reminded me of a similar situation I was in over a year ago as I attempted to rescue a boat of girls. My jump that night came up short.

Not tonight.

I landed next to Garrett, started to pitch forward, and felt his hand squeeze me back. I glanced behind me. Wayne cut back on the throttle as I had instructed him, and *Impulse* fell off. He would stay within a hundred feet until I stopped the yacht, and then he would approach us for a tie-up.

Garrett's SIG Sauer exploded in my right ear. I instinctively hit the deck, and a man tumbled on top of me. With my left hand, I grabbed the stainless-steel handle on the port side of the walkway up to the main deck. With my right, I snatched the man's arm to keep him from going in the drink. Garrett bounded up the steps. I hauled the man to the main deck and turned him over.

"Won't be telling us anything," I muttered under my breath. I quickly went through his pockets but found nothing other than a St. Christopher's cross around his neck.

"Either him or you," Garrett said.

I spun around. "I thought you went to the bridge."

"I did."

"And?"

"Came back to give you a heads-up. The blonde's inside— no one has the wheel. If there's more crew, they're hiding. I'm going hunting. Boat and blonde are yours. I vote you slow us down."

Garrett took off for the lower deck, and I sprinted into the main stateroom.

Southern Breeze. Seventy feet of top shelf. Teak floors. Mahogany walls. Recessed lighting. Flat-screen TVs the size of my bed. Overstuffed couches. A bamboo coffee table sat on an oval rug the color of sea coral. Six steps at the front of the stateroom led up to the pilothouse.

The blonde. She *was* the sunbather I'd seen earlier. She stumbled down the steps in a gold sundress with spaghetti straps and a ruffled scoop neck. At the sight of me, she abruptly halted her forward motion, although her head didn't get the memo. She held a gun in both hands and waved it at my head. The gun had my full attention.

"One move," she said in a plastered voice, "and I'll kill you. Swear I will. Swear it, I really do." *Really* came out like a *Saturday Night Live* skit about Baba Wawa.

I didn't believe her, but I had to consider the downside.

CHAPTER 33

"I'm here to help you," I said.
She was three sheets to the wind, but that wasn't necessarily good news.

"Stay back," she blurted. I hadn't moved.

"Do you know where Paretsky—"

"He's an aaaaass." She brought the gun up. A single shot from below. Garrett? He must have located the rest of the crew.

"I need to know where he is." I took a bird step forward. "He's a dangerous man."

"Don't, don't, don't." She raised the gun even higher.

The gun was a minor nuisance compared to what I saw approaching—the tip of Egmont Key. We were bearing straight in toward the lighthouse. Seventy feet of fiberglass and eighty-four thousand pounds, barreling at thirty knots into six inches of water—that was if we were lucky. We could crash into the sunken concrete that shrouded Egmont. Blondie started to tumble but caught herself with her right hand on the varnished rail that led to the pilothouse. Her left still clutched the gun.

I put my hands up, palms out. "I need to slow the boat down, OK? I'm going to walk over to the—"

"Don't." She aimed at my eyes. "Please, just don't."

I let my breath out slowly and tried to hold her glassy eyes. "What's your name?"

"Paige, with an *i*."

"I have to, Paige. We—"

"Last name Godfrey."

"—will both die if this boat is not stopped. Shoot me if you want, but at least save yourself and wait until I stop the boat."

"I chust might do that." She sloshed out the words as she waved the gun toward the helm, as if to give me permission. "Let you save me and then kill you. What do ya think of that?"

She teetered sideways away from the steps, nearly losing her balance. I cleared the steps to the helm in one stride. I eased the throttles back, spun the wheel to starboard to clear the shallow waters, and then cut the throttles to neutral. We were in an area where we could safely drift. I returned to the stateroom. Paige stood off by one of the flat-screen TVs.

She said, "What was the question again?"

"Paretsky. Do—"

"Aaaaass."

"Do you know where Renée Lambert is?"

"That wacko? Why?" Her knees started to buckle. She reached out to the TV and steadied herself.

"I think she's in danger—"

"Goody, goody gumdrops."

The gun had been slipping. I snuck another bird step in her direction. "Do you know where she is?"

"She's like one of those things, you know…ah, shit… what do you call it? Boomerang. Yeah, boomerang love. You know what that is, don't ja? It just keeps comin' back, baby.

Keeps on comin' back." She waved the gun like she was swatting away a fly. "Thought he was over her, but nooo, she just kept comin' back, like a boom-boom-boomerang. Hey, ya know what? She thinks he's gonna kill a bird."

"Who?"

"Alex, baby, who do you think we're talking about?"

"Why would she—"

"Why the questions? Don't ja wanna do me?" Her eyes rolled and then settled back, but like Magic 8 Balls, they weren't exactly centered. "That's all he ever wanted."

I was wasting time with her in her present state. I took a step toward her and demanded, "Do you know where Paretsky was headed when he left the boat tonight?"

She smacked her lips together. "Got me, babe. Where?"

"Did he say anything about the Guardian?"

"Who?"

"A man he knew was killed tonight. He went by the name of the Guardian."

"Never heard of him or this Paret—"

I snatched the gun with my left hand and slapped her sharply across the cheek with my right palm. She would have hit the deck, but I cradled her in my left arm. The right strap of her dress slid down over her arm as it struggled to contain her breasts. She was soft and warm, and her hot, moist breath smothered my face. I backed her away.

"Don't lie to me. The Guardian? Did you know him?"

"Fuckin' hit me."

"Where's Paretsky?"

"You *hit* me."

"I'm sorry. I need—"

"A liar and a hitter."

"Where's—"

"Your girlfriend Renée? Ya know what? If he finds her she's a gon—"

She crumpled like a marionette.

I caught her with both arms and carried her to an overstuffed couch which had a blue anchor pillow in one corner and a map of the British Virgin Islands pillow in the other. I tried to prop her up, but she kept toppling over like a Raggedy Ann doll. I settled her in the Virgin Islands.

Her eyes popped open just as I stepped back. "Why ja hit me?"

"I need to find Paretsky. We'll talk in the morning."

"I'm not a bad girl."

"I know you're not. We'll—"

"Kill a bird. Believe that?"

I grabbed her shoulders and jerked her face up to mine. "The hell you talk—"

"Don't hit me. Don't hit me. Don't hit me."

I pulled back.

"The guy you asked me about?" Her eyes tried to focus, but they were rolling like waves. "The Guardian? Name is Paulo," she spat out, giving the *P* most of the weight. "That's his name. That's what you want, right? Whatja think, we called him the Guardian all the time? Silly. Hey, I'm a good girl. You know that?" She tried to straighten herself out, but her head was too heavy. "Alex said Paulo was dead. Did you kill him?"

"You need to help me find Pa—"

"Hey…" She straightened up again, like a heavyweight fighter refusing to go down. She focused her eyes, summoning whatever bit of sobriety remained in her. "You never told me your name."

"Travis. Jake Travis."

"Travis. Jake Travis. Travis Jake. Well, howdy, JT." Her head flopped to the side. "Wanna guess what *I* had to drink tonight?"

"We'll talk in the morning."

I positioned the pillow behind her head. She sank into the couch, but then her eyes widened as they focused on something behind me. Her head fell back, and her eyes rolled shut.

"Oh, God, I gotta stop the hard stuff," she moaned. "You're not gonna believe this, JT."

"What?"

"No way."

"Tell me."

"JT?" She opened her eyes for the last time that evening. "There's a cowboy on the boat."

With that, Paige Godfrey was out for good.

CHAPTER 34

"You won't pump any information out of her until morning," Wayne commented as he stepped into the stateroom.

"How's Garrett?"

"Got two hog-tied. Too bad he was so quick on the draw with that first fellow."

"You mean when he covered my ass?"

"I suppose."

"She secure?"

He glanced at Paige. "Looks like she's in the pen to me."

"My boat, not the slopped broad."

"Oh. Got her hog-tied, too. Maybe not like you told me, but she's not taking off on her own."

Wayne went over to a wooden bar cart and poured himself a drink. At both our previous meetings, he'd stuck with water. A drink didn't sound half bad; indeed, it sounded wholly good at that moment. I joined him at the bar and poured a couple of shots into a glass tumbler that outweighed a bowling ball.

He winced as the Southern Comfort found its mark and helped himself to another pour. Piloting *Impulse* at night into the aft deck of *Southern Breeze* might have been just a tad out of his comfort zone.

He gave his singular nod. "I need to call this in to my group."

I ignored him and gave him time for another swig. Maybe a little liquid gold would enlighten him. I returned to the helm. Mexico was still over a thousand miles away, but it was time to stop drifting.

The Egmont Key lighthouse was at ten o'clock off my port side. I turned the wheel to the starboard and headed up the coast. I'd piloted big boats before, but it took a few minutes to get a feel for *Southern Breeze*'s controls and familiarize myself with the electronics. The Garmin chartplotter sported the same controls that my unit had, except it displayed a fifteen-inch screen versus my ten-inch. I steered *Southern Breeze* into the main channel. I needed to talk to Garrett, who I assumed was searching the boat. Then what? Let him take *Impulse* back to my dock while I docked *Southern Breeze* at Morgan's inside dock? She'd fit, but it would be tight. The tide shouldn't be a problem, as low tide was still over three hours out and a foot over mean. MacDill could send over a crew to scrub her for leads, but she'd draw a lot of attention. I didn't want that and killed the plan before it hatched.

Wayne was at the bottom of the short flight of steps. "I need you up here," I said. "Keep her straight. I'm going to find Garrett."

"I need to call this in to my people," Wayne repeated as he joined me at the helm.

"I don't think so."

"You got a dead body, gunfire, and—"

"We don't have Paretsky."

I put the boat in neutral and faced Wayne. Garrett entered the pilothouse through the side port door and propped his SASS up against the instrument panel. "Secure," he said.

"Two tied up and the body on the aft deck. No other bodies on board."

"They know anything?" I said.

"Doubtful. Hired deckhands out of George Town. I fired a single shot to emphasize that the party was over. Been with the boat for over a year. Paretsky's had it for the past six months, and he's been on and off it over that time. They confirmed his ID when I showed them a picture. They never knew the man's name beyond Alex."

"Wayne feels it's his patriotic duty to," I cut Wayne a look, "how did you phrase it? 'Call this in.' That right?"

"I'm a federal—"

Garrett said, "Our people will handle it, not yours. You're either with us or not. You have no—"

"What he's trying to say, John," I cut Garrett off before he roped Wayne into a corner and forced him to come out blazing, "is that you're out of your saddle here. We got this."

Below and behind us in the stateroom, Paige snored like a man.

Wayne said to me, "What's your plan?"

"*We* call it in. MacDill decides what to do, but I'll suggest that we anchor. It will draw less attention. They can scour the boat for leads to Paretsky. The sooner, the better. We take off on *Impulse.*"

Garrett said, "We settled?"

Paige snorted.

Wayne gave Garrett a glance and then came back to me. He nodded. Twice.

We anchored five miles off Bunce Pass. Wayne and Garrett brought the two deckhands into the stateroom for further questioning. Garrett had untied them, hoping to gain a little cooperation. He had questioned them briefly, and I wanted to see if I could pump more information out of them before we surrendered them. I gave them the physical description, minus the wig and glasses, of the man who attacked me in the elevator. They confirmed that he was the man they knew as Paulo Guadarrama. They were never privy to conversations between Paretsky and Guadarrama. Paretsky had taken off on the dinghy earlier that night and not informed them where he was going. They had not seen Guadarrama in the last forty-eight hours.

Guadarrama had made the arrangements to charter the boat. They were instructed to address Paretsky as 'Mr. Alex' at all times. No last name. They reiterated that they never heard him addressed by any other name. Mr. Hoover was a blank. I brought up a picture of Renée Lambert. She was not familiar to them.

"What's going to happen to us?" the skinny one with a blue plug in his left lobe said. They sat next to each other on a white leather couch. Each wore a black T-shirt with *Southern Breeze* in baby blue across the front.

"Not up to me."

"What's your guess?" Skinny said.

"If you're telling me the truth? You'll be back at Rackman's in a few days with a good story, a drink in your hand, a woman on your lap, and a Cayman sunset. If you're lying or being the least bit disingenuous, you'll never see the Caymans again." I knelt down in front of him. His Caribbean-green eyes were wide, the skin around them etched with tributary crevices. He'd never known a cloudy day. "What's your name?"

"Sallinger. My friends call me Sally."

"Is there anything else, Sally, you'd like to add or tell me at this time?"

He hesitated. "What's dis...dis—"

"Not a hard-core lie, but lacking truth and sincerity." He nodded in approval.

His buddy looked like he drank a six-pack every night. Six-Pack said, "Maybe you should tell 'em, Sally, 'bout Lynette and the moustache. I think they might be interested, might fall under that 'dis' word."

"Why do I care about Lynette and the moustache?" I said.

"'Cause if you're looking for Mr. Alex," Sally said, "it might just help you a bit."

"Just might at that," Six-Pack added.

"Why don't you do that, Sally?" I pulled up a matching leather chair and sat across from my two new friends. I leaned in, elbows on my knees, hands clasped in front of me. "Lynette and the moustache."

"Well." Sally shifted his weight so he sat higher. "We was in Sint Maarten, you know, moored off Philipsburg, and they, that is Mr. Alex and Paulo, went ashore. We took them in the tender."

"When was this?"

"Well, let's see. Mr. Alex, he was on and off a lot, sometimes only staying a few days. Must have been right before we picked up Ms. Paige. So, maybe like three, five weeks back?" He turned to Six-Pack. "That sound about right?"

"It was a Sunday."

"How you remember that?" Sally furrowed his eyebrows.

"Dunno. Never track the days. But I always know when it's Sunday. I call Mom."

Sally turned back to me. "There you go. It was a quick trip over there and back." He leaned in toward me. "Listen,

I can't incriminate myself here, can I? I mean, if I help you out, you're not going to bust me for running a little Mary Jane, are you? I'm not saying that I—"

"Couldn't care less."

"OK, well then. So we drop them off, and we head over to Benny's Beach Bar. Big charity bash going on. Place was jammed. Girls cover their body with whipped cream and a guy, or a girl, it don't matter, gets a lick for a five. A ten spot gets you a long lick, and for twenty—"

"Stick to the story."

"OK, right. So, we pick up our supply there, you know?" He shrugged. "Some of it's a little more advanced than weed, but nothing big, man. It's a way to like, augment—I think that's the word—our income. We just run it for friends and—"

"Get to why I care about this story."

"OK, right. Well, we're—"

"Who's 'we'?"

He tilted his head toward Six-Pack and continued. "OK, so we're in the back room, and I peer out the door, and there's Mr. Alex at the bar. He don't drink, you know? And I think, what's Mr. Alex doing here? Paulo was there, but he was turned, like he was looking out for Mr. Alex's backside."

"You said the place was packed?"

"Well, I said it was ja—yeah, packed will do. But they was all lookin' at the girls. I gotta tell you," he pitched a few degrees toward me, "when it gets down to just a little whipped cream left? I've seen C-notes fly like seagulls in a hurricane. There was this one time—"

I raised my hand, palm out, and said, "Lynette and the moustache."

"OK, I got it. So Mr. Alex, he pulls out an envelope and hands it to this stiff next to him. Real Caribbean Joe, you know? Tan slacks, button shirt, dark shades—he was the whole package, man. Now I'm in the back room with—I don't need to tell you my guy, do I?"

"No," I lied. I wanted the story out of him as fast as possible. MacDill would get to the finer points.

"I ask my man who the guy with Mr. Alex is, 'cause I never seen him before, and my buddy says he's seen him once or twice with different dudes, none that you would ever want to cross."

"Was Paretsky disguised in any manner?"

"Who?"

"Mr. Alex."

"Yeah, that's just it." He nodded in excitement. "Mr. Alex had this woolly worm across his lip. Me and Ace—"

"Ace?"

He nodded again toward Six-Pack. Six-Pack, who was relaxed deep into the couch, smiled at me. His teeth had come in every way but straight. It was a pretty bad deck that carried him as an ace. His T-shirt was half tucked in. A worthless stevedore. I refocused on Sally. "We thought he was, you know, sporting it to pick up a girl. He had a collared shirt and sunglasses that P. Diddy would kill for."

"You hear anything?"

"Naw. Was too far away, and the crowd was whippin'." He cocked his head and smiled. "Hey, you get it? They was covered with whipped cream, and I said that—"

"Lynette," I prompted him.

"OK, sure, Lynette."

"Who is she?"

"The owl. That's what everyone called her."

ROBERT LANE

"Sally, you've got to dig deep and get crystal clear for me real fast."

"OK. You see, Benny's got this big, hollow, wood owl that watches over the bar. Used to call her Squeaky, but one day someone calls her Lynette, you know, after that girl who tried to kill President…oh hell, I don't even re—"

"Ford. Lynette Fromme. Nickname was Squeaky."

"Right, man." He nodded in approval. "You got it. So the name sticks. Benny, he starts calling the owl Lynette, but the old salts still call her Squeaky. You know when that was?"

"Fromme's assassination attempt with an empty chamber? September 1975."

"No, man. I mean when they started calling the owl Lynette?"

"No. Why?"

Sally shook his head. "I don't know, man. Thought maybe you'd been there and—"

"Move along."

"OK. So I tell my buddy that's the guy that we work for, you know? Tell him we're on the *Breeze*. You could see her out in the harbor from the bar. I'll tell you something, this here's a nice boat." He glanced around the stateroom. Probably never spent as much time in it as he was now. "For my money, seventy-foot is perfect. It's a great combination of size and agility. It don't take much crew, easy to keep spotless, effortless to dock—those bow thrusters, they suck tit big-time—and all the size anyone needs unless they got the larger dick syndrome, you know, just want to watch other people watch them as they motor in. Some of these guys— trust me, this ain't my first boat—that's all they care about. Here I come, mama, look how big I am. I'm telling you—"

"Sally?" I cut him off.

256

"Yeah?"

"You seem like a nice guy."

"Thank you. I do try to—"

"I am going to bash in your teeth unless you get to the point. And if you say 'OK' one more time, you will die here and now. Understand?"

"O—" He nodded, shuddered, and shriveled down like an admonished dog.

"Tell me about Lynette, the squeaky owl."

Six-Pack, without altering his position in the corner of the sofa, laid the ace on the table. "Lynette, the squeaky owl, watches over the bar. Benny got tired of missing booze and finally relented. He put a security camera, pretty much frowned upon in that part of the world, in the owl's mouth. You can't even see the thing when you're looking for it. But Mr. Alex and his business partner? They were right under it. Passing envelopes. Opening envelopes. Smile, baby; your ass is on high-def Candid Camera. I'm telling you—you get that tape; you read their lips."

Told you he was worthless.

I stood up and said to Six-Pack, "The man stupid enough to draw on my friend." He nodded. "Who was he?"

"Mr. Guadarrama knew him. He didn't come with the boat; he came with the men. Understand? Like the three of them had chartered boats before."

That explained why he greeted us with a gun. "Anything else?"

Sally said, "That picture of that girl you showed us?"

"This one?" I again brought up a picture of Renée Lambert on my phone. He nodded.

"Yeah. I don't want you thinking that I'm being dis... in...jenny...ous. Is that it?"

"Close enough."

"We had time off one night in Saint Pete. But I think I saw her go on the boat. Paulo was with her. I asked Paulo about it later. He said she was Mr. Alex's girlfriend."

"Still can't believe you did that," Six-Pack said.

"What?" Sally glanced at his friend.

"Asked Paulo about her. Told you, we wanted nothing to do with him."

"She," Sally nodded to my phone, "is a fine-lookin' woman. I'd die to walk with a woman like that. She looks out of Mr. Alex's league. When a man walks with a woman that ain't in his league—I'm not just talkin' looks—he knows it. You know what I mean?"

I did. I said, "OK, anything else?"

"See," Sally said, wiggling around as if he had to use the bathroom, "you do it too."

"Do what?"

"You said, 'OK.' I mean, if that's my worst fault, all I'm saying is—"

I gave him a playful slap across his left cheek. "You're OK, Sally."

I left them and called in the coordinates to MacDill. We waited until we saw two boats approaching, and then we abandoned ship. Garrett carried Paige onto *Impulse* and laid her on the deck along the starboard side, her feet toward the bow. We planned to question her in the morning and then sacrifice her to MacDill. He placed a boat cushion under her head. I would have laid her the other way so that her head was higher than her feet as we cruised, but it didn't matter. Wayne stood off to my right, his left hand back to home position on the white-powder aluminum railing. I planted myself behind the wheel, my left foot not more than six

inches from Paige's head, and took *Impulse* through the channel at five thousand rpms.

Garrett called in the information on Benny's Beach Bar.
Hopefully, they still had the tape. I wondered what Paige
would divulge when she woke up. With luck, once sober she
would be a fountain of information about Paretsky's operation and Renée Lambert. I felt as if I were transporting a
great vessel, a Greek goddess, who would clear my questions,
balance my universe, and bring peace to my soul. She stirred
on the deck. I looked down at her.

She vomited on my new shoe.

CHAPTER 35

The next morning I returned from my run and found Paige—sitting in my chair—and Kathleen and Morgan in the screened porch. What part of "Get her the hell out of my life" did he not comprehend?

I ignored them and went to the side of the house, where I rinsed off under the outdoor shower. A steady, warm breeze, like a hair dryer on low, blew the palm fronds in a uniform direction. They looked like thin girls with big hair, bending over. My palm trees never had a gender, but at that moment they were all girls. I changed into shorts and a T-shirt with a pocket and joined them on the porch. My insides had not cooled down yet, and despite the shower I broke into a seeping sweat.

"I told you to keep her away until I called," I said to Morgan as a greeting to the trio.

"He didn't have a choice," Kathleen cut in before Morgan could answer. "I'm giving a lecture today, and I didn't feel like canceling or being a no-show." Her voice had a hard, dismissive edge to it. What'd I do now? She wore beige shorts, an emerald-green, silk T-shirt, a thin necklace, and sandals. Her hair was tied behind her, and I wondered if I would ever see it down again. She sat between Morgan and Paige, who still wore her gold dress and still sat in my chair.

Paige didn't look so hot.

I could say she resembled a French call girl the morning the *poilus* flagged taxis to the western front, or the last underweight sophomore to stumble out of a Florida State frat party, or Madison Avenue's stock "before" picture rolled out for cosmetic accounts or—

Paige didn't look so hot.

I said to Kathleen, "What part of a man taking an elevator up to kill you did not scare common sense into you?"

Kathleen stood and launched herself toward me. "You certainly have no problem with exerting *your* free will." She knifed a look at Paige. "Nice to know I was missed." She bolted out the door.

"Her?" I blurted out. "She's a…she's a—"

"She's a what?" Paige demanded. "Last night's trick? Like I told her; all I know is that I woke up in your bed, and you were already gone. I don't remember anything. Oh, gee," she cocked her head to the side, "maybe I do. You slapped me. You slapped me hard and then kissed me. Like that really makes up for it." She shook her head. "Swear to Almighty. I must have a word tattooed inside each thigh. *Losers* on one and *welcome* on the other."

She buried her face in my favorite coffee cup. The cup had silhouettes, set against the US flag, of Mickey, Goofy, and Donald marching in procession. Her feet touched my Tinker Bell alarm clock, and she rocked it gently with her right big toe, nearly tipping it over. I often set the alarm to commence the drinking portion of the day. Her toenails were painted like coquina shells, each one layered with strands of soft colors. How long did that take?

We worked things out, but it wasn't easy, and I'm sure not rehashing it. Kathleen finally accepted that Paige— although Paige claimed total memory loss outside of the slap and kiss and in no manner came to my defense—and I had not slept together. She was only in my bed because my guest bedroom was without a bed. Would Kathleen harbor future doubts, assuming we had a future? I'd had no idea that a new bed could have made that much difference in my life. Next time the deliveryman calls, you bet I'm jumping all over that, survey and all. Garrett came in around the third inning and backed me up, but not before he played ignorance long enough to entertain himself, watch me squirm, and nearly dynamite the whole mess.

What I had done was place Paige gently into my bed and, still feeling guilty about the face slap, given her a light kiss on the forehead. I slept on the couch. I prefer to believe that her recollection of my kiss was a testament to the life force of my lips rather than her inability, as a drunk, to totally check out.

Morgan joined Kathleen at the end of the dock. Garrett said we had about fifteen minutes. I started in on Paige, who, not to make a big deal of it, still sat in my chair (it faced southwest) and drank from my mug. I had a list of questions to fly through. I paced the room as I fired them.

"Where did you meet him?"

"Do we have to do this now?"

"Where did you meet him?"

"Key West."

"When?"

"Couple weeks a—"

"Tell me all about him."

She blew her breath out the right corner of her mouth. She'd make a good Popeye. "He paid me to be pretty. Invited me on board. Said we'd do some cruising. Thought it'd be cool, you know? Said he was just back from Sint Maarten and London before that. Sounded like a good life."

"Tell me about Paulo Guadarrama, the Guardian."

"Why the monotone questions—you always like—"

"Answer me."

She puffed out a breath that flipped her bangs. "On and off the boat. Held meetings but never talked much in front of anyone. Got the feeling that he stayed nearby. They yakked together on the phone."

"Do you recognize this girl?" I held up a picture of Renée Lambert.

"Nope."

"Do you know the name Renée Lambert?"

"Nope."

"Did he tell you where he was going last night when he left the boat?"

"No—"

"Do *not* use that word again." I took the chair next to her and leaned into her space. Her breath smelled like toothpaste. Probably used my brush. A strand of hair fell over her left eye. I reached out and tucked it behind her ear. Her shoulders trembled. A gold earring in the shape of a ship's anchor hung from her left earlobe. Her right ear was naked.

"Last night." I placed my hands on my knees; I didn't trust them. "You told me that you recognized Renée Lambert, knew the name, and gave me a lecture on boomerang love. Sound familiar? Listen to me, Paige Godfrey." I shifted my weight even closer to her. Her eyes never left mine, but she shrank away as if the chair was gathering her in. "I think you're a good girl who stepped onto a bad boat. Just how bad that boat was you'll find out in a few minutes when some men come to haul you away for what they refer to as official questioning. Are you with me so far?"

"I didn't do anything. I just—"

"I know. Tell the truth, and you'll be fine. Lie, and that face slap will seem like child's play. Now let's give it another try, shall we? Do you recognize this girl?" I held up the picture of Renée Lambert, but my eyes never lost contact with hers.

"Yes."

"Do you know the name Renée Lambert?"

"Yes."

"Why did you just lie?"

"You scare me—what the hell do you think?"

"Spill it."

"She's his ex." She wiggled up in her seat and brought her knees up under her, Indian style. Her coquina toenails disappeared under her smooth, tan legs. "You know, he picked me up when she dropped out." She shrugged her shoulders. "I was the next one."

"When was the last time you saw her?"

"Paulo brought her in, I don't know, less than two weeks ago. They—Alex, Paulo, and Renée—start yelling at each other. They accused her of taking something. I tried to listen, but they were in the stateroom. I got bits and pieces."

"Sally and Ace told me they never saw her." Sally told me he saw Paulo and a girl who looked like Renée board the boat, but he wasn't positive.

"They weren't on the boat. Shore leave."

"Why was she there?"

"Dunno. Like I said, Paulo hauled her in one evening. He still liked her."

I assumed Paulo hauled her in the night he tracked her down at the Valencia. "Alex still liked her?" I said to clarify her last statement.

"Yeah, you could tell. He was taken with...Renée." She glanced out toward the water. "I was—whatever. Give me a refill, will you?" She reached over and handed me the mug with my three buddies on it. I got up and went to the kitchen. When I returned, she had just finished raking her hands through her hair. She stopped when I entered the porch. I put the mug in front of her. She sat poised, with her legs crossed.

"You told me last night," I took my seat but didn't lean into her as I had done before, "that Renée said something about Alex killing a bird." I was eager to move on to Paretsky but first wanted to clear the air about last night's comments.

Paige gave a nervous nod. "First of all, I haven't a clue what I said last night, so don't trot out that lead again." A brief smile and a nose crinkle. It was a classic combination, and I'm sure it opened about any door she desired. "After the shouting match, on the way off the boat, Renée grabbed me. Told me to get off, said she thought they were danger-ous men. You know, save yourself. Stuff like that. Like I was going to let the ex tell me what to do? But I knew," she left me and gazed over my shoulder, "that I was on a bad boat."

"What exactly did she say about the bird?"

"Not much. Apparently, Alex was going to kill some bird, and I'm telling you, that girl—and she's a wacko—was pissed. That's not what they questioned her on, though. Like I said, they thought she'd stolen something. The bird thing was on her own." She puffed out her cheeks and then lurched forward and gave a dry heave.

I went to the kitchen and returned with a bottle of water and a banana. "Here." I placed them in front of her. "Eat. Drink." She handed me back the water. I unscrewed the cap and gave it back to her. She ate the banana and took a long sip from the bottle.

"Tell me about last night," I said. "About Alex and Paulo."

She swallowed and draped the peel across the Copacabana ashtray on the end table. "Paulo, I don't know about. Alex left about seven or so. I invited some people over that I met at the Valencia. We drank pretty heavy—bet you didn't figure that out—and Alex suddenly said he had to leave."

"Did he tell you where he was going?"

She explained that Paretsky had abruptly left the *Southern Breeze*, returned a short time later, and departed again with a suitcase. He'd returned within half an hour, placed the suitcase in the dinghy, and slipped away.

"You question him on the suitcase?"

"Said he'd be back later, that Paulo was dead. Creepy and calm—just told me. That's when I went in my room and got my peashooter. The captain chased everyone off the boat and had Sally and Ace untie us. We took off."

"Any way of contacting Paretsky?"

"No, sir. I do not." She flashed a tease smile. Her color was starting to come back, and I saw a little bit of the woman I'd first noticed, whose body I'd wanted to smear oil on.

"They're here," Garrett cut in.

I dropped to my knees so my face was in front of hers. I placed my hands on the arms of her chair, boxing her in. "He's a dangerous man. Tell me something that will help me out here."

"I just don't know that much." She brought up her right hand and twirled her hair. She was not the wealth of information on Paretsky I had hoped for. My disappointment weighed on me like a backpack of bricks. "Do I look as bad as I feel?" She glanced at Garrett.

"You look swell," I said.

"I was asking *him*." She came back to me. "I can help *you*, though."

"How?"

"That girl?"

"What girl?"

"Your woman."

"Kathleen? What about her?"

"The part where you squirmed and explained that we didn't really sleep together?" She paused, as if I might have already forgotten the conversation from ten minutes ago.

"Yes?"

"She knew that. She knew before you came in the house. She *is* ticked at you, but it has nothing to do with me." Her pug nose crinkled up. How many men fell for that siren song?

Garrett again. "They're waiting." I shot him a look. A few minutes wouldn't hurt.

"She say anything else?"

Paige smiled, brought up both hands, and swept her hair back. "I'm a mess. Mind if I take a shower?" She shifted her gaze from me to Garrett.

"She say any—"

"It's Jake, right?" She stood up, and I did likewise, backing away to allow her space. She was taller than I thought. "All this stuff about Alex, yet you drop him in a nanosecond when I mention Kathleen. And the hippie?"

"Morgan?"

"Whoever. I heard them before I got up. They were talking about you. And if you want to know about what, you'll need to ask them, slap man."

She spun to leave. Garrett took a step toward us. "No shower. There's a truck in the street. They'll take you to Mac-Dill Air Force Base, where you'll be questioned—"

Paige slipped off her dress. No bra.

"—further on your knowledge of Alexander—"

She wiggled out of her panties in a playful manner.

"—Paretsky and any other knowledge that—"

With her right foot, she flung her panties into the air, caught them with her right hand, and tossed them onto Tinker Bell. *My* Tinker Bell alarm clock.

"—you might possess."

"I'll be in the shower," Paige said and kept her eyes on Garrett. "In the event you want to drag me out. Otherwise, boys, I'm gonna need thirty minutes." She sashayed out of the screened porch. She did a full-body turn just before she took the corner to my bedroom. No tan lines.

"Jake?"

"Yes, Paige?"

"Was there a *cow*boy on the boat last night?"

"Yes, Paige, as a matter of fact, there was. A real John Wayne."

She gave a slow, comprehending nod, as if, at least for her, life's big answer was finally laid out. "I wondered where they went."

CHAPTER 36

Garrett greeted the men in the SUV, returned, and asked me to fix two plates of scrambled eggs. I've seen Garrett pin down seven men while medics attended the wounded behind him, but he can't crack an egg. He disappeared back out the front door with the plates. Paige emerged from my bedroom, looking more like the million-dollar girl that Paretsky had enticed aboard in Key West and who I had salivated over while nursing a Bloody Mary at the Valencia. Her gold sundress wasn't as wrinkled as it'd been earlier, and I wondered what trick of the trade she knew.

"One more for you." I put down my empty coffee cup. "In Key West, did he ever leave the boat? Take you to dinner, shopping?"

"Listen," she glanced down and smoothed out her dress, "did I have any shoes on last night?"

"No. I've got an extra pair of flip-flops you can have."

"I'm a buyer. My other stuff on the boat?"

"It'll be returned. Key West."

"Right-o." She punched her fist out. "You do like your questions. That's how I met him. But I believe the only time and reason he left any boat was to pick up the next blonde. We had drinks at Casa Marina. Even got him to sit around one of the fire pits one night. But that was it. My turn."

"Sure."

"Your friend, Mr. Greek God. He single?"

I handed her my card. "Ask him, when he gives you the flip-flops."

"I might if I get the courage. He's a little intimidating."

"You said I scared you, but you came around."

"Silly." Paige crinkled her nose again. Back in the game. "Bad boys—*real* bad boys—don't wear shorts."

Garrett came back in and escorted her to the black SUV in the street. My own truck occupied the driveway. Morgan and Kathleen returned from the dock, and Morgan said he'd be back in a minute.

"Morgan's running me over to the college," Kathleen said. Her voice dull, all business. "After that, if you want, I'll go back on his boat. Your call."

Casa Marina would have cameras on the bar. A chance for some clear shots of Paretsky. Maybe he goofed and paid with a credit card. I should have asked Paige how the bill was settled. Between Lynette and Casa Marina, Alexander Paretsky was like a pinfish with a ten-foot cast net sinking around him. I needed to—

"I'm talking to you."

"Back on the boat." I dropped my thoughts and put a hand on each of her shoulders. I wanted to pack her up and stick her in my pocket. "But after your class, and after we get a chance to talk."

I placed my hand on her cheek and down to the edge of her mouth. Paige Godfrey was a beautiful woman, but I'd trade a full-body view of her for a single smile from Kathleen. Any day. Any time.

"Let's walk the beach," I said, "this evening. Sunset. You can tell me that everything's going to be OK. Even if it's a lie."

"You'd live with a lie?" She rolled her tongue inside her left cheek.

"To my judgment day. I would revel in your—"

"Touching." She patted me on my left shoulder like an object that needed minor attention. I didn't mind the interruption, as I had no idea where I was going with that line. I felt awkward standing next to her, and I had never felt that way before. I couldn't remember the last time we'd had forward momentum to our relationship. That's right—London. Before I lied. Before I told her (for those not keeping track) for the second time to go back to her books.

"You think a sunset stroll will win the girl?" she said.

"Don't you ever get tired of thinking?"

Her eyes narrowed, and her shoulders slumped. "I do. I really do. All the time."

"Let's give it a break. Walk the beach. Watch the sun slip away. If I get lucky, you'll let me hold your hand, although I'll lie in school tomorrow and say I copped a feel."

The world's most important person smiled at me.

Za-za-boom, baby. I'm comin' up now.

Morgan returned, and Kathleen climbed on his Harley. She leaned in and wrapped her arms around him. As the bike roared away, the black SUV that had escorted Paige passed them coming back. It pulled up to the curb in front of me. The rear window that held my reflection eased down, and Paige Godfrey appeared.

"The bird?"

"What about it?"

"Remember I said that Renée told me that Alex was going to kill a bird? That wasn't entirely it. She said that Alex *arranged* for him be killed, you know, like assisted suicide. I was like, what do you mean? She said this bird had

killed her mother and wanted to die. Crazy, right? Birds killing people? Assisted bird suicide? You can understand why
I tuned that wacko out. But, Travis, Jake Travis, you wanted
details, so there you go. Alex helped a cardinal die. The cardinal killed some other lady. Screwed-up world, isn't it?"

The window whizzed up and closed with a thud. I stared
at myself until the SUV lurched forward. I was dying for
someone to tell me something I didn't know.

I nearly got my wish.

CHAPTER 37

A few hours later, everybody in the Milky Way had clear shots of Alexander Paretsky camped out at Benny's Beach Bar sporting a ridiculous, slightly crooked Chaplin moustache. More important, we were able to lift numbers and addresses from the papers that Paretsky and his business partner exchanged. His compatriot was identified as an arms dealer who worked both sides of the fence. The outdoor bar at Casa Marina also came through. He paid by cash, but the pictures were gold. I told the group at MacDill to flip on the Garmin in *Southern Breeze*. It would track the boat's movement in the event that Ace and Sally couldn't recall the exact time and place of each port, although I knew that Ace was solid for one day a week.

We had recently gained access to the bank accounts of the arms dealer and had not shut him down for this very reason—to scoop more garbage into the net. They would pull the same play on Paretsky: don't let the mark know that you have his banking information. Track his movement and gather names, associates, and more bank digits. Once you have a man's banking information, you have him by the nuts. You milk it for all you can, pick the time and place, and step out of the shadows with force, timing your move to have extracted as much information as possible from him before he caused further damage. The downside? Although we knew where his money, or at least some of his money, was, Paretsky was still loose. The animal I'd been dispatched to kill was out there and likely knew that he was being cornered.

I called PC, who was still canvassing Donald Lambert's neighborhood. I knew if he found anything he would call, but I wanted to check that box. Nothing new. I told him to stand down. We never found the boat the Guardian used to approach Donald Lambert's house. He likely wired it miles away, and no way could we cover that much territory. The hard fact is that in any investigation, the majority of your casts don't even register a nibble.

I hit Wayne's number and told him what Paige said. He already knew. Whatever loop I was in, he was there as well.

Rondo called.

"You get my message?" he asked.

"No, tell me."

"I sent you a text last ni—"

"Busy night. What do you got?" I was by my outdoor shower, holding my left shoe under the spray, a bottle of water in my right hand, and my phone wedged between my shoulder and ear. Should have done it last night; stuff really sticks.

"Renée Lambert. She responded to the message board. Wants to meet you."

"When?" A great blue heron landed on the edge of my seawall. It glided down to the low-tide beach and set up shop. The bird feeds itself, and its species survives by being motionless, a stark contrast to humans. Sounds like that should mean something, but I don't think it does.

"Said she's in town today. Your pick, but make it public."

I told Rondo to have her meet me at the pink hotel, high noon, beachside bar. Not to worry, I'd recognize her.

Renée Lambert for lunch. Kathleen tonight. Alexander Paretsky on the run. I needed all three to drop into place: Kathleen back in the fold, Renée Lambert willing and able to explain the big bang theory—or at least what the cardinal's sin was—and Paretsky dead. Maybe Renée would even have a clue as to Paretsky's location.

A lone woman in a sailboat, one of my favorite things to see, glided past the end of my dock. She tacked south. All dreams are south. Bet she was off to Somewhere Island to moor in Brigadoon Bay. I wondered if I would ever get there—if a certain someone would buy into that.

I changed into a button-down, silk shirt, taking my good, sweet time with the buttons, linen pants, and sandals. A real bad guy today.

It hit me as I skipped out the door. *A stark contrast to humans.*

Paretsky wouldn't be motionless. He would either flee or fight. He was either a thousand miles away or watching me. There was a distinct possibility that the only thing I'd accomplished was to make him aware of my presence while I was dicking around making certain I didn't ruin another shirt.

CHAPTER 38

The only ones who'd gotten breakfast that morning were the two men who collected Paige. I was famished. I slammed the truck door and scampered across the street. The pink, Moorish-style hotel was built in the 1920s by an Irishman from Virginia, named after a character in a play by a French dramatist that was turned into an English opera, and is set in a town named for its Russian counterpart.

Give me a jingle if you have a clue what that means.

I rounded the towel stand and helped myself to a plastic cup of citrus water from the cooler. The towels were no longer neatly folded and stacked but heaped together in the bin. Clean ones were hustled out from the laundry, still warm, in a gallant effort by the laundry regiment to keep up with demand. I nearly tripped over a rug rat chasing a ball that had escaped the pool. The resort was over capacity with oiled mannequin skin. Waiters scurried with trays on their shoulders, and a singer, with his back to the gulf and a harmonica mounted in front of his mouth, strummed "Hollow Man," although the tempo was too slow.

She was at the bar. Her dark hair shrouded her back, and she sat erect as if she were bracing for a cat one. The high barstools on either side of her were taken. Guests were stacked up two deep, jockeying for position to flag the attention of frenzied bartenders. I angled in next to her.

"Renée?"

She spun her head. "Yes? Mr. Travis?"

"It's Jake. Follow me. I know a quieter spot."

I pulled back her heavy barstool and then switched positions so that I led. I led her past the second pool, rimmed with people sitting on the edge and nursing colored drinks; I led her past the boardwalk that gave way to the beach where a Cornhole game was taking place with the enthusiasm normally reserved for Saturday-night football rivalries; I led her past the shower where I rinse after my morning run, through the gate, and I led her to the second, smaller bar that was adjacent to the restaurant. A couple vacated their seats as we approached. Without breaking stride, I led her to the empty high chairs and pulled one back.

"My," she adjusted herself in the chair, "are you always so lucky?"

"Luck's a big part of my plan." I took the chair next to her. I *was* lucky. Guadarrama had gotten the jump on me, and I'd lived to fight another day.

Although we were outside, we faced the inside of the bar. A pass-through window was in front of us. I slid the debris from the previous couple over the mahogany surface and into the restaurant. It was cooler in the restaurant, and it was like inserting my hand into a refrigerator.

"You were a hard lady to find." I shifted my weight and signaled the bartender.

"That was a big part of *my* plan."

It worked out well that she was to my right, as I had trouble hearing on my left. The bartender halted in front of us across the counter, in the cool air. She hastily cleared the dishes that I had shoved into her territory. We ordered drinks.

Renée wore beige shorts and a blue, button-down shirt that was tucked in. Layers of necklaces were visible above the top few open buttons. She hit me as the type of woman who, despite her youth, had not only grown weary of the stares but also did as little as possible to elicit them. Then again, her mother had committed suicide, and her lover turned out to be an international assassin who had caused the murder of her father. I wasn't sure she'd put all those pieces together, but I wouldn't bet against it. She took her right hand, reached across the back of her neck, and pulled her hair over her right shoulder. She crossed her right leg over her left leg and demanded, "Who are you?"

The drinks arrived. I reached for my beer as if it was the culmination of every thought I'd had since my eyes first greeted the day. Renée kept her guarded, yet curious, eyes on me.

"I'm—"

"How do you know about Renée Sutherland?"

"I—"

"Are you with a law agency?"

I took a slow drink. I gazed out toward the sparkling waters of the Gulf of Mexico. Above the gulf, a highway of birds kept vigilant watch for any fish foolish enough to approach the surface. I turned back to her. Her eyes were waiting for me.

She cocked her head. "Sorry." She reached for her chardonnay and took a sip, seemed to consider whether to place it back down or not, and went in for seconds. "I've been," she gave a dismissive shake of her head, "under a lot of stress." She arched her eyebrows. "That's a colossal understatement."

"My condolences for your father."

"You knew him?"

"Only briefly. If I'd been on my guard a little more, you would still have him. I..."

Nothing accentuated my failure to protect Donald Lambert as much as having to face his daughter. It had been foolish of me to not prepare for this moment with her. Her presence amplified the poignancy of my failure.

"I'm sure you did what you—"

"I could have done better." I bitterly cut her off. "How did you learn?"

She briefly explained that after her father didn't return phone calls, she'd called the police, who confirmed his death. After that she went underground, afraid to talk to anyone.

"My question stands." She used her elbows to shift higher into the chair. "I got your messages on the WAP members' board, but who *are* you?"

I told her I was a contract worker for the government looking into Paretsky's affairs. She listened without comment. I kept it brief. I doubt she fell for half of it.

"Do you know where he is?" I asked.

"No."

"Positive?"

"Not a clue."

"Hungry?"

"Excuse me?"

"Would you like lunch?"

"I could use a bite."

Thank God.

I leaned in and snatched a menu for her. We ordered fish tacos and iced tea with lemon. I kicked off my sandals, offered a silent prayer for the food to come quickly, and said, "What's your story?"

"What do you want to know?"

"Alexander Paretsky."

She took a supportive sip from her wineglass, placed it back on the wooden counter, and uncrossed her legs. I reached over the bar, grabbed a few cardboard coasters, and scattered them in front of us.

"I met him, Alexander—Alex—a year or so ago. Charming. Rich. Polite. Considerate. Smart. Got the snapshot? I enjoyed his company, although he was more into me than I was into him."

"How do you know that?"

Renée's lips curled up in a smile that disappeared just as quick. "We know. Trust me." She seemed to consider me and then added, "Don't worry, that's the way we like it."

Am I that transparent?

"Alex and I were staying in his London flat. It was a beautiful Sunday, early summer. He asked if I wanted to go to a carnival. Alex, for a man so twisted, was...so romantic. He said that Sundays in June were the best days of the year, and Sunday morning the best part of the day." She shook her head and studied her glass. "How do you even reconcile that with the monster he was? Looking back, I really had no clue. We ended up at Granville Estate. Because you posed online as Renée Sutherland, I assume, Mr. Tra—"

"It's Jake."

"I assume, Jake, that you know about Cardinal Antinori?"

"I did my homework. I also had a lengthy conversation with Cynthia Richardson."

"You met with Cynthia?" Her eyes widened.

"I did."

"Where?"

"At the estate and later in London."

"When?"

"Recently."

"Why?"

"To see if the murder of your father had anything to do with the murder of Cardinal Antinori."

"Did you meet her daughter?"

"Lizzy."

"She's named after my mother. Do you know that?"

"So I learned."

She brushed back strands of hair that had escaped her right shoulder. She had a mole, a Hershey's pellet, just below her left ear. "Did Cynthia tell you about my mother and the cardinal?"

"Only that they exchanged harsh words when your mother visited two years ago. I understand that you lost her around six months ago."

"Yes, she was troubled...had been for a long time. I wouldn't exactly say they exchanged harsh words. My mother, from what she told me, planted her feet and screamed in the good cardinal's face. I doubt in his life he'd ever uttered anything that he thought bore resemblance to harshness. That, you see, was part of the issue."

The fish tacos arrived. Each plate held three lined up on a stainless-steel rack. I took a shark bite out of one of mine. She was more considerate of hers.

"Alex and the carnival," I prompted her rudely when she was in midchew.

She finished at her own pace. "Alex said...excuse me." She paused for a sip of iced tea. "He said he knew the cardinal and that he was a financial supporter of his works. But when we pulled into the estate, he told me that he went by the name of Mr. Hoover—you know, like the vacuum cleaner? Said I needed to play along. I asked why, and he just chuckled and said because he erased all the dirt. But that day changed everything. After the cardinal had private words with me, I knew, or at the very least was highly suspicious, that Alex was not the romantic Sunday-morning man I thought he was."

"What were your thoughts when he told you he went by another name?"

"He traveled a lot internationally; it wasn't like we were together twenty-four-seven, so I just went with it." She paused, and I gave myself an A for not barging in. I wondered if she was good for all three of her fish tacos. Mine were disappearing like a plate of glazed donut holes at a Boy Scout meeting. "But I knew it was wrong," she continued. "You know, those nagging feelings you get but pay no attention to?" Her words drifted off, and I had a good idea where her mind was sailing. Renée Lambert's actions and decisions had resulted in the death of her father. We would have to cross that river.

"Strike you as an odd pair, Antinori and Paretsky?"

"You notice the physical resemblance?"

"Perhaps. Both slight men." I also recalled the almost feminine eyebrows both men had. I harbored deeper suspicions—my snowflakes were piling up fast. I gave her the opportunity to share my suspicions.

"Did Alex divulge anything else about his relationship with Antinori?"

"Like what?"

"Any passions, pastimes, commonalities?"

"Not really." She didn't take the bait. "I didn't think they were friends as much as they were acquaintances. Alex was a lot younger and certainly wasn't the church type. My mother, who shared most everything with me, had already poisoned me about the late cardinal. I wasn't even sure I wanted to meet him."

"Poisoned you?"

"She said Antinori said some horrible things to her as a child when he counseled her over the death of her child-hood friend, Renée Sutherland. Things that, although she was never specific with me, she never got out of her head. I've always blamed him for her madness. The church planted a disease in her mind, and it festered and eventually, despite her best efforts, took her. When Alex introduced us, I cut him off; the words just spit out of my mouth. I proclaimed myself Elizabeth Lambert's daughter. Told him that I was named after Renée Sutherland, and what do you think of *that*?"

"How did that fly?"

"I rang his—no, I ruffled his feathers. Right? I can tell you this: he was one dazed cardinal."

"What did he say?"

"Paretsky or Antinori?'

I shrugged. "Both."

She raised her left index finger as if to signal to give her a minute. She stuffed the remains of the second taco into her mouth. I took the occasion to finish my third. She rinsed hers down with wine.

"Antinori first. He apologized. Tripped over his words. Said he tried to explain to my mother, to make up. He seemed horrified that I was with Alex. And Alex? Baffled. Just stood there."

"I'm not following. Paretsky didn't know you had family connections to Cardinal Antinori and Granville Estate?"

"No. I mean, I thought about telling him, you know, on the drive up, but I didn't. No way..." She shook her head. "No way of knowing what would have happened if I had told him. Maybe he would have turned around. You have no idea how many times I've played that in my head. I should have told him on the way there. Maybe he…" Her jaw tightened.

"Don't," I said, but the river was upon us.

"Maybe he would have changed his mind. My actions killed my father, not your lack of guard."

"There's no way of—"

"Oh, *please*," she flared up. "If I had told Alex on the way to Granville Estate that my family had some history there? He would have spun on a dime. But I didn't. No reason. Just didn't. Terrible, isn't it?" She had been staring past me, but now her eyes focused on mine. "That something so…so defining, so *ending*, could be caused by something so casual. An omission, a slip…not even an act or words, but merely the lack of either."

I reached out and touched her left shoulder. "It does no good." I thought I should and could do better, but sometimes all I've got just isn't that much. Maybe I should adopt Porky Pig as my mascot, and when people look to me expecting more I can just roll out, "That's all, folks!"

I withdrew my hand from my awkward gesture, shifted my weight, and drained my beer. I pushed my plate away. I don't tolerate a dirty plate in front of me on a table. Renée reached into a small handbag and dabbed her face with a tissue.

"What happened?" I said and leaned into her. "The private words you mentioned. What did Antinori say on the grounds of Granville Estate that caused you to reevaluate Paretsky?"

"I need a minute. The restrooms?"

I told her where, and then, like in the song, I watched Renée walk away.

What if she didn't come back?

Worse than that—what if she didn't hold the key to why Cardinal Antinori used me to kill him? I had one person pegged as my last hope in the event that Renée came up short. Someone whose measured words to me indicated not only a conflicted mind but also, I'd convinced myself, a desire to tell me.

CHAPTER 39

I fidgeted and kept an eye on the door, as if that would do any good. The bartender cleared my plate. I told her to leave Renée's as it still held a surviving fish taco, which I greatly coveted. I ordered another round.

A man with a cane came through the door. I recalled sharing a raspberry parfait over glasses of chardonnay with Kathleen at Les Deux Magots and observing a man with a cane. The Caned Man, she had named him. I wondered if someday I would be a man with a cane strolling through a hotel door. If, one day, young lovers at a sidewalk café would observe me with distant curiosity.

Two animated teenage girls were next.

A man and a small boy.

Renée.

She strode toward me, tall and poised, with a natural swing in her arms. There was a lot of plastic skin around the pools and the beach, and that made it a relief to look at her. *If nearly every woman is wearing a bikini, then the one that draws the eyes is the one in the shorts and button-down shirt.* You never know when one of life's great truisms will unveil itself to you. I'd have to pass that on to Morgan. He's a great scholar of the gospels.

She reclaimed her seat, nodded at the new glass of chardonnay that was already sweating, and said, "Thank you."

"You were saying?"

"Where were we?"

"The grounds of Gran—"

"Right. Alex and I drifted apart, and Antinori was upon me. Grabbed my arm and told me that Mr. Hoover was a very dangerous man and I needed to get away from him. He said I needed to run. Run away."

I recalled telling Kathleen the same thing and reined that thought in before it took a dark turn.

"Did he say anything more specific?"

"He gushed apologies about my mother but said he was doing me a great favor by divulging that Mr. Hoover was a sick man. Told me only God could save him. We ended up behind the high striker—you know, you swing a big hammer and try to ring the bell? I think Antinori sensed my skepticism. Unsolicited, he gave me dates that Alex had traveled. Cities he'd been to. Knew he'd recently made a couple of round trips down to Key West, where he kept a boat. I told him that I knew him as Alexander Paretsky."

"Did Antinori display any recognition of that name?"

"Claimed to have never heard it, but I thought he was lying. I figured he was covering for himself at that point."

"And Cynthia? Did you see her at the carnival that day?"

"No. That was disappointing. I assumed she'd be there, and I did look, but I never found her. It was all very fast after that. The cardinal's words frightened me, alarmed me. I realized that I'd gotten myself into a situation that I needed to extract myself from. Alex had a friend, called him his guardian. His real name was Paulo Guadarrama. Paulo was Alex's bodyguard slash partner. He often referred to Alex as the Pope, like a kind of nickname. I think he, Paulo, killed my father, but the police aren't telling me much. Did you happen to meet him?"

"Briefly." I wasn't into self-incrimination and wanted to move on to a central question. "I'm curious, though, like everyone. Do you know why Cardinal Antinori was in Kensington Gardens and how it was arranged?"

"I do."

"You do?" I was amazed the wind didn't die and the sea pause its relentless assault upon the shore.

"A few weeks after the carnival, Alex left his computer on one day when he went downstairs to get coffee. His apartment had two floors. His calendar was up, and 'Kensington Gardens, Giovanni, sunrise' was entered on a date. I asked him what that was about."

"He wasn't mad at you?"

"Kidding, right? Fucking furious. But what could he do? I was walking by and saw it. He told me to forget about it.

"The next day he took me to brunch. Told me that something might happen in Kensington Gardens, but it would not be what it seemed. He said that Cardinal Antinori wanted a favor. Alex asked me if I thought we should be able to choose how we die. I didn't like the talk. I remember looking at my spinach quiche and thinking, 'Why can't I just enjoy it?'"

"A favor?"

"His words. I believe I countered with, 'What kind of favor?' He took some time with that. Then he told me." She looked intently at me, her eyes steady, her voice flat. "He told me that someone was going to kill the cardinal on that date, but he thought he would be killing him, Alex. The cardinal had told Alex he wanted to die, but he couldn't take his own life. And so they would, you know, switch out. Said it was an elaborate plan that had been set up months before. That he,

Alex, had been dressing as the cardinal, knowing that some people who wanted him dead were tracking him—at that point I was afraid for my own life.

"He'd told Antinori that he had an inside source, and on a specific morning, someone would be there waiting to kill him—Alex—and Antinori could be there instead." She took a breath and pulled her hair over her shoulder again, although it wasn't necessary. "Alex told me, yapping over quiche, that he and Antinori had grown close, that Antinori was trying to convert him, forgive his sins, stuff like that, but instead Alex was going to grant the cardinal's wish and arrange for his death. He thought there was great irony in that. I was...shaking, petrified."

I tried to hold her eyes, but I couldn't. I took a drink of beer. I always knew. I'd known it since that morning when his eye cut through the fading dark. I knew it when the colonel stared me down on my dock. Here was something I didn't know: someone using me irritated me more than the actual act. That wasn't right, and now *that* disturbed me.

"He lectured me that I could tell no one. But, as he's telling me this? I'm thinking, to hell with the quiche. I've got to get myself away from this man. He spoke of these things in the same manner, the same inflection, that he spoke about Sunday mornings in June. Alex and Paulo were taking off the next day to Key West. The plan was for me to join them after I attended the FTA conference and saw my father. He said he'd bring the boat up to Saint Pete. I told him not on my account."

"*Southern Breeze.*"

"Yes. The following day, while Alex was out, I packed. I noticed a flash drive that he had left out. That never happened. He was meticulous about things like that. I picked it up, on a whim—just like that," she flicked her right hand into the air, "and I bolted out the door. I had on my new Secret Circus jeans. They are so tight, I thought for sure he'd see it.

"I flew to Tampa. Paulo was hot on my trail, but they had no proof that I had taken the flash drive. The cleaning service and the plumber were in that day. I was fortunate that there was so much activity. I'm alive today because of a leaking spray nozzle in the kitchen sink and Alex's obsession with cleanliness—and with me. Paulo tracked me down at the Valencia—middle of the reception on the upstairs veranda—accused me of taking the drive, and escorted me to the boat, but I maintained an indignant innocence."

"You scribbled a note in the ladies' room that night and handed it to Tracy Leary."

Renée's eyes widened. "My God, did I put her in danger? Is she—"

"She's fine. We talked to people you came in contact with. That's all. She passed us the note."

"I was worried, confused. If something happened to me, I wanted to leave a clue. But then I thought I might put her in danger, so I handed her that note that I'm afraid made little, if any, sense. I wanted to explain to her, but we were interrupted."

"You took the flash drive to your father the next day."

Her eyes flashed anger. "Thank you."

"I'm so—"

"Don't."

"Did you know where he hid it?" I eyed the last fish taco. Bet it was cold by now. A fly tried to move in on it, and I waved it away.

"He didn't want me to know. I take it you found it, or we wouldn't be sitting here."

"The bait bucket."

Renée smiled and drifted away for a few seconds. I wondered if she'd fished with her father at the end of the dock. Donald Lambert had said he used to have a second chair at the end of his dock, but that he didn't use it much anymore. "You do know, if you'd never taken it to your father, they would have gone after him anyway."

"You're just saying that." She blinked back tears.

"I'm not."

I gave her a moment and then went back in. "Your father said he couldn't get in contact with you." I'd decided that Donald Lambert, not knowing my intentions, had kept me off her trail until he could hold me in more trust—a day that never came.

"The part where I bolted out the door with the flash drive? I left my phone by my bed. I realized it halfway to the airport, but my heart was pounding out of my chest. I just got a new phone."

"You called him from another phone?"

"Showed up in a cab one night."

Slammin' Tammy Callahan.

I said, "The night Paulo escorted you on board *Southern Breeze*—they let you walk?"

"I know, right? I think they bought my story. It also occurred to me that maybe the whole 'arrange a murder' deal was off, but I was too afraid to bring it up. Plus, they never had me alone. There was another woman—"

"Paige Godfrey."

"Whoever." She wrinkled her face and flipped up both hands. "Alex said he was lonely, and he picked her up and would dump her in a second. I told him he didn't get it; it was over between us. On the way out, I tried to save her. I told her that Alex was an assassin. Was arranging for a cardinal to die, to be murdered. But Bimbo didn't follow me. Probably thinks I'm a wacko."

"Her exact word."

"Excuse me?"

"She called you a wacko."

She nodded. "Tell her I give a fuck." That was twice. She must be fond of the *f* expletive. Renée Lambert would turn heads in a graveyard, but if she and I went on a dinner date, it would be one and out. It's like that sometimes.

Another gnat avoided my backhand. "Listen, you going to eat that last taco?"

"Pardon?"

"The last taco?"

She spread her hands, gave me an incredulous look, and leaned away from me. "By all means."

I reached over and took a bite.

"He wanted to die," I said after I swallowed unchewed, cold fish taco. "Why? Because he sexually abused your mother when she came to him for counseling years ago?"

"*No.* Why would you think that?"

"Everyone's saying he uttered some words to your mother when she was a young girl. That's the story your mother sold, even to you. I don't buy what everyone sells. I think your mother, ashamed of what occurred, altered the story. It was easier for her to explain. Less shame. Easier for her to hear, to live with."

"Nothing of the sort, I assure you. It was what he said, not what he did."

"You're positive?"

"Don't challenge me."

"What did he tell her?" Hard to believe I was wrong.

"That, I don't know."

"You don't—"

"Alex said Antinori would rather die than carry the weight of his words. He had carried them too long. There were other issues. Alex thought Cardinal Antinori was bipolar, you know, people who soar high and then crash? Such people are often larger than life, but they fight dark demons. Evidently, Cardinal Antinori went down one too many times, and he couldn't get up. Breaks my heart. He felt that all his good deeds, all his ideological shifts, meant nothing. His life, his religion, was constructed around beliefs that he had long ago jettisoned. Alex said they had long conversations and that he, the cardinal, wondered what current beliefs would be tossed out and discarded at some future date. I had a hard time giving a shit."

"Certainly your mother told you something. Gave you some clue."

"I said she shared *most* everything with me. Not that. She only said that he said horrible things to her. Things that no twelve-year-old should ever hear. Said she didn't want to prejudice me against the church. Against God."

"How'd that work out?"

She spit out a puff of air.

"There is one who knows," she added. "My mother told me she confided in her."

"She told me she didn't know. That I needed to ask you."

"Then you need to explain to her that the game's up, and she needs to get off her high, stuffy, proper British ass and tell you. For both of our sakes."

CHAPTER 40

I remember that night because Kathleen wore a summer dress that raked the sand as we strolled the beach at sunset and kicked the remnants of waves as they thinned out over the sand. I remember that more than John Wayne coming on like a bull, his long leather coat taking flight behind him. He flew over the dunes, his Civil War cannon blazing at me. I remember that dress more than I remember thinking that Garrett would never get a good shot off; we were too close. I remember the dress more than the bullets, the pain, the blood, the sand that washed into my eyes as I lay dying on the beach where I run. A coquina shell was the last thing I saw, and Paige Godfrey's toenails was my last thought. Kathleen's wet dress the last thing I felt. Her hand the last thing I reached for.

It was the second time that a cowboy came in handy.

Renée and I parted, and I headed back to the house. Garrett and I assumed that Paulo was sent to kill Kathleen, and Paretsky likely fingered me as the one who erased his accomplice. The assumption had strength, as the disc contained my address. We also assumed that Paretsky knew we were on to him and that, at least as of yesterday, he was still in our neck of the woods. We discussed our plan. Garrett said he'd contact Wayne. Morgan had a date with Tracy Leary, who was in town visiting family. He was taking Tracy, her sister and husband, and their recently divorced neighbor on a sunset sail that would conclude with a campfire on a beach. Pretty much his favorite thing to do. He offered to cancel, but I said no.

It was late in the afternoon when Kathleen came around to the screened porch and flitted in the room. The door bounced behind her.

"You going to fix that?" She settled into her seat, and I poured her a glass of red wine.

"Check the fridge; pretty sure it's on your list."

"Good luck with that," she said and studied the glass of wine. "Sophia and I met for drinks at Mangroves." She took a sip. "I've probably had enough."

"Sad words."

To the southeast, in front of us, the sky had morphed to pewter, and the clouds and bay were one color, indistinguishable from each other. Sheets of rain rolled over the distant land like a freight train, but I doubted it would hit us. That track rarely runs over water. Hadley III leapt onto her lap.

The dress.

It was one of those full, body-hugging wraps of cotton. A female cocoon. She had never worn one like that before. It touched the rug when she sat. Low in the front, but not too low. Lower in the back. Thin straps. Layers of beads crossed her chest. That laid-back, chic hippie style like you might see on a summer night at Tanglewood or Blossom, or what a redhead Irish lassie might wear to a fall, Sunday-afternoon sidewalk art show. Cream with wide blue stripes. Big fat deal, right? Different things jingle our chains, and I'm telling you, mine was clanking like a drunken brass circus band, all the clowns blaring their horns.

"Nice dress."

"It's new. You like?"

"I do." Her hair was in a ponytail. It was the color of the sun in the western sky as it fought through thin, late-afternoon clouds. "Won't it get dirty on the beach?"

"And God invented dry cleaners." Her toe nudged Wayne's badge. "What's this?"

I leaned over and picked it up. "John Wayne's badge."

"Naturally. You going to wear it?"

She hadn't a clue to whom I was really referring, nor could I summon the energy to explain. I thought of Wayne's comment. Maybe if I wore it, I'd be an honest man tonight. I started to pin it on, but I didn't feel like putting a hole in my T-shirt, so I wedged it in the pocket. It was a tight fit. "Still mad at me?"

She took a sip of wine and ran her hand down Hadley III's back. "Why? You have a box you're waiting to check off?"

"That reminds me." I retrieved the gift-wrapped package from Harrods and took my seat.

"Pulling out all the stops, aren't you?"

"Haven't a clue what you're talking about."

She unwrapped the box and lifted out the dress she had coveted but passed on. "Thank you." She folded the dress, placed it back in the box, and gazed at me with a thin smile. "You remembered."

"I can't forget."

We tested the ground a little bit more with talk of her day. When that ran its course, I filled her in on my meeting with Renée Lambert.

"The cardinal knew you were going to be there and that you would kill him; you've assumed as much. But why wouldn't he, the cardinal, say something to you? Why just— what was it he said?"

"Forgive me my sin." I stretched my legs out on the glass table.

"Forgive me my sin," Kathleen repeated. Her legs joined mine on the table, her feet sticking out from the bottom of her dress, her right big toe almost touching my calf muscle. Not quite there. Not yet. "Morgan thinks," she continued, "that he was a man without faith. That all he had ever believed in was destroyed and he felt he was better off dead than facing the crowd and renouncing not only his beliefs but those of his flock as well."

"Morgan came up with that?"

"Uh-huh."

Kathleen was not an *uh-huh* type girl. First the dress and now her speech. How long had we been apart?

Hadley III fled Kathleen's lap and pounced on top of the grill. She maneuvered her hindquarters down like she was a chicken getting ready to lay an egg.

"Despite Renée's adamant denial of my thesis…" I inched my leg so that we touched—there we go, everything's back to good. "I still think Antinori abused her mother. When she circled around in his life two years ago, he was confronted with his past. She committed suicide six months ago, and he couldn't live with that."

"Your theory is that Cardinal Antinori sexually abused twelve-year-old Elizabeth…"

"Maiden name is Masterson."

"Decades later, unable to shake his demons, he voluntarily walks the plank."

"You're on board now. You know what they said about Elvis's death?"

"I think you're going to tell me."

"Great career move. If Antinori was about to get busted for something he did to Elizabeth Masterson, then his early exit off the stage was brilliant."

"I see. You're a real buckaroo, did the man a favor, is that it?"

"In no way did I imply that."

"What's next, you going to tell me the church's PR department ordered the hit?"

"Just say it."

She shrugged her left shoulder. "I don't agree."

"About?"

"The whole sexual abuse line. You're wrong."

I don't handle those words well.

She continued. "You're limiting your explanation to your understanding of the world. Plus, the sexual abuse angle doesn't account for the cardinal's theological shift. It was wrong then; it's wrong now. Morgan thinks it was a shift in his beliefs, that—"

"Shift in beliefs? For Christ's sake, Antinori got a stiff one and stuck it—"

"You don't know that. Besides, it's always physical with you, isn't it?"

Here we go. "Be my guest."

"Pain. You always think it's physical. That's how we got here. You can't imagine damage being done—person to person—that's not physical. Words are feathers, and swords are steel; laugh at me, for I don't feel."

"The heck that—"

"My variation of 'sticks and stones.' Worst lie ever taught to children—that words don't hurt."

I give myself a lot of credit here. Despite the wine and vehement internal disagreement over her last comment, I remained silent. There was nothing I could say that would advance my case or make me look good. I clammed up, shut down, and sat back. It was the new me; I would no longer talk, just drink.

I took a swallow of wine, not bothering to let my taste buds get even a hint of the grapes. I leveled my eyes at her hazel-greens and let my breath out. "No. I do not think that."

Her tongue poked out her left cheek. "Morgan says he lost his faith. Besides, there is nothing that points in your theory's direction. To the contrary," she said, placing her wineglass on the side table between us. "Antinori was forthright in discussing the church's shortcomings."

"Nothing focuses your attention like the shadow of the gallows. Antinori was one step ahead of the law and went to the only place where that long arm did not reach. How do you know so much about Antinori's past?"

"Morgan."

"Morgan's not always right."

"Name one time when he's been wrong."

So she scored a point; you can't always pitch a shutout.

I drained my glass. Hadley III flew off the grill and cornered a gecko. She maimed it and brought it under Kathleen's chair.

"I don't like her doing that," she said.

"But you still like the cat, right?"

She let that hang for a few seconds. "Give it up, doofus, you have more free will than a cat."

"You'd be surprised."

"Probably would be. Ready for the sunset stroll?"

I stood up. "I've got to get my gun."

"My, you must really be disgusted with words. What's the game plan, plug holes in a dictionary?" She stood and faced me. "Or do you plan to take potshots at sandpipers?"

"Garrett called right before you slammed the screen door that you're supposed to fix. Paretsky's still breathing. He knows me. He knows you. Garrett will be shadowing us, as will John Wayne. Don't ask. I think we'll be fine. For all we know, Paretsky's boarding a private plane to George Town as we speak. Or he might seek revenge. You still want to walk with me?"

"What would you do?"

"What?"

"Revenge or flee?"

"I'd live to fight another day." *Why do I keep lying to her?*

"Am I in danger?"

"You might be bait. It's hard to—"

"*Am I in danger?*"

"Any time you walk with me."

"The sun waits for no one."

"Can the bravado act. You don't need to pre—"

I needed a few quick steps to catch up with her.

CHAPTER 41

She left her shoes—I was shoeless—in the truck, and we trudged over the quarter-moon boardwalk that spanned the sea oats. I couldn't spot Garrett or Wayne. I didn't really think that Paretsky would try to seek revenge on a public beach, and if I had I certainly wouldn't have brought Kathleen along, but after my elevator ride, I thought it better to err on the side of caution.

The bullcrap we tell ourselves. A couple of days ago I smuggled her off on a sailboat, but now I felt she was safer with Garrett, Wayne, and me? Fleeing was never a permanent solution.

The sea breeze was from the east; therefore, we were on the leeward side of the island. The sky was clear in the west, and the air was like a blanket that came out of the dryer too early, still warm and wet. We arrived at the water's edge and headed north, saving the southern trek, my preferred direction of travel, for the return trip.

"We missed it," Kathleen said. The water had already swallowed the top of the sun. The blue sky was now infected with yellow, red, and black.

"Hope it comes back tomorrow."

"That could be an issue."

"Make our troubles small."

"Yes." She looked at me and smiled. "Make our troubles small."

She was on the lower ground, and I switched places with her so I didn't tower over her. She wasn't fond of crushed shell on bare feet, so I wandered a few inches into the gulf so she could be on the smooth, concrete sand. The gulf lay flat and barely had the energy to deliver any of its waves onto the shore. A black skimmer glided over the surface and dropped its lower beak. It made the tiniest wake you would ever see. We chitchatted about the cloud formations and how, often, a half hour after the sunset the sky blazes, and the real show begins. We held hands.

"You know," I started in, "I plumb forget what we had a disagreement over."

"For starters, while on vacation, by omission, you lived a lie."

"Been thinking about that. Doesn't it just make us even? After all, you lied when we first met."

"That was different."

"You lied when we first met."

"That doesn't apply to this situation."

"You lied when—"

"Stop it. We'll call it a draw, but it doesn't excuse the gist of the matter: your condescending attitude toward me."

"Right. And I called that horseshit."

"You did."

"I misspoke. Double horseshit."

"Man oh man, that's the extent of your progress? Way to strive for middle ground."

"I don't do middle ground. There's you and the universe that surrounds you."

"See." She stopped and faced me. She tugged at my hand to free hers, but I wouldn't have it. "You say stuff like that, and I get it, I more than get it. But words just can't make everything good."

"Triple horseshit. You're telling me that words can make things bad but are incapable of making things good? Convince me of that."

A woman jogger danced around us. A human being exercising during prime drinking time. Swear to almighty God, what's this world coming to?

"Words of criticism sting and linger. Words of praise fade away."

"Where are you *get*ting this stuff from?" We resumed our pace.

"Me."

"I don't—"

"Don't argue with me; it has always been that way. People feel pain more acutely than joy—it's the same with words. It's the callous and thoughtless words that lurk and hurt; they contaminate our pots of self-esteem and foster doubt. Such words trump our good words and intentions."

"I'm not disagreeing, Ms. Marc Antony. Did you ever consider that just, perhaps, my hastily misspoken words did not accurately convey my thoughts?"

"Your thoughts?" She swung her head toward me. "What exactly did you mean when you told me to crawl into books?"

I stopped and, still holding her hand, turned to face her. "Run away from me. Run far. Run fast. Never look back. What type of person goes on vacation and kills another man? Who hides that side from his lover? What man is foolish enough to dream of a grandiose world, a romantic Eden where love, anchored in a calm harbor, rests beyond the reproach of stormy words and steamy flesh, where it's—whatever, who-ever, some-ever. You get the picture, right?"

"Some-ever? Little over your head there?"

"Not a bad side to err on."

"Pretty slick recovery, I'll give you that."

"I—"

"You're telling me that you say something mean and… what? It's a subliminal attempt to drive me away from you?"

"Sure—I'll go with that."

"That," she splashed water at me with her feet, "is horse-crap."

"Doing what I can, here."

She punched me on the shoulder with her free hand. We continued our pace.

A couple in shorts, T-shirts, and tennis shoes pounded past us. Evening power walkers. No acrimony against them, and not to belabor the point, but the Eleventh Commandment (am I the only one to read the Good Book?) clearly states that sunsets—that's generally 4:00 to 10:00 p.m.—are explicitly reserved for alcohol consumption. Wouldn't surprise me if someday all these evening-exercise sickos turned to salt.

"Did I ever tell you," I tugged at her hand, "I was sorry for what I said?"

"Hmm…pretty sure that never happened."

"Did so." Was she right?

Was she?

I showed sympathy by saying sorry to Rondo over his loss and to Cynthia over the death of her childhood friend, mended fences with Morgan, and apologized to Paige for slapping her; I even tossed the word out to Lambert's bird—

a frickin' bird—but not to Kathleen? *You always think it's physical. That's how we got here.*

"Did so." I opted to stage a weak defense.

"Did not."

"Did so."

"Nope."

I tossed out the white flag. "I'm sorry." I leaned in, placed my free hand on her shoulder, and gave her a kiss. "I'll stand here until the sun comes around and say it over and—"

"Please don't." I let her go, although I still held her hand.

"Are you really?" she asked timidly, which was an unfamiliar tone for her.

Wayne's badge weighted down my T-shirt pocket. *You tell me if the badge makes the man or the man makes the badge.*

"It was a poor decision. I thought it was best not to tell you at the time. I was wrong. I—"

"That's not what I'm referring to." She went from timid to disgusted in record time.

"The books?"

"Yes, birdbrain, the books."

"Major-league sorry about that. Begging your forgiveness."

"Accepted."

"Really?"

"Really."

"You know," I said as I felt old man swagger rising up from his dormant position, "I wondered if there was any chance—we're talking a tiny little possibility—that you were just a tad—remember, we're dealing in minuscule, nuclear measurements—too sensitive to that remark?"

"You waste no time going on the offensive, don't you?"

"Microscopic chance."

"How big is that?"

"A particle of dust in the universe."

"Hmmm…sure."

"Sure?"

"Blame rarely fits neatly on one set of shoulders."

Somewhere, at that precise moment, there was a men's club nailing a plaque with my name on it upon a wall. In the far corners of the earth, dissident armies were laying down their arms, raising their glasses, and toasting me. If only for that moment, the male population of the planet enjoyed peace and camaraderie that transcended all political, ideological, and religious divides as they chanted my name, harmony echoing throughout the universe.

"That's it? All this time putting the weight on me, and just maybe a little of it belongs on you?"

"Don't get bloated. Dust in the universe."

"Ever going to come clean with that minor detail?"

"The night you came clean at the Valencia? That was a lot for one dinner. I told you I needed time."

"How about the other times that—"

"Don't be so persnickety."

"Persnickety?"

She gave a playful shrug of her shoulders. "Doesn't excuse your remark. I'm a woman. I have a right, an obligation, to demand that you pay more attention to details—in this case, words. It's my right to be persnickety."

"Persnickety. Just how much did you and Sophia indulge in?"

She stopped and faced me. "Persnickety, persnickety, persnickety. That answer your question?" She nailed each syllable with astonishing accuracy and verbal agility. She'd make a good trumpet player.

We'd walked about half a mile, and I didn't want to make it too difficult for Garrett and Wayne to track us in the shadows. "On three?"

She said, "One...two...three." We pivoted and trekked south.

Darkness settled fast. The days had become notably shorter as the sun slipped farther south, answering the prayers of those in the southern hemisphere, or, perhaps, chasing its own dreams. Another couple passed us. Swimsuits, T-shirts, and red Solo cups. Finally, hope for the species.

"Do you?" Kathleen halted and faced me.

"What?"

"Want me to run. Run far. Run fast. Sail away. Never look back. Do you want me to do that?"

"You ever worry as a kid that something terrible was going to happen?" She gave me a quizzical stare. "Die young," I continued. "Fall out of the air the first time you flew, show up to class buck naked, or—"

"What does this—"

"Play along."

She brushed away a strand of hair that had found freedom in the breeze. "I read *Death Be Not Proud*. I was very young. It haunted me for years, the thought that everyone would continue with his or her life and mine would be genetically programmed to end early. Not your aforementioned panic plunge from the sky or trying to spell *persnickety* at a sixth-grade spelling bee and realizing that I had forgotten to get dressed, but the lingering knowledge that you would be gone before twenty. Knowing that it was all out there and would continue as if you had never stepped on the stage." She shuddered. "I was too young when I read that book. I kept thinking, what if that happens to me? It was, still is, my worst thought: slow knowledge of impending early death." Her head had drifted down. She snapped it up. "But that's life, isn't it? And you?"

"If you ever were to run, far and fast—sail away—that would be the saddest thing in my world."

"Oh, great." She halted as if we'd hit a red light. "And you hung me out there totally absorbed with myself. What does any of this have to do with you living a lie while on our vacation and your crass book remark?"

"Despite the weight of my poor judgment, my callous decision and ignorant words were inconsequential to the core."

"The core?"

"The core. Where even radioactive words have no effect." My conversation with Wayne at the airport and the book of Corinthians took over my mind. I added, "Where all is forgiven and love endures."

Really? That didn't sound like me at all. But it was something that if I didn't believe, I should.

"You really are pulling out all the stops. You might convince me to buy into that."

I dropped her hand and reached behind her with both my arms. I hiked up her dress, lifting her so that her legs rested on my hips and her face was with mine. The bottom of her dress was soaked, and it bled onto my shirt.

"Are you back?" I said.

"I never left."

We kissed, and I was already anticipating waking up with her in my bed, covering her with a blanket, and quietly leaving her in the predawn hours while I ran and swam, and flirted with the top of the world. Only then was I beginning to understand the depth of her absence.

I lowered her back down. She smoothed her dress with both hands, and I thought of Paige Godfrey when she had caressed her own dress. We continued our walk, and Kathleen placed her head on my shoulder. It felt funny. I wasn't sure she'd done that before. I'm not sure she could have done anything better.

It was nearly black now, and the streetlights from Gulf Boulevard ran straight until they stopped at the channel. Twenty-eight lights. We continued south on the beach and back toward the truck. I wondered if Garrett and Wayne had stayed around for the show or called it a night.

Another couple approached, and the man was also on the water side. He wore tan slacks, and the woman was in shorts and a loose blouse. At least the guy wore a T-shirt with a pocket. Nice T-shirt, not beachwear. A baseball cap was pulled low over his face. I thought of the fishing boat we'd come across on Tampa Bay and the captain who wore his cap at night. Why? They passed on the higher ground as Kathleen and I drifted toward the water to accommodate them.

Kathleen said, "Let's throw a beach party. You know—"

Revenge or flee? She had asked what I would do. *I'd live to fight another day.* I had lied to her and foolishly believed my own lie. The real question was: what would Paretsky do? In that regard, he likely wasn't that different from me.

The couple that had just passed. Not the couple—the man. A T-shirt with a pocket—not that different from me. Why had I looked at the man, when a woman was with him? A cap pulled low over his face. Too low. Sun was gone.

Bad men don't wear shorts. The picture of Paretsky on the boat...tan slacks.

A hundred feet down the beach, John Wayne sprang from the sea oats, his gun drawn, his leather coat trailing him like an unwanted accomplice. Wayne's gun cracked the night as Kathleen babbled about grilling lobsters over an open fire.

I spun around, reaching for my gun. The woman had kept walking—*she was in on it*—and was several paces beyond the man who stood, feet apart, pulling a gun out of his pocket. Paretsky. I caught Garrett out of the corner of my eye, crouched low by the concrete bench at the Twenty-First Street walkover. His SASS aimed at me. *We're too close. He'll never get a shot off.*

I wanted to turn back and see where Wayne was but didn't dare take my eyes off Paretsky. I started to raise my gun, but he was ahead of me. It was a hundred-yard dash, and he had a fifty-yard head start. I was cooked.

He aimed at Kathleen.

CHAPTER 42

My life was down to one act.

Garrett's SASS sliced the night, and two more reports echoed from the direction of Wayne. Wayne was shouting, but I couldn't make out what he said.

Kathleen had ceased talking, and her eyes held the first seeds of confusion and panic. I threw myself on her. I had to get her covered and on the ground. I twisted so that my back was to Paretsky, but I was too late and felt a blistering pain in the left side of my chest. My momentum carried me over her, and we tumbled onto the sand. Another shot, and my lower left side burst into heat. I kept my concentration on Kathleen. With Wayne riding in and Garrett poised, once I had her on the ground, Paretsky was done.

I fell on top of her just as another bullet shaved my head, and then the darkness came fast.

No, no, no—not on the beach where I run.

A coquina shell washed into my eye. I thought of Paige Godfrey's toenails. Sand swirled into my mouth, but I couldn't close it. I was broke and didn't work anymore. Kathleen's dress wiped across my face. It was red. She called my name. She called it again. I reached out for her hand, but I couldn't find it.

We had come undone.

CHAPTER 43

Cynthia Richardson sat at the end of my dock along with Morgan and Kathleen. She had flown in the previous night, and I invited her over for a dinner of gag grouper and Morgan's seafood gumbo. I scuttled back to the house to fetch another bottle of wine.

Wayne's badge rested on top of Tony Bennett's 1965 album *Songs for the Jet Set*. A sizeable dent warped its surface. The bullet from Paretsky's gun that should have found my heart met its match in that Viking badge. I can't say that wearing a badge makes me an honest man. I can say it saved my life. If I could only have one, I'd choose the latter over the former.

My left side had taken a few other hits. If I were a boat, I'd no longer be listing to the port but would be dry-docked in the yard for major repairs. As it was, I vacationed three nights in the hospital. Paretsky crumbled under the combined fire from Garrett and Wayne. Garrett told me that he took a shot at Paretsky when I was still standing, and the three of us were clustered on the beach. He saw that Paretsky had the draw on me and didn't debate my situation. He also believed that Wayne had gotten off a shot a split second before, which jibed with my memory.

I remember nothing after the dress wiping across my face.

As for Kathleen, here's a clue: when you take one for your woman (we're talking real lead here, not some symbolic goo),

THE CARDINAL'S SIN

it does a world of good toward showing the meaning of *I will fucking die for you*. That I was the one who led her into that danger was something that she insisted I let slide. No need, she said, to be so persnickety.

We never identified the woman Paretsky was walking with, and that bothered me. I don't like loose ends, but at least I'd whittled my original questions down to one: what was Giovanni Antinori's sin?

Renée had nuked my theory of sexual abuse, but I had a strong contender up my sleeve, not that anyone gave me a chance of being right. It wasn't the sexual thingumajig or the unknown words that Antinori laid on a twelve-year-old mind. Furthermore, I had great faith in my hypothesis. That put me on the opposite side of seven billion people, but I liked my odds. Always have.

My hypothesis, although conceived in the cardinal's eyes as he lay dying, was far more than hocus-pocus. It packed substance. Uranium weight.

My first night back, at 2:38 a.m., I left Kathleen in our sheets and wandered onto the screened porch. It was there—in my favorite seat, watching the red, pulsating channel marker, stroking Hadley III, who for some inexplicable reason had leapt up on my lap—that it came to me. I remembered my dream in which a wallet-sized picture of Kathleen floated above my head. The zeppelin dream. There was another picture I'd wanted to see, but I'd forgotten about it. I tossed the cat, got up, and scrounged around in my dresser, using my phone as a flashlight. Kathleen never stirred. I found it and returned to the screened porch. I flipped on the lamp and stared at the picture of the young woman that had been in Antinori's hand.

Cynthia's words from the Red Lion, when she was talking about her daughter, Lizzy, flooded over me. *All I managed to do was go from a brunette to a blonde, and that took me thirty years.* No wonder I hadn't made the connection earlier.

But I did now.

No doubt.

"I know you," I said to the picture and smiled. "I know you," I repeated. "And I know your secret." How would I explain how it had come into my possession? I couldn't. That line could never be crossed.

I rejoined the triumvirate. Morgan had hauled out chairs from the patio table, and we perched four across with the ladies in the middle. Cynthia was next to me, her white sweater curtaining the back of her chair. I had on lightweight long pants, which, according to Kathleen who'd insisted I wear them, would make Cynthia feel more comfortable and not so out of place. I lost. I planned to do more than my share of losing.

I'd explained on the phone to Cynthia that Renée Lambert was in the dark, same as me; her mother never told her the exact words the cardinal had pronounced that cast such a pall over her life. I informed her that, despite her assertion in the Red Lion that she didn't know what Antinori had said to Elizabeth years ago, both Renée and I believed she did. I recalled her denial at the pub; it had come too fast, and she'd glanced away from me. Renée's need for closure was the trump card, although I was highly suspicious that Cynthia was the one who needed closure. I e-mailed her flight confirmation, which made *no* a tougher word to say.

And Renée? She had no desire to hear firsthand from Cynthia the opening scene that set her family on its tragic trajectory. Her mother's demons had destroyed not only her own life, but in a sense her father's as well. She requested only a phone call that could finally put to rest the question that had bothered her for so long: what did Giovanni Antinori, as a young priest, say to her mother all those years ago that drove her mad and damaged her mind beyond repair? As to whether that led Antinori to embrace death, she didn't give a fuck. Her words, not mine.

I reclaimed my seat with the opened bottle of red, and Cynthia said, "Aren't you hot in those long pants? It's so... *sticky* here."

Kathleen and I exchanged glances, and she gave me a dreamy smile. I have no idea what a dreamy smile is, but that one's going in my pocket.

"I wasn't allowed to wear shorts."

"I see. I hate to think I'm making you uncomfortable. Really, Kathleen," she glanced over to her, "it certainly matters not a bit to me."

"It's good for him," Kathleen said, "to practice on the side of caution when being considerate of other people's positions."

"Well, I won't get between you, although, obviously, here I am."

The sun, behind us in the west, illuminated mushrooming thunderheads that formed over the land. Distant lightning bolts battled one another for my attention; they wouldn't win tonight. Cynthia Richardson would either share the cardinal's words to Elizabeth or not. She was the end of the line. Time for me to let go, pack up, and move on.

"Goodness," Cynthia said. Her eyes fixed on the quiet, late-afternoon water that mirrored the sky with liquid clouds of orange and black, as if there were two skies. "You live like this?"

"Worse," I replied, "Morgan grew up in this."

"A sailboat. That sounds so…adventurous." Cynthia glanced over at Morgan. He had regaled us at dinner with tales about his upbringing on the water.

"It was," Morgan replied. "I was raised on a sailboat, reading books as we chartered from one port to the next. I had no choice in that. It was as if I'd won an enormous lottery. In all of history, no finer gift could be bestowed upon a child."

"Not all are nearly so fortunate," Cynthia said.

"I was blessed," Morgan said, strengthening her comment. I was thinking of how to bring up the subject of Cardinal Antinori when Cynthia said, "Certainly not the case with the group of girls I grew up with."

"About that little knot," I said, taking her cue.

"A knot, indeed. How was your meeting with Renée Lambert?"

"Enlightening, to a degree." I explained what Renée had told me. "But," I added, "she came up short on the central question. Her mother told her the church, specifically Giovanni Antinori, damaged her, but she never fully explained what that damage was for fear of alienating her daughter from the church."

"Elizabeth Lambert didn't want to raise her daughter to be angry at God."

"So the world's told me," I replied. "You claimed that you weren't particularly close to Elizabeth Lambert, some comment about how men find a common ground so—I believe the word was 'effortlessly'—but I think you and Elizabeth had plenty to discuss when you reunited with her two years ago."

Cynthia shifted her weight as a pelican miraculously survived a smacking dive into the water. "Yes, well, about that—rather violent bird, isn't it?" She gave me a nervous smile. "It wasn't my most honest moment, but really I had no idea what you were fishing for."

"Your most honest moment."

"I realize that, but first, I think—and I *have* thought about it—that the church is not wholly to blame here. I think Elizabeth had other issues. I'm in no way defending the church, or Giovanni, but it was likely a case of strong words cast upon a weak mind. Heaven knows that Elizabeth wasn't the first to hear those words. And the man who cast those words? He wasn't the first to alter his beliefs, but his dark moods deformed his own mind, and her mind never surmounted its youthful impressions. Their meeting was a tragic affair for both."

"We hear words differently, though, don't we?" Kathleen added.

"We do. What rolls off one person sticks like glue to another."

Kathleen shot me a look that could only be interpreted as the world's largest *I told you so.* No need to pocket that.

"Those words," I said. "Words that stuck and led to Elizabeth's darkening mind, to her death, that Antinori never forgave himself for—what were they?"

"I recall from our pub visit," Cynthia said, "that you know history. Am I correct?"

"Bits and pieces."

"Are you familiar with Catholicism?"

"I light candles for my liver."

"Yes, well." She couldn't suppress a smile. "I was thinking more in line with ideological thinking. Vatican Two?

The ecumenism? Do you carry a remedial, and I don't mean to imply the negative connotation that word carries, understanding of those issues?"

"The Catholic church's coming to terms with an official position." Morgan stepped in, and I was glad for the hand-off. He had far more interest in the topic. "Specifically, how to view and accept others who are outside of the Catholic church. For many followers, but not all, the church for centuries considered that its Christian offshoots—Protestants, Lutherans, Baptists, the list goes on—were not part of the true church."

"Yes," Cynthia agreed. "We could debate the finer points, but why spoil such a night? Suffice to say, prior to this ideological shift, there existed some radical views within the church; in many cases, non-Catholic Christians were treated with even greater disdain than those who were never introduced to the one true church. Those lucky souls were excused under the doctrine of invincible ignorance.

"Giovanni's family was old school." She took a sip of wine and looked at Morgan. She knew her audience. "He was raised under strict beliefs. Beliefs that for the majority of his career he felt compelled to follow. Compelled by his faith, his parents, his unwillingness to plot his own beliefs."

"He dropped it two years ago," Morgan said, picking up the pace, "didn't he? His old faith, his upbringing?"

"He did."

"Triggered by his meeting with Elizabeth Lambert."

"That is correct. But bear in mind, it had been boiling underneath for some time."

"Antinori was raised to believe that non-Catholic Christians were essentially not even Christians," Morgan continued as my surrogate questioner. "Is that right?"

"Yes. His childhood, unlike yours, Morgan, was greatly encumbered with rooted thoughts and beliefs. His mind never set sail. Nor was it in his nature, until much later, to pick up anchor and question such things."

I shifted my weight, and Kathleen landed another glance.

"You're doing quite well, Mr. Travis," Cynthia said. "I know you prefer the straight road, and so we now find ourselves upon it. Giovanni was raised to believe that all non-believers went to hell. Invincible ignorance gave you a free pass, but for those who professed to be Christians but did not belong to the Catholic church, well then, a particularly nasty little corner of Dante's inferno awaited them. Mad, isn't it? In many ways we are such a disappointing species, considering the size of our brains.

"Renée Sutherland died at age twelve. Elizabeth's parents were devout Catholics. The Sutherlands were Protestants. Elizabeth and Renée were very close. Played at each other's houses nearly every day. As I told Mr. Travis in London, we all lived on the same street. We had a bunny, a white bunny— just the cutest thing—that we raised jointly. You know, one week at each house."

I recalled Cynthia staring at the girl with the white rabbit in the basket of her bicycle when we were at Granville Estate. It had frozen her, and now she stared blankly at the waters of the bay.

"Elizabeth's parents," she continued, "sent her to a very young and dashing Father Antinori for counseling. He, he said...he told her..."

She hung her head and rested it in her right hand, her elbow propped on the arm of the chair, her eyes open but dead, staring at the composite dock. I thought of Lambert's eyes taking in his popcorn ceiling. Kathleen reached over and draped her arm around Cynthia's back. We all knew what was coming. She shouldn't have to say it. She'd lived with it. It destroyed her childhood friend.

"He told young Elizabeth," Morgan said, "not in a mean way, but sitting there in his robe of authority, that twelve-year-old Renée Sutherland would burn in hell."

"Forever and ever." Cynthia raised her head. "*So* ridiculous, isn't it?" She blurted it out in a half laugh, half cry. "That a twelve-year-old with a white bunny would suffer God's eternal punishment. Oh..." She shook her head. She blew out her breath. "Giovanni had no courage of thought, no stomach for the questions. A stupid man.

"Thank you, Morgan. I knew none of this at the time, of course. Indeed, not until Elizabeth confided in me two years ago. When Elizabeth saw Antinori at the carnival, she broke. Unleashed hell in his face. She told me afterward that she'd suffered decades of nightmares. Twenty-four years of counseling. Can you imagine? It never erased the images in her head, her dreams, her life. She hid the root of her problem from both her husband and her daughter—thought she could tough it out herself. Was embarrassed, ashamed, she told me, that she couldn't overcome an imbecile's words.

"He was never the same after that—after she screamed at him. *Then* he found the courage of thought, of words. *Then* he publicly amended his beliefs, although privately those beliefs had already been severely altered. *Then* he became the people's cardinal. As if he were madly scrambling to atone for his past transgressions and his blunt unwillingness to question the doctrine that had been drilled into him as a child."

"He did have courage," Morgan said. "It just came too late for Elizabeth."

"Nothing, Elizabeth told me, could stem the images of her childhood friend, Renée Sutherland, burning in hell. No drugs. No two dozen years of Tuesday four o'clock sessions. No support groups. Nothing. Elizabeth said, when she went to bed, she feared the night. She disowned belief in any organized religion and never forgave her parents."

Morgan, contemplating his words, said, "He told young Elizabeth that her friend would live in hell, and in doing so he inadvertently sent Elizabeth there as well."

"Bravo, Morgan," Cynthia exclaimed. "And he knew it. Knew that he created hell." She swayed her head from side to side. "No way, as a young priest serving a supposedly loving God, did he ever see that coming. Elizabeth told me, when we met two years ago, that they, the church, in well-publicized settlements, fork over millions—billions, actually—to the victims of sexual abuse. 'What about me?' She beseeched me as if I would know the answer. 'What about the damage they've done to me and thousands like me?' What was I to say to her? Nothing. I had nothing to say."

"And that tipped Antinori?" I interjected.

"He was already in a depression over Mr. Hoo—yes. In a way, I suppose, Elizabeth gave him a way out. When Giovanni learned of her death...what a pit he went in. He wasn't able to crawl out of his depressive state. I couldn't convince him to forgive himself. I don't believe he ever saw the sun again. He told me once that he didn't fear death but regarded it with curiosity—to see if everything the church believed in was true or not. He decided to take that great litmus test. He wanted to die."

The conversation rambled on about the evolution of religion, although I wasn't a participant. I was stuck on a comment Cynthia had made and shut everything else out.

Eventually, Morgan and Kathleen excused themselves. Earlier I'd drawn Morgan aside and told him that I desired time alone with Cynthia. She and I sat in silence and watched as a cloud—microscopic particles of water—drifted under the moon until it was shrouded and only half its light filtered through.

"He was murdered, Ms. Richardson," I said, evenly drawing back to her earlier remark concerning Antinori. "What leads you to believe he wanted to die?"

Cynthia glanced at me with apprehension. "I mis—"

"You did not. How do you know the cardinal wanted to die? Did you talk with him or Mr. Hoo—"

"No. It's not that. I..."

"I what?"

"I saw—in his diary—the day he took his fatal stroll? It was marked."

"How so?"

"You know Latin? I don't know why you would, but for some reason I assume you do."

"Eat, drink, and be merry?"

"That's Ecclesiastes. Why always the jesting?"

"Tell me how it was marked."

"*Incepto ne desistam.*"

"May I not shrink from my purpose."

"Very good."

"This was not his official diary, is that correct?"

"It was his personal diary."

"Did Father McKenzie ever see it?"

"Not that I know."

"Would you know?"

She hesitated. "Yes, Mr. Travis. I would most definitely know." I wanted to make sure McKenzie, despite pissing in his robe, was in the dark. I didn't like the man and was quite certain he felt the same way about me.

"Anything on the following dates?"

"Meetings, appointments. But that doesn't tell us anything, does it?" She intensified her eyes. "But this does. And the Latin? He never put anything in his calendar in Latin. It's the only entry.

"Don't you see?" Her voice skipped up two notches on the excitometer. "He knew he was going to die. He *went* to the gardens to die. It's the man who killed him who didn't know his part in the tragedy. I can only conclude that a man was dispatched to kill someone else—who that person might be, I prefer not to know—but his guilt should at least be muted by the knowledge that Giovanni desired and sought the outcome."

"Yet," I said, taking tentative bird steps with my words—I'd been taken to school on how important those instruments were—"when we departed from the Red Lion, you wished his assassin to live in a conscious inferno."

"I might have been hedging myself a bit there, and, well, you see, I have…mixed opinions of you. Besides, you were getting too close. I wanted to push you away. You were so… inquisitive with your battery of impatient questions. The diary—I suppose it could be used to show Giovanni's intent, but I doubt that absolves someone of murder. I don't know what to make of it—if I should go to the police."

"Have you?"

"Have I what?"

"Gone to the police?"

"No." She leaned in just a tad and held my eyes. "What do you think?"

"About?" I feigned not following her logic.

"Someone being misled to kill a man being absolved of such an act."

"Small chance."

The Queen's Bench wouldn't give a Jolly Roger that I thought I was killing someone else. If I were the director of public prosecutions, I'd go after me on two charges—the man I killed and the man I conspired to kill.

Wanting to drop that subject, I said, "Did he consider his words to Elizabeth to be his greatest sin?"

She hesitated, her eyes bolted on mine as if to acknowledge the theme shift, then said, "His sin?"

"If a man was to have one sin, hypothetically, would that have been his?"

"He considered his inability to break away from early doctrine, and consequently the suicide of Elizabeth Lambert, to be a great flaw, one he took his life over. But I don't believe he saw it as a sin—it wasn't in that arena—it was more of a malignant regret."

"Regrets and sins? Aren't they differences without distinction?"

"I assure you they are not in the same family."

"Mr. Hoover, as I mentioned in my e-mail, is dead."

"You do jump tracks quickly, don't you? Yes, so I read in your e-mail."

"You don't seem too—"

"He was a greatly disturbed man." It came out fast. We held eye contact until she shuddered and broke away. She could never divulge her secret. The damage would cause irreparable harm to the late cardinal; it would have been a career buster in the early years, no reason to do so now. His reputation had already suffered massive body blows as his unsolved death spurred dark, unsubstantiated rumors of a double life.

And my secret? There would be ice caps in the Gulf of Mexico before I incriminated myself. Yet I felt an obligation to the man's outstretched arm, his supplicating eyes. I didn't wish to hurt her or pour salt on the wound, but I'd been searching for answers ever since Garrett proclaimed that I'd clipped the wrong bird. Besides, her secret, unlike mine, wasn't a felony.

I said, "When you were young..."

She sprang up as if my words had catapulted her out of her chair. She darted over to the side of *Impulse*, her back toward me, her face against the port side of my boat, her world shrinking. I went to her. I skipped to the end.

"Your son arranged for his father to die."

Her body quivered, and I felt like total shit. Why not let her go in peace? But I wasn't about to let myself feel too bad. She wanted this—saw it coming from the moment I met her. If not, I'd blame Antinori. If he thought he could allow someone to kill him without affecting others in his life, then he was indeed a stupid bird.

"My son."

"Mr. Hoover. Alexander Paretsky. The man whom, when we met, you did a credible job of claiming not to know, even acted surprised when I showed you his picture."

She spun, blew out her breath, and then pursed her lips. "Yes, I know." She perked up as if it wasn't a big deal, no more than being told that a restaurant had run out of the daily special. A flag bearer, if there ever was one, for her nation.

"At first I did deny, didn't I? But you said he 'posed'— your word, Mr. Travis, for you are not the only one with gifted ears—a threat to Renée, and then you added, 'perhaps even fatal.' Well, I scrambled then—decided to come clean, at least in my knowledge of him. I was on pins and needles that whole conversation, gauging what to say and what to hold back. I wanted to protect Giovanni's reputation and Renée's life. An impossible balancing act. And you? I should have guessed you'd already be there. Tell me, though, how *did* you connect the dots?"

"I synthesized. Your sabbatical to France. Alexander Paretsky's strange appearance in Antinori's life. Similar facial features. Right age. A photograph when you were in your early twenties, your eyes steady on Antinori when everyone else played to the camera."

And a picture of you in Antinori's dead hand—no need for synthesizing that. But those words stayed safely locked inside my head.

She cocked her head. "A photograph?"

"Taken at the high—"

"Yes, yes, I know the picture. You made your assumption from those items?"

"Yes. Why?"

"It's that you don't seem that...sensitive to me."

"I occasionally malfunction."

She stiffened. "I seriously doubt that. Let's be done with it, shall we? Mr. Hoo—Alexander—was a bad man, despite his unrestricted gifts. Yes, Giovanni and I...loved each other since the day I walked in as his twenty-year-old secretary and placed a cup of tea on his desk, and his hand found the cup before I withdrew mine. I gave birth in France and put my baby up for adoption. A child, *that* child, was the last thing I, or he, needed. Alexander tracked me down and then show-ered the church with money. After a fund-raising dinner one night, the three of us found ourselves in the vestibule. As Giovanni draped a checkered scarf around Mr. Hoo—Alex-ander's neck, Alexander said, 'Thank you, Father.' A passing guest corrected him, reminding him that Giovanni was a cardinal. Alexander smiled, and his eyes rotated back and forth between Giovanni and myself. There was no denying the men had similar features. The three of us just froze there... oh, such a weight fell on us, or was lifted. I still can't decide.

"It became clear that Alexander Paretsky had no ill intentions whatsoever toward Giovanni or me. Giovanni kept him from me, told me that Alexander was a deeply disturbed and troubled man, that our union was not to blame for such a man. As bad as that sounds, I got the distinct impression that Giovanni was holding back, that Alexander was far worse than I could imagine. Do me a favor?"

"Perhaps." I recalled her using the exact phrase in London when she wanted to be kept apprised of Renée Lambert. As if her questions were queued up long before she met me.

"Oh, no. That entirely won't do. I need far more. I deserve more."

"What may I do for you?"

"Alexander? I don't want to know. Whatever you may know. Is that bad? Innocent ignorance?"

"No. Not at all."

"I mean, I had nothing to do with his up—"

"You can stop right there."

"Thank you."

I said, "When Paretsky showed up with Renée Lambert at the carnival on a Sunday afternoon, she searched for you but told me she couldn't locate you."

"I couldn't face her. Imagine, Alexander dating Elizabeth's daughter—what a vile web. I saw them arrive, and I left with haste. Giovanni told me that Renée approached him and harshly criticized him for his words to her mother. It was, as they say, the final nail."

I admired the irony; Elizabeth's daughter gave her mother's tormentor the final nudge to end his life. I wondered if Antinori told Cynthia that he told Renée to run away from Paretsky. I'd decided that Antinori, as Cynthia suspected, attempted to shield Cynthia from the hard truth about Alexander Paretsky's career choice. Per her wish, I wasn't about to enlighten her with more than she already suspected.

"One more," I said.

"Yes?"

"The day I met Father McKenzie—why did you track me down and demand to meet?"

"What do you think?"

"Although you didn't know me, you knew I was coming. You flipped down the edge of my business card on your desk to accentuate the moment and then hopscotched after me when I was finished with McKenzie. You pined for this day."

"This day." She exhaled. "I'm so terribly drained from self-examination, but I suppose you're spot-on. I was more action that day, at least initially, than thought. And now, Mr. Travis, perhaps, on this day, we can engage in a little quid pro quo."

"Such as?"

"I too need closure and possess my own assumptions. I don't claim to match your zip, and perhaps I don't share your accuracy, and I certainly don't want to be presumptuous here, but, as you just suggested, I knew you were coming and—hear me out—this is what really spurred me to change my tune regarding my recognition of Mr. Hoover. You let slip—you mentioned when we met that you were in London when Giovanni was—accidentally, of course, as he was not the intended victim—but mur...killed."

"Me and ten million other lost souls."

"But only one of those is with me now and—"

"It's an uncaring world."

"—dropping pieces, one after another, neatly and deftly into the puzzle." Her teary eyes pleaded with me. "I would like to know, that's all, if he said anything. Expressed any feelings."

I said nothing.

"He wouldn't tell me. The night before? He was withdrawn, and then on the way out the door, he kissed me. He kissed me like—when they say the heart never grows old… you just can't imagine." She took a step toward me. "It wasn't over, don't you see? You're too young to know, but mark my words; passion has no end, nor does it dim.

"He thought of renouncing his vows. Oh, the talks we had. Move to a country cottage where our biggest concern would be dry firewood. A parallel life that we all dream about. I wouldn't have it. He needed his career, his center, but he wanted me. Sometimes I think it would have been better for him if we'd never met. He got so very angry when I said that, but our feelings—oh, look at your face—it is stone. Don't you see? Can't you *feel*?"

"You need to leave."

"Was it quick? Last words? Give me *some*thing. What we had wasn't a youthful fling. A day has not passed without either of us thinking of the other. The second doubts, career considerations, my ruined marriage. You have no idea. Listen to me babble. Surely you can malfunction for just—"

"Go."

"I'm not accusing you. If it wasn't you, perhaps you know who—"

"Good night."

"Please, oh, *please*."

Closer now. I thought of the colonel sticking his face in mine while we were on the dock. Why the dock? Perhaps because, on a dock, directions and choices are severely limited; there's only one route, and that is the only time in this impaired world where truth stands a chance.

Her batting eyes were no match for her tears. "I'm begging you. This is the day. I will not have another."

I remained silent but felt the civil war within.

She shuddered so deep my pilings sympathized. She wiped her eyes with her right hand and gave me a final pleading and disappointed look. A dismissive shake of the head. A step back. I was all she had, and I was no good. No good at all.

Kensington Gardens. His eyes. I was the last thing he saw in the world. I received his final message. I'd become convinced that Giovanni Antinori desired more from me than just to end his life. He'd given me a duty, a charge. This man, whom I did not know. This man, who used me. Haunted me. Who made me his Judas.

"I don't think"—my emotions grabbed the reins while my intellect stood idly by, pretending not to notice—"his greatest sin, or regret, was his harsh words. They may have led him to his depression and death, but I believe there were sadder, more tragic things in his life."

"You think this?" It came out in a child's voice, with bewilderment and awe and begging for more, as if the last spark of hope had ignited a small and promising flame.

I fondled the picture in my pocket. Should I give it to her? Make up some story that I found it in a London gutter? Sure. Why not? Forget it: sentimentality is acceptable, stupidity is not. Not with murder.

With my hand firmly on the picture, I said, "From what I've read in the papers—you understand—he loved a young woman, a woman who took thirty years to change her hair color. A woman he returned to, yet he never left. A woman who, despite your allegation that he was a weak man, he nearly gave up every belief he possessed in order to walk with. A woman whose love drove him to the wilderness for six months of contemplation. A woman he had a son with. A son she gave up for adoption and sacrificed for his career. When Giovanni came down from the Swiss Alps, he chose God over his heart. His unexamined beliefs caused him to harm another person so severely that he became disillusioned with his life, his choice, and saw no sense in moving forward. The forgotten son turned out to—to have issues, yet he appeared, as in a Greek tragedy, at the end to orchestrate his father's assisted suicide. But Giovanni couldn't tell you, the love of his life—the night before the deed—he kept it to himself. The greatest sin from that lot? All bets are off. The man had a bundle. For my buck?

"I think he failed to follow his heart, and no greater sin, or betrayal to himself, can a man have. *That* was his sin. His singular regret. His final words before he went quickly and painlessly to his god. This, mind you, is from what I've read in the papers."

I was winded. That was a verbal marathon for me.

As I spoke, Cynthia's graduation photograph, like a battery, charged and added conviction to my words. Could I be positive what the man's greatest sin was? It didn't matter. I'd made up my mind. It would bother me no more. I had other things to do with my life. Heck, I had furniture being delivered tomorrow. Definitely wasn't going to miss that.

Her eyes softened. "Did he say any—"

"We're finished."

"I won't—"

I stretched out my hand. "Enjoy your time in the Sunshine State, Ms. Richardson."

She gave a slow, understanding nod, shook my hand, limply at first but then warmly, and strolled down the dock. Halfway to my house, she came back around.

"Thank you." She didn't wait for my acknowledgment. It was an absurd two-word combination to the man who, in an attempt to kill her son, had murdered the love of her heart.

I took her graduation picture out of my pocket and, without looking, let it slip into the bay. The tide was going out.

Was that quadruple horseshit I'd just laid down? Disloyalty to one's heart being a man's greatest sin? Does that trump damaging words, committing sins of the flesh in the eyes of your father's god, a bastard, evil son, and all that other gobbledygook? Maybe not, but that's what I got out of the whole mess that started when I killed a man in London who did not die.

And if the other seven billion nut cases in the world don't agree with me?

I like my odds.

Always have.

For an excerpt of Robert Lane's, *The Gail Force,* coming soon from Mason Alley Publishing, please turn the page.

THE GAIL
FORCE

ROBERT LANE

It do seem to me that the life of man is merely a pattern scrawled on Time, with little Thought, little care, and no sense of design.

Only for a little we live, and feel ourselves truly alive, with truth, and the Angel flaming sword comes to slash us out. Beauty and music there is.

Richard Llewellyn
How Green Was My Valley

CHAPTER 1

The Fat Man

Karl Anderson knew he'd made a mistake when he got a sex change and neglected to inform his wife.

"What the—?"

"It's me babe."

"What the—?"

"Hey, you know we talked about it and—"

"Carl, you dumbass. What—?"

"It's Colette."

"What?"

"Colette. You know, French. Thought we'd make a cute couple. Whatdaya think?"

"Oh, babe." Riley Anderson put down her grocery bag of fresh produce, fish wrapped in white paper—that she suspected was not as fresh as the fish it wrapped—and a loaf of French bread. She strode over to her husband and combed her hand through his hair, tenderly tucking a few loose strands behind his left ear. "You're a blonde, babe. We talked about it? Remember? You'd look *so* much better as a brunette. Besides, a blonde French—they even make them?"

"Don't know why not."

"Name one."

"One what?"

"Blonde French. Come on, Karl. They don't exist. It's like a happy Eskimo or—"

"Catherine Deneuve."

"Cather—OK, so you got one, but dead or alive, right? And look at your shoes, you got to start thinking differently."

"I'll be fine. Pretty sure she's still alive. Born in '43."

"You didn't, you know," Riley said with a coy smile, "touch the private equipment, right?"

They stood in a seaside bungalow, the late afternoon sun filtering through the slats of the venetian blinds, and casting shadowed lines upon the wall. A spiritual sea breeze swept through two sets of opened patio doors, ushering in air that hung heavy with the gummy scent of salt water. The front doors faced the Caribbean and the side doors the courtyard and pool, one floor beneath them. "Some island south of Florida," the government man in the buttoned dark suit had retorted to Riley's earnest question. That was three nights ago when they'd been dropped off at two a.m., in the middle of a weed-infected runway.

"No shit, Sherlock. Which one?" Riley had demanded.

"Brig-a-fuck-a-doon."

"Gotcha. Hey, thanks for the heads up. Now give me my phone."

"We've been over this. They can trace you. No phone."

"How long we gonna be here?"

"Until I knock on your door."

"Yeah? Will if I don't let you in, congratulate me. It means I'm finally showing signs of intelligence."

Karl had stepped in before Riley got wound up. He was always calming her emotions and outbursts, like throwing a blanket on a fire. He believed his wife's bravado stemmed from her diminutive statue but he wasn't the type of man who gave thought to such trivial things. He simply loved her every way times ten.

"You know I didn't. It's just another precaution. We might even have fun with it." Karl replied to his wife and gave her a kiss. Their first kiss had been had been outside the pre-fabricated junior high classroom in Marion, Indiana when they were fourteen years old. He folded her, all five feet and one inch and a little south of one-ten, into his chest.

She jerked back. "Boobs?"

"Fakys. I'm thinking this might be a pristine opportunity for you to see if you swing both ways, you know, snuggle up to daddy big tits, might find it rocks your boat. Make a real sorority girl out of you."

Riley smiled, glanced up at her husband and said, "I don't think so, baby. You've been rocking my boat ever since the day you grabbed my shoulders, stuck you lips on mine, and than dashed off faster than the Easter bunny being chased by a pack of starving coyotes."

While not poetic, and certainly not the finally crafted lyrical notes she would, if presented the opportunity, have chosen, nonetheless, it was a fine thing for Riley Anderson to say to her husband as they were the last words he would hear her say. The last words she ever heard him say were coming around the corner like a de-railed freight train.

Karl Anderson, who towered over his wife, gathered her back in and lifted her off the floor. He faced the open patio door. Riley, before looking up to his face, eyed the grocery bag on the kitchen counter. She wondered how she should prepare the fish, but knew that Karl would likely step in and cook dinner. Maybe she'd slice up the French loaf, make garlic bread and croutons. Karl Anderson loved crispy croutons. Later, she would wonder if she *hadn't* glanced at the damn groceries if she would have seen the panic—the sadness—in her husband's eyes a split second sooner, and if that split second, of all the seconds the banged-up world had ever known, would have make a difference in their lives.

When she did glance up, Karl Anderson was not looking at the object of his heart, but at the open patio door where a rotund unwelcomed guest stood blocking the salt air, the sun, the view, their future.

Karl, like a Polish weight lifter, jerked his wife over his head, took a giant leap towards the side patio that fronted the pool below, and heaved his wife over the patio rail and, with luck, into the pools' deep end.

"Run baby run," he screamed while he prayed that once in her life the little fireball would do the sensible thing and listen to him. That was assuming he didn't miss and Riley went kerplat on the concrete pool decking. Karl spun and dove for the shelter of a desk. Like a runner on third knowing he was cooked, he closed his eyes, thinking it would be less painful when the bullet found him.

It wasn't.

"Tsk, tsk, tsk," the Fat Man said upon entering the villa. He glanced behind him. "Find her. Go." Two men were with him. The one that had shot Karl sprinted down the concrete stairs.

"*Mr.* Anderson," the Fat Man took several steps into the room. "Might I be mistaken or have you sprouted a pair of shapely—although the right one seems to be slightly off kilter—breasts since out last meeting."

"Eat me."

"Yes, yes, yes. If only you knew. Why not now Johnnie, while he's still breathing?"

Johnnie Darling, who resembled the product of an inces-tuous relationship, slithered around his boss, and snapped away with a Nikon D810.

"Fat little shit," Karl Anderson blurted out. His left hand grasped his Tommy Bahama shirt that Riley had sprung on him yesterday as a present. He tired to stem the bleeding that was turning the gold silk shirt into a rust colored pre-monition of death.

"Why the animosity?" The Fat Man tapped his cane on the floor. "Is that what the end brings you? It is differ-ent with all of us. You should understand. Our minds are so similar in some departments, but apparently—and this, most unfortunately does not bode well for you—sadly dif-ferent in others. But what a marvelous picture you make, especially now that you've made yourself such a conflicted creation. You know how I feel about art. It stimulates our senses. That which we are rarely exposed to, that we dream about and participate only through the voyeurism of our dreams, stimulates the most. So considerate of you, and, I might add, so utterly unselfish, to be our *objet d'art.*"

"Go fuck yourself."

Click. Click Click.

The Fat Man prodded Karl Anderson's shirt with is cane. He nudged the blond wig off to the side, taking care to keep some of it on Karl's head.

Click. Click. Click.

"Hmm. This is exquisite. Exquisite indeed. Death comes to what? A man? A woman? We don't know, Johnnie, what Mr. Anderson is trying to be. Perhaps one of your own. Death does not care, does it Mr. Anderson?"

Click. Click. Click

The Fat Man stepped around Karl, and toddled into kitchen, his back to Karl, "I thought we were getting along splendidly. The beauty of numbers, their unlying simplicity, their brutal honesty. It's disappointing when those we trusted, our confidants, turn and drive a spike into our hearts. So sad. All of this, brought about by you."

Karl groaned.

The Fat Man picked up the bag of groceries. He positioned a chair before Karl, sat, and bent over, his face close to Karl's.

"Look at me," the Fat Man said.

Karl did not. Karl Anderson decided to go deep inside himself, to choose his place of death, to envision the dimpled face of his sweet Riley as the last thing he would see. *Did I throw her too far? I was afraid of coming up short. A short putt never goes in—oh God, please, I hope she hit the water.*

"I said," the Fat Man poked Karl's chin with his cane, "look at me."

Karl did not.

"Very well then." He propped his cane against the side of the chair.

Click. Click. Click.

The Fat Man gave a dismissal gesture with his hand. "Be done Johnnie, until the closing shot. Why Mr. Anderson? Why couldn't you let me go? I told you that if you kept our secret you would live. If not, you would create this egregious situation. What part of that simple statement did you not comprehend?"

Karl curled into a fetal position and coughed up blood.

The Fat Man opened the grocery bag. "Now you understand, don't you? And your little Riley? My! What a throw that was. My guess is that she's bleeding out on the pink pool paver bricks. Pink. Pool. Paver. Bricks. What do you think, Karl? Or is it Pink. Paver. Pool. Bricks? Remember our number games? Of course you do. I got it right the first time, didn't I? Words with the fewest letters lead the way. We resort to the alphabet for a tiebreaker. 'Pink' before 'pool' as 'i' comes before 'o.' Remember? We constructed whole sentences in such a manner, although paragraphs were beyond the scope of even our minds. I will miss your stimulating company. I digress. Riley.

"Perhaps that wasn't her fate; there's always the cabana, a somewhat softer ending. You know which one I'm talking about, don't you Karl? Yes, that's right. The one were the lady in the black bathing suit was spreading oil on her breast yesterday as if she were making love to them. Remember now? Judging by the trajectory, I think that is where your little trinket might have landed. Johnnie, would you be so kind as to glance out the door. Take a few shots of Mrs. Anderson. Show them to Mr. Anderson in you viewfinder."

Johnnie Darling went to the side patio door and peered down. He shook his raisin head at the Fat Man.

"Not there? Really—quite an amazing throw then. I'm sure Eddie will rope her in. Pity for her that she didn't hit the bricks. Didn't think of that, did you Karl? Really, have you nothing to add?"

Karl tightened his position, his arms and legs drawing into his center, as if in death, life compresses into you, growing small, dense, and close. Then, like a flickering flame reacting to a kindly puff, it is gone.

The Fat Man opened the bag. "I greatly admire your courage to control your last moments. Superb, actually. One never knows until the bitter end what kind of strength lies dormant in a man. With you, it is bottled animosity and structured silence. Think of the picture in his mind right now Johnnie. The greatest art is that which we never see. Pity. Are you tuned-in Karl?"

The Fat Man unwrapped the fish. "I shall dine on your wife's shopping tonight. Let's see Johnnie, French loaf, fresh produce, kiwi—excellent—such an integral component for a Caribbean salad. Yellow tail snapper. Enough for two, which means just enough for me." He wrapped the fish and stood as he he'd lost all interest. "I fear we've overstayed our visit, and we do want to be going before the police arrive; although I told them to give me an hour. One shot, Johnnie. With both instruments. Don't cheat and rely on the camera."

The Fat Man turned to leave.

"Shwell ill you."

He turned and was surprised to see Karl Anderson's eyes nailing his own. "Pardon me."

"Riley. She'll kill you."

"I think not. Johnnie."

Johnnie shot Karl Anderson once in the forehead. He circled the corpse twice and settled on a position. He took his time with the Nikon. Johnnie Darling always took his time with the last shot.

Click.

CHAPTER 2

Every thing's a game. Sometimes you win. Sometimes you lose. Sometimes you don't know what game you're playing.

I was twenty feet outside the wake of my boat, *Impulse*, getting ready to cut my Connelly slalom back across the double wake. I'd been clearing both wakes by launching off the first, and hugging my knees as high as possible before letting the ski slap the water. I rocketed off the first wake and spotted the manatee in my landing zone just as I made out another boat zeroing dead into *Impulse* and Morgan, who was at the helm.

What the heck?

As Morgan swerved to avoid a collision with the oncoming boat, I threw the ski out to miss the manatee. My takeoff had been fine, the landing—not so much. My head and chest slammed into the water and my legs flew up behind me, bending my torso in a direction in which it was not designed to bend. My body somersaulted. When I broke the surface in the bay, my house was less than a half-mile off to my left. The boat that had been tracking us like a torpedo, was idling up to Morgan. I glanced to the right and—wouldn't you know it, there was my house again.

Little dinged up. Got my bell rung. It happens.

Legs—check. Neck pain—the usual. No major problems. It was just my head, an over-rated component of the body, that was malfunctioning. I leaned back in my vest, my face sticky with salt, and took in the blue Florida sky, allowing my mind time to get off the mat.

Morgan pulled *Impulse* up along me. The other boat was a deck boat with a wake board tower and a female head peering over the wheel. A wide red strip on the side begged for wax. *Stringer's boat?*

"I needed to cut sharp," Morgan explained. "No choice. You fall? I didn't see."

"Flipped over a manatee."

"Out here?"

"Have a chat with it, will you? What's with the kamikaze boat?"

"That's my no choice. She wants a few words."

"Now?" I glided the ski over to Morgan. He reached over and snatched it out of the water. I lowered the ladder and climbed over the transom and onto the deck. *Impulse* was a center console Grady White, but Morgan and I installed a tow bar that spanned her twin engines with a ring in the middle.

"Apparently it's important," he said.

"Stringers boat, isn't it?"

"It is."

"He on it?"

"No."

"Crap." I reached into my pocket and pulled out my phone.

Morgan smiled. "You'll find out if the new water proof case is what it's billed to be."

I shook my head in disgust. It had not been my intent to test the new cover. I was rough on phones and merely wanted the toughest case. It flicked to life. After drying it, I placed it on the console in the shade.

I took a healthy swig from a bottle of water, and yanked up my swim trunks. Morgan maneuvered *Impulse* along side of the wake tower boat as it sat rolling in the chilly waters of Boca Ciega bay. A double-barrel early season cold front had blasted through last week and the eighty-degree water temperature of the summer had been tamed to the low seventies. I pulled a couple of veteran fenders from under the front seats and tied us together while the woman on the other boat was content to watch.

"Kill the engine," I told her.

"You Jake Travis," she demanded and did as instructed.

"You with the IRS?"

"What? No."

"D.E.A.?"

"The wh—no, nothing like that."

"St. Pete parking? I'll pay—"

"Listen to me. You have to find my husband before he kills more people."

"You're husband's a killer?"

"No. Before the Fat Man kills more people. I'm pretty sure he murdered my Karl, even though he changed his name to Colette and we were going to make a run for it as a gay couple."

"Your husband had a sex change?"

"Not really. A fake you know?"

"Fake?"

"Boobs, wig, shit like that. People do it all the time. Games and stuff. But that wasn't our angle. You need to stop him."

I leaned against the rear bait well and took another swallow of water. My block palace was to my left, bridge to my right, sun high, water low, ten toes. I wasn't nuts, but this lady was driving me there.

The lady? Petite. Maybe a c-note in weight. A bikini top I failed at not staring at and shorts that covered a waist that never bothered to grow. She had a nasty bruise on her right shoulder; just all shades of purple, red, and black, like a tattoo with no form. I could probably ball her up and toss out of my life. Not a bad thought. She ruined my Sunday morning ski and drink. It's rude to interrupt church time.

Morgan brought out a bottle of Taittinger from a cooler and gave me an inquisitive nod that I affirmed. He popped the cork—a gorgeous sound to hear on the open water—and poured two glasses. I offered mine to Pixie, wanting to be polite and at the same time wondering why.

She stared at it. "Are you listening?"

I shrugged and took a drink. I'd been looking forward to my Sunday morning Champagne ski run since last Sunday.

"I am listening. The Fat Man killed your husband who was trying to become a woman. Correct?"

Pixie shook in her head in disbelief. "How can you stand there? He's a monster, a brutal killer. My husband is gone and your drinking champagne?"

"I offered."

Pixie jumped over the sides of the boats, charged up to me, snatched my fine crystal flute and tossed it into the bay. It bobbled like a sad cork. You don't think corks can be sad?—you didn't see this one.

"We were supposed to be in protective custody." She started in while I pondered my glass drifting out of my life. "Someone knew. He's connected, beyond what we ever suspected. I'm pretty sure he killed Karl and know he's killed countless more. And you can bet your wet ass he's coming after me. Are you my guy, cause if not I'm not burning any more time here. God damn it, I am talking to you."

I turned to her. "Have a seat Pixie."

"It's Riley. Riley Anderson."

I extended my hand and we shook. Her hand was like a small stone that got lost in mine. "Jake Travis. Have a seat, Riley Anderson."

PRAISE FOR ROBERT LANE'S JAKE TRAVIS NOVELS

The Second Letter

Gold Medal winner of the Independent Book Publishers Association's Benjamin Franklin Awards, Best New Voice: Fiction

"...a winning hero in Jake Travis, someone who is super killed, super fit, glib, oddly bookish, funny as a stiletto."

Phil Jason, Florida Weekly

"Lane's story makes a worthy new entry into the suspense genre...a book whose high stakes action, mystery, and sparkling characters could easily remain relevant for years to come."

Foreword Clarion Reviews

"There's a new mystery kid on the block. Lane not only provides thrills, but does it while keeping his sense of humor...the reader could not ask for more."

BookLoons

"...filled with believable, likable characters, witty dialogue and page-turning drama."

Blueink

Cooler Than Blood

"Lane delivers a confident, engaging Florida tale with a cast of intriguing characters. A solid, entertaining mystery."

Kirkus

"...entertaining and enjoyable."

SceneSarasota

"...gripping and highly enjoyable...Jake is at once a classic noir character...a fascinating protagonist."

Foreword Clarion Reviews

"...evokes the underbelly of West Coast Florida with authority...every bit as satisfying as a Myers and Coke at the end of the dock at sunset."

Les Standiford, author of Water to the Angels, and Last Train to Paradise

Be sure to read these previous stand-alone Jake Travis novels from Robert Lane:

The Second Letter

Cooler Than Blood

Learn more at http://www.robertlanebooks.com

Visit Robert Lane's Author page on Amazon: http://www.amazon.com/Robert-Lane/e/B00HZ2254A/ ref=dp_byline_cont_ebooks_1

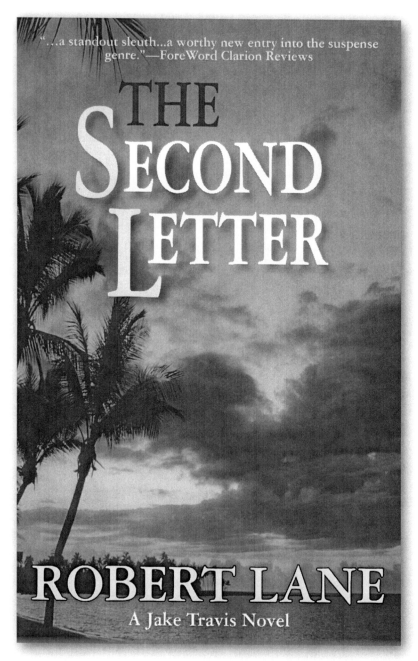

"...a standout sleuth...a worthy new entry into the suspense genre."—ForeWord Clarion Reviews

THE SECOND LETTER

ROBERT LANE
A Jake Travis Novel

COOLER THAN BLOOD

"...gripping and highly enjoyable...
a fascinating protagonist."
ForeWord Clarion Reviews

ROBERT LANE

A Jake Travis Novel

15

002B/333/P

9 780692 356517